John Duncombe

Select Works of the Emperor Julian, and Some Pieces of the Sophist Libanius

Volume the First

John Duncombe

Select Works of the Emperor Julian, and Some Pieces of the Sophist Libanius
Volume the First

ISBN/EAN: 9783337276959

Printed in Europe, USA, Canada, Australia, Japan

Cover: Foto ©Andreas Hilbeck / pixelio.de

More available books at **www.hansebooks.com**

SELECT WORKS

OF THE

EMPEROR JULIAN,

AND

SOME PIECES

OF THE

SOPHIST LIBANIUS,

TRANSLATED FROM THE GREEK.

WITH

Notes from PETAU, La BLETERIE, GIBBON, &c.

TO WHICH IS ADDED,

The HISTORY of the EMPEROR JOVIAN,

From the French of the Abbé De la Bleterie.

By JOHN DUNCOMBE, M. A.

IN TWO VOLUMES.

Him Poefy, Philcfophy, deplore.
The fcepter'd Patriot, who diftinctions wav'd,
Lord of himfelf, by Pagan rites enflav'd;
Whom all, but Chriftians, held their common friend,
Whofe very errors had a virtuous end.   Irwin.

VOLUME THE FIRST.

L O N D O N,
Printed by J. NICHOLS;
For T. CADELL, in the STRAND.
MDCCLXXXIV.

[iii]

CONTENTS of VOL. I.

PREFACE.

THE Abbè de la Bleterie publifhed, in 1735, *La Vie de l' Empereur Julian*, 12mo. * To this he added, in 1748, *L' Hif-toire de l' Empereur Jovien, et Traductions de quelques Ouvrages de l' Empereur Julien*, in two volumes, fmall 8vo. Both thefe works are executed with uncommon elegance and judgement, and have been very ferviceable to me in the following tranflations. With great fagacity the Abbè has explained and enlightened feveral ambiguous and obfcure paffages; and many others he has happily illuftrated, though, in general, by endea-vouring to give the idea of his author as he prefumes "Julian himfelf would have ex-"preffed it, if he had written in French,"

* Bleterie's Life is indeed a very elegant one, and writ with much candour and impartiality. He is no deep man in the learning of thofe times, but his good fenfe gei erally enables him to feize the right. WARBURTON.

<table><tr><td>VOL. I.</td><td>b</td><td>his</td></tr></table>

his verfion is too free and paraphraftical. If I have fteered between the extremes of thofe " literal verfions," thofe " homely copies," which he condemns, and the beautiful, but flattering, likenefs which he has drawn, I fhall have fucceeded to my wifh, being defirous of reprefenting this Imperial author juft as he is, as far as the idiom of the two languages will admit, in which the Englifh, in point of analogy to the Greek, has the advantage of the French. Moft of the annotations of M. de la Bleterie I have adopted, and the rather, as few of them have before appeared in Englifh. A tranflation of his " Life of Julian," by fome ladies *, was publifhed in 1746, under the infpection of Mr. Bowyer; but the " Hiftory of Jovian" has till now been to our country " a fountain " fealed." Were the learned Abbè ftill living, I fhould, however, defpair of fatisfying him in this attempt, having traced him more clofely than he has tranflated Julian, or wifhed to be tranflated himfelf.

The occafion, and the motives, that engaged me in this undertaking being the fame

* Mrs. Williams, a blind lady, affifted by two fifters of the name of Wilkinfon. *Anecdotes of Bowyer*, p. 185.

with

with thofe of this French academician, I
cannot fo well exprefs them as in the fame
words :

"Having lately met with the works of
"Julian, notwithftanding the juft horror
"with which I was infpired by his apof-
"tacy, I found them equally eloquent and
"ingenious, and perhaps more worthy to
"be read than many of the ancient Pagan
"writers. Befides, his morality being more
"refined than theirs, becaufe it has retained
"a tint of ours, I perceived in his writings
"a multitude of particulars ufeful for hiftory,
"and others, contrary to the intention of
"the author, very advantageous, and highly
"honourable, to religion. It feemed griev-
"ous to me, that ill-founded fcruples fhould
"prevent tranflating into our language
"that which deferved it. ' The Emperor
' Jovian,' faid I to myfelf, ' very zealous
' as he was for the faith, did not think the
' adorning the tomb of Julian, and honour-
' ing, even in the afhes of that apoftate
' prince, his rank as a man and an emperor,
' incompatible with the true fpirit of Chrif-
' tianity. Would it therefore be criminal
' not to neglect the productions of his ge-
' nius, and to draw them from the obfcurity

' of the learned languages ?' The excellent
" Latin version of Father Petau * has already
" placed Julian within the reach of those
" who are not sufficiently acquainted with
" Greek to read the original; and the cele-
" brated Satire of THE CÆSARS, published
" in French by M. Spanheim †, with a long
" and

* PETAU DIONYSIUS [or PETAVIUS], a Jesuit, was one
of the most learned men of his age. He was born in the
city of Orleans, and honoured it by his merit. He was a
vast genius, formed for literature, and rendered himself
a prodigy of knowledge. For, besides the learned languages, which he wrote and spoke with the greatest fluency,
there never was a divine more profound, an historian better
informed, an orator more eloquent, a critic more judicious,
a poet more ingenious and more flowery. In short, of
nothing in literature he was ignorant. His excellent works
leave no room to doubt this truth. Father Petau entered
among the Jesuits in the year 1605, which was the 22d of
his age. He was professor there of eloquence, and afterwards of sacred literature, and during the forty-eight years
that he lived there in a most exemplary and edifying manner,
he was the ornament of his society, the friend of all men
of learning, the admiration of foreigners, and, in a word,
one of the most excellent geniuses in France in the XVIIth
century. F. Petau died in the college of Clermont, at
Paris, on the 11th of December, 1652, aged 69. See his
Life, written by another great man, Henry de Valois, his
intimate friend, with the funeral elogiums of the learned.
Besides numerous other works, he printed, in 1613, XVI
orations of Themistius, in Greek and Latin, with notes
and conjectures of his own; and in 1634 [rather 1630], he
published the works of the Emperor Julian, 4to. &c.
MORERI.

† SPANHEIM EZEKIEL, the eldest son of Frederick Spanheim, professor of divinity at Leyden, was born at Geneva,
in

" and learned commentary, has inſtructed
" the moſt intelligent, without offending the
" moſt ignorant *."

Of all the remaining works of Julian, both
thoſe which are here tranſlated, and thoſe
which are not, M. de la Bleterie has given
the following very accurate account :

" Independently of thoſe faults of his
" age, which Julian has not ſufficiently
" avoided, I mean a taſte for declamation,
" and the malady of quoting inceſſantly the
" ancients, eſpecially the divine Homer,
" whether by way of ornament, or even of
" proof, I queſtion whether the two PANE-

in the year 1629. For proofs of his extenſive learning
ſee his work *de præſtantiâ et uſu numiſmatum*, his Diſſerta-
tion on a medal of the Abderites, his five letters to Morell,
a famous antiquary and medalliſt, which have been printed
with the *Specimen univerſæ rei nummariæ antiquæ*, which the
ſame Morell publiſhed at Leipſic, in 1695; his notes on
Callimachus, and on the CÆSARS of the Emperor Julian,
and ſome other treatiſes, whoſe title may be ſeen in
Moreri, Paris edition, 1695. You may there alſo find a
ſeries of all the employments to which he was ſucceſſively
raiſed at the courts of various princes, till he was ſent for
the fourth time to the court of France [by the Elector of
Brandenburgh], after the peace of Ryſwick. He continued
at Paris from that time to the beginning of the year 1701,
when he was ſent ambaſſador to England by his maſter, the
new king of Pruſſia [with the title and dignity of Baron].
He died there Oct. 28, 1710, aged 81.   BAYLE,

* *Preface à la Vie de Julien,* p. 1—3.

b 3

" GYRICS

" GYRICS ON CONSTANTIUS * would afford
" much pleasure [to a modern]. Notwith-
" standing the beauties of narration, which
" Julian has the art of diffusing, they err
" essentially as to their subject. Equitable
" readers would blame the author for having
" been obliged to employ so much art and
" genius to erect into a hero a prince of
" moderate talents, whom he hated, and
" feared. But would they forgive a trans-
" lator for fatiguing posterity by the irksome
" repetition of praises, which fear and ne-
" cessity rendered excusable in the mouth of
" an orator who pronounced them on pain
" of death?

" THE PANEGYRIC ON THE EMPRESS
" EUSEBIA † is a memorial of the gratitude
" of Julian. He does not speak there, how-
" ever, sufficiently from the heart. It is a
" frigid, didactic, monotonous elogium. As
" the author quotes in it some particulars of
" antiquity, that are less known now than
" they were then, the generality of readers

---

* *Orat.* I. *Orat.* II. These two panegyrics contain many facts, and excellent principles of government. Julian wrote the second in Gaul. Some Pagan phrases occur in them, which would induce us to think that he retouched them after he had declared himself a Pagan. *Life of Julian.*

† *Orat.* III.

" would

" would think the piece too learned, and
" would not fail to fay, that Julian intended
" to convince his benefactrefs that he made
" ufe of the library which fhe had given him.
" THE DISCOURSE IN HONOUR OF THE
" SUN-KING *, *in Solem Regem*, is an elo-
" gium on the *Logos* of Plato. Julian has
" fome remarkable expreffions on the fub-
" ject of that intelligence, the eternal pro-
" duction of the Sovereign God, of whom
" it is the living image, which, from all
" eternity, according to Julian, arranged the
" univerfe, which preferves and will always
" preferve it, which, holding the fame place
" in the intelligible world that the fun
" holds among corporeal beings, is the
" fource, the centre, the light of the fub-
" altern Gods, and of all the fpirits to which
" virtuous fouls will be reunited after death;
" which manifefts its power, and refides, in an
" efpecial manner, in the ftar whofe rays
" enlighten the material world. This work
" is ufeful and curious to fuch as wifh to
" know fundamentally the philofophical pa-
" ganifm of the Platonifts of that time, and
" the fyftem of religion which Julian formed

* *Orat.* IV.

b 4

" to

" to himfelf. But this long difcourfe pre-
" fents fuch a confufed mixture of meta-
" phyfics and phyfics; it has fo much ver-
" bofity, fo little juftice and precifion, that
" it can do no honour but to the fecundity
" of Julian, who compofed it in the fpace
" of three nights.

" He employed only one in making the
" ELOGIUM ON THE MOTHER OF THE GODS*.
" It was compofed at Peffinuntus in Phrygia,
" where was a temple of that Goddefs, ap-
" parently to revive the zeal of the people.
" He tortures his genius and imagination to
" explain allegorically the fable of Cybele
" and Atys, with the ceremonies of their
" worfhip. All thefe efforts terminate merely
" in publifhing, with the tone of an enthu-

* *Orat.* V. One of the orations of Julian is confecrated
to the honour of Cybele, the Mother of the Gods, who required from her effeminate priefts the bloody facrifice fo
rafhly performed by the madnefs of the Phrygian boy. The
pious Emperor condefcends to relate, without a blufh, and
without a fmile, the voyage of the Goddefs from the
fhores of Pergamus to the mouth of the Tyber; and the
ftupendous miracle, which convinced the fenate and people
of Rome that the lump of clay, which their ambaffadors
tranfported over the feas, was endowed with life, and fentiment, and divine power. For the truth of this prodigy he
appeals to the public monuments of the city; and cenfures,
with fome acrimony, the fickly and affected tafte of thofe
men, who impertinently derided the facred traditions of
their anceftors.   GIBBON.

" fiaft,

" fiaft, a romance of very obfcure phyfics.
" If I perfectly underftood it, I fhould not
" have tranflated it, on account of the ob-
" fcenity of the poëtical fable, from which
" Julian, neverthelefs, endeavours to deduce
" even fome moralities.

" The Discourse entitled against igno-
" rant Cynics *, *contra imperitos canes*, is
" alfo an *impromptu* which he compofed in
" two days, at his leifure hours, indignant
" at the irreverence and audacioufnefs of a
" diffolute Cynic, who, not contented with
" leading a voluptuous life, ridiculed the
" fingularities of Diogenes, and treated him
" as a coxcomb. Julian undertakes the apo-
" logy of the mafter, and exerts himfelf
" againft the difciple, with all the warmth
" of a man, who, in order to be a new Dio-
" genes, wanted only the wallet and ftaff.
" I think that this piece, though inferior to
" thofe, which I have tranflated, would not
" difpleafe in French.

" I will not fay the fame of the Discourse,
" which is addreffed to another Cynic, na-
" med Heraclius †. This philofopher, ha-
" ranguing in the prefence of Julian, had de-

<hr>

* *Orat.* VI. † *Orat.* VII.

" livered

" livered an allegorical fable, in which he
" modeftly took upon himfelf the part of
" Jupiter, and gave the Emperor that of the
" God Pan. Julian was ftill more hurt by
" the little refpect with which the Cynic
" mentioned the Gods. He was very near
" impofing filence on this profane declaimer.
" But having then made an effort of patience,
" as well from regard for the audience, as
" for fear of being confidered as he faid, as
" a fufpicious man, who is feared at every
" thing, he indemnifies himfelf by giving
" fcope to his zeal in a long difcourfe; whofe
" object is to prove that a Cynic, an enemy,
" by his profeffion, to all diffimulation and
" difguife, ought not to compofe fables ; or,
" if he will compofe them, that they fhould
" at leaft be ferious, inftructive, religious.
" This difcourfe, which would be clearer,
" if the fiction which fhocked Julian were
" known to us, contains fome curious par-
" ticulars relating to the origin and nature
" of fable, on the ancient and modern
" Cynics, &c. But what feems there moft
" worthy of attention is a fable by Julian,
" which I fhall prefently mention.

" Julian

" Julian was only Cæfar when he com-
" posed the piece entitled, A CONSOLATORY
" DISCOURSE ON THE DEPARTURE OF SAL-
" LUST *. It is the same Salluft whom
" Julian afterwards made Præfect of Gaul,
" and who muft not be confounded with the
" Præfect of the Eaft. Under Conftantius
" he had a considerable employment in Gaul.
" His talents and fidelity having rendered
" him the intimate and confidential friend
" of the Cæfar, the jealoufy and intrigues of
" the court did not fail to difplace and recall
" him. Julian, who was fenfible of all the
" greatnefs of his lofs, endeavours, in this
" difcourfe, to confole himfelf, and to com-
" fort his friend, for fuch a cruel feparation.
" He regrets not only the charms and de-
" lights of an union founded on the love of
" virtue and the public good, but alfo the
" affiftance of another felf, who partook his
" engagements, his pains, and his pleafures,
" of a true man, whofe like he defpairs to
" find, who loved him without intereft, re-
" proved him without arrogance, and told

*Orat. VIII.

" him

" him the truth without difguife. He
" makes a very rare and moft refpectable
" confeffion, efpecially in the mouth of a
" prince; he fays, in exprefs terms, that he
" owes to Salluft all his reputation. In this
" work are fentiment and principles; but
" they are a little choaked by the quo-
" tations and examples of antiquity. The
" piece was compofed to be publifhed, though
" the author was apprehenfive that it would
" not. On that account he confines himfelf to
" generals. It is plain, that, full of vexation,
" and pierced with a grief which he conceals
" in the bottom of his foul, he choofes to
" tell Salluft any thing but what he tells
" him. If he fpeaks to him of Scipio, Lælius,
" Cato, Pythagoras, Plato, Democritus, Pe-
" ricles, Anaxagoras, &c. it is becaufe he
" dares not fpeak of what interefts him moft.
" Thofe who cannot be ignorant are reduced
" by fervitude and conftraint to pedantry:
" witnefs moft of the Greeks who wrote
" under the Roman empire. Julian, as a
" private man or the Cæfar, lived in a
" moft dreadful conftraint. This perhaps
" is one of the caufes of that mifplaced
" erudition

" erudition which disfigures many of his
" works *.

" He could, however, forego erudition
" when he pleafed, as we may be convinced
" by reading his Manifesto againft the Em-
" peror Conftantius †. This work has no-
" thing pedantic, but the being addreffed to
" the Senate and People of Athens,
" whom Julian treats as he would have
" done the Athenians in the time of Mil-
" tiades, Ariftides, and Themiftocles. The
" piece is written in a folid, noble, perfuafive
" manner, without declamation, without di-
" greffion, without a fingle quotation, even
" from Homer, and gives occafion to prefume
" that the faults which are juftly blamed
" would not have been found in the other
" works of Julian, if he had only exercifed
" his pen on happy fubjects ‡.

" A long Fragment § of inftruction was
" addreffed by him, in quality of Sovereign
" Pontiff, to a Pagan prieft. It feems at if

* This Oration is omitted by M. de la Bleterie, but is
tranflated in the following work.

† Epift. ad S. P. Q. A.

‡ I have alfo tranflated this Epiftle. M. de la Bleterie
has omitted it from " motives of delicacy," having interwoven almoft the whole of it into his " Life of Julian."

§ Fragmentum Orat. aut Epist.

" Julian

" Julian there pretended to reduce Paganifm
" into a fyftem; and that the inftruction was
" divided into two parts, the firft of which
" concerned, if I may fo exprefs myfelf, the
" doctrine and the morals, and the fecond
" contained the rules of difcipline. It is, in
" general, a valuable and a very honourable
" teftimony to our religion, as, on one fide,
" the reformer of Hellenifm thinks nothing
" more proper to render it refpectable than
" to borrow, if he could, from the Chriftian
" church, her difcipline and manners; and,
" on the other, he fubftitutes to revealed
" facts fome extravagant fables. He rejects
" what Mofes informs us of the creation of
" Adam, in order gravely to utter a theurgic
" tradition, according to which, Jupiter,
" in arranging the univerfe, let fall fome
" drops of blood, and of that facred liquor
" formed mankind. In truth, religion is
" well avenged of its enemies by the very
" abfurdities which they prefer to its tenets;
" *and fending them ftrong delufion, they fhall*
" *believe a lie.* Such a one, who ridicules
" the fable of Julian, if he does not believe
" our facred fcriptures any more than Julian,
" admits, as to the origin of man, and a mul-
                                        " titude

" titude of other points, fome hypothefes,
" which, by being invefted with a meta-
" phyfical jargon, are not lefs irrational than
" his pretended tradition. In this fame
" FRAGMENT the author avows that he
" would have rebuilt the temple of Jeru-
" falem; and we are fenfible of all the im-
" portance of that avowal. The account of
" the rules which he prefcribes to his pontiffs
" is copied from the idea of what the church
" requires of her minifters. On the fubject
" of public entertainments, obfcene books,
" and romances, of that fenfelefs philofophy
" which denies or calls in queftion the ex-
" iftence of God, his providence, and the
" immortality of the foul, he explains him-
" felf in fo ftrong and Chriftian a manner,
" that nothing more would be wanting to
" ruin him in the opinion of fome perfons,
" if the hatred which he expreffes for the
" religion itfelf, of which he has preferved
" thofe remains, did not make him find fa-
" vour in their fight. Neverthelefs, how
" ufeful foover this FRAGMENT might be,
" my hand could not have a fhare in copy-

3   " ing

" ing the blafphemies which Julian there
" utters againft our infpired writers *.

" The Books against the Christian
" Religion † which this prince compofed
" during the long winter-nights, were an
" abftract of what unbelievers oppofed to
" Chriftianity, and efpecially of the objec-
" tions of Celfus, Hierocles, and Porphyry.
" Though the work was weak and immetho-
" dical, the delicacy and agreeablenefs of the
" ftyle, as well as the purple of the author,
" gave it a great reputation. The Pagans pre-
" ferred it to every thing, and with their Ju-
" lian in their hands went forth to attack the
" Chriftians. Superficial minds took, as ufual,
" witticifms for reafons, trite fophiftries for
" incontrovertible arguments, and the fre-
" quent quotations of fcripture, with which
" the author paraded, as a proof that he was
" deeply verfed in facred literature, and that
" he had not ceafed to believe it without
" knowledge of the caufe. The Chriftians,
" diftracted by domeftic controverfies, ne-
" glected to anfwer it; for infidelity is al-

* Omitting thofe " blafphemies," I have extracted the
ufeful and inftructive part of this Fragment, under the title
of The Duties of a Prieft.

† S. Cyrilli contra Julian. libri X.

" ways

" ways a gainer by our difputes. They had
" a fpecious pretext. Origen, Eufebius of
" Cæfarea, Methodius, and Apollinarius had
" anfwered it before. But the fimple were
" fcandalifed ; and not being able to difcern
" of themfelves whether the filence of one
" of the parties concerned proceeded from
" weaknefs or contempt, were tempted to
" afcribe the victory to him who was the
" laft fpeaker. About the year 400, Philip,
" of Side in Pamphylia, deacon of the
" church of Conftantinople, under St. Chry-
" foftom, endeavoured to avenge the honour
" of religion. The anfwer of Philip is loft ;
" and the opinion, which Socrates gives of
" another work by the fame author, affords
" us no reafon to regret it. At length, fifty
" or fixty years after the death of Julian, St.
" Cyril of Alexandria, though very inferior
" to that prince in the art of writing, at-
" tacked the expiring refuge of Paganifm,
" and deftroyed it. This father has preferved
" us a part of the work which he refuted.
" Thefe paffages are lefs valuable to unbe-
" lievers than they perhaps imagine. They
" will find there fome very mortifying con-

" feſſions *. Divines obſerve there ſome un-
" ſuſpected teſtimonies of the antiquity of
" ſome tenets †, of ſome cuſtoms and ex-
" preſſions. The refutation by St. Cyril,
" which he dedicated to the Emperor Theo-
" doſius the Younger, is learned, profound,
" deciſive againſt Julian and Paganiſm ; but
" the peruſal of it would be more agreeable,
" if his pen were as elegant as that of Julian.
" Beſides, St. Cyril wrote for readers who
" were perſuaded that, if Paganiſm was falſe,
" Chriſtianity muſt neceſſarily be true. For
" this reaſon he applies himſelf leſs to anſwer
" directly the objections of Julian than to
" prove the weakneſs, or rather the nothing-
" neſs, of Paganiſm. This method, which
" was then ſufficient, would not be ſo well
" adapted to the neceſſities of our age, in
" which the ſame objections are unhappily
" too often repeated by men equally hoſtile
" to all religion. A direct refutation of
" theſe too famous books would be an em-

* _Cyrill. contr. Jul. l._ vi. 10.
† _Ibid. l._ x. Theſe paſſages are quoted in _La Vie de
Julien, pp._ 244, 245.

" ployment

" ployment truly worthy of a philofophical
" divine *.

" It is ufelefs here to mention fome other
" works, which have not reached us. I will
" now give an account of thofe which I
" have tranflated.

" THE CÆSARS † are deemed unqueftion-
" ably the mafter-piece of Julian. I exprefs
" myfelf too freely, both as to his perfon
" and his writings, to be charged with that
" kind of idolatry which is too common in
" tranflators. I venture therefore to fay, that
" profane antiquity does not afford any piece
" which is comparable to this, for the merit
" of the fubject, and very few which ought
" to be preferred to it for the merit of the
" execution.

" A Roman Emperor, who has had the
" advantage to be a private man, a mind
" filled, and perhaps a heart penetrated, with
" great maxims of government, a philofo-
" pher notwithftanding all impediments,
" born with much tafte and genius for rail-
" lery, ready to feize the ridiculous, and never
" letting it efcape; in others, not even in

* Mr. Gibbon is pleafed to call this " a ftrange Centaur."
Vol. II. p. 369.
†, *Cæfares, five Convivium.*

                    " himfelf,

" himfelf, knowing how to diftinguifh thofe
" light clouds which conftitute the difference
" between the middling and the good, the
" excellent and the perfect, between qualities
" which are eftimable and thofe which are
" only brilliant, nourifhed with the reading
" of Plato and Ariftotle, and fpeaking their
" language like themfelves, affembles in one
" piece all the Emperors who reigned before
" him for the fpace of about four hundred
" years.

" It is a moving picture, in which the
" fpectator fees rapidly paffing before his
" eyes, but without confufion, thofe mafters
" of the world defpoiled of their grandeur,
" and reduced to their vices and their virtues.
" By the aid of a fimple and ingenious fiction,
" Julian makes thofe who have difhonoured
" the purple difappear with ignominy ; and
" among thofe who deferve to be placed
" in the number of fovereigns he chooſes
" the moft illuftrious to make them contend
" for pre-eminence. Though he feems to
" leave the queftion undetermined, it is fuf-
" ficiently clear that Marcus Aurelius is the
" hero of the piece ; that Julian gives him
" the preference, and means to announce to
" the

" the universe that he has taken that philo-
" sophical Emperor for his model.

" Such is the general plan of the Satire,
" or rather of the Judgment, of THE CÆSARS.
" I do not think that in any work so short
" are to be found at once so many characters
" and manners, so much refinement and fo-
" lidity, so much instruction, without the
" author ever assuming a dogmatical tone,
" so much wit and pleasantry, without his
" ever ceasing to instruct. In a word, it
" seems to me that THE CÆSARS ought to
" undeceive, or at least to embarrass, those
" who have voted an exclusive esteem to the
" productions of ancient Greece.

" The work, however, is not exempt from
" faults. Not to mention some railleries
" that are either frigid, or seem so to us,
" nor a few groundless and too severe sen-
" tences which Julian pronounces on certain
" Emperors, in whose memory no one at
" present is much interested, the no less un-
" just than indecent manner in which he
" treats his uncle, Constantine the Great, is
" inexcusable. In spite of his inclination,
" not being able to avoid making him enter
" into competition with the most distin-

c 3   " guished

" guifhed Emperors, he omits nothing that
" can ridicule and degrade him.

" This vifible partiality, produced by his
" hatred of our religion, and by other caufes
" which I have taken care to develope in
" the remarks, can injure only Julian.
" Neither his envenomed ftrokes, nor thofe
" of Zofimus, will prevent Conftantine
" from being regarded as a prince of fupe-
" rior merit, and highly worthy of the title
" of Great ; any more than the extravagant
" elogiums of the Greeks, who give him the
" title of " equal to the apoftles," will
" ever perfuade us that all his actions were
" conformable to the fanctity of the gofpel,
" of which he declared himfelf the pro-
" tector. Without diffembling either his
" faults or failings, I have detected the ca-
" lumnies by which a paffionate enemy en-
" deavours to blacken him ; and I have
" done it folely for the intereft of the truth
" of hiftory ; for I am far from thinking,
" with this unjuft cenfor, that the blows
" aimed at Conftantine can fall upon re-
" ligion. If he has the glory to be the in-
" ftrument which God employed to refcue
" it from oppreffion, he is not, after all,
" either

" either its founder or apoſtle. Without the
" Emperors, and in ſpite of their efforts,
" when Conſtantine embraced it, it had ſo
" much prevailed, that he has been ſuſpected,
" though falſely, of having embraced it from
" policy." When we have the happineſs to
" profeſs a religion ſo auguſt, ſo divine,
" fixed on immoveable foundations, there
" would be puſillanimity, not to ſay cow-
" ardice, in thinking it dependent on, or
" reponſible for, the reputation of its firſt
" protectors. God, the ſupreme diſpoſer of all
" events, and *who calls things that are not*
" *as though they were,* could, and yet he did
" not, have made Theodoſius have reigned
" before Conſtantine, and have placed St.
" Lewis at the head of our Chriſtian kings.

" I muſt obſerve, that in THE CÆSARS
" is a ſort of contradiction. The author
" there ſuppoſes the Gods ſuch as the poets
" repreſent them, yet he often recurs to the
" ideas of the philoſophers. This is not
" a fault peculiar to him. It cannot be in-
" ferred from hence that he meant to ridi-
" cule religion, nor that he was a free-
" thinker. He conſidered the fables of the
" poets as fictions, which being taken lite-

" rally

" rally would have diſhonoured the Deity;
" but perſuaded that they muſt be turned
" into allegories, being a deiſt in ſpeculation
" to a certain point, but a zealous pagan in
" practice, he conformed to the eſtabliſhed
" language. This mixture of poetical and
" philoſophical Paganiſm was not unuſual.
" No one was hurt by it. We are juſtly
" ſhocked at it, and ſhould be much more
" ſo, if reading the ancients had not fa-
" miliariſed us to ſuch abſurdities.

" It is more than ſixty years * ſince M.
" Spanheim, ſo well known in the republic
" of letters, undertook to tranſlate THE
" CÆSARS into French. This learned fo-
" reigner was unacquainted with the refine-
" ments of our language; and his verſion
" no more reſembles the original than a
" ſkeleton does a human body †. To the
" text he has added ſome remarks, has ſup-
" ported his remarks by proofs, and en-
" riched them both with medals; the whole
" with ſo much profuſion, that the ſmall

* In 1683.

† In like manner, Mr. Gibbon ſtyles this French verſion " coarſe, languid, and correct." " The Abbé de la
" Bleterie," he adds, " has more happily expreſſed the
" ſpirit, as well as ſenſe, of the original, which he has illuſ-
" trated with ſome conciſe and curious notes."

" work

" work of Julian is in a manner loft in a
" quarto of above fix hundred pages. It is
" a mafter-piece of typography, a treafure
" of ancient literature ill-digefted, and of
" numifmatic erudition. This book is or-
" namental to libraries, but it alarms the
" generality of readers, whom the fight of
" fo prolix a commentary infpires at leaft
" with indifference for a text which, they
" fuppofe, requires fo many illuftrations.
" Every one is not obliged to know that
" commentators do not labour merely to
" give the meaning of their author; that
" they often choofe him only for an oppor-
" tunity of emptying their common-place-
" books, and that they are generally as dif-
" fufe on the moft eafy paffages as they are
" fuccinct, or even filent, on real difficulties.
" The Misopogon * is a fatire lefs diver-
" fified, but more fingular, than The Cæsars.
" Julian, driven to extremities by the inha-
" bitants of Antioch, inftead of avenging
" himfelf, or of pardoning them, like a
" prince, undertakes to avenge himfelf like
" an author; and no author, I fancy, ever
" conceived fuch a project of revenge. He

* Misopogon, five Antiochus.

" pretends

" pretends to turn his ill-humour against him-
" felf; he exaggerates his own imperfections,
" and reprefenting the good qualities that he
" may have as extravagances, he oppofes them
" to the vices of Antioch, which he ironically
" exhibits as virtues.

" Julian draws himfelf more extraordi-
" nary than he really is, but he muft have
" been very extraordinary to draw himfelf
" in fuch a manner. If the work be defi-
" cient in dignity, it abounds with ftrokes,
" fallies, principles, and manners. Genius
" fparkles throughout the whole; but the
" pleafantry is too cauftic and bitter. It is
" the laugh of a man in a paffion, who acts
" the part of a philofopher, and cannot fup-
" port it to the end. He leaves at laft the
" ironical tone, to affume that of invective
" and direct reproach. I think I may
" affirm that this fatire flowed from the pen
" of Julian in a fit of chagrin and anger,
" and that he employed no more time in
" compofing it than was neceffary to write
" it. But fuch as it is, it is an *unique*, and
" without having read it we cannot be fuf-
" ficiently acquainted with Julian.

" A Fable,

" A FABLE *, which I have taken from
" the difcourfe to the Cynic Heraclius, will
" I doubt not be read with pleafure. Julian,
" in order to give him the model of an
" inftructive and religious fable, defcribes,
" in an allegorical fiction, but which it is
" impoffible to miftake, the misfortunes of
" his family, the dangers which he incurred
" in his childhood, his fyftem in religion
" and government. Though it is in profe,
" it is an excellent piece of poetry.

" The letters of celebrated men are ge-
" nerally the moft curious parts of their
" writings. Many of the EPISTLES † of
" Julian difplay his mind, his genius, his
" ideas on goverment and religion; others
" throw light on hiftory, facred and profane;
" and there are fome billets which prove
" that he was very capable of fucceeding in
" the laconic ftyle. Among his Epiftles are
" fome of his laws. Two or three more I
" have taken from the Theodofian Code.
" No Emperor made fo many laws in fo
" fhort a reign : excepting thofe which re-

* *Ex Orat.* VII.

† *Epiftolæ.* Of the LXXI. Epiftles, thofe to Themiftius,
Conftantius, and the Athenians, included ; M. de la Bleterie
has tranflated only XLVII.

" gard

" gard Christianity, his are esteemed by the
" lawyers ; but unfortunately the Codes of
" Theodosius and Justinian scarce ever give
" more than the enacting part of the law,
" and not the preamble, in which the genius
" and eloquence of the legislator were dis-
" played.

" I have inserted in its place the EPISTLE
" TO THEMISTIUS *, which the editions
" place at the end of the Orations. It is in
" fact a treatise in the form of an Epistle, in
" which the author, seeing the rocks that
" surround the throne, expresses his anxieties
" and apprehensions, lays down excellent
" maxims concerning the duties of a sove-
" reign, and acknowleges his incapacity with
" a modesty highly laudable, if it be sincere.
" We perceive in this work a strain of de-
" clamation, and somewhat rather vague.
" It were to be wished that the author had
" applied a little more the principles which
" he draws from Aristotle and Plato. But
" it should be considered that Julian, when
" he composed this treatise, had just been
" declared Cæsar by Constantius, and that
" this new dignity had only increased his

* *Epistola ad Themistium.*

" slavery.

" flavery. The piece is free enough for the
" time when it was written. Julian ven-
" tures to fpeak there as if he were inde-
" pendent, or at leaft as if he would one day
" be fo."

With a well-grounded confidence the learned writer adds, " Though the public is
" prejudiced againft notes, and regards them
" as fuperfluities which only ferve to en-
" large the volumes, I venture, however, to
" intreat them to caft their eyes on mine.
" They are extremely laboured, and, I pre-
" fume, nothing will be found in them ufe-
" lefs or trifling. I have entered into gram-
" matical difcuffions only when I thought
" them important, and to fhew that I could
" tire the reader by that kind of erudition
" as well as others. If fome fhould think
" that I ftop too often to parry the weak
" thrufts that Julian makes at Chriftianity,
" I will own, that, writing in a Chriftian
" nation, I am afhamed to be obliged to re-
" fute what deferves only contempt. But as
" for thofe who fhall think thefe precautions
" exceffive, I beg them to examine whether
" they do not contribute to make them ne-
" ceffary.

" ceffary.   *I am become a fool in glorying; ye*
" *have compelled me* *."

The comment indeed of this learned foreigner is frequently fuperior to the text; and the whole is fuch a fund of critical, hiftorical, and Chriftian knowledge, that it cannot but be acceptable to an Englifh reader. I muft add, that I am alfo much indebted to the elegant (I am forry I cannot fay, unexceptionable) *Hiftory of the Decline and Fall of the Roman empire*, as will appear by the frequent quotations from that work in the notes. The Epiftles of Libanius to Julian, which are alfo inferted, and two Monodies on fubjects mentioned in thefe works, will give fome idea of the ftyle of that fophift.

Befides the *Hiftory of Jovian*, an abftract of an Effay, by the Abbé de la Bleterie, " on " the rank and power of the Roman Em- " perors in the Senate," which has not, to my knowledge, appeared in Englifh, is annexed.

Chrift-Church,
Canterbury, 1783.   J. DUNCOMBE.

The following fhort Annals and Pedigree of Julian may ferve to illuftrate the hiftorical events occafionally mentioned in his writings.

* *Preface à l'Hiftoire de Jovien*, p. x.—LXIII.

A N-

ANNALS

OF THE

PRINCIPAL EVENTS

IN THE

LIFE of JULIAN.

FLAVIUS CLAUDIUS JULIAN was born at Constantinople. His mother, Basilina, died a few months after.   A. D. 331. Nov. 6.

His father, Julius Constantius, and most of his relations, were massacred by order of the Emperor Constantius. His half-brother, Gallus, is banished into Ionia; and he is sent to Nicomedia, where he is educated a Christian by the bishop Eusebius, and officiates as a lecturer in the church. He is put under the tuition of Mardonius, an eunuch.   337.

He is taken from school, and confined six years with Gallus in a castle in Cappadocia.   345.

Gallus is created Cæsar, and goes to reside at Antioch.   351. Mar. 5.

Julian

A. D. 351. Julian visits Edesius at Pergamus, and is perverted to Paganism by Maximus, who initiates him at Ephesus.

He is sent to complete his education at Constantinople under Ecebolus and Nicocles.

354. Dec. Gallus is deprived of the purple, and put to death in Dalmatia. Julian is conveyed to the court of Milan.

355. May. He is sent to study at Athens, where he is initiated into the Eleusinian mysteries.

Oct. He is recalled to Milan.

Nov. 6. He is declared Cæsar, and soon after marries his cousin Helena, sister to Constantius. Writes his 1st panegyrical oration on Constantius.

Dec. 1. Sets out for Gaul with 350 soldiers. Winters at Vienne, and there probably composes his Epistle to Themistius.

356 Jan. 1. Enters on his 1st consulship with Constantius (the viiith). Writes his iid panegyric on that prince.

June 24. Arrives at Autun. Twice defeats the Alemanni, and retakes Cologne.

Winters at Sens, where he repulses an attack of the enemy.

357 Jan. 1. Enters on his iid consulship, with Constantius (the ixth.)

Defeats

Defeats the Alemanni at Strasburgh, takes A. D. their king, Cnodomar, prisoner; &c.   357. Aug.

Passes the Rhine at Mentz.

Subdues the Franks. Winters at Paris.   Dec.

Defeats the Salians and Chamavians. Passes 358. July. the Rhine again. Two kings of the Ale- manni surrender and sue for peace. Winters at Paris. Writes his consolatory oration on the departure of Sallust.

Passes the Rhine a third time, surprises six 359. kings, who disputed his passage, and rescues 20,000 prisoners. Restores the ruined cities of Gaul.

Winters again at Paris. Sends Lupicinus to Britain, to repulse the Scots and Picts.

Enters on his third consulship with Con- 360. stantius (the Xth.)   Jan. 1.

The flower of the Gallic army being or- April. dered by Constantius to march into the East, they mutiny at Paris, and proclaim Julian Emperor.

He passes the Rhine a fourth time (at Bonn) July. and subdues the Attuarii. Declares himself a Pagan.

Winters at Vienne, where he celebrates his Oct. fifth anniversary, Nov. 6, 361. Loses his wife.

Passes the Rhine a fifth time, and again defeats and reduces the Alemanni.

VOL. I.   d   Marches

A. D.
361

Marches against Constantius, and seizes the pass of Succi.

Writes from Sirmium, and Naissus, to Athens, and the other cities of Greece.

Nov. 3.†   Constantius died at Mopsocrene in Cilicia, aged 45.

Dec. 11.   Julian enters Constantinople, and restores the Pagan worship. Winters there, and writes the Cæsars.

362.
May 15.xii   Leaves Constantinople. In his way, visits the temple of Cybele at Pessinus in Phrygia, where he writes his vth oration.

June.   Arrives at Antioch, where he winters.

Dec.   Composes his books against the Christian religion.

363.
Jan. 1.   Enters on his rvth and last consulship, with Sallust, præfect of Gaul. Attempts in vain to rebuild the temple of Jerusalem.

Feb.   Writes the Misopogon.

March 13.   Leaves Antioch, and marches against the Persians, joining his army at Hierapolis, where he passes the Euphrates.

April 7.   Passes the Chaboras, and enters the Persian territories.

Besieges and takes by assault Perisabor and Maogamalcha in Assyria.

---

† Ammianus says, Oct. 3. But Idatius, Socrates, Cedrenus, the Alex. Chronicle, and others, say as above.

Transports

Transports his fleet from the Euphrates to the Tigris.

A. D. 363.

Forces the passage of the Tigris, but, unable to reduce Ctesiphon, and deceived by a Persian deserter, burns his fleet and magazines, and advances into the inland country, where he is severely distressed by famine.

June.

Retreats towards the Tigris. 16.

Repulses the Persians at Maronga. 21.

Receives a mortal wound in a skirmish, of which he died in the succeeding night, aged 32. 26.

His remains, by his own desire, were interred at Tarsus in Cilicia.——

PEDIGREE

PEDIGREE OF JULIAN.

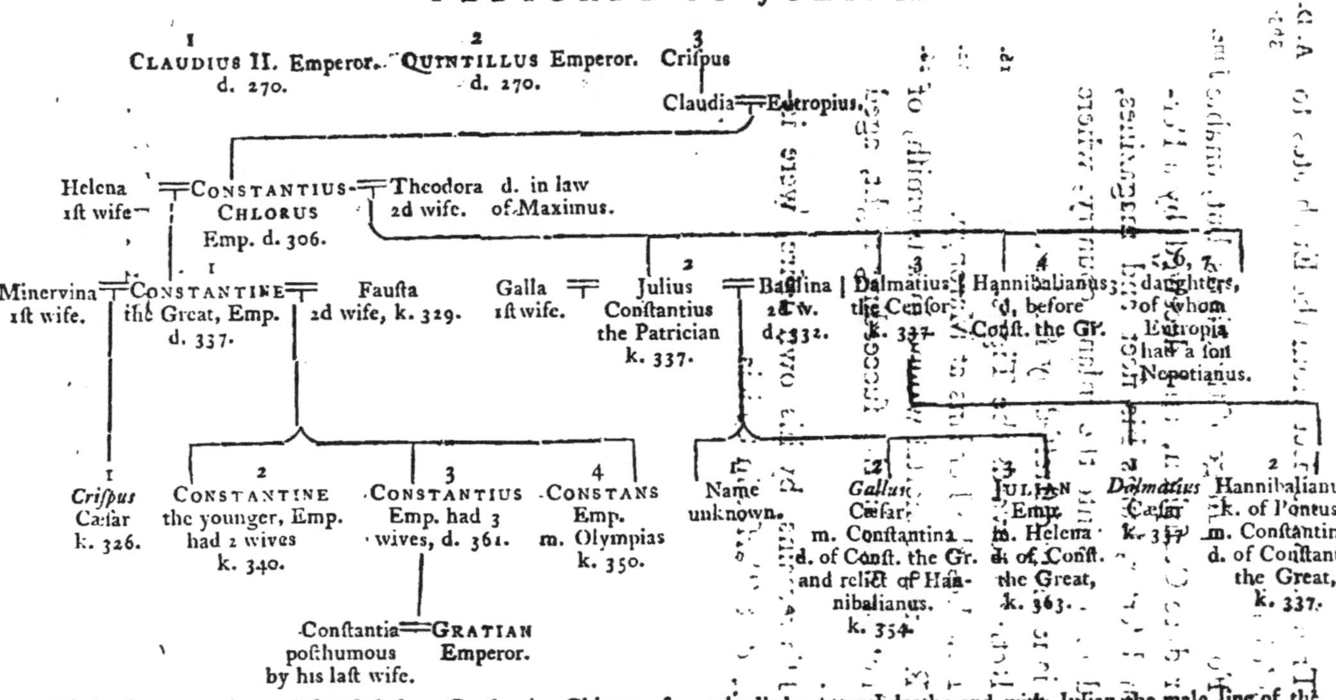

Of the fourteen princes descended from Constantius-Chlorus, five only died a natural death; and with Julian the male line of the Flavian or Constantine family ended.

SELECT WORKS

OF

JULIAN.

GALLUS * CÆSAR TO HIS BROTHER JULIAN HEALTH †.

THE neighbourhood of Ionia has afforded me great joy, having difpelled the concern and indignation that I felt at a former report. What that was I will inform you. I heard that

you

A. D. 351 or 352.

---

* Gallus was the elder brother of Julian, by a different mother, and having with him been fecreted from the murderers of their relations in 337, they were banifhed by the Emperor Conftantius into Ionia, from whence, in 345, they were conveyed to the caftle of Macellum in Cappadocia. There they were not only educated Chriftians, but officiated as lecturers in the church of Nicomedia. Six years after, viz. on March 5, 351, Gallus was declared Cæfar by Conftantius, and married to his fifter Conftantina. He then went to Antioch, to prefide, with a delegated authority, over the three great diocefes of the Eaftern Præfecture, and from that city this Epiftle was

you had departed from your former religion tranfmitted to you by your anceftor ‡, and, hurried
away by mad and wicked advice, had embraced a
vain fuperftition.   How did I grieve at this information! For as I confider your good actions, whenever they are celebrated, as advantageous to myfelf, fo I efteem your bad deeds (which Heaven
avert !) as much or more detrimental.   But the
anxiety which this intelligence gave me, has been
removed by the arrival of our father Ætius *, as

he

probably written, Julian being then in Ionia, whither
Gallus had difpatched Ætius to ftrengthen him in the
Chriftian Faith. Conftantius, in the mean time, was march-
ing towards the Weft. The fubfequent imprudence of
Gallus, and his fatal cataftrophe in 354, are related by
Julian in his Epiftle to the Athenians.

† The learned F. Petau fuppofes this Epiftle to be
fpurious, without affigning a reafon.   Meffrs de Tillemont
and Spanheim think it genuine. In fact, we find nothing
in it which does not agree with what we know from other
hands.   La Bleterie.

‡ Gallus had fome reafon to fufpect the fecret apoftacy
of Julian, and, in a letter to him, which may be received
as genuine, he exhorts Julian to adhere to the religion of
their anceftors; an argument, which, as it fhould feem, was
not yet perfectly ripe.   Gibbon.

The grandfather of Gallus and Julian, Conftantius
Chlorus, the father of Conftantine the Great and Julius
Conftantius, had been very favourable to the Chriftians,
and perhaps was a Chriftian in his heart. Nothing more
is neceffary to authorife, in fome degree, the expreffion
ufed by Gallus, his grandfon.   La Bleterie.

This conftruction, it muft be owned, is rather forced.

* Ætius, a Syrian by birth, a brafier, a goldfmith, an
empiric, having ftudied the categories of Ariftotle, fet up
for a divine. He carried the principles of Arianifm as far

as

he affures me, on the contrary, to my great joy, that you are zealoufly employed in houfes of prayer †, and can hardly be removed from the tombs of the martyrs, but are totally attached to our worfhip. I muft apply to you that expreffion of Homer: "Be this your aim ‡." Continue thus

as they would go; and, reviving the blafphemies of Arius, he plainly taught that the Word was only a creature. This occafioned his being ftyled *The Atheift*, not only by the Catholics, but even by the moderate Arians. Leontius, bifhop of Antioch, did not fcruple to ordain him a deacon; and Gallus took him for his oracle in divinity. Ætius was the dupe of Julian, who carried his diffimulation fo far as to embrace a monaftic life. Libanius fpeaks of this hypocrify as if it were an innocent ftratagem. " Though " Julian," fays he, " had changed his religion, he ftill " profeffed the fame, not being allowed to difcover his " real fentiments. This was the reverfe of the fable of " Æfop. The lion borrowed the fkin of a vile animal. " Julian knew the better part, but he acted outwardly the " fafeft." *Liban. Oral. Parent.* We fee that the panegyrift was no more fcrupulous than the hero on the article of fincerity, even in the affair of religion. *Ibid.* The death of Gallus was followed by the exile of Ætius. But he was recalled by Julian. See an Epiftle from him to that prelate (as he was afterwards) the XXXIft.

† Σπυδαζειν σε ιφη ιις οικυς ευχων. In the Latin tranflation it is, *Te in domibus ftudiose verfari.* " That you are " ftudioufly employed in houfes;" which, by omitting *precum* (ευχων) conveys no meaning.

‡ Βαλλ' υτως, *Sic jaculare.* Iliad. VIII. 282. Thus, always thus, thy early worth be try'd. *Pope, 340.*

Thefe are the words of Agamemnon to Teucer, who was fhooting his arrows with fuccefs againft the Trojans. It fhould be remarked that the Greeks, and thofe who fpoke Greek, whether Pagans or Chriftians, quoted Homer on every occafion, and made continual allufions to fome paffages of this poet. The Pagans, and Julian in particular, had the fame refpect for Homer that we have for the canonical books. LA BLETERIE.

to delight all who love you, remembering that nothing is preferable to religion. For the perfection
of virtue inftructs us to deteft the fallacy of falfe-
hood, and to adhere to truth; which is principally
apparent in piety towards God. But a plurality of
Gods is productive of endlefs diffenfions and un-
certainty. One only Deity by his fole power governs the univerfe *, not, like the fons of Saturn,
by lot and partition, but becaufe he is felf-created
and has almighty power, not acquired by force,
but exifting before all things. This is the true
God, and to him all worfhip is due. Farewell.

Julian Cæsar to the Philosopher Themistius †.

A. D.
355 or 356.
I Earneftly wifh to realife the expectations, which,
you fay, you have formed of me. But in this
I fear I fhall fail, as you promife much more for
me than you ought to others, and efpecially to yourfelf.

---

* We read in the text, Το δι μονον συν ινι υπαργον ον βασιλιυιι
τυ παντος, which gives no meaning. I think that we fhould
read συν ινι υπαργω. Gallus will then fpeak like an Arian,
like a faithful difciple of Ætius. The Chriftianity both of
Julian and Gallus was in all appearance only Arianifm.
                                        La Bleterie.

† This philofophical Epiftle " on the dangers of fovereign
power" was written foon after Conftantius had raifed Julian
to the dignity of Cæfar. It muft not be forgotten that
this was not only a defignation to the empire, but alfo an
                                        actual

felf. For long ago, on my fuppofing a competition between myfelf with Alexander and Marcus
[Aurelius], I was wonderfully fearful and apprehenfive of falling far fhort of the fortitude of the
firft, and of not making the leaft approach to the
perfect virtue of the other. On thefe confide-
rations, an idle life feemed to me moft defirable;
and recollecting with pleafure the Attic fables, I
wifhed to fing them to my friends, as porters in
the ftreets thus alleviate the weight of their bur-

actual affociation in a confiderable part of the imperial
power. The Greeks gave the Cæfar the title of βασιλευς
δευτερος, or even, as they did the Emperor, fimply that of
βασιλευς. I fhall prefently mention why I cannot adopt the
conjecture of F. Petau, who imagines that Julian compofed
this treatife when the death of Conftantius had made him
mafter of the empire. And I fhall examine, in the fequel,
whether the Themiftius, to whom Julian writes, be the
fame whofe works we have. La Bleterie.

Philofophy had inftructed Julian to compare the advantages of action and retirement; but the elevation of his
birth, and the accidents of his life, never allowed him the
freedom of choice. He might perhaps fincerely have preferred the groves of the Academy, and the fociety of
Athens; but he was conftrained at firft by the will, and
afterwards by the juftice, of Conftantius, to expofe his
perfon and fame to the dangers of Imperial greatnefs; and
to make himfelf accountable to the world, and to pofterity,
for the happinefs of millions.

Julian himfelf has expreffed thefe philofophical ideas
with much eloquence, and fome affectation, in a very
elaborate Epiftle to Themiftius. The Abbé de la Bleterie,
who has given an elegant tranflation, is inclined to believe,
that it was the celebrated Themiftius whofe Orations are
ftill extant. Gibbon.

Petau ftyles this, " not an Oration, but an Epiftle;" but
" becaufe it is longer than an epiftle," he places it among
the Orations.

B 3

thens.

thens. But you, by your late epiſtle, have augmented my fears, and have propoſed to me a much more arduous contention, by ſaying, that God has placed me in the ſame ſituation that Hercules and Bacchus were placed of old, who at the ſame time philoſophiſed and reigned, and freed almoſt the whole earth and ſea from the vices with which they were overwhelmed. You alſo adviſe me, baniſhing the thoughts of ſloth and idleneſs, to conſider how I ſhall act with propriety in this ſuppoſed contention. You then mention all the legiſlators,- Solon *, Pittacus +, Lycurgus ‡; and you add, that the world may reaſonably form greater expectations of me than it did of them.

On reading this paſſage I was ſtruck with aſtoniſhment, knowing that you think it by no means allowable to flatter or falſify ; and as to myſelf, being conſcious of no ſuperior talents, either natural or acquired, except my love of philoſophy. Of the calamities, which have hitherto rendered this love imperfect, I ſay nothing. I knew not therefore what conſtruction to put on theſe expreſſions, till this was ſuggeſted to me by Heaven, that you meant by thus praiſing to exhort me, and to diſplay the magnitude of thoſe trials to which every ruler muſt neceſſarily be expoſed.

* One of the wiſe men of Greece, the lawgiver of Athens. See Plutarch and Diogenes Laërtius.

+ Another of the wiſe men, contemporary with Crœſus, a philoſopher of Mitylene. Some of his precepts are preſerved in Auſonius *de Sapientia*.

‡ The lawgiver of Sparta. See Juſtin and Plutarch.

But

But this is rather a difcouragement than a recommendation of fuch a ftate.

Suppofe that a man navigating your ftrait *, and that not with eafe or expedition, fhould be told by one skilled in divination, that he fhould traverfe the Ægean, and afterwards the Ionian fea, and at laft the main ocean. " Here," the prophet fhould fay, " you fee towns and harbours, but " there you fhall difcern neither watch-tower, nor " rock, happy if you difcover fome fhip at a diftance, " and can hail the crew. You fhall often pray to " God for a fafe return to land, even were your " life immediately to end; fatisfied, if after having " reached the haven, and reftored your fhip to the " owners, and the mariners to their families, you " might commit your body to your native earth †." This might happen, but that it would muft till the laft moment remain uncertain. Do you think, that, after having heard this, fuch a man would even choofe to dwell in a fea-port town? or rather, bidding adieu to riches and the profits attendant on commerce, to his domeftic connections, to foreign friendfhips, and to the furvey of diftant cities and coun-

* It is difficult to conjecture what ftrait he means. I fufpect it, however, to be the Bofphorus, and that Themiftius was then at Conftantinople.   PETAU.

If I were fure that this Epiftle was addreffed to the celebrated Themiftius, I fhould affirm, that this ftrait was that of Conftantinople.   LA BLETERIE.

† The ancients thought drowning the moft difhonourable of deaths. Hence thofe paffionate exclamations, under fuch an apprehenfion of Achilles in the Iliad, and Æneas in the Æneid.

B 4

tries,

tries, would he not think the advice of the son of Neocles *, "Live privately," the wiseft that could be given?

'Of this you feem fo apprehenfive, that you endeavour, by reproaching Epicurus, to prejudice me againft him, and to eradicate that opinion. Thefe are your words; "that he, a man of no bufinefs, "fhould praife idlenefs, and thofe Peripatetic "difputations, might well be expected." But that Epicurus was in this miftaken, I have been long and am firmly perfuaded. Whether indeed it is proper to urge any one to public adminiftration, who is naturally unqualified and of mean abilities, may deferve farther enquiry. For even Socrates is faid to have withdrawn many from the forum who feemed not calculated for it; and he endeavoured, in particular, as Xenophon relates, to diffuade Glaucon, and the fon of Clinias †, but could not reftrain the impetuofity of that youth.

Shall we then compell thofe who are confcious of their own deficiencies, and urge them to be confident in fuch undertakings as depend not fo much on virtue and a right difpofition, as on fortune, who governs all things, and often forces us to follow her direction? Chryfippus ‡ in other things

seemed

---

* Epicurus.

† Alcibiades.

‡ Chryfippus is ftyled by Cicero "the moft fubtle inter-"preter of the Stoic dreams, and the fupport of the Por-"tico." His chief ftudy was logic, which he carried to a trifling degree of fubtlety. Of his works, which filled 705 volumes,

feemed wife, and was juftly fo efteemed; but his ignorance of fortune and chance, and other like caufes, which happen independently of our actions, is not eafily reconcileable with what time has evidently taught us by many examples. For in what particular fhall we ftyle Cato *, or Dion Siculus †, happy? Perhaps for their difregard of death, but certainly not for their leaving the works in which they at firft engaged imperfect, works to which they had diligently attended, and for which they would willingly have fuffered the fevereft calamities. When difappointed, they behaved, it is faid, with moderation, not repining at fortune, and derived no fmall confolation from virtue; but they could by no means be ftyled happy, having failed in their greateft undertakings, unlefs in the fenfe of the Stoics. To which it may be anfwered, that to be praifed and to be happy are not the fame thing; and if all creatures naturally defire

volumes, fome titles only remain. He died about 200 years before the Chriftian æra, and was honoured by the Athenians with a ftatue in the Ceramicus. His death is faid to have been occafioned by an immoderate fit of laughter at feeing an afs eat figs. Chryfippus defired the afs might have a glafs of wine to wafh them down, and was fo diverted with his own conceit, that it coft him his life. He is faid to have been a very copious and learned writer, but obfcure and immoral; though one would be inclined to think, from the refpect with which he is mentioned by Epictetus, that this latter accufation is groundlefs.

Mrs. CARTER.

* Of Utica.

† A nobleman of Syracufe, attached to Plato, by whofe counfel he freed his country from the tyranny of Dionyfius. He was afterwards affaffinated by one of his friends.

happinefs,

happinefs, it is better for us to be declared happy than to be praifed for virtue. Subftantial happinefs by no means depends on fortune. Thofe who are engaged in government cannot indeed breathe, as the faying is, without her * * * † as if philofophy could form a general, and place him above the reach of chance, like the pure, incorporeal, and intelligent world of ideas, whether they are produced in reality, or formed falfly. He indeed who is, according to Diogenes,

Of city, country, houfe depriv'd,

has nothing more to lofe. But how can one whom cuftom has called forth, and as Homer, the firft of writers, fays,

—— Who mighty nations guides,

Directs in council, and in war, prefides ‡, confiftently place himfelf out of the reach of fortune? And if he be really fubject to it, with what confideration and prudence muft he act, fo as

—————

† Before this paffage we have placed aftericks, as fomething here is wanting. But in our MSS a fragment was inferted of another epiftle, which, if I miftake not, Julian wrote to Arfacius, a High Prieft, in which he gave fome directions relating to religion and the worfhip of the gods. This we have extracted, and publifhed feparately, in another place; but what follows feems addreffed to Themiftius.   PETAU.

The above-mentioned Fragment of an oration, or epiftle, (fo ftyled) is characterifed in the preface, and that unobjectible part of it, which contains " The Duties of a " Prieft," is detached and inferted, under that title, among thefe " Select Works."

‡ Iliad, II. 25. Pope, 27.

to fuſtain with equanimity, like a ſage pilot, the ſtorms that aſſail him on every ſide?

If admiration be due to thoſe who withſtand her attacks with fortitude, much more is it deſerved by thoſe who receive her favours with moderation. By them the greateſt of kings, the conqueror of Aſia, was ſubdued, as in cruelty and inſolence he far ſurpaſſed Darius and Xerxes, after he had conquered their dominions. By theſe weapons the Perſians, Macedonians, Athenians, Syracuſans, the Lacedæmonian magiſtrates, the Roman generals, and, laſtly, many emperors, were attacked and totally deſtroyed. It would be endleſs to enumerate all who have fallen a prey to wealth, ſucceſs, and luxury. And why ſhould I mention thoſe, who, overwhelmed by misfortunes, from freemen have become ſlaves, from noble mean, and from ſplendid abject? Would to Heaven, that human life afforded no ſuch inſtances! But ſuch there have been, and ſuch there always will be, as long as the world exiſts.

But that I may not ſeem ſingular in thinking that Fortune has the chief ſway in human affairs, I refer you, intelligent as you are and my inſtructor, to Plato, in his admirable book on Laws; and to convince you that I have not weakly imbibed this idea, I will tranſcribe the paſſage*: "God, and, with
"God,

---

* All this paſſage is taken from the fourth book of Plato *de Legibus*, which, in ſome places, we have corrected from
Plato

" God, Fortune, or Opportunity, govern all things
" human, but a third muſt be annexed; Art muſt
" attend them, as an aſſociate." He then proceeds to ſhew, that every king, every ſovereign
artificer of great actions, ſhould be a kind of King-
God. " Saturn," he ſays, " knowing (as we have
" before obſerved) that human nature is not of it-
" ſelf capable of governing mankind with ſupreme
" power and abſolute authority, without giving
" way to inſolence and injuſtice, then * placed at
" the head of our ſtates, as kings and magiſtrates,
" not men, but genii of a divine and more ex-
" cellent nature ; as we act with regard to our
" flocks and herds. For we never make an ox
" the ſuper-intendant of oxen, nor a goat of
" goats ; but they are governed by us, a ſupe-
" rior race. In like manner †, the God, being
" a lover of mankind, has ſet over us a race of
" ſuperior beings, who, with great eaſe both to
" themſelves and us, undertake the care of us,
" and, diſpenſing peace, innocence ‡, and juſtice,

Plato himſelf. Others, which Julian ſeems to have expreſſed differently, we have remarked in the margin.
PETAU.
Petavius obſerves, that " this paſſage is taken from the
" fourth book *de Legibus* ;" but either Julian quoted from
memory, or his MSS. were different from ours. Xenophon
opens the Cyropædia with a ſimilar reflection.   GIBBON.

The variations, which are ſpecified in the notes, are few
and immaterial, being chiefly verbal.

* The word τοτε (" then") is not in Plato.

† Αρα, a kind of expletive, occurs here in Plato.

‡ Και ελευθεριαν και αφθον (" and freedom and plenty"), is
added in Plato.

" preſerve

" preferve mankind in tranquillity and happinefs.
" And this is agreeable to truth and reafon; for
" thofe ftates * which are governed, not by a God
" but by fome mortal, have no ceffation from evils
" and oppreffions. We fhould therefore exert our
" utmoft efforts to imitate the life that was led in
" the reign of Saturn, and, with as much immor-
" tality as we have remaining, to govern, by his
" directions, both in public and private, our fami-
" lies and our ftates, confidering † the law as the
" application of the divine mind. But whether
" one man, or a few, or a number of people ‡,
" govern any ftate, if their minds are enflaved by
" pleafure, and through a defire § of indulging it
" they trample on the laws, there is no chance
" of fafety."

I have tranfcribed this whole paffage of Plato
on purpofe to prevent your furmifing, that I
quote the words of the ancients fraudulently or
erroneoufly, and without regard to the connection.
But what fays this paffage really on the fubject?
You fee, that, though a prince be by nature human, he fhould, in his conduct, be a divine and
fuperior being, and entirely banifh from his

* There is alfo a fmall difference here; οσων πολεων and
αρχη in Julian, ως οσον αν πολεων and αρχει in Plato.

† Ονομαζοντας in Julian, επονομαζοντας in Plato.

‡ In other words, and nearer to the original, " a mo-
" narchy, an oligarchy, or a democracy."

§ There follows in Plato ϛιγυσαν δε υδεν· αλλ' ανυητω και
απληϛω κακω νοσημαλι ξυνεχομενην αρξει δε, κ. τ. λ. which Julian
perhaps, for the fake of brevity, omitted. PETAU.

foul

foul every thing that is mortal and brutish, except what muft necessarily remain for corporeal ufes. If any one, reflecting on this, fhould dread being engaged in fuch a ftate of life, would you rather recommend to him the Epicurean tranquillity, the gardens and fuburbs of Athens, and the myrtles and cottage of Socrates? But I never preferred them to toils and dangers *. Thefe labours I would willingly recount to you, and the hazards to which I was expofed from my friends and relations, when I was firft inftructed by your precepts, were you not well acquainted with them. To my conduct in Ionia, in oppofition to one who was my relation by birth, but much nearer by friendfhip, and in favour of a man who was a foreigner, and little known to me, you are alfo no ftranger. Did I not go abroad for the fake of my friends? In behalf of Carterius, I need not tell you, I went unfolicited, and intreated the affiftance of my friend Araxius †. On account of the effects of the excellent Areta, and the injuries which fhe had fuffered from her neighbours, did I not travel twice within two months into Phrygia; though my body

---

* The facts which Julian produces to prove that he never wanted courage fully convince me that this Epiftle was prior to his refidence in the Gauls. How many marks of firmnefs, how many valiant deeds, might he not have alleged, if it had been written after he was proclaimed Auguftus?   La Bleterie.

He might probably compofe it at Vienne, where he paffed the winter after his being appointed Cæfar.

† Ammianus mentions Araxius towards the end of b. xxvi, and relates, that, having efpoufed the party of Procopius, when he was killed he was banifhed to an ifland, and afterwards fet at liberty.   Petau.

was

was infirm in confequence of a diforder contracted
by former fatigues? Laftly, before my journey
into ,Greece, while I continued with the army,
many would fay, with the utmoft hazard, recollect
what kind of letters I wrote to you, whether they
were in a plaintive ftrain, or exhibited any marks
of littlenefs, meannefs, or fervility. When I
went again into Greece, did not I congratulate
my good fortune, as if it had been a feftival,
affirming, that the change was moft delightful to
me, and that, according to the faying, I had
gained

   —Gold for brafs, what coft a hundred beeves
   For the low price of nine * ?

Such was my joy on being allowed to refide
in Greece, though I had neither a houfe, nor
any land, not fo much as a field or a garden
there. But perhaps you will fay, that though
I may feem to bear adverfity with firmnefs, yet I
am abject and pufillanimous in profperity, as I
prefer Athens to the fplendor that now furrounds
me †, regret that indolence, and, on account of
my numerous avocations, deteft my prefent ftate
of life. But a better opinion of us fhould be

* Iliad. vi. 236. thus paraphrafed by Pope, 292.
   For Diomed's brafs arms, of mean device,
  , For which nine oxen paid, a vulgar price,
   He gave his own, of gold divinely wrought,
   A hundred beeves the fhining purchafe bought.
 † The Cæfars had all the marks of the Imperial power,
excepting the diadem.   La Bleterie.

formed of us, not only with regard to idleneſs and employment, but according to that maxim, " Know " thyſelf," and

> That trade which he has learn'd let each man
> praᶜtiſe.

To govern ſeems to me more than human; and a king, as Plato ſays, " ſhould be of a ſuperior nature."

I will now quote a paſſage from Ariſtotle, to the ſame purpoſe; not " to carry owls to Athens *," as the ſaying is, but to ſhew that I have not entirely negleᶜted his works. In his Political Diſcourſes †, he thus expreſſes himſelf : " If any one " ſhould think it beſt for a nation to be governed " by a king, what ſhall be determined in regard " to his children ? Muſt his deſcendants alſo reign ? " If they muſt, however incapable, much inconve- " nience may enſue. But will not the ſovereign " in poſſeſſion leave the government to his ſons ‡ ? " That he will not can ſcarce be ſuppoſed, as " being a taſk too arduous, and requiring a grea-

---

* Γλαυκα Αθηναιοις αγων, *Noᶜtuas Athenis ducens.* To the ſame purpoſe is out Engliſh proverb, " carrying coals to " Newcaſtle." Equally needleſs was any information from Ariſtotle to Themiſtius.

† *Ariſtot. de Republicâ, lib.* III. *cap.* 15.

‡ In Ariſtotle it is Αλλ' ꙋ καʈαλειψει τꙁς υιεις διαδοχꙁς ο βασιλευς, επ' εξυσιας εχων τꙍτο ποιησαι; " Will not the king " leave his ſons his ſucceſſors, if he has it in his power ?" The inſtance of Marcus Aurelius and his degenerate ſon Commodus (ſee the Cæſars, p. 161.) ſeems a caſe in point, The " taſk" of diſinheriting ſuch a monſter was too arduous, " the virtue" too exalted, even for that philoſopher.

" ter degree of virtue than is the lot of human
" nature."

Afterwards, fpeaking of a king who governs
according to law, of which he is the minifter and
guardian, and ftyling him, " not a king," but
ranking him in another clafs, he adds *, " As to
" abfolute monarchy †, or arbitrary power, fome
" think it inconfiftent with nature for one to be lord
" of all ‡. For all men, being by nature equal, have
" the fame natural rights §." And, a little after,
he fays, " Whoever therefore would have reafon
" govern, would have God and the laws govern.
" But whoever would give the government to man,
" would give it to a wild beaft ‖. For fuch is con-
" cupifcence, and anger alfo debafes ** the beft men.
" Law therefore is reafon, exempt from paffion."

The philofopher, you obferve, feems here to
diftruft and reprobate human nature. For he fays,
in effect, that human nature is by no means
equal to the eminence of fuch an exalted ftation.
He thinks it difficult for a prince to prefer
the general good of the ftate to that of his

* *De Republ. l.* iii. *c.* 16.

† Παμβασιλεια.

‡ Both the prince and the philofopher choofe, however,
to involve this eternal truth in artful and laboured obfcurity.
                                        GIBBON.

§ There follows in Ariftotle, Και την αυτην αξιαν καια φυσιν ειναι
(" And, according to nature, the fame rank.")

‖ Ο δε ανθρωπονκιλιυων, προσιβησι και θηριον. The MS. of
Voffius, unfatisfied with " a fingle beaft," affords the ftron-
ger reading of θηρια (" beafts"), which the experience of
defpotifm may warrant.   GIBBON.

** Αρχονίας και (" magiftrates and") is inferted in Ariftotle.

children, He says, that " it is unjuft for one to
" govern many of his equals." And at laft, in
the clofe of his difcourfe, he adds, that " law is
" reafon, exempt from paffion;" and that " go-
" vernment fhould be entrufted to law alone, and
" not to any man. For the reafon that men pof-
" fefs, even if they are virtuous, is debafed by
" anger and luft, moft favage beafts."

This doctrine of Ariftotle feems perfectly agreeable to that of Plato. Firft, he thinks that the governor ought to excell the governed, not only in
virtue, but in nature; which is not eafy to find
among men. And alfo, that he fhould, to the utmoft of his power, obey the laws, not thofe which
were enacted on a fudden emergency, or compiled
by men who were not entirely governed by reafon;
but by fuch, as, having pure minds and fouls, had
a view not only to prefent offences and contingen-
cies, but from the nature of government, and alfo
the nature of juftice and of guilt, after obtaining
all poffible inftruction, framed laws for all the people in general, without refpect to friend or foe, to
neighbour or relation. And this is much preferable, as they meant to promulge and tranfmit
their laws, not to their contemporaries only, but
to pofterity and foreigners, with whom they never had, nor expected to have, any connection or
intercourfe. I have heard that the wife Solon,
though by his civil inftitutions he made the people
free, incurred much reproach by confulting with

his friends as to cancelling of debts *, and thus giving them an opportunity of improving their fortunes. So difficult it is to avoid such fatalities, even though a man were to enter into the public service unimpassioned.

As such are my apprehensions, I often regret my former state of life, and, in deference to you, I reflect that you have said, not only that those great legislators, Solon, Lycurgus, and Pittacus, were proposed for my emulation †, but also that I must quit the shade of philosophy for the open sunshine. As if you should say to a man, who, for the sake of his health, had used moderate exercise at home, " You must now repair to Olympia ‡, and " exchange your domestic recreation for the games " of Jupiter ; where your spectators will be the " Greeks resorting from all parts ; and, in parti- " cular, your fellow citizens, for whom you must " enter the lists; and also some Barbarians, whom " you must astonish, in order to render your country " as formidable to them as you can." This would immediately alarm him, and make him enter the lists with terror. Suppose me now affected in the same manner by your epistle. Whether my opinion on the subject be just or not, whether I am a little

* Before the resolution which Solon had taken to extinguish debts transpired in public, some of his friends borrowed large sums, well knowing that they should be excused from paying them.   LA BLETERIE.

† See p. 7.

‡ A town of Peloponnesus, where was a temple of Jupiter, in honour of whom the Olympic games were celebrated there every fifth year.

C 2

mis-

miftaken, or totally err, I expect to learn from you.

The matters in your epiftle as to which I am doubtful, and therefore wifh you to explain, my deareft and moft refpectable friend, fhall now be mentioned. You " prefer," you fay, " an active " to a philofophical life;" and you appeal to the teftimony of the wife Ariftotle, who makes happinefs confift in acting well; but " whether a po- " litical or a contemplative life fhould be preferred, " he was," you fay, " rather undetermined." For, in fome places, he gives the preference to contemplation; in others, he commends the " architects," as he ftyles them, " of illuftrious deeds." " Among " thefe," you fay, " are kings." But Ariftotle never ufes the word which you have introduced. And the contrary may rather be inferred from the paffage that you have quoted. For inftance: " We think thofe acquit themfelves moft properly " in all external actions, who are, as it were, men- " tal architects." This may be fuppofed to mean law-givers, or political philofophers, and all who act merely by thought and reafon, rather than the artificers of civil tranfactions; for whom it is not fufficient to confider, and devife, and inftruct others in their duty; but every thing that the laws direct, or circumftances may require, they muft undertake and execute themfelves; unlefs we call himan architect, who is

——— in m ghty actions fkill'd *,

* Μεγαλων επιςορα εργων. Odyff. xxi. 26.

as Homer poetically ftyles Hercules, the greateft
of fuch artificers.

But if we admit this to be true, and think thofe
only happy who have adminiftered public affairs,
fuch as have ruled or reigned over many, what then
fhall we fay of Socrates? As to Pythagoras *, and
Democritus †, and Anaxagoras ‡ the Clazomenian,
they, perhaps you will fay, were in another refpect happy, on account of their contemplations.
But Socrates, rejecting a fpeculative, and preferring an active life, could not govern his own wife,
nor his fon, nor indeed reftrain two or three dif-
orderly citizens. Will you fay, that he was not
active, as he was not a ruler? On the contrary, I
maintain, that the fon § of Sophronifcus performed
greater actions than Alexander ‖; for to him I afcribe

---

* A philofopher of Samos, who travelled as far as India,
through Ægypt, in fearch of knowledge; and on returning opened a fchool in a remote part of Italy (Magna Græ-
cia), in the reign of Tarquin the Proud. See Cic. *Tufc.
Quæft.* IV. 1. He held the tranfmigration of fouls, and
was thought by his fcholars infallible.

† Of Abdera, from his ridiculing the eager purfuit of
welath and honour, known by the name of the laughing
philofopher. Yet his own father was fo rich, that at one
time he feafted Xerxes and his army. He died at the age of
99 years. See Cic. *de Fin.* v. 29. and *Acad.* IV. 17.

‡ A man of high birth, and a higher mind, the preceptor of Pericles. See the Confolatory oration on the de-
prture of Salluft.

§ Socrates. His father was a ftone-cutter of mean fortune, and his mother (Phænarete) a midwife.

‖ Julian is right in preferring Socrates to the conqueror
of Afia, the wifeft and moft enlightened of philofophers to
the fcourge of mankind. But whatever he may fay of
pretended philofophical converfions, as rare as defective,

C 3

men

men derived very little advantage, from the instructions of Socrates: witness the deplorable state in which the nations by whom philosophy was most cultivated were with regard both to religion and manners before the publication of the gospel. It was reserved for twelve men, of the dregs of the people, and of a nation which Athens and Rome considered as barbarous, to effect in the world a reformation which philosophy had never attempted and deemed impossible. If men had had for apostles only Socrates, and the philosophers of different sects proceeding from his school, the world would still have been what it was formerly. In the midst of the profoundest darkness, some men, a little less blind than the vulgar, and often more vicious, had a glimpse of a small number of truths, which served as food for their pride, and exercise for their tongues, rather than as a rule for their conduct. Some considered every thing as problematical, even the existence of God, and the principles of morality. Others, raving at vice, dishonoured virtue, and affronted public decency. Some performed virtuous actions, but from fanaticism and self-love. Many concealed, and badly concealed, under the philosophical cloak, some abominations which now we dare not name. The most enlightened, through want of zeal for the truths with which they were best acquainted; and besides not being able to support them but by subtle and far from popular arguments, held them in captivity. They had not the courage merely to propose to the multitude the fundamental tenet of the unity of God. The people, without instruction, without principles, without manners, without an idea of the duties of man, rushed headlong into all the horrors of idolatry; and the pretended sages, such as Socrates, Plato, Cicero, Seneca, &c. had the meanness to worship in the temples the same Gods whom they ridiculed in their schools and in their writings: or at the most like Julian, and the Platonists of his time, by the aid of some arbitrary system they formed a monstrous mixture of the tenets of the divine unity together with the speculative and practical follies of polytheism. It is even more than probable, that the general corruption and the various revolutions that happened in the world would have absolutely extinguished the weak lights of philosophy if Christianity had not come to strengthen, purify, and extend them, and to place within the reach of the dullest minds both what the philosophers could not, and what they dared not, teach. Probably the nations which dismem-

bered

the military fkill of Xenophon *, the fortitude of Antifthenes †, the Eretrian ‡ and Megarean § philofophy ; a Cebes ‖, a Simmias **, a Phædon ††, and innumerable others ; not to mention the colonies that we have received from Athens ; from the Lyceum, the Porch, and the Academies ‡‡. Who is now preferved by the victories of Alexander?

bered the Roman empire would again have plunged us into barbarifm, if the Chriftian religion had not civilifed them. Will thofe who oppofe it never have the equity to confider, that without it they would certainly have been abandoned to the moft foolifh fuperftitions, and perhaps have been in a ftate fimilar to that of the favages of America ?   La Bleterie.

* Of the " military fkill" of Xenophon there needs no other proof than the retreat of the ten thoufand Greeks, which he conducted.

† The founder of the fect of the *Cynics*, which Diogenes, one of his principal hearers, rendered fo confiderable. *Patientiam*, fays Cicero (*de Orat.* iii. 17.) *et duritiam in Socratico fermone maximè adamarat.* He ftyles him alfo (*ad Attic.* xii. 38.) *hominis acuti magis quàm eruditi.*

‡ From Menedemus, becaufe he was of Eretria [in Eubœa] the Eretrians were fo called; all whofe good was placed in the mind, and the quicknefs of its apprehenfion, by which truth is difcerned. *Cic. Acad.* iv. 42.

§ From Euclid, a difciple of Socrates, who was of Megara [in Achaia], his followers were ftyled Megareans, who maintained that only to be good which was fingle, and always the fame.   *Ibid.*

‖ Of Thebes. He wrote three dialogues, whofe titles are preferved by Diogenes Laertius (*Vit. Philof.*) The firft of them, his *Table*, is ftill extant.

** Of Thebes alfo. Laertius enumerates twenty-three of his dialogues.

†† Phædon of Elis was firft a flave, but being emancipated he ftudied philofophy, and became the chief of the fect called Elean.

‡‡ The fchools of Ariftotle, Zeno (or the Stoics) and the Academics.

C 4

What

What nation is more wifely governed, what individual is improved, by them? Many you may find whom they have enriched, but none whom they have made wifer, or more temperate, either in themfelves, or towards others: on the contrary, they have fomented pride and infolence; while all who are now reformed by philofophy, are reformed by Socrates. In this opinion I am fupported by Ariftotle, who feems to mean the fame, by faying, that " the theological work *, which he was com-
" pofing, required as great abilities as thofe which
" fubverted the Perfian empire." In this I think he reafoned right. For victories are principally owing to courage and fortune, and, if you pleafe, a kind of prudential cunning. But he who conceives true ideas of God is not only endued with perfect virtue, but it may juftly be doubted whether fuch a one fhould be ftyled a man or a God. For if it be true, that all things are fo conftituted as to be beft known by thofe who are connected with them, he who is acquainted with the divine nature may, in like manner, be deemed a pure intelligence.

But fince I am returned to the comparifon between a contemplative and an active life, from which I had digreffed, and which, at the beginning of your epiftle, you wifhed to decline; I will

* Τη θεολογικη συγγραφη, " On the nature of God." The fequel fhews, that it fhould be thus tranflated. I know not what this work of Ariftotle is; and Julian, if I miftake not, is the only one who has mentioned it. La Bleterie.

mention the fame philofophers that you did, Areus *, Nicolaus †, Thrafyllus ‡, and Mufonius ||.   Not one of thefe had the government of his country; though Areus, it is faid, refufed the præfecture of Ægypt, which was offered him. But Thrafyllus, being the intimate friend of that cruel tyrant Ti-

* A philofopher and a man of learning, who, with his two fons, Dionyfius and Nicanor, was attached to the perfon of Auguftus, whofe confidence he poffeffed.   Seneca fays, that he was the comforter of Livia, when fhe feemed inconfolable for the lofs of Drufus. *Senec. Confolat. ad Marciam.*   LA BLETERIE.

† A friend of Auguftus, M. Agrippa, and Herod the Great, who learned of him philofophy.   At the defire of that king of the Jews, he wrote an univerfal hiftory.   He did honour to philofophy by his difintereftednefs and generofity.   He anticipated in every thing the wants of his friends, and faid, that " money, like inftruments of mufic, " was only ufeful to thofe who employed it."   He compofed the Life of Auguftus, or rather the hiftory of his education.   We have only fome fragments of his works, which are in the extracts of Conftantine Porphyrogenetus, publifhed by M. de Valois.   *Ibid.*

‡ A Platonic philofopher and a celebrated aftrologer. It appears in Tacitus, *Annal.* vi. with what addrefs and prefence of mind he contrived to efcape the cruelty of Tiberius, and to gain his confidence.   *Ibid.*

|| C. Caius Mufonius Rufus, a Roman knight.   Not contented with profeffing the Stoic philofophy, he endeavoured to diffufe it among the young nobility of Rome, and fpeaking freely of the conduct of Nero, that tyrant committed him to a dreadful prifon, from whence he fent him firft into the ifland of Gyaros, and afterwards to the ifthmus of Corinth, there to work in chains.   A friend commiferating his fituation, " I had rather be here," faid Mufonius, " than act on a ftage like Nero."   After the death of his perfecutor, he returned to Rome, and was the only philofopher whom Vefpafian did not expell.   As Julian fays, that Mufonius fuftained the cruelty " of tyrants," he was again perfecuted by fome other befides Nero; no doub by Domitian. *Ibid.*

berius ,

berius, unlefs he had exculpated himfelf by the difcourfes that he has left, would have contracted a perpetual and indelible ftain. Thus civil government was of no fervice to him. Nicolaus was the artificer of no great deeds, and he is better known by his writings concerning them. Mufonius alfo, by fupporting with fortitude and fubduing by firmnefs the cruelty of tyrants, became diftinguifhed, and was no lefs happy than thofe who governed the greateft kingdoms. As for Areus, when he refufed the præfecture of Ægypt, he willingly deprived himfelf of the greateft happinefs, if he thought an active life the greateft. You yourfelf too are inactive, as you neither command an army *, nor harangue the people, nor govern any

nation

---

* Indeed the Themiftius, with whom we are acquainted, was not a warrior. Nor did he harangue the people; no one, I imagine, had then that privilege, except the Emperors and Cæfars. He was not Præfect of Conftantinople till the reign of Theodofius. Neverthelefs, the manner in which Julian here mentions the Themiftius, to whom he is writing, would make one think, that he was rather a mere philofopher, concentered in his fchool, than the celebrated Themiftius, who had been made fenator of Conftantinople two months before Julian was named Cæfar, and who had always the ambition to be at once a philofopher and a ftatefman. Befides, the Themiftius to whom the epiftle is addreffed, appears to have been one of the moft intimate friends of Julian; and Themiftius the fenator, in an oration pronounced in the reign of Theodofius, in which he boafts of the regard which the Emperors had had for him, intimates that Julian did not love him, becaufe, he fays, that prince had been forced (by truth, no doubt) to acknowledge him for the firft of philofophers. In fhort, what is ftill of more confequence,

Julian

nation or city: but does it follow, that you are not wife? And if you should form several philosophers, or only three or four, you would contribute more essentially to the happiness of mankind than many kings united. A philosopher acts no inconfiderable part; he is not, as you have said, the director only of public counsels, nor is his action confined to thinking. But if he confirm his words by his deeds, and appear such as he would have others to be, he will urge to action

Julian was not Cæsar when Themistius was made senator; yet Themistius, in the discourse where he thanks Constantius for his new dignity, congratulates the Emperor on having taken Julian for his colleague. These difficulties are very strong; but may it not be said in answer, 1. That Themistius was perhaps one of the senators who were styled *allecti* or *immunes*, and who enjoyed all the privileges of senators, without being obliged to exercise the functions? 2. Themistius was at least as good a courtier as philosopher. Policy therefore did not allow him to boast, in the reign of Theodosius, of having been the friend of Julian. He rather chose to have it then believed, that, if that prince had given him great marks of esteem, it was not so much from inclination and choice, as because he could not refuse them. The vanity of Themistius, which is very apparent in the oration in question, concurred with policy to make him speak this language. 3. It is true, that the letters by which Constantius made Themistius senator were read in the senate of Constantinople on the first of September, 355, and that Julian was not declared Cæsar till the sixth of November following; but the acknowledgement in which the new senator mentions the association of Julian was, as appears by the discourse itself, pronounced some time after the letters of Constantius had been read at Constantinople, and when it was just known that Julian was Cæsar. Nothing hinders our supposing that two months and a half, or three months, intervened between the reading of those letters and the discourse in question. La Bleterie.

.with .

with more perfuafion and effect than thofe who excite to it by command.

But I muft now return to the fubject with which I began, and conclude an epiftle already perhaps too long. This is the fum of it; that it is not for the fake of avoiding fatigue, nor of purfuing pleafure, nor from a love of floth and idlenefs, that I am averfe to public bufinefs; but, as I faid at the beginning, from a confcioufnefs of my not having fufficient knowledge or genius, and alfo from an apprehenfion of throwing a reproach on philofophy (whom though I love I have not won, and who by the men of this age is already too much flighted), having written fomething formerly, and now being corrected by your admonitions.

May God grant me fuccefs, and prudence to deferve it! I have now the utmoft occafion for the affiftance principally of the Supreme Being, and alfo of you philofophers, for whofe credit I have expofed myfelf to danger. If God fhall by my means grant to mankind a bleffing * beyond my abilities alone to procure, you will have no reafon to be offended at my difcourfes. For as I am confcious of nothing good, this only excepted, that having nothing, I do not think that I abound †, I con-

---

* This bleffing was particularly the re-eftablifhment of Paganifm. La Bleterie.

† Οτι μηδε οιομαι τα μεγιστα εχειν, εχων γε ουδεν. As both Julian and his correfpondent were, no doubt, well acquainted with the writings of the Apoftles, I will hazard a conjecture that this was intended as a fneer on an expreffion

of

continue to act, as you obferve, in the fame manner; and I intreat you not to form high expectations of me, but to fubmit every thing to God. So if any faults fhould be committed, I fhall be blamelefs; but if all things fhould fucceed to my wifhes, I fhall be grateful and moderate, not arrogating to myfelf the deeds of others, but afcribing, as is juft, every thing to God *; and knowing that my acknowledgements are due to him, let me exhort you to return him yours alfo.

of St. Paul, in 2 Cor. VI. 10. Ὡς μηδὲν ἔχοντες, καὶ πάντα κατέχοντες, *As having nothing, and yet poffeffing all things.* The expreffions at leaft are very fimilar.

* That piety of fpirit, that true magnanimity, which Julian here profeffes, has been nobly exemplified, while I am writing this, by a modern commander, the retriever of the glory of the Britifh flag, whom we find, in the midft of the moft brilliant fuccefs, " giving God the glory," and not fcrupling to declare, that " It has pleafed God, " out of his Divine Providence, to grant to his Majefty's " arms a moft complete victory," &c. See Sir George Rodney's Letter in the London Gazette of May 18, 1782.

A CONSOLATORY ORATION ON THE DEPARTURE OF * SALLUST †.

A. D.
358.

UNLESS, my dear friend, I communicate to you what has occurred to me in private, since I heard of your approaching departure, I shall

* One MS. adds, τυ αγαθωτατυ, ("the excellent.")

† This is a farewell encomium on Salluſt, who was going into Illyricum and Thrace, he being one of the few who was dear to Julian, and his confidential friend. He wrote this Oration when he governed the Gauls with the title of Cæfar, during the life of Conſtantius. The time when Julian celebrated the departure of Salluſt with this Oration may be afcertained from a paſſage in the Epiſtle to the Athenians, where he mentions, that Conſtantius removed Salluſt from the Gauls, becaufe he was his friend.

PETAU.

This Oration exhibits to us a picture of an excellent temper, on the eminence to which Julian was now exalted, in not being able to be feparated from the deareſt and moſt ufeful guide and companion of his life without the utmoſt regret.

SPANHEIM.

Salluſt was an officer of great merit, by birth a Gaul. What employment Conſtantius had given him in the Gauls is not known, but it was certainly one that was confiderable. He was a Pagan, a man of learning, of great ability in bufinefs, and of diſtinguiſhed probity; fufficient recommendations to the friendſhip of Julian. Salluſt had the rare talent of giving advice without petulance, and without that air of confidence, which too often renders the truth, and always thofe who fpeak it, difgufting. The freedom with which he reproved the prince was foftened

by

shall think myself deprived of some consolation;
or

by respect, cordiality, and tenderness. Julian revered him
as a father, and all the good that Julian did was attributed
to Salluft, without exciting any jealousy in Julian. The
intrigues of Florentius and some other officers induced the
Emperor to recall Salluft, on a pretext that was honourable
to him; but, in reality, to mortify Julian, who was left at
the discretion of persons unworthy of their posts, and his
professed enemies. He was extremely concerned at the loss
of Salluft. To assuage his grief, he addressed this discourse to him, in which he takes leave of him in an affecting
manner, with testimonies of the sincereft friendship and
esteem. Afterwards, when he was Emperor, he made him
Præfect of the Gauls.   LA BLETERIE.

On his entering the Persian territories [April 13, 363],
Julian received a letter from his old friend Salluft [then in
Gaul], conjuring him not to take the field till he had ap-
peased the Gods, who seemed, by various prodigies, to
declare against the Persian war. But the die was caft. *Ibid.*

See also Epiftle XVII, and what M. de la Bleterie says
farther of this difcourfe in the Preface.

The measures of policy, and the operations of war,
muft submit to the various operations of circumftance and
character, and the unpractifed ftudent will often be perplexed in the application of the moft perfect theory. But
in the acquifition of this important fcience Julian was
affifted by the active vigour of his own genius, as well as
by the wifdom and experience of Salluft, an officer of
rank, who foon conceived a fincere attachment for a prince
fo worthy of his friendship; and whofe incorruptible in-
tegrity was adorned by the talent of infinuating the
harfheft truths, without wounding the delicacy of a royal
ear.   GIBBON.

This excellent minifter was fpeedily recalled by the
jealoufy of the Emperor; and we may ftill read a fenfible
but pedantic difcourfe, in which Julian deplores the lofs of
fo valuable a friend, to whom he acknowledges himfelf indebted for his reputation.   *Ibib.*

This Salluft muft be carefully diftinguifhed from the
venerable Præfect of the Eaft, who had the fingular honour of twice refusing the empire, once after the death

or rather I shall imagine that my dignity * affords me no advantage unshared by you. For having participated with each other in much joy, and in much grief, both in words and deeds, in public and in private, at home and in the field, for the present evils, be they what they may, we must both have recourse to the same remedy. But who will supply us with a lyre like that of Orpheus, or with songs like those of the Sirens, or with the drug Nepenthes † ? Whether this was a fiction

derived

of Julian, and again on the death of Jovian. Julian honoured the consulship with the name of the Præfect of Gaul (A. D. 363.)   *Ibid.*

The fourth Oration of Julian, *In Solem Regem*, composed in three nights, is addressed to the same Sallust, and towards the conclusion he mentions a former work (now lost) " on the Κρονια," or *Saturnalia*, which was also inscribed to him, and of which one paragraph (quoted in the first note on the Cæsars, p. 145.), is preserved by Suidas.

* Of Cæsar, which Constantius had conferred on him at Milan, Nov. 6, 355. See the Epistle to the Athenians, p. 77.

† Odyf. IV. 221. On the arrival of Telemachus at the court of Menelaus at Sparta,

> ———— With genial joy to warm the soul,
> Bright Helen mix'd a mirth-inspiring bowl;
> Temper'd with drugs of sovereign use t'asswage
> The boiling bosom of tumultuous rage,
> To clear the clouded front of wrinkled care,
> And dry the fearful sluices of despair.
>
> . . . .
>
> These drugs, so friendly to the joys of life,
> Bright Helen learn'd from Thone's imperial wife,
> Who sway'd the sceptre, where prolific Nile
> With various simples cloaths the fruitful soil, &c.

FENTON.
Julian

derived from Ægyptian lore, or was invented by the poet himself, and interwoven in his sequel of the Trojan calamities, as if Helen had learned it in Ægypt, it expresses what ought to be the language of those who wish to dispel, not the miseries which the Greeks and Trojans mutually inflicted, but mental sufferings, and to restore chearfulness and tranquillity. For pleasure and pain seem to flow from the same source, and in their turns succeed each other. And those events which occasion great labour and trouble, in the opinion of the wise, give a mind, that is rightly disposed, not more pain than pleasure. Thus from the bitterest herb that grows on Hymettus * the bee extracts sweet juice, and works it into honey. Such bodies, as are healthy and robust, are nourished by any kind of food, and that which is generally deemed unwholesome, far from impairing, increases their strength. But on those, whose constitutions, by nature, education, or study, are weak, and through their whole life, valetudinary, the slightest attacks make violent impressions, So, in regard to the mind, those who are thus [susceptible, must be

Julian refers to the same passage in his xxxviith Epistle. And Milton thus alludes to it, in his Mask of Comus :

Not that Nepenthes which the wife of Thone,
In Ægypt, gave to Jove-born Helena,
Is of such power to stir up joy as this,
To life so friendly, or so cool to thirst.

* A mountain of Attica, famous for excellent honey.
Ubi non Hymetto mella decedunt.　　　Hor.

Vol. I.　　　　　D　　　　　contented

contented *] with being moderately well, and though they are not endued with the strength of Antisthenes † or Socrates, or the fortitude of Callisthenes ‡, or the temperance of Polemo ||, yet if they can be serene in such trials, perhaps in greater difficulties they may be chearful.

As to myself, sensible how much I suffer and shall suffer from your journey, my concern was equal to that which I felt on first leaving my preceptor §. For I immediately recollected the labours which we have shared, our pure and unfeigned affection, our innocent and unreserved

---

* Imperfect. The translator has supplied the chasm by conjecture.

† A philosopher and teacher of rhetoric at Rhodes, who, on hearing Socrates, bade his scholars seek a new master, for he had found one. He was the founder of the Cynic sect, and the master of Diogenes.

‡ A philosopher and disciple of Aristotle, who frequented the court of Alexander the Great. On his opposing that prince being worshipped in the Persian manner, he was accused of a pretended conspiracy, and cruelly exposed to lions.

|| Polemo was a profligate young rake of Athens, and even distinguished by the dissoluteness of his manners. One day, after a riotous entertainment, he came reeling, with a chaplet on his head, into the school of Xenocrates. The audience were greatly offended at his scandalous appearance; but the philosopher went on, without any emotion, in a discourse on temperance and sobriety. Polemo was so struck by his arguments, that he soon threw away his chaplet; and from that time became a disciple of Xenocrates; and profited so well by his instructions, that he afterwards succeeded him in the Socratic school.

Mrs. CARTER.

§ The eunuch Mardonius. See the Misopogon.

con-

converfation, our concurrence in all things laudable, the alacrity and refolution with which we uniformly oppofed the wicked, and the firmnefs with which we conftantly maintained our purpofe, having one and the fame mind, fimilar manners, and being united by the ftricteft friendfhip. Befides, I recollected that expreffion,

—— On the field Ulyffes ftands alone *.

For I now much refemble him, fince God has removed you, like Hector †, far from the darts which have been launched at you by fycophants ; or rather at me, endeavouring to wound me through you; as thinking no method fo certain as that of depriving me, if poffible, of the fociety of a faithful friend, an alert defender, and a fharer, with the utmoft alacrity, in all my dangers. You, I think, at being denied a participation in my cares and labours, are no lefs affected than I am ; but on

* Il. xi. 401. Οιωθη δ' Οδυσευς. Pope, 509. It has before been remarked, (p. 3. note.) that it was fafhionable for the Greeks in general, and Julian, their admirer and imitator, in particular, to quote Homer at random on every occafion. The above expreffion is applied by the poet to Ulyffes, when Diomed had been wounded by Paris, and obliged to quit the field.

† Il. xi. 164. This paffage is again quoted and applied, with more propriety, by Julian to himfelf in his Allegorical Fable. That Hector was removed from the battle was a defirable circumftance to Ulyffes ; not fo the defertion of his friend Diomed. To this therefore the removal of Salluft from Julian feems more applicable.

my account, and for my safety, are rather more anxious than myself. For as I never preferred my own intereſt to yours, I have always experienced from you the ſame attention. I am therefore juſtly and deeply concerned, that to you, who, with reſpect to others, can ſay,

> " I heed them not, for my affairs are proſperous,"

I alone ſhould occaſion grief and anxiety. But in this, it ſeems, we are equal ſufferers; you, however, lamenting only on my account, but I conſtantly regretting the loſs of your ſociety, and recollecting the friendſhip which we mutually pledged to each other, cemented firſt and principally by virtue, and afterwards by the obligations, not from you to me, but thoſe which were largely conferred on me by you. This friendſhip we bound not by oaths, or other ſuch ties, like Theſeus and Pirithous *, but by a perpetual concurrence in opinion, in being ſo far from uniting to injure any one, as never to converſe on the ſubject. But if any thing happened advantageous to an individual, or the common good was in view, this engaged our private diſcourſe.

That I have abundant cauſe to lament, on being ſeparated, for ever ſo ſhort a time, not only from a friend, but, God knows, a faithful aſſiſtant,

* The ſworn friendſhip of theſe two heroes was proverbial. See the Life of Theſeus in Plutarch.

Socrates,

Socrates, I doubt not, the great herald and teacher
of virtue, would allow; as far as his fentiments
may be conjectured from Plato. For thefe are his
words: " Rightly to govern a ftate, I deem a moft
" difficult tafk; for it cannot be governed without
" faithful friends and counfellors; and fuch can-
" not eafily be found," And if Plato thought
this more arduous than digging through Athos,
what can we expect, who in wifdom and knowledge
are more unequal to him than he was to God?
But I not only regret the mutual affiftance which
we gave to each other, in civil adminiftration, and
which enabled us more eafily to fupport whatever
happened unexpectedly either by accident, or by
the machinations of our enemies; but the approaching lofs of my chief folace and delight rends
and afflicts my heart. For what friend equally
benevolent have I now remaining? Whofe fincere
and innocent confidence fhall I be able now to endure? Who will advife me prudently, reprove me
mildly, confirm me in virtue without pride and
arrogance, and ufe freedom of fpeech without
afperity; like thofe, who from medicines extract the
naufeous, and leave the ufeful? Thefe advantages *
I have derived from your friendfhip. Deftitute of

* In the original, Αλλα τετο μιν εκ της σης φιλιας το ονειδος
εκαρπωσαμην; literally, " But I have reaped this *difgrace* from
" your friendfhip." Perhaps we fhould read το ονειον (*utile*).
The Latin tranflator renders it by *famam hanc* (which may
be taken either in a good or bad fenfe); and Mr. Gibbon
(fee his fecond note, p. 31.) by " reputation."

D 3

that,

that, how shall I compose numerous orations?
Who, when, in despair, I am hazarding my life,
from regret of you, of your counsels and benevolence, will persuade me to be resigned, and to
submit with fortitude to whatever God decrees?
For this, in concurrence with him, the great Emperor * seems to have determined. By what
method, by what charms, can the mind be enabled
to support such anxiety and distress with moderation? Shall we imitate the discourses of Zamolxis †, and mutter his incantations, which, when
Socrates had introduced them at Athens, he obliged beautiful Charmides ‡ to sing, before he would
cure him of his head-ach? Or if these, as being
too vast, and intended for greater trials, like large
machines in a small theatre, are unmanageable, yet,
from former occurrences, collecting, as it were, from
a variegated meadow, some choice and beautiful
flowers, shall we solace our minds with narrations,
interspersing with them some strictures from philosophy? As draughts that are too luscious are ren-

* Constantius.

† A Gete, and servant of Pythagoras, who, at his return, civilised his countrymen, and by them was reputed a
God.

‡ An Athenian, the son of Glaucon, famous for his
beauty. See the Dialogue of Plato so named, in which
Charmides is an interlocutor. "If," says Socrates, "what
" Critics here say be true, if you are extremely tem-
" perate, you have no more occasion for Zamolxis, or the
" incantations of Abaris, the Hyperborean; that alone will
" be a sufficient remedy for your head." Charmides is also
mentioned by Plato in his Theages, Protagoras, and
Banquet.

dered

dered more palatable by the infufion of certain drugs, fo when fuch narrations are feafoned with fome apt maxims of philofophy, thofe parts of ancient hiftory which feem tedious are ftripped of their redundant loquacity.

What firft? What next? What laft fhall I relate * ?

Was not Scipio, loving Lælius, and being equally loved by him, fo clofely connected with him, that he undertook nothing without having previoufly confulted and advifed with him? which occafioned the envious traducers of his actions to fay, that Lælius was the author of them, and Africanus only the performer. The fame report prevails in regard to us, and I hear it, I confefs, with great fatisfaction. For to adopt the good advice of another feemed to Zeno † a proof of greater virtue

than

---

* Odyff. IX. 14.

† Zeno, the founder of the Stoic fect, was born at Citium, a fea-port town in the ifland of Cyprus. He was originally a merchant, and very rich. On a voyage from Tyre, where he had been trading in purple, he was fhipwrecked near the Piræum. During his ftay at Athens, he happened to meet, in a bookfeller's fhop, with the fecond book of Xenophon's *Memorabilia*; with which he was extremely delighted; and afked the bookfeller where fuch kind of perfons, as the author mentioned, were to be found. The bookfeller anfwered, pointing to Crates, the Cynic, who was luckily paffing by, " Follow him ;" which Zeno did, and became his difciple. But his difpofition was too modeft to approve of the Cynic indecency ; and forfaking Crates, he applied himfelf to the Academics, whom he attended for ten years, and then formed a fchool of his own. There was a conftant feverity, or perhaps aufterity, in his manners, his drefs, and his difcourfe ; except at an

D 4 enter-

than originally to conceive what is juſt and right thus altering a line of Heſiod:

That man is beſt who follows good advice *,
from

———— who counſels wiſely for himſelf.

Yet I do not approve the alteration; as I think the ſaying of Heſiod much more true. But better than either is that of Pythagoras, from whom that proverb originated, "With friends all things are "common." This indeed does not refer to money only, but includes a communion of minds and underſtandings. So that what you ſuggeſt is no leſs the property of him who adopts it; and in ſuch parts of yours as I performed, you are juſtly entitled to a ſhare. But let thoſe actions be aſcribed to whom they will, they belong to another; and

entertainment, when he uſed to appear with chearfulneſs and eaſe. His morals were irreproachable; and he was preſented by the Athenians with a golden crown, becauſe his life was a public example of virtue, by its conformity with his words and doctrines. He lived ninety-eight years, and then ſtrangled himſelf, becauſe, in going out of his ſchool, he happened to fall down, and break his finger.

DIOGENES LAERTIUS.

* Οὗτος μὲν πανάριστος, ὃς ευ ειπαντι πιθηται.

In the Works and Days of Heſiod, ver. 291. we read,

Οὗτος μὲν παναρίστης, ὃς αυτω παντα νοηση.

(In Julian, πρὸ δ᾽ εαυτω) to which latter hemiſtich, it ſeems, Zeno ſubſtituted part of ver. 293, viz.

Εσθλος δ᾽ αυ κακεινος, ὃς ευ, κ. τ. λ.

He too is good, who follows good advice.

Heſiod and Livy thought, that he who counſelled wiſely for himſelf, was the firſt of men. and that he who followed the good advice of others was the ſecond. But Zeno preferred the latter.

of

of their fuggeftions the invidious can make no advantage.

I now return to Africanus and Lælius. After Carthage * was deftroyed, and all Libya was fubjected to Rome, Africanus difpatched Lælius with the intelligence of his fuccefs. Scipio was concerned at being thus feparated from his friend; yet he did not think his grief inconfolable. Lælius too, it is probable, was afflicted at departing alone; yet this calamity did not feem to him infupportable. Cato alfo took a voyage, leaving his intimate friends at home. Pythagoras too travelled into Ægypt, and fo did Plato and Democritus, without any companion, leaving behind them many whom they highly efteemed. Pericles made war againft Samos †, unaccompanied by Anaxagoras, and conquered Eubœa ‡; by his counfels indeed, for he was his

---

* By mentioning Libya afterwards, Julian feems to mean Old Carthage; but C. Lælius, as we learn from Livy (xxvii. 7.), was difpatched to Rome by Scipio Africanus the elder, with the account of " the conqueft," not deftruction, " of New Carthage, the capital of Spain, in one " day." He was indeed difpatched, many years after, by the younger Scipio, from Africa, with Syphax and other prifoners, and with the intelligence of the victory of Zama: but it does not appear that he was fent with the account of the deftruction of Old Carthage. Julian, trufted much to his memory, which fometimes deceived him.

† Making war with the Samians, Pericles gained a naval victory, and at laft took their city.

‡ Eubœa having rebelled againft the Athenians, he invaded it with a fleet and army, and reduced it to their obedience. See his Life in Plutarch.

pre-

preceptor *; but, like other neceffaries, he did not
take him perfonally with him to the field.   It is
reported, that the Athenians feparated him unwillingly from, the fociety of his preceptor.   But,
like a wife man, he bore the frenzy of his fellow-
citizens with firmnefs and moderation; thinking
that his country, greatly; though not juftly, offended at their connection, fhould, like a parent,
be obeyed, and perhaps thus reafoning with himfelf : (you muft confider what follows, as the words
of Pericles.) " The world at large is my city and
" country, and my friends the Gods and Genii,
" and all the good, whoever they are, and where-
" ever they refide. But the place of our birth
" deferves refpect, as this is the law of God, and
" what fhe commands ought to be obeyed, and
" not oppofed, left, as the proverb fays, we kick
" againft the pricks †.   The yoke of neceffity,
" as it is ftyled, is implacable.   Yet it is not to
" be deplored and lamented, even when its weight
" is the heavieft, but the burthen itfelf is to be
" rightly eftimated.. She now commands Anax-
" agoras to leave me ; fo that I fhall fee no more
" my beft friend, on whofe account I was dif-
" pleafed with the night for fecreting him from me,
" and returned thanks to the day and the Sun for

---

* In the Phædrus of Plato, Socrates fays, that " Pe-
" ricles had this advantage of all other orators, that he
" had been a hearer of the philofopher Anaxagoras."
                                         Cic. Orat. 4.

† Προς κεντρα λακτιζειν. The fame proverb is ufed in the
Acts of the Apoftles, ix. 5.

" re-

" reſtoring to my ſight the chief object of my
" love. If nature, O Pericles, had given you
" no more ſight than ſhe has given to birds, had
" your grief been ſtill more poignant, it would not
" have been ſtrange. But as ſhe has not only
" breathed into you a ſoul, and implanted a mind,
" by whoſe recollection you diſcern, though abſent,
" many things that are now tranſacting at a diſ-
" tance, but has alſo endued you with reaſon,
" which, diſcovering many future events, reveals
" them, as it were, to the eyes of your mind, and
" a fancy, which, diſcloſing things preſent, ſub-
" mits to her judgement and inveſtigation not
" thoſe only which are the objects of ſight, but
" thoſe alſo which are many miles diſtant, more
" plainly even than ſuch as are at our feet,
" as it is ſaid, and before our eyes; what avail
" ſo much affliction and diſquiet? To produce au-
" thority for what I ſay, ' The mind ſees, and the
" mind hears,' ſays the Sicilian *. A being ſo
" acute, and endued with ſuch wonderful ſwiftneſs,
" that Homer, in order to expreſs the incredible
" velocity of one of the Gods, ſays,

* Ο Σικελιώτης. What author is here meant I cannot
aſcertain. If Julian himſelf had been the ſpeaker, we
might ſuppoſe him to refer either to Theocritus, (whom,
in Epiſtle III. he ſtyles ο Σικελιώτης ποιητης) or Diodorus Siculus. But Pericles could not, without a great ana-
chroniſm, quote a bard, who was above two hundred years,
or an hiſtorian, who was near five hundred years, ſubſequent to himſelf.

" As

" As some way-faring man, who wanders o'er
" In thought — *.
" Assisted by this, you may easily discern from
" Athens one who is in Ionia ; from the Gauls
" those who are in Illyricum and Thrace ; and
" him who is in the Gauls from Thrace or
" Illyricum. For, though plants, when removed
" from their native soil in an improper season,
" cannot be preserved, yet men, when they travel
" from place to place, do not, in like manner,
" soon decay, or change their disposition, or' de-
" viate' from the right principles which they had
" previously imbibed. Therefore if we do not
" love with more ardour, we certainly should not
" abate in our benevolence. Luxury is attended
" by lasciviousness, but poverty by virtuous love.
" Thus we shall be happier by the increase of
" our mutual affection ; and 'shall see ourselves
" fixed, like statues in their niches, in the mind
" of each other. Now I shall behold Anaxagoras,
" and then Anaxagoras will behold me ; for no-
" thing prohibits our seeing each other ; not the
" flesh and nerves, the face and form, or a bodily
" reprefentation, (though nothing perhaps will
" prevent even these appearing to our minds), but
" the virtue, the actions, the discourses, the con-
" versations, the meetings that frequently cc-
" curred between us ; when we not unskilfully

* Il. xv. 80. Pope, 86. Homer here compares the
flight of Juno, from Ida to Olympus, to a man travelling
in idea.

" joined

" joined in the praife of education, and juftice,
" and of that underftanding which directs all
" things human and divine; and alfo on civil
" government, and laws, on virtuous conduct, and
" ingenuous ftudies, we made fuch obfervations
" as our memories fuggefted.   Reflecting on thefe
" things, and ruminating on fuch reprefentations,
" we fhall difregard the delufions of nightly
" dreams; nor will the fenfes, affected by a bad
" habit of body, prefent to the mind vain and
" empty vifions.   For, inftead of employing the
" affiftance and miniftration of the fenfes, the
" mind will meditate on thefe fubjects, and thus
" inure itfelf to the contemplation and compre-
" henfion of incorporeal objects.   For by the
" mind we affociate even with the Almighty, and
" are naturally enabled to behold and inveftigate
" things that efcape our fenfes, that are in place
" far diftant, and even things that have no place *.
" And fuch a vifion all whofe lives have rendered
" them worthy of it, conceive in their minds and
" perfectly enjoy."

* Thus Shakefpeare :

The poet's eye, in a fine frenzy rolling,
Doth glance from heaven to earth, from earth to
            heaven,
And, as imagination bodies forth
The forms of things unknown, the poet's pen
Turns them to fhape, and gives to airy nothing
A local habitation, and a name.

Midfummer Night's Dream,   Act V. Sc. I.

Pericles

Pericles, being endued with true magnanimity, and educated free in a free city, might folace himfelf with fuch fublime meditations. But I, born " in thefe degenerate days *," confole and beguile my mind, and affwage the bitternefs of my forrow, by arguments more human; thus endeavouring to apply fome remedy to the many anxious and diftreffing ideas which on that fubject perpetually affail me; like a charm againft the bite of a wild beaft, deeply wounding my heart and vitals. Of all my afflictions this is the principal; I am now left alone, deprived of a fincere, focial intercourfe, and an unreferved communication. For I have none remaining whom I can confult with equal confidence. But cannot I eafily converfe with my felf? Or cannot fome other engage my thoughts, and oblige me to regard and attend to fubjects not of my own choofing? Is not this fimilar to writing on water, or boiling a ftone, or inveftigating the traces of the flight of birds? Our converfing on fuch fubjects none can hinder. And perhaps God will fuggeft fomething better. For it is impoffible that a man who gives himfelf up to the Almighty fhould be entirely neglected and deferted by him. But God with his own arm defends him, endues him with ftrength, infpires him with courage, inftills into his mind what he fhould do, and deters him from what he fhould forbear. A divine voice

* Οιοι νυν βροτοι εισ'. Il. v. 304. An expreffion often quoted by our author.

accom-

accompanied Socrates *, forbidding him to do

* The notion of Socrates having a fupernatural attendant, either an evil fpirit, as fome of the Fathers imagined,
or a good one, as others have conceived, has been lately
difcuffed, in " an Effay on the Dæmon or Divination of
" Socrates," by Mr. Nares, who maintains, " that the
" divinations of Socrates were perfectly analogous to thofe
" in common ufe at the time in which he lived ; but that
" he, from a fcrupulous exactnefs in his expreffions, (and
" probably alfo with a defire to inculcate, as frequently
" as poffible, the notion of a conftantly active and fuper-
" intending providence) chofe rather to refer his divi-
" nation always to its primary and original caufe, the
" Gods, than to their fecondary and unconfcious inftru-
" ments, the omens by which it was conveyed. In con-
" fequence of thefe ideas, he appropriated to the fubject
" an expreffion, which firft the malice of his enemies, and
" fince the miftaken zeal of his friends, have wrefted to
" his difadvantage, as if he had pretended to a communi-
" cation with fome attendant Dæmon ; than which nothing
" could be more remote from his ideas. It appears, in-
" deed, that he conceived the particular fignal, or omen,
" by which he was directed, to be fomething in a manner
" appropriated; or at leaft more accurately obferved and
" attended to by him than by others. But in this there is
" nothing repugnant to the common notions of prophetic
" warnings in his and every age, nor in the leaft fubverfive
" of what has been here advanced. From this reprefen-
" tation of the matter it will appear, that there is, in
" the hiftory of this extraordinary man, nothing which
" can countenance the vague and romantic notion of
" attendant tutelar dæmons ; nor any thing which can
" in the leaft invalidate our conceptions of his ftrict in-
" tegrity and open difpofition : a conclufion, which every
" lover of philofophy will doubtlefs embrace with pleafure,
" if the arguments and authorities which form the foun-
" dation of it be deemed of fufficient ftrength." The author fupports this ingenious hypothefis by paffages to the
fame purpofe from Plato, Xenophon, and Plutarch.

If Julian had not been more a Greek than a Roman, he
would have mentioned alfo, on this occafion, Numa and
his nymph Egeria.

3

whatever was improper. And Homer says of Achilles, " His mind was infpired *," intimating, that our thoughts are fuggefted by God, when the mind, by reflection, converfes firft with itfelf, and then privately with God, without interruption; for the mind requires not ears to learn, nor God a voice to teach, what is neceffary, but, without fenfation, a participation of the Almighty is given to the mind. How, and in what manner, I have not leifure now to examine; but that this is effected there are fure and faithful witneffes, not fuch as are ignoble, and to be claffed with the Megarenfians, but thofe who have had the firft reputation in wifdom. Therefore, as we expect that God will be for ever prefent with us, and that we fhall again have a mutual intercourfe, the violence of our affliction ought to abate. Even Ulyffes, who fo much lamented his confinement in an ifland for feven whole years, though I praife him for his bravery on other occafions, I admire not for his grief on this. For what availed his gazing on the fea, and fhedding tears †? Not to be dejected and difpirited by misfortunes, but to act with intrepidity in the midft of danger and deftruction, feems indeed more than can be expected from man. But it

*. By Juno. Il. I. 55. Thus alfo Virgil, *Hic mentem Æneæ genitrix pulcherrima mifit. Æn. xii. 554.*

† Odyff. v. 82. All on the lonely fhore he fat to weep,
And roll'd his eyes around the reftlefs deep ;
Tow'rd his lov'd coaft he roll'd his eyes in vain,
Till dimm'd with rifing grief, they ftream'd again.
Pope, 105.

is

is unjuſt to praiſe, and not to imitate, the ancients, or to think that God readily aſſiſted them; but will overlook thoſe of this age whom he ſees attached to virtue, ſince on that account he was pleaſed with them. It was not for perſonal beauty; or Nireus * would have been more beloved by him. Nor was it for ſtrength; as the Læſtrygons † and Cyclops ‡ were greatly ſuperior in ſtrength to Ulyſſes. Nor was it for riches; for then Troy would have remained in ſafety. But why ſhould we labour to inveſtigate the reaſon of the poet's ſaying that Ulyſſes was beloved by God §, when we may hear it from himſelf?

Becauſe, in every uſeful art refin'd,

His words were eloquent, and wiſe his mind ‖.

It is plain therefore, that, if we have theſe endowments, the Almighty will not deny us his ſupport, but, according to the oracle given of

* Il. ii. 671. Nireus is here mentioned as the moſt beautiful of the Greeks, Achilles only excepted; but his name never occurs again; for
— few his troops, and ſmall his ſtrength in war.
It is remarkable, that Nireus is introduced by Euripides [Iphigenia in Aulis] as accompanying Ulyſſes, though their manners were unſuitable, and their dominions [Syma and Ithaca] far diſtant. In the vith book of Quintus Calaber, Nireus falls by the ſpear of Eurypylus.   WODHULL.

† Odyſſ. x. 119, &c.

‡ Ibid. ix. 125, &c.

§ Θεοφιλη Διι φιλος (beloved by Jupiter) in Il. xi. 419, 473.

‖ Odyſſ. xiii. 332. [Minerva] by ſaying to Ulyſſes, that ſhe would never overlook nor deſert him, " Becauſe, &c." ſhews that of all we have, virtue only is eſteemed by God and divine.   *Plutarch. de audiendis Poetis.*

old to the Lacedæmonians, invoked, or not invoked, God will be prefent with us.

Having thus fought confolation, I now return
to that circumftance, which, though at firft it
feems trivial, is generally thought of no fmall
importance. Alexander is faid to have wifhed for
Homer, not as a friend indeed, but as a herald,
as he was to Achilles, and Patroclus, and the two
Ajaces, and Antilochus. But he, always defpifing
what he had, and coveting what he had not,
flighted his contemporaries, and was never fatisfied
with what was granted him. If he had been indulged with Homer, he would probably have requefted the lyre of Apollo, on which he played at
the nuptials of Peleus *, thinking it not a fiction
of the genius of Homer, but a true fact related
in verfe, like thefe.

> Aurora now, fair daughter of the dawn,
> Sprinkled with rofy light the dewy lawn †.

And, The Sun arofe ‡.

And, Crete, a fruitful foil §.

* Il. xxiv. 62. Juno fays to the Gods,
To grace thofe nuptials, from the bright abode,
Yourfelves were prefent; where this minftrel-god
(Well pleas'd to fhare the feaft) amid the choir,
Stood proud to hymn, and tune his youthful lyre. POPE.
This harmonious banquet is alfo celebrated by Eu-
ripides, in one of the choruffes of his Iphigenia in
Aulis. Apollo is there introduced foretelling the glory of
Achilles.

† Il. viii. 1. Pope.
‡ Odyff. iii. 1.
§ Ibid. xix. 172, Fenton.

And

And other similar passages of the poets, which are plain and obvious, as some of the objects still remain, and some of the facts are still transacted.

But whether the excellence of his virtue, and a wisdom, by no means inferior to his great superfluity of worldly happiness, inflamed his mind with such ambition, that he coveted more than any one else; or whether the excess of his valour and intrepidity tended to arrogance, and bordered on ostentation; must be left to the discussion of those who would compose his panegyric or satire; if any share of the latter can be thought his due. I, on the contrary, always satisfied with what is present, and not in the least desirous of what is absent, contentedly acquiesce in having my merits proclaimed by a herald who has been a spectator and a fellow-combatant with me in all *, but whose judgement partiality never biasses, nor prejudice perverts. Sufficient is it for me to profess my friendship; in other respects I shall be more silent than those who are initiated by Pythagoras †.

But here I must advert to the general report, namely, that you are going not only among the Illyrians, but also to the Thracians, and those

---

* Sallust himself, no doubt, on whose representation of his conduct Julian might indeed safely rely.

† The scholars of this philosopher in their probation were enjoined silence, and were only to hear; which time was called ἐχεμυθία. *Gell.* i. 9. See the Epistle to Themistius, p. 21. note *.

Greeks

Greeks who dwell near that fea *. This, being the place of my birth and education, has infpired me with a great regard for thofe people, and their country, and cities; and an equal regard perhaps they retain for me. To them, I am confident, your arrival will be moft acceptable, and that they will think it a happy exchange, as you have left me here. By faying this, I mean not to infinuate that I wifh it; on the contrary, if you could return hither immediately, by the fame road, I fhould be much more gratified. But as it muft happen, I am confidering how to fupport it with firmnefs and equanimity, while I congratulate them on feeing you juft come from us. On your account, I reconcile myfelf to the Gauls; deeming you worthy of being ranked among the firft of the Greeks, in juftice and other virtues; as being alfo an adept in oratory, and far from a novice in philofophy, in which the Greeks alone are perfect; inveftigating truth, as its nature requires, by reafon, and not fuffering us to be deluded by idle inventions, and incredible fables, like many of the Barbarians.

And now (to difmifs you with aufpicious omens) where-ever you go, may the benevolent God be your guide, and Jupiter the friendly and hofpitable receive you, conducting you fafely by land, and, if you embark, fmoothing the waves! May you be loved and honoured by all men; fo that they may rejoice at your arrival, and lament at your

---

* The Propontis, which laves Conftantinople, where Julian was born. It divides the Hellefpont and the Thracian Bofphorus.

depar-

departure! Still retaining your affection for us, may you never want the society of a friend equally faithful! May God also conciliate to you the favour of the Emperor; may he regulate every other circumstance to your complete satisfaction; and grant you a safe and speedy return to your own country and to us! In these prayers for you I unite with the good and virtuous. Let me add,

> With health, with joy, to his lov'd native shore
> May the kind Gods my honour'd friend restore *!

* Ουλι τε, και μεγα χαιρι· θιοι δι τοι ολϐια δοιιν,
    Νοϛησαι οικον δι φιλην ις πατριδα γαιαν.

The first line is taken from ver. 401, and the second is an alteration of Νοϛησαντα in ver. 404, of Odyss. xxiv. with the addition of most part of ver. 562 of Odyss. x.

Besides the warmth of affection that breathes through this whole composition, several parts of it, especially the conclusion, in the original, are poetical without being turgid.

JULIAN CÆSAR TO THE EMPEROR CONSTANTIUS *.

A. D.
360.

EVER retaining one and the fame opinion, I
have adhered to what I faithfully purpofed,
not lefs from principle than by the covenant of
treaties, as has evidently appeared in various inftances. As foon as I was created Cæfar, you expofed me to all the tumults and horrors of battle;
yet, contented with a delegated authority, like a
faithful apparitor, I filled your ears with frequent
accounts of fucceffes anfwerable to your wifhes;
never dwelling on my own dangers, though by
continual proofs it may appear, the Germans being
every where fcattered and difordered, that I was
always the firft in labours, but the laft in re-
frefhment.

* The Gallic legions being ordered by Conftantius to
march into the Eaft, a tumult arofe (as Julian himfelf relates more particularly in the fucceeding epiftle to the
Athenians); and from the fubordinate dignity of Cæfar he
was exalted by the army to the fupreme rank of Auguftus.
This epiftle, written foon after that event, is preferved by
Ammianus.

He compofed, in his own name, and in that of the army,
a fpecious and moderate epiftle, which was delivered to
Pentadius, his mafter of the offices, and to his chamberlain
Eutherius; two ambaffadors, whom he appointed to receive
the anfwer, and obferve the difpofitions, of Conftantius.

GIBBON.

But,

But, with your leave, I will inform you whether any innovations have now been made, as you imagine. The foldiers, wafting their lives in many and fevere wars, without advantage, have formerly held confultations, raging and impatient of a ruler in the fecond place, being fenfible that no recompence can be made them by the Cæfar for their daily fatigues and frequent victories ; their refentment has been appeafed by no increafe of honours, not even by a year's pay now due, to which this alfo has been unexpectedly added; their being ordered to the moft diftant parts of the Eaftern world, men accuftomed to frozen climates were to be feparated from their wives and children, and were dragged forth indigent and naked. Being therefore more bitterly enraged than ufual, affembling in the night, they befieged the palace, exclaiming JULIAN AUGUSTUS with loud and repeated cries. I trembled, I confefs, and withdrew; and while I could, fought fafety by filence * and retirement. But no refpite being allowed, guarded, as I may fay, by the free fortrefs of my breaft, I went forth and prefented myfelf to them, thinking that my authority or mild words might allay the difturbance. Their fury was wonderful, and it went fo far, that, on my endeavouring by intreaties to conquer their obftinacy, rufhing clofe up to me, they threatened inftant death. At length fubdued, and conjec-

* In the original, *fimulatione*. I prefer the correction of Gelenius, *mxffatione*.

turing *, that, when I was killed, another perhaps would be declared prince, I assented, thus
hoping to appease the tumult.

. This is the substance of what has happened, which
I request you to accept with complacence. And
think not that any thing is misrepresented, or credit
the evil reports of the malicious, who are accustomed to promote the revolts of princes for their
own advantage ; but banishing flattery, the nurse
of vice; cultivate the most excellent of all virtues,
justice ; and receive with good faith the equitable
terms which I offer, considering them as beneficial
both to the Roman state and to us, who are allied
by consanguinity, and by the eminence of superior
rank. These requests, (excuse me) as they are founded in reason, I am less anxious for your granting
than for your approving and thinking them just and
proper. I am ready also with chearfulness to obey
your commands. What may be necessary I will
reduce into a short compass.

I will furnish Spanish horses † for your chariots,
and some Letian ‡ youths, sprung from Barbarians on

* In the original, *Mecúmque ipse contestans.* In the margin
of the Royal MS. *conjectans* is written in the same hand.
VALOIS.
The translator has adopted the latter.

† Zonaras says the same thing. And he adds, that
Julian inscribed his letter with the name of Cæsar, not
Augustus, lest Constantius, offended at it, should immediately disdain it : which Julian also confirms in his Epistle
to the Athenians. *Ibid.*

‡ The Leti, or Læti, were some half-barbarians, who
dwelt in the Gauls ; or (as our Ammianus subjoins) *cis
Rhenum edita barbarorum progenies. Ibid.*

this fide the Rhine, or, at leaft, from vaffals who have revolted to us, to be incorporated with your provincials and targeteers.   And thefe, as long as I live, I promife to fupply, not only with gratitude but delight.   Prætorian præfects, of diftinguifhed equity and merit, fhall be given us by your clemency *.   As for the other ufual magiftrates, and the directors of the war, it is proper, that they fhould be left to my nomination, and alfo the guards.   For, when they can previoufly be learned, it is abfurd for the manners and tempers of thofe who are ftationed by the Emperor's fide to be unknown to him.   The following rule, without the leaft hefitation, I would eftablifh: Gallic recruits, juft enlifted, fhould not be fent, either voluntarily, or by force, to foreign and far diftant countries, and oppreffed with daily fatigues or vexatious accidents, left the youth fhould be totally exhaufted, being afflicted with the recollection of paft, and finking under impending, dangers.   Nor can it be proper to oppofe the Parthians with auxiliaries drawn from hence, fince the barbaric fury is not yet quelled, and (if you will permit me to fpeak the truth) thefe provinces, harraffed by continual misfortunes, require external and powerful affiftance.   In giving this advice I ftudy, I am convinced, the public good, requefting and intreating; for I know, not to arrogate more than my ftation warrants, what embarraffed and defperate

* A term of refpect, like "majefty," &c.

affairs

affairs have been retrieved by the agreement of princes mutually complying with each other; and the example of our anceftors will fhew, that rulers, thinking in this and the like manner, have, as it were, difcovered the method of living happily, and of endearing their memory to the lateft times *.

* In this negociation Julian claimed no more than he already poffeffed. The delegated authority which he had long exercifed over the provinces of Gaul, Spain, and Britain, was ftill obeyed under a name more independent and auguft. The foldiers and the people rejoiced in a revolution, which was not ftained with blood. Florentius was a fugitive; Lupicinus a prifoner. The perfons who were difaffected to the new government were difarmed and fecured; and the vacant offices were diftributed according to the recommendation of merit, by a prince who defpifed the intrigues of the palace, and the clamours of the foldiers.

GIBBON.

" To this oftenfible epiftle he added," fays Ammianus, ".private letters, *objurgatorias et mordaces*," which the hiftorian had not feen, and would not have publifhed. Perhaps they never exifted.   *Ibid.*

Thefe " ftinging" letters, Zonaras fays, were not fent by Julian at that time, but afterwards, when Leonas, who had been ambaffador to Julian, returned unfuccefsful to Conftantius. " Leonas therefore, defpairing of being able to " execute any part of his commiffion, returned with the " letters of Julian, in which he impudently upbraided the " Emperor, as having been very criminal towards his re- " lations, and threatened that he would revenge their in- " juries."   VALOIS.

The ambaffadors found Conftantius at Cæfarea in Cappadocia. On reading the letters with which they were charged, this prince flew into a dreadful paffion; and viewing them with a look that feemed to threaten their lives, he commanded them to withdraw, without condefcending to give them any further audience, or to afk them any queftions. He was very near quitting the Perfian war to march directly againft Julian. However, he only difpatched a Quæftor, named Leonas, to him, with a menacing letter, and recalled his principal officers. LA BLETERIE.

THE

THE EMPEROR JULIAN TO THE SENATE AND PEOPLE OF ATHENS *.

THOUGH many actions have been performed by your anceftors, for which you, as well as they, are juftly renowned, and though many trophies have been erected by all Greece in general,

A. D. 361.

and

* Julian wrote this epiftle foon after his being pro-claimed Emperor in the Gauls ; and while he was marching with his army againft Conftantius. For Libanius affirms, that he then wrote letters to feveral cities of Greece, in order to exculpate his affuming the empire to other na-tions. " He was fo much more folicitous," fays that orator, in his Panegyric on the confulfhip of Julian, " to " exculpate himfelf than to gain a victory, that, while he " was expofed to the greateft dangers, he apologifed for him-" felf by the Greeks, to all mankind, writing epiftles to " them, according to the feveral difpofitions of each city, " fome longer, and fome fhorter, as might fuit thofe to " whom they were addreffed." This epiftle therefore explains the motives of his con-duct, and fully defcribes the patience with which he had hitherto borne the repeated injuries and provocations of Conftantius, and the great reluctance with which, by the concurrence of the army, he was exalted to the empire. Indeed, of all the remains of that apoftate, none feems to me more worthy of publication and the perufal of the learned, efpecially of thofe who ftudy hiftory. For it ac-curately relates that whole tranfaction, throws light on many parts of this fubject tranfmitted to us by Ammianus and others, and alfo contains feveral hiftorical facts and circumftances not to be found elfewhere. The great regard which Julian had for Athens and the Athenians, and the

reafons

and by your city in particular, when fhe contended fingly either with the neighbouring ftates, or with the Barbarians, none of her deeds are fo diftinguifhed, no acts of her heroifm fo illuftrious, as not to be rivalled by the other cities. In fome, they have co-operated with you; others they have performed unaided and alone. But left, by mentioning particulars, I fhould feem to draw an odious comparifon, or to give an invidious preference, in order to ferve my caufe, as is ufual with orators, who by faintly praifing, really de-

reafons why he reforted thither, Gregory of Nazianzus declares in his fecond oration στηλιτ.   Petau.

After having made himfelf mafter of the pafs of the Succi, in his march againft Conftantius, while Julian refided at Naiffus in Illyricum, waiting for his troops, and making new levies, he wrote to feveral cities of Greece, among others to Athens, Lacedæmon, and Corinth, not only to engage them in his intereft, but alfo to juftify his procedings.

In particular, he made it a point of honour and religion to take for judges the Athenians, fo celebrated in antiquity for their love of juftice, by carrying his caufe to the tribunal of Areopagus, where the Gods had formerly appeared. Of all his manifeftoes we have only that which was addreffed to them. It is an eloquent and perfectly well-written piece.   La Bleterie.

The moft authentic account of the education and adventures of Julian is contained in this epiftle, or manifefto, It deferves the praifes of the Abbé de la Bleterie, and is one of the beft manifeftoes to be found in any language.   Gibbon.

His epiftle to the Senate and people of Athens, feems to have been dictated by an elegant enthufiafm, which prompted him to fubmit his actions and motives to the degenerate Athenians of his own times, with the fame humble deference, as if he had been pleading, in the days of Ariftides, before the tribunal of the Areopagus. *Ibid.*

preciate

preciate, and decry, the, merit of their opponents, this only I will say of you, to which of all that tradition has transmitted the other. Greeks can produce nothing parallel. You obtained the dominion over the Lacedæmonians, not by the force of your arms, but by the fame of your justice. Aristides * the Just was formed by your laws. And these proofs of your virtue, splendid as they are, you have confirmed by still more splendid facts. For in mere matters of opinion we are liable to mistake, nor is it unusual to find, among many wicked men, one who is virtuous. Is not Deioces † celebrated among the Medes, Abaris ‡ among the Hyperboreans, and Anacharsis § among the Scythians; of whom it was remarkable, that, though they lived in nations notoriously unjust, they nevertheless cultivated justice? The two last sincerely; the first was prompted by interest to dis-

* See his Life in Cornelius Nepos.

† He determined with so much prudence the differences of the Medes, that he deserved to be chosen their king. He built, according to Herodotus, the city of Ecbatana, and reigned forty years, from the year of the world 3358 to 3398.   MORERI.

‡ A Scythian, who wrote Apollo's Northern Journey in verse, oracles, predictions, &c. Jamblichus says, he was a scholar of Pythagoras, which does not agree with what the ancients affirm of Abaris being prior even to Solon. *Ibid.*

§ Another Scythian, contemporary with Solon, of whom he learned philosophy at Athens.

He was the only philosopher of his nation, whence the proverb, *Anacharsis inter Scythas.* At length he was killed by his brother the king of Scythia, for endeavouring to introduce the Athenian laws. See Diogenes Laërtius, in his life, *l.* 1.

semble

femble it. But it is difficult to produce a whole city and nation, who practife juftice, both in word and deed, except yourfelves. Of many inftances that have occurred among you it may be fufficient to mention one. When Themiftocles *, after the Perfian war, had formed a plan of privately fetting fire to the naval arfenals of the Greeks, and dared not publickly to propofe it, but faid, he would communicate the fecret to any one whom the people by their fuffrages would elect, they named Ariftides. He, on hearing the propofal, concealed the particulars, and only informed the people, that " nothing could be more advan-
" tageous, but at the fame time more unjuft, than
" the advice of Themiftocles." Upon which, the city immediately difclaimed and declined it; a fignal inftance of magnanimity, and highly becoming a people educated under the eye of the wifeft Goddefs!

If thefe things happened among you in ancient times, and a fmall fpark, as it were, of the virtue of your anceftors has ever fince been preferved, you ought, when you hear of any great action, to confider, not the furprifing fingularity of it, like that of a man walking with as much ftrength and agility as if he had wings, but whether its motives were juft and right. And if fo, both in public and private it will receive your deferved applaufe; if not, it will with reafon be difregarded and condemned. Nothing is fo nearly allied to wifdom as

* See his Life in Plutarch.

juftice.

juſtice.   Thoſe therefore who defpife it you ſhould baniſh as profaners of your Goddefs.   Though you are not ſtrangers to my affairs, this is the occaſion of my prefent addrefs.   If any thing ſhould chance to have efcaped your knowledge (and ſome particulars probably may, even of thofe in which you all are interefted), it may thus be communicated to you, and by you to the other Greeks.   And let me not be charged with trifling, if I endeavour to comprife in my difcourfe thoſe fcenes which have lately been prefented to the eyes of all men, as well as former tranfactions, as I wiſh to have every thing that relates to me generally known.   I will begin with my anceſtors.

That the family of my father, and that of Conſtantius, had the fame origin, you need not be informed.   Our fathers were brothers, having the fame father.   How that moſt humane Emperor acted afterwards towards me, who was fo nearly related to him, and how he unjuſtly put to death fix of his own and my coufins, as well as my father, his own uncle, together with another uncle of us both, and alfo my elder brother * ; and after having

ing

* He fays, that " fix coufins and two uncles" were ſlain by Conſtantius.   The latter, I find in the hiſtory of thoſe times, were [Julius] Conſtantius, the father of Julian, and Dalmatius, both fons of [Conſtantius] Chlorus, by Theodora, the daughter-in-law of Maximian-Herculius, and brothers of Conſtantine.   [See the " Pedigree of Julian."]   But the hiſtorians mention only " three" coufin-germans, viz. Dalmatianus and Hannibalianus, the fons of Dalmatius, and Nepotianus, the fon of Eutropia, the fiſter of Conſtantine.   The others were killed, foon after the death

of

ing intended to deftroy me * and another brother †, changed our fentence into banifhment, from which he afterwards releafed me, but deprived him, juft before he was killed, of the name of Cæfar; all thefe dreadful tragical events why fhould I relate? efpecially, as he is faid to have repented, and to have been much afflicted, attributing to them his want of children, and alfo his ill fuccefs in the

of Conftantine, by a confpiracy of the foldiers. Nepotianus was flain after the death of Conftans, not, however, by Conftantius, but by the tyrant Magnentius. So fay Socrates, Zofimus, Eutropius, and Victor. I read therefore of but " two" coufins flain by Conftantius. The reft let the diligent and learned inveftigate.　　　　Petau.

* We learn, from this paffage, what is mentioned, as I recollect, by no other writer, that Julian had, befides Gallus Cæfar, another, and that an elder brother, whom he here plainly diftinguifhes from Gallus, and mentions to have been killed, before Gallus was Cæfar, by Conftantius. Who he was, or what was his name, I profefs myfelf to be ignorant. But fo was Socrates.　　　　*Ibid.*

Julian here charges his coufin Conftantius with the whole guilt of a maffacre, from which he himfelf fo narrowly efcaped. His affertion is confirmed by Athanafius, who, for reafons of a very different nature, was not lefs an enemy to Conftantius. (tom. 1. p. 856.) Zofimus joins in the fame-accufation. But the three abbreviators, Eutropius and the Victors, ufe very qualifying expreffions, " *finente* " *potius quam jubente ;*" " *incertum quo fuafore,*" " *vi militum.*"
　　　　Gibbon.

† Socrates (III. 1.) fays, that " Gallus was fuffered to " live, becaufe, on account of his weak conftitution, it was " thought that he could not live long ; and Julian, becaufe " he was only eight years old." But in this, Socrates is not quite accurate. For Julian was not " eight," but only " five" years old ; as he died in the 31ft year of his age, in that of our Lord 363. But Conftantine died in 337.
　　　　Petau.

Perfian

Perſian war *. Such rumours, at leaſt, were circulated among the courtiers, in the hearing of me
and my late brother Cæſar Gallus, for ſo he was
then ſtyled. Having put him alſo to death, in
defiance of all laws, he neither ſuffered him to be
entombed with his anceſtors, nor his memory to be
honoured. But, as I ſaid before, we were informed and convinced, that ſome of theſe crimes
originated from miſapprehenſion and miſinformation, and others from the overbearing inſolence
and compulſion of a turbulent and mutinous army.
Such reports often reached us in our confinement
in a certain Cappadocian farm †, to which no one
was allowed acceſs: there we were both placed ;
my brother, recalled from exile ; and I, almoſt a
child, removed from ſchool. Why ſhould I mention thoſe ſix years ‡, in which we were educated
in a kind of foreign country, and as ſtrictly guarded as if we had been in Perſia, no ſtranger, nor

---

* In the reign of Conſtantius, Sapor vanquiſhed the
Romans in nine battles, invaded Meſopotamia, took Amida,
Singara, &c.

† Ammianus (xv. 2.) relates, that " Julian was accuſed of
" going from the farm of Macellum, in Cappadocia, into
" Aſia, for the ſake of liberal ſtudies, and, in his way
" through Conſtantinople, of ſeeing his brother." This αγρος,
or farm, he afterwards calls κτημα, and thus the Latins term
a farm *poſſeſſio*. PETAV.

Mr. Gibbon, in different places, ſtyles this farm " an
" ancient palace, ' " a ſtrong caſtle," " the reſidence of
" the kings of Cappadocia :" " the ſituation," he adds,
" was pleaſant, the buildings ſtately, the incloſures ſpa
" cious." It was at the foot of Mount Argæus, not far
from Cæſarea, the capital of the province.

‡ From 345 to 351.

any of our friends, being admitted to us; where, fecluded from all liberal ftudies, and debarred all intercourfe with families of rank, we were forced to affociate only with our domeftics? From thence, by the affiftance of the Gods, I was at length happily releafed; but my brother was moft unfortunately inveigled to court. If there was any thing ruftic and uncivilifed in his deportment *, it was owing to that mountainous education. He therefore who doomed us to it is juftly chargeable with the blame. Thanks be to the Gods, philofophy has purified me; but this blefling was denied to my brother. For after he had exchanged the country for the court, and had been invefted with the purple, he immediately became an object of envy; nor did that envy ceafe, till, not contented with ftripping him of the purple, it had accomplifhed his deftruction. Yet though he might be

* This opinion of Julian concerning his brother is expreffed by Libanius, in his panegyric on the confulfhip of Julian, p. 234, where he mentions fome letters, in which he, a private man, admonifhed Gallus, then Cæfar, of his duty: " If his brother had attended to his letters, we " fhould now have had two princes. For he who did " not reign dared to admonifh him who did. But when " he, who might have alleged fomething in his own de- " fence, had been put to death unheard, an inclination " appeared of preferring fome charges againft the other, " as if he had killed him; but that not being practicable, " his life was fpared to be harraffed by fatiguing journeys, " thus fuffering, though innocent, the punifhment due to " guilt." The difpofition of Gallus is alfo mentioned by Nazianzen, in his *Steliteut.* l. " Though of a paffionate " temper, he was unaffectedly pious."   PETAU.

deemed

deemed unfit to govern, furely he was not unworthy to live. And even allowing the expedience
of depriving him of life, he fhould not have been
denied the ufual privilege of criminals, that of
being heard in his own defence. The law does
not forbid him who has the right of imprifoning
robbers to put them alfo to death; deprived of
all their honours, and reduced from a princely to a
plebeian rank, it fays, that they fhall be executed
without a trial. What if he could have produced
the perfons who impeached thefe traitors *? For
in fome of their letters that were fhewn him,
heaven knows what charges were contained! Thus,
incenfed by an unbecoming weaknefs, he was rafhly
betrayed into paffion. He did nothing, however,
that deferved death; but, you may fay, that it is
a rule univerfal, both among Greeks and Barbarians, that he who has received may revenge an
infult. True—yet Conftantius revenged it too feverely. But he did nothing more than is ufual.
" It is ufual," he once faid, " for an enemy, when
" enraged, to go any lengths." But to gratify an

* See in Ammianus (XIV. 1. 7.) a very ample detail of
the cruelties of Gallus. His brother Julian infinuates
that a confpiracy had been formed againft him; and Zofimus names the perfons engaged in it; a minifter of confiderable rank, and two obfcure agents, who were refolved
to make their fortunes.   GIBBON.

Julian perhaps here refers to the maffacre at Antioch of
the Imperial minifters, Domitian and Montius, by the command of Gallus.

F 2   eunuch,

eunuch *, his chamberlain †, and alſo his maſter-
cook, Conſtantius ſacrificed to his moſt inveterate
enemies ‡ his couſin-german, the Cæſar, the huſ-
band of his ſiſter §, the father of his niece, whoſe
                                              ſiſter

* Euſebius, who ruled the monarch and the palace with
ſuch abſolute ſway, that Conſtantius, according to the
ſarcaſm of an impartial hiſtorian, poſſeſſed ſome credit
with his haughty favourite : *Apud quem (ſi verè dici debeat)*
multa Conſtantius potuit. Amm. xviii. 4.   GIBBON.

† A favourite eunuch, who, in the language of that age, was
ſtyled the *præpoſitus* or præfect, of the ſacred bed-chamber.
His duty was to attend the Emperor in his hours of ſtate,
or in thoſe of amuſement, and to perform about his perſon
all thoſe menial ſervices which can only derive their ſplendor from the influence of royalty. Under a prince, who
deſerved to reign, the great-chamberlain (for ſuch we may
call him) was an uſeful and humble domeſtic; but an artful domeſtic, who improves every occaſion of unguarded
confidence, will inſenſibly acquire over a feeble mind that
aſcendant which harſh wiſdom and uncomplying virtue can
ſeldom obtain.   *Ibid.*

‡ The Emperor was eaſily convinced that his own ſafety
was incompatible with the life of his couſin ; the ſentence
of death was ſigned, diſpatched, and executed ; and the
nephew of Conſtantine, with his hands tied behind his
back, was beheaded in priſon, like the vileſt malefactor.
Ibid.
    This event happened " near Pola in Iſtria," ſays Am-
mianus, " where Criſpus, the ſon of Conſtantine, was for-
" merly killed." Near Flanona, or Flavona, in Dalmatia,
(not far from Pola) ſay Socrates and Sozomen.

§ Gallus had married Conſtantia [rather Conſtantina],
the daughter of Conſtantine, and ſiſter of Conſtantius.
Julian mentions his having a daughter by her ; and alſo
that Conſtantius had before married the ſiſter of Gallus.
Theſe two circumſtances, related, as far as I know, by him
only, were before unknown. The firſt of theſe is deduced
from this paſſage a little corrected. For αδελφιδης (" niece")
ſhould evidently have been written, inſtead of αδελφιδους
                                              (" nephew.")

fifter he himfelf had married, and who was connected to him by fo many domeftic ties. Me, not
without difficulty, he difmiffed, after removing me
to various places, and keeping me in confinement,
feven months. And if fome God, to infure my
fafety, had not ingratiated me with his beautiful
and excellent wife, Eufebia *, I could not have
efcaped his refentment. Though the Gods will
atteft that my brother, when he purfued thofe
meafures, was never feen by me, even in a dream;
for neither was I with him, nor did I vifit him,
nor was I in his neighbourhood. And when

("nephew.") Gallus had the fame father as Julian; his
mother was Galla, the fifter of Rufinus and Cerealis, whom
the Confulfhip, fays Ammianus (l. xiv.) had ennobled. Conftantius feems to have married the daughter of this Galla
before Eufebia, and I know not whether it was fhe with
whom Conftantius celebrated his nuptials in the life-time,
and by the management, of his father, as related by
Eufebius, in his Life of Conftantine. That Conftantius
had more wives, is affirmed by Ammianus. And Victor
fays, in his Epitome, ", of his wives, of whom he had
" many, he loved Eufebia moft." Eufebia is generally mentioned as the firft; and Fauftina [or Faufta] as the fecond
and laft, by whom he had a pofthumous daughter, Con-
ftantia, who was married to the Emperor Gratian. PETAU.

* A woman of beauty and merit, who, by the afcendant fhe had gained over the mind of her hufband, counter-
balanced, in fome meafure, the powerful confpiracy of the
eunuchs. She was a native of Theffalonica in Macedonia,
of a noble family, and the daughter, as well as fifter, of
Confuls. Her marriage with the Emperor may be placed
in the year 352. In a divided age, the hiftorians of all
parties agree in her praifes. GIBBON.
In culmine tam celfo humana, is her panegyric by Ammianus, " In fuch an exalted ftation not inhuman," gives an
imperfect idea of it in Englifh.

F 3

I wrote

I wrote to him, which was feldom, my letters were fhort. I therefore gladly took refuge in the houfe of my mother. For as to the eftate of my father, of none of his poffeffions had I the leaft fhare, no land, nor a houfe, not a flave, the worthy Conftantius having feized all my paternal inheritance, without giving me the mereft trifle. Having defpoiled Gallus of the effects of his mother, he gave him a few of his father's.

Moft part, at leaft, if not the whole, of his behaviour to me, before he conferred on me that moft refpectable name *, but in fact impofed on me a fevere and laborious flavery, you fhall now hear. Having thus with great difficulty, and beyond my expectation, efcaped, and being happily fheltered under the roof of my mother, a fycophant, from the neighbourhood of Sirmium +, falfely reported, that new commotions might be expected there. You have heard, no doubt, of Africanus and Marinus; nor can the name of Felix have efcaped you, and what was their fate ‡.

As

* Of Cæfar.

+ The capital of Illyricum, at prefent Sirmifch or Sirmick, a fmall town, almoft ruined, in the Lower Hungary,
LA BLETERIE.

‡ Ammianus (xv. 3.) mentions a drunken and treafonable entertainment at Sirmium, given by Africanus, governor of the fecond Pannonia (A. D. 354), in confequence of which, on the information of Gaudentius, the fycophant here meant, all the company were arrefted. Marinus, a tribune, and the principal delinquent, ftabbed himfelf in a tavern, on the road, at Aquileia. And the reft were put to the torture at Milan, and afterwards imprifoned. This, doubtlefs, is the incident to which Julian alludes. A perfon
named

As foon as Conftantius received this intelligence, and had alfo been affured by Dynamius, another informer from the Gauls, that Sylvanus * would foon revolt againft him ; alarmed and terrified he fent for me, and after ordering me to retire for a fhort time into Greece, he fuddenly recalled me. He had never feen me before, except once in Cappadocia, and once in Italy, at the earneft intreaty of Eufebia, that I might be affured of fafety. Yet I was fix months in the fame city † with him, and he promifed to fee me again. But that heaven-detefted eunuch ‡, his trufty chamberlain, was ignorantly and undefignedly my friend, by preventing my frequent accefs. Conftantius himfelf perhaps might not wifh to fee me ; neverthelefs, all my misfortunes were owing to that favourite, as he was apprehenfive, that, if we

named Felix was made mafter of the offices by Conftantius, but rejected by Julian. And there was another who was Count of the facred largeffes. But probably this Felix was one of the riotous company abovementioned.

* For an account of this revolt fee a note in the fucceeding page.

Οσοι υπω τυ Νειλυ, και εν αυτω πολεμον αναφανεισθαι. This I cannot underftand. What follows is related more at large by Ammianus and Zofimus. See alfo *Orat*. III. " on Eu-" febia." PETAU.

Thefe words may be thus corrected : Οσον υπω τον Σιλεανον αυτω πολεμιον αναφανεισθαι. Zofimus mentions the fame Dynamius at the end of l. ii. But he is miftaken in afcribing to him the death of Gallus Cæfar ; as Dynamius calumniated Sylvanus, not Gallus. VALOIS.

This correction is adopted by the tranflator.

† Mediolanum, or Milan.

‡ Eufebius above-mentioned, whom Julian, when he was Emperor, put to death.

F 4

fhould

ſhould be acquainted, a friendſhip might enſue; and if my fidelity had been approved, I might have been inveſted with ſome place of truſt.

As ſoon as I returned from Greece, the bleſſed Euſebia, by the eunuchs of her houſhold, ſhewed me many acts of kindneſs. And ſoon after, on his arrival, after terminating the war with Sylvanus *, I

---

* In the ſummer which preceded the elevation of Julian (Sept. A. D. 355.) this general had been choſen to deliver Gaul from the tyranny of the Barbarians; but Sylvanus ſoon diſcovered that he had left his moſt dangerous enemies in the Imperial court. A dexterous informer, countenanced by ſeveral of the principal miniſters, procured from him ſome recommendatory letters; and eraſing the whole of the contents, except the ſignature, filled up the vacant parchment with matters of high and treaſonable import. By the induſtry and courage of his friends, the fraud was, however, detected, and, in a great council of the civil and military officers, held in the preſence of the Emperor himſelf, the innocence of Sylvanus was publickly acknowledged. But the diſcovery came too late; the report of the calumny, and the haſty ſeizure of his eſtate, had already provoked the indignant chief to the rebellion of which he was ſo unjuſtly accuſed. He aſſumed the purple at his head-quarters of Cologne; and his active powers appeared to menace Italy with an invaſion, and Milan with a ſiege. In this emergency, Urſicinus, a general of equal rank, regained, by an act of treachery, the favour which he had loſt by his eminent ſervices in the Eaſt. Exaſperated, as he might ſpeciouſly allege, by injuries of a ſimilar nature, he haſtened, with a few followers, to join the ſtandard, and to betray the confidence, of his too credulous friend. After a reign of only twenty-eight days, Sylvanus was aſſaſſinated. The ſoldiers, who, without any criminal intention, had blindly followed the example of their leader, immediately returned to their allegiance; and the flatterers of Conſtantius celebrated the wiſdom and felicity of the monarch who had extinguiſhed a civil war without the hazard of a battle.　　GIBBON.

was

was allowed to go to court, induced by what is called a Theffalian perfuafion upon force *. For on my refolutely declining all intercourfe with the palace, the courtiers convening, as if they had been in a barber's-fhop, fhaved my chin, and throwing over me a military mantle, transformed me, as they thought, into a very ridiculous foldier. For none of the finical ornaments of thofe wretches were fuitable to my tafte. I walked about therefore, not like them, ftaring on every fide, and with a haughty gait, but poring on the ground, as I had been taught by my preceptor †. This was at firft the fubject of their laughter, but foon after of their fufpicion, which at length gave place to envy. But I muft not omit, that I refided among them, and that I did not difdain even to lodge

* This proverb, Θιτταλικη πειθαναγκη, is alfo quoted by Julian, in his firft Oration, and by Eunapius. But, as to its origin, the collectors of proverbs are filent. PETAU.

Spanheim fuppofes it to originate from the impoftures, perfidy, and magic of the Theffalians, which were alfo proverbial. Our Englifh proverb, which is not unlike it, " Patience on force," has an addition, which may perhaps afford a clue; " is a medicine for a mad horfe;" the inhabitants of Theffaly being anciently famous for their horfemanfhip. Πειθαναγκη is applied by Cicero to Cæfar, *ad Attic.* IX. 13.

† Mardonius, an eunuch, mentioned afterwards more particularly in the Mifopogon.

Julian himfelf relates, with fome humour, the circumftances of his own metamorphofis, his down-caft looks, and his perplexity at being thus fuddenly tranfported into a new world, where every object appeared ftrange and hoftile.
GIBBON.

with

with thofe whom I knew to have been the affaffins of all my relations, and whom I had reafon to fufpect of meditating alfo my deftruction. What floods of tears I fhed *, and what lamentations I uttered, when, extending my hands towards your citadel †, I intreated and implored Minerva to protect her fervant, and not to deliver him up to his enemies, many of you, who were prefent, can atteft; and, above all, the Goddefs herfelf knows, that I petitioned death of her at Athens in preference to that journey. That the Goddefs did not abandon me, nor deliver me up, the event has fhewn. On the contrary, fhe has every where been my guide, and was conftantly with me,

---

* Libanius, in his panegyrical Oration on the confulfhip of Julian, p. 235, has taken this, and fome other paffages, almoft in the fame words, from this Epiftle. PETAU.

† This was the temple of Minerva at Athens. The Emperor affigned Athens for the place of his honorable exile, which is implied in what Julian fays above of his "fhort retirement into Greece." He was fent thither in May, 355, and there "fpent fix months amidft the "groves of the Academy (as Mr. Gibbon expreffes it) "far from the tumult of arms, and the treachery of "courts, in a free intercourfe with the philofophers of "the age, who ftudied to cultivate the genius, to en- "courage the vanity, and to inflame the devotion of their "royal pupil. Gregory Nazianzen was his fellow-ftudent; "and the fymptoms, which he fo tragically defcribes, of "the future wickednefs of the apoftate, amount only to "fome bodily imperfections, and to fome peculiarities in "his fpeech and manner. He protefts, however, that "he then forefaw and foretold the calamities of the "church and ftate." St. Bafil was another of his fellow-ftudents.

borrowing

borrowing guardian-angels * from the Sun and Moon †.

What follows may be also worth relating. On my return to Milan, where I resided in one of the suburbs, Eusebia frequently sent me friendly messages, and urged me to write to her, on any subject, with the utmost confidence. This induced me to compose this letter, or rather petition, with an adjuration : " So may you have children and heirs, " so may God bless you with both, as you send " me home ‡ immediately § !" After this, I was apprehensive of not being able to convey it safely

---

* Julian did not yield till the Gods had signified their will by repeated visions and omens. His piety then forbade him to resist.   GIBBON.

He here declares himself a Pagan, which may serve to correct the hasty assertion of Ammianus, who supposes Constantinople to have been the place where he first discovered it.   *Ibid.*

† Julian, however, seems to have " borrowed" these angels from the Christian Scriptures, with which he was well acquainted. On the angels of the Sun he descants at large in his ivth Oration *ad Solem Regem*, and they are also mentioned by Iamblichus, in his Life of Pythagoras, and by Proclus on the 2d book of Hesiod.

‡ So he styles Asia Minor, where he had been educated.

§ Julian animated his army, not only by presents, but by constantly swearing by the importance of the enterprize in which they were engaged. " So may we subdue the " Persians !" " So may we repair the shattered Roman " world !" As Trajan is reported frequently to have confirmed what he said by swearing, " So may I see Dacia re- " duced to a province !" " So may I master the Danube " and Euphrates with bridges !" and the like.
                                        AMMIANUS.

into

into the palace. And therefore I befought the Gods to inform me by night whether I fhould fend it to the Emprefs, or not. They threatened me, if I fent it, with the moft ignominious death. I appeal to all the Gods for the truth of what I affert. In obedience to them, I fuppreffed it. But from that night I imbibed an idea which it may not be improper to mention. " Now," faid I to myfelf, " I undertake to oppofe the Gods, and " imagine that I can judge for myfelf better than " they who know all things." Human wifdom, " confining its view to the prefent, may think " that it judges well, when, in fome inftances, " which rarely happen, it commits no miftake. " But no one deliberates on events that will hap- " pen three hundred years hence, as that is im- " poffible, or on occurrences that are long paft, " that being needlefs; but only concerning objects " that are prefent, and of which the beginnings " and feeds, as it were, now exift. But the wif- " dom of the Gods, obferving the moft diftant " events, or rather all things, always directs what " is right, and does what is beft. As they are no " lefs the caufe of the prefent than of the future, " muft they not neceffarily be acquainted with the " prefent ?" Thus far then the laft advice feemed to me much the moft prudent; and viewing it in the light of juftice, I added, " Would you not be " provoked at being defrauded of any part of your " property, or, on your requiring its attendance,

" if

" if any one of your domeſtic animals * ſhould
" abſcond? And will you, who pretend to be a
" man, and that not of the common, vulgar herd,
" but of the rational and temperate, defraud the
" Gods of your ſervice, and not ſuffer them to dif-
" poſe of you as they pleaſe? Beware leſt you act
" not only fooliſhly, but contemptuouſly, with re-
" gard to the divine laws? What occaſion is here
" for fortitude? The pretence is ridiculous. Will
" you then condeſcend to cringe and flatter, in
" order to preſerve your life, inſtead of removing
" every obſtacle, and allowing the Gods to act as
" they pleaſe; dividing your ſolicitude for yourſelf
" with them †, as was the wiſh of Socrates; com-
" mitting every thing to them, poſſeſſing and
" uſurping nothing, but chearfully accepting
" whatever they beſtow?" Thinking this advice
moſt ſafe and prudent, as it was ſuggeſted by the
Gods (for by avoiding preſent evils to expoſe myſelf
to future dangers ſeemed the utmoſt raſhneſs), I
deſiſted and obeyed. Immediately I was honoured
with the title, and inveſted with the robe ‡, of

Cæſar.

* In the original, καν ιππος, καν προβατον, καν βοιδιον, (" a
" horſe, a ſheep, or a heifer.")

† Διελομενον προς αυτας [τας Θεας] την επιμελειαν την εαυτυ.
This language Julian perhaps rather learned from Chriftianity : Πασαν την μεριμναν υμων επιρριψαντες επ' αυτον [τον Θεον]
κ. τ. λ. *Caſting all your care upon him,* &c. 1 Peter, v 7.

‡ Ammianus, xv. 8. " Saying this, he thus accoſts Julian,
" ſoon after he had been arrayed with the purple, and de-
" clared Cæſar, to the great joy of the army, but ſome-
" what dejected, and with his brow contracted." He means
there-

Cæſar. Of this ſlavery was the conſequence, and every day, how great, O Hercules, was my apprehenſion, how imminent my danger ! Barred gates, guards, ſervants ſearched, leſt they ſhould convey letters from my friends, and a ſtrange houſhold ! I was with difficulty allowed to bring with me to court, as my perſonal attendants, four domeſtics, two of whom were boys ; and of the two others one only, my librarian *, from conſcientious motives, was privately, to the utmoſt of his power, my aſſiſtant. The other, who of my many friends and companions alone was faithful, was my phyſician †. Not being known to be alſo my friend, he was

therefore the purple which was common both to the Cæſar and the Auguſtus.   PETAU.

After the inveſtiture of the Cæſar had been performed, the two princes returned to the palace in the ſame chariot ; and during the ſlow proceſſion, Julian repeated to himſelf a verſe of his favourite Homer, which he might equally apply to his fortune and to his fears :

Ελλαϐε πορφυρεος θανατος, και μοιρα κραταιη. Il. v. 83.
——————— the *purple* hand of death
Cloſ'd his dim eyes, and fate ſuppreſs'd his breath.
                                               POPE, 108.

The word " purple," which Homer had uſed as a vague but common epithet for death, was applied by Julian to expreſs, very aptly, the nature and object of his own apprehenſions.   GIBBON.

* Euemerus. He was employed in the care of a valuable collection of books, the gift of the Empreſs, who ſtudied the inclinations, as well as the intereſt, of her friend.
                                                         Ibid.

† Oribaſius. See the firſt note on Epiſtle XVII: which is addreſſed to him in confidence. The elogium of " ſin-" gular fidelity" is applied by the Latin tranſlator to the librarian. The original, I think, warrants my applying it, as is more probable, to the phyſician.

                                                         my

my fellow-traveller. Such were my fears and apprehensions, that the visits which were offered me by many of my friends, whom I much wished to see, I chose to decline, lest I should involve them in my misfortunes *. But this, though connected with my subject, is rather foreign to it.

With three hundred and sixty soldiers Constantius sent me into Gaul, which was then in confusion, in the middle of winter †, not so much to command his armies there, as to be subordinate to his generals. For they had express orders to be as much on their guard against me as against the enemy, lest I should attempt any innovations. Every thing being thus settled, about the summer solstice ‡ he allowed me to join the army, bearing

his

* Julian represents, in the most pathetic terms, the distress of his new situation. The provision of his table was, however, so elegant and sumptuous, that the young philosopher rejected it with disdain. Amm. xvi. 5. GIBBON.

† Libanius, in his panegyric on the consulship of Julian, says the same, viz. that "less than four hundred soldiers "were given him, in the depth of winter;" and what follows he has transcribed, as has before been observed, from this Epistle. Ammianus (xv. 8.) says, that "Julian was "declared Cæsar on the 6th of November [355]; soon after "Helena was given him in marriage; and on De- "cember 1, he set out for Gaul." Marcellus and Sallust were sent with him, and to them all the management of the province and of the war was entrusted, lest Julian should attempt any innovations. PETAU.

‡ I cannot agree with the learned [Latin] translator, who, for " summer," affirms we should read " winter solstice." For this passage is not to be understood of that year, towards the end of which Julian was sent into the Gauls; but of the subsequent year, when he entered on his first consulship

with

his robe and image. For he had both said and written, that " he did not mean to give the Gauls " a king, but one who should exhibit to them his " dress * and image."

The first campaign, as you have heard, having been ill-conducted †, and no advantage gained, at my return into winter-quarters, I was exposed to the utmost danger. For I had not the power of assembling the troops; this was entrusted to another, and a few only were quartered with me. My assistance being requested by the neighbouring towns, after sending them most of my forces, I

had

with Constantius; which was the year of Christ 356. At the summer solstice the Gallic soldiers used to set out on expeditions.   VALOIS.

* Σκημα, not οχημα (" carriage") the common reading.
Ibid.

† Julian was made Cæsar in the consulship of Arbetio and Lollian, A. D. 355. Towards the end of that year, [as above mentioned], he was sent into Gaul, and wintered at Vienne, where he entered on his first consulship, with Constantius (the 8th time) for his collegue, at the beginning of the year 356, which was the first year of his Gallic government. This campaign, Julian complains, was unsuccessful, and that no advantages were gained. But if we refer to Ammianus, we shall find that less indeed than accorded with the inclination and impetuosity of Julian, yet much, nevertheless, was done against the Barbarians. While he was at Vienne, hearing that the Germans were making incursions in order to ravage Gaul, and had with difficulty been repulsed at Augustodunum [Autun] he determined to pursue them. After defeating and dispersing them, he recovered Colonia Agrippina [Cologne]. And he so terrified the kings of the Franks, that he compelled them to make peace. "Rejoicing" (adds Ammianus) "at these first fruits of conquest, he went into " winter-quarters at Treves, a then convenient town of

" the

had ſcarce any left *. So affairs were circum-
ſtanced. But the general in chief †, having in-

"the Senones." I ſuſpect therefore that Julian wrote
[ου] κακως δε, ως ακηκοαλι, [" not] ill conducted, as you have
" heard;") and, ſoon after, πραχθεντος [τινος] σπυδαιε, (" and
" [ſome] advantage gained.") But wintering at Sens, with
a few ſoldiers, the enemy aſſembled on a ſudden, and be-
ſieged the town; and Marcellus, maſter-general of the
cavalry, who commanded in the next cantonment, neglected
and refuſed to aſſiſt him. Yet in twenty days the Barbarians raiſed the ſiege, and retired. This we collect from
Ammianus xvi. 4.   Petau.

Ammianus appears much better ſatisfied with the ſucceſs
of this firſt campaign than Julian himſelf; who very frankly
owns that he did nothing of conſequence, and that he fled
before the enemy.   Gibbon.

* In the original, αυτος απελειφθην μονος, " I was left
" alone."

† As ſoon as Conſtantius heard how perfidiouſly Marcellus had acted at Sens, " abſolving him from his military
" oath" (theſe are the words of Ammianus) " he ordered
" him to retire to his own houſe; and he, as if he had been
" grievouſly injured, plotted ſomething againſt Julian,
" truſting that the ears of Auguſtus would be open to every
" charge." But the eunuch Eutherius, the moſt faithful præfect of his chamber, being diſpatched by Julian, refuted this
calumny. This Marcellus was a native of Serdica, whither,
when he was diſplaced, he retired. So ſays Ammianus, as I
have corrected him. The common reading is neither perfect,
nor conveys that ſenſe. For, after a long digreſſion, ariſing
from the eunuch Eutherius, on the wickedneſs of the
eunuchs, Ammianus, returning to Marcellus, expreſſes
himſelf thus: *Nunc redeam unde diverti. Superato, ut dixi,
Marcello,* everſâque Serdicâ, *unde oriebatur,* &c. Read *rever-
ſoque Serdicam.*   Petau.

The ſon of this Marcellus aſpiring to the empire was
put to death by Julian in 361. Libanius ſpeaks rather
more advantageouſly of the military talents of Marcellus.
And Julian intimates [above] that he would not ſo eaſily
have been recalled, unleſs he had given other reaſons of
offence to the court.   Gibbon.

curred the difpleafure of the Emperor, was fuper-feded and difmiffed, for inability; and, becaufe I had acted with clemency and moderation, my talents and abilities were not deemed equal to the command. For I thought it by no means right to ftruggle with my yoke, or officioufly to affume the general *, by obtruding my advice, unlefs when I faw fomething hazardous attempted, that I thought fhould have been omitted, or neglected, that fhould have been done. But having more than once received fome [im]proper † treatment, I determined for the future to be filent, and contented myfelf with the pageantry of the robe and image. For to that I thought I had a right.

Conftantius imagining that the Gallic affairs would foon wear a better afpect, not indeed that the alteration would be fo great, gave me the command of the armies ‡ in the beginning of fpring. As soon

* Ζυγομαχειν, ουδε παραστρατηγειν.

† Καθηκοντως ("properly") in the original. Ου ("not") feems neceffary to be prefixed, implying, that he afterwards was quiet, becaufe he had once or twice been treated ill. Petau.

‡ When Julian was appointed general, and what was the nature of his commiffion, deferves enquiry. He himfelf fays, that it happened after Marcellus was difmiffed, and fent to Serdica. But he alfo mentions, that, after he obtained this command, he rebuilt Colonia Agrippina (Cologne) and another town, Tabernæ, with fome other towns of Gaul, to the number of forty-five, recovered from the Barbarians. Very different is the account given by Ammianus. For he affirms, that Julian recovered Colonia before the end of the firft year of his being in Gaul, that is, in the confulfhip of Conftantius (the 8th time) and Julian,

foon as the corn was ripe, I took the field, many of the Germans dwelling fecurely near the towns that they had deftroyed in the Gauls. There were forty,

Julian, of our Lord 356, before Marcellus was commiffioned by Conftantius, which happened towards the end of the fame, or the commencement of the enfuing, year. Marcellus was fucceeded by Severus, a man well verfed in the art of war, good-natured, and unaffuming; at the acquifition of whom Julian expreffed much pleafure, and declared " that he would obey his able directions," (fays Ammianus) " as a foldier fhould an [obliging] leader." The fenfe requires *morigerus*. Barbatio alfo was fent with him, who was to attack the Barbarians in another quarter with twenty-five thoufand men. He was mafter-general of the foot, and Severus of the horfe, as Ammianus informs us, l. xvi. But if we compare the words of Julian with the hiftory of Ammianus, we fhall find, that the command of the army was given him in the fecond year of his being in the Gauls, viz. A. D. 357, when he engaged the Alemanni and king Cnodomar," after the corn was ripe." For in that year he acted as general, at leaft, of that army which Severus had commanded. And fo far was; Barbatio, who commanded the other, from obeying him, that he neglected and refufed to affift him, when he was in danger. Therefore his faying, " he gave me the command " of the armies," I do not think true of them all... Nor fhould it be omitted, that, even in the firft year, when Marcellus was ftill in Gaul, the Cæfar Julian was not fo obnoxious to the generals as not to be entrufted with fome command. For Ammianus relates (xvi.) that, in that year, which was 356 of Chrift, when Julian went to Rheims, " he ordered the army to be collected in one body," in order to difguife his force; " which army was then com- " manded by Marcellus, the fucceffor of Urficinus;" and alfo that Urficinus himfelf was ordered to wait in the fame place the event of that expedition. But though he had the title of governing the province, and managing the war, yet the mafters-general of the forces, as Conftantius had ordered, did not implicitly obey him, but in general, were refractory. Add, that Julian here oratorically depreffes

forty-five fuch towns that were difmantled *, befides villages and fmaller fortifications. The Barbarians then poffeffed all the territory on this fide
of the Rhine, from its fources to the ocean. Thofe
who were the neareft to us were three hundred
ftadia † diftant from its banks. A diftrict thrice
as extenfive was left a defert by their devaftations,
where the Gauls could not pafture their cattle.
Some towns were alfo deferted by their inhabitants,
though the Barbarians had not yet approached
them. Finding Gaul thus diftreffed, I recovered
the city of Agrippina [Cologne] on the Rhine,
which had been taken about ten months before,
and alfo the neighbouring caftle of Argentoratum
[Strafburgh] near the foot of Vofegus ‡; and we

his fituation below the truth, as if he had then no other
employment than carrying about the Imperial image.
Zofimus fays, (l. iii.) that " Conftantius permitted Julian,
" at his departure, to regulate the Gauls as he fhould
" think expedient." This Conftantius feems to have done
openly; but privately he ordered his præfects to watch
all his words and actions, and fometimes to obey perverfely.
See the Oration of Libanius on the confulfhip of Julian.

PETAU.

* Zofimus (l. iii.) fays, that " forty towns in Gaul,
" which the Barbarians had deftroyed, were rebuilt by
" Julian " And he alfo mentions, how much they had over-
run Gaul. Libanius enumerates as many as Julian, taking
all that hiftory from this Epiftle. *Ibid.*

† Near forty miles.

‡ One of the principal mountains in Gaul, now Mount
Vauge, which feparates Burgundy from Lorrain, and alfo
divides Lorrain from Alface, ftretching towards the north.
It gives rife to the rivers Maefe, Mofelle, and Sar.

CLUVIER.

7

fought

fought not ingloriouſly *. Of this battle, no doubt, you have heard †. The Gods then giving me the captive king of the enemy ‡, I did not envy Conſtantius the glory of the action. Though I was not allowed to triumph, I had it in my power to have ſlain my enemy, nor could I have been prevented leading him through Gaul, expoſing him in the towns, and thus inſulting the misfortunes of Cnodomar. None of theſe meaſures, however, I approved, but immediately ſent him to Conſtantius, who was then juſt returned from the Quadian and Sarmatian war §. While I was fighting, he was travelling alone, and holding an ami-

* Και εμαχεσαμην ουκ' ακλεως. The very words of Horace, on a different and leſs glorious warfare, l. III. ode 26, *Et militavi non ſine gloria.*

† Julian himſelf ſpeaks of the battle of Straſburgh with the modeſty of conſcious merit. Zoſimus compares it with the victory of Alexander over Darius; and yet we are at a loſs to diſcover any of thoſe ſtrokes of military genius which fix the attention of ages on the conduct and ſucceſs of a ſingle day. GIBBON.

‡ Meaning Cnodomar, who, in his flight, falling from his horſe into a moraſs, and being taken priſoner, was ſent to Conſtantius. See Ammianus (l. XVI. 12.) "Six thouſand "of the Germans," he ſays, "were killed in this battle, "beſides thoſe that were drowned, and only two hundred "and forty-three of the Romans." PETAU.

§ The events of this war are related by Ammianus, (XVI. 10. XVII. 12, 13. XIX. 11.) The Quadi, a fierce and powerful nation, were reduced to ſue for peace; and the Sarmatian exiles, who had been expelled from the country by the rebellion of their ſlaves, were reinſtated. Conſtantius, after this ſucceſs, received the name of Sarmaticus. GIBBON.

cable intercourse with the nations that border on the Danube. Yet not I, but he, triumphed *.

Another year succeeded, and a third, in which all the Barbarians were driven out of Gaul, most of the towns were rebuilt, and many loaded vessels arrived from Britain. Having collected a fleet of six hundred ships †, four hundred of which I had caused to be built in less than ten months, I brought them all into the Rhine; no easy task, on account of the irruptions and neighbourhood of the Barbarians. This had seemed so

---

* Constantius, though he was forty days journey distant, arrogated to himself the glory of this victory, describing the battle, as if he had been present, in letters crowned with laurel, which he sent to the provinces, and never mentioning the name of Julian.   AMMIANUS.

† Zosimus reckons eight hundred, which, he says, were built of materials found on the banks of the Rhine; that they might sail to Britain, and bring back corn and provisions to supply the garrisons. I know not that Ammianus mentions so many ships being built. He says, indeed, in his xviith book, that Julian fortified the towns that had been destroyed by the Barbarians, and built granaries in the room of those which were burnt, where the provisions accustomed to be brought from Britain might be lodged.   PETAU.

If we compute the six hundred corn-ships at only seventy tons each, they were capable of exporting a hundred and twenty thousand quarters (see Arbuthnot's "Weights and Measures"); and the country, which could bear so large an exportation, must already have attained an improved state of agriculture. These barks were framed in the forest of the Ardennes.   GIBBON.

Some of these vessels, as appears from Ammianus, must have been freighted with provisions, as well as with corn, which would reduce the quantity of the latter.

imprac-

impracticable to Florentius *, that he had agreed to give two thoufand pounds weight of filver † to permit a free paffage. Conftantius, on being informed of this (for they correfponded concerning this propofed prefent), exprefsly ordered me to agree to it, unlefs I thought it abfolutely difgraceful. But how could I poffibly think otherwife, when it feemed fo to Conftantius himfelf, though he was always very obfequious to the Barbarians? No payment therefore was made; but marching againft them, the Gods being prefent and propitious, I furprifed part of the Salians ‡, I reduced the Chamavians ‡, and took great numbers of

cattle,

---

* Prætorian Præfect of Gaul, an effeminate tyrant, a crafty and corrupt ftatefman, incapable of pity or remorfe.　　　　　　　　　　　　　　GIBBON.

† Five *aurei* (fomewhat more than eleven fhillings each) were the legal tender for a pound of filver.　　GREAVES.
Confequently two thoufand pounds of filver would amount to 5500l. fterling.

‡ Ammianus (XVII. 8.) relates, that, in the year when Datianus and Cerealis were confuls, Julian undertook an expedition againft the Salian Franks, who had formerly fettled near Toxandria [from the neighbourhood of Tongres to the conflux of the Vahal and the Rhine] whom, terrified at his fudden approach, he forced to furrender. Afterwards, he fubdued the Chamavians [a people near Munfter]. Treating the Salians with lenity, he marched againft the Quadi, whom, on account of their notorious robberies, he juftly deftroyed. And then happened that remarkable ftory of the king of the Chamavians, which is related by Eunapius, and more briefly by Zofimus. PETAU.
See it alfo in the Abbé de la Bleterie's *Vie de Julien*, p. 82 — 4. and in Mr. Gibbon's Roman Hiftory, II. p. 171.

　　　　　　　　　　This

cattle, with many women and children. This ir-ruption so much alarmed the Barbarians, that hoftages were immediately fent me, and the free importation of corn was fecured.

To relate every circumftance would be tedious. In fhort, thrice, while I was Cæfar *, I paffed the

This difference of treatment confirms the opinion, that the Salian Franks were permitted to retain the fettlements in Toxandria.   GIBBON.

It is pretended, that the name of Toxandria is ftill pre-ferved in a village, in the territory of Liege, called Tef-fender-loo.   LA BLETERIE.

* In the years 356, 358, and 359. Ammianus treats elo-quently of the two latter. The firft he does not mention; but it may be inferred from what he fays in his xvith book, where, relating the actions of the year 357, he fays, that what chiefly induced Julian to give battle to the Germans and Cnodomar was, that " in the year juft " ended, the Romans making large incurfions beyond the " Rhine, no one appeared in defence of his own home, " nor ftood his ground; but the Barbarians, removing to " a diftance, fubfifted with difficulty, blockading all the " roads with trunks of trees, during the inclemency of " winter." Which words mean, that Julian made war on the Germans beyond the Rhine in the year above-men-tioned, and therefore at the approach of winter. And this happened at the time when he recovered Agrippina [Cologne].   PETAU.

It was not enough for Julian to have delivered the pro-vinces of Gaul from the Barbarians of Germany. He af-pired to emulate the glory of the firft and moft illuftrious of the Emperors; after whofe example, he compofed his own Commentaries of the Gallic war. Cæfar has related, with confcious pride, the manner in which he twice paffed the Rhine. Julian could boaft, that, before he affumed the title of Auguftus, he had carried the Roman eagles beyond that great river in three fuccefsful expeditions.
                                    GIBBON.

Rhine.

Rhine. Twenty thousand captives * I rescued from the enemy on the other side of that river. In two battles and one siege, I took a thousand prisoners, and those not of a useless age, but men in the prime of life. Four bands of the most chosen † foot I sent to Constantius, with three others, not inferior, of horse, and two most distinguished cohorts. I now, such was the will of the Gods! took all the towns: before, I had taken near forty. I invoke Jupiter, and all the tutelar Gods of cities and of nations, to attest my attachment and fidelity to him. I have acted towards him as I would wish a son of my own to act towards me. The respect that I shewed him exceeded that of any former Cæsar to any other Emperor. I may boldly dare him therefore to allege any thing against me, even to the present moment, on that head. Some ridiculous pretences he has invented. "He has de-"tained," says my adversary, "Lupicinus ‡, and

---

* He meant, no doubt, in different campaigns.
La Bleterie.

Zosimus relates the whole transaction at large. See *Legationum excerpta ex Eunapio.*   Petau.

† What one of our modern generals calls "the *elite* of "the army." But why "the *flower* of the army" should not found as well, or why our brave garrison of Gibraltar should not make "*sallies*" as well as "*sorties*," &c. is difficult to conceive. These military Gallicisms were ridiculed long ago with great humour in the Tatler.

‡ This Lupicinus, master-general of the cavalry, on the death of Severus, was gone to Britain at the time when Julian was made Emperor by the army; but as he was of a haughty and enterprising spirit, lest he should take any steps against the new Emperor, a notary was dispatched to Boconia [Boulogne] to observe that coast.   Ammianus.

" three

" three * others." And fuppofing I had even put them to death, traitors and confpirators as they were, it ftill would have become him to have fmothered the refentment which their fufferings might have excited, for the fake of friendfhip and union. Thefe men, not in the leaft hurt, I fecured as dangerous difturbers of the public peace, and though I expended upon them much of the public treafure, I plundered them of nothing. But what would have been their punifhment, if Conftantius had been injured, and inflicted it? And does not he, by his refentment againft me, on account of thefe men, who bear not the leaft relation to him, arraign and deride my folly, in having been fo obfequioufly attentive to the affaffin of my father, of my coufins, and, in a word, the executioner of my whole family and kindred? Confider alfo the deference that I have paid him ever fince I became Emperor; as appears from my letters.

. How I behaved to him before that time, I will now inform you. Being fenfible that I fhould incur the whole danger and difgrace of every fault, though committed by others, I intreated him, that, if he had determined to declare me Cæfar, he would give me the beft and ableft counfellors. Inftead of which, he gave me at firft the vileft. When one of them, the moft abandoned of

all,

* Of the other three nothing certain can be affirmed. Florentius feems to have been one of them, who, Ammianus

all *, * * * * † he liftened indeed very readily, and gave me with reluctance an excellent officer in Salluft ‡. On account of his virtue, he foon became invidious. But not being fatisfied with him alone, and obferving the different manner in which Conftantius treated the others, confiding in them, and not regarding him, embracing his right hand and his knees, " Though I am not acquainted," faid I, " or ever was, with any one of thefe, yet " knowing them by report, and in deference to " you, I will confider them as my friends, and " efteem them as old acquaintance. It is not " proper, however, that my affairs fhould be con- " fided to them, or that theirs fhould be embroiled " by mine. I requeft you, therefore, to direct me, " by fome written rules §, what you would wifh

anus fays, at the very beginning of Julian's government fled from Vienne, where he then was, to Conftantius. Julian " leaving his family and effects untouched, and al- " lowing him the ufe of a public carriage, ordered him to " return in fafety into the Eaft."   PETAU.

If Florentius fled to Conftantius, how could he be one that was " detained by Julian ?"

* Meaning Marcellus, of whom above.   *Ibid.*

† Imperfect.

‡ We are ignorant of the actual office of this excellent minifter, whom Julian afterwards created Præfect of Gaul.
                                                    GIBBON.

§ When Julian was fetting out, Conftantius gave him a letter, in which he not only prefcribed rules for his conduct, but alfo limited his diet, and the amount of his daily expences. Ammianus, l. xvi. 5. " Laftly, as he conftantly " perufed the letter, which Conftantius, as if he had been " fending a fon-in-law to fchool, had written with his own " hand, regulating, with too much freedom, what fhould " be expended on the Cæfar's table," &c.   PETAU.

                                                    " me

" me to avoid, and what to do. Then, with the
" utmoſt reaſon, you will praiſe me if I obey,
" and puniſh me if I tranſgreſs.   But I am firmly
" of opinion, that I ſhall in no inſtance controvert
" your commands."

The innovations that Pentadius immediately attempted *, it is needleſs to mention. I oppoſed them all; conſequently he became my enemy. Soon after, by perverting another, and then a ſecond, and a third, and by bribing againſt me Paul † and Gaudentius ‡, notorious ſlanderers, he ſucceeded in having Salluſt, who was my friend §, recalled, and Lucian immediately appointed to ſucceed him. Florentius alſo was irritated by my oppoſing his in-

---

* At his complaining of Pentadius I am much ſurpriſed. For Ammianus mentions Pentadius (l. xx.) and ſays, that " he was maſter of the offices to Julian, and " was ſent by him, when he was made Emperor, to Conſtantius, with Eutherius, his chief chamberlain." He cannot therefore be the ſame, who, Julian here ſays, was his enemy while he was Cæſar.   PETAU.

† Paul was a notary, born in Spain, famous for cruel informations under Conſtantius, who was burnt alive, with Apodemus, when Julian was Emperor. See Ammianus, (l. xix. and xxii.)   *Ibid.*

‡ Gaudentius alſo was a notary, and having been ſent into the Gauls as a ſpy on the actions of Julian, was afterwards put to death by him at Antioch. Ammianus, (l. xxii.)   *Ibid.*

Their executions [thoſe of the two former] were accepted as an inadequate atonement by the widows and orphans of ſo many hundred Romans, whom thoſe legal tyrants had betrayed and murdered.   GIBBON.

As to Gaudentius, ſee the third note on Epiſtle X.

§ See the Conſolatory Oration on his departure, p. 30, &c.

fatiable.

fatiable avarice *. They therefore perfuaded Conſtantius, already perhaps jealous of my actions, to remove me from the command of the forces. And he wrote letters filled with invectives againſt me, and threatening deſtruction to the Gauls. Soon after, it appeared that he had ordered all the flower of the army, without exception, to be withdrawn from Gaul, charging Lupicinus and Gintonius † with this commiſſion, and commanding me in no reſpect to oppoſe them.

In what words ſhall I now relate the works of the Gods? It was my intention, they can witneſs, diveſting myſelf of all regal ſtate and magnificence, to reſt in peace, and never more to act in public. I only waited the return of Florentius and Lupi-

---

* See Epiſtle XVII.

† "Sintula, then tribune of the ſtables to the Cæſar," ſays Ammianus, (l. xx. 4.) "was joined in commiſſion "with Decentius, a tribune and notary, to conduct the "troops out of the Gauls." Of Gintonius I do not remember to have read. But of this hiſtory ſee more in Ammianus and Zoſimus, and alſo in the Oration of Libanius on the conſulſhip of Julian.   PETAU.

Julian was ſurpriſed by the haſty arrival of a tribune and a notary, with poſitive orders from the Emperor, which they were directed to execute, and he was commanded not to oppoſe; that four entire legions, the Celtæ, the Petulants, the Heruli, and the Batavians, ſhould be ſeparated from the ſtandard of Julian; that, in each of the remaining bands, three hundred of the braveſt youths ſhould be ſelected; and that this numerous detachment, the ſtrength of the Gallic army, ſhould inſtantly begin their march, and exert their utmoſt diligence to arrive, before the opening the campaign, on the frontiers of Perſia.   GIBBON.

cinus,

cinus, the one being in Britain *, and the other at Vienne. In the mean time, a great difturbance was raifed among the natives and foldiers, an anonymous libel being difperfed in a neighbouring town, among the Petulants and the Celts (the legions fo named) filled with invectives againft Conftantius, and with complaints of his having betrayed the Gauls. And the author of that paper no lefs lamented my difgrace. This being circulated, a general difaffection enfued, and thofe who were moft in the interest of Conftantius ufed their utmoft endeavours to perfuade me to detach the troops as foon as poffible, before the like libels were difperfed among the reft of the army. (Not one of my friends was then prefent). They were Nebridius †, Pentadius, and Decentius ‡, the latter

* Ammianus (l. xx. 1.) The valour of Lupicinus, and his military fkill, are acknowledged by the hiftorian, who, in his affected language, accufes the general of exalting the horns of his pride, bellowing in a tragic tone, and exciting a doubt whether he was more cruel or avaricious. The danger from the Scots and Picts was fo ferious, that Julian himfelf had fome thoughts of paffing over into the ifland.

GIBBON.

† Prætorian Præfect. This faithful minifter fingly oppofed the folemn engagement of the troops to devote themfelves to the fervice of Julian. Alone and unaffifted, he afferted the rights of Conftantius in the midft of an armed and angry multitude, to whofe fury he had almoft fallen an honourable, but ufelefs, facrifice. After lofing one of his hands by the ftroke of a fword, he embraced the knees of the prince whom he had offended. Julian covered the Præfect with his imperial mantle, and protecting him from the zeal of his followers, difmiffed him to his own houfe,

with

latter of whom Conftantius had difpatched for that purpofe. My reply, that " we ought to " wait for Lupicinus and Florentius," was totally difregarded, they all infifting that the oppofite plan fhould be purfued, unlefs I meant to confirm and corroborate former fufpicions. " Befides," they added, " the detaching the troops will now be " deemed your meafure; but when thofe minifters " return, Conftantius will impute it not to you, " but to them, and confequently will reprobate " your conduct." Thus I was perfuaded, or rather compelled, to write to him. For he may be faid to act by perfuafion, who has the liberty of refufing ; but thofe who can be compelled it is needlefs to perfuade; as they act not by choice, but neceffity. There being two roads, it was next , debated which fhould be taken. I propofed one ;

with lefs refpect than was perhaps due to the virtue of an enemy. The high office of Nebridius was beftowed on Salluft. *Ibid.*

Nebridius had before been Count of the Eaft, and, from being quæftor to Julian, was made by Conftantius præ-fect of the Gauls, in the room of Florentius, who had been removed to the præfecture of Illyricum. Florentius refufed to return from Vienne, dreading the refentment of the army. Nebridius retired in a private ftation into his native country, Tufcany. Pentadius is mentioned above.

‡ There is fome corruption in this paffage, for neither were they abfent, nor friends to Julian. On the contrary, they adhered to Conftantius. Petau.

The prefent reading may be fupported either by omit-ting the preceding paragraph, or by putting it (as in the tranflation) into a parenthefis. " Nebridius, &c." will then refer to the friends before mentioned, of Conftantius, as they certainly were.

but they compelled me to adopt * the other;
left my oppofition fhould excite fome tumult and
diforder in the army ; and when a difturbance was
once begun, a general confufion might enfue. An
apprehenfion this, which feemed by no means
groundlefs. The legions approached. I, as ufual †,
went out of the city to meet them, and urged
them to purfue their march. They halted one
day ; till when I was a ftranger to what they had
been concerting. Jupiter, the Sun, Mars, Minerva, and all the Gods know ‡, that I had not the
leaft fufpicion of their intentions till the evening
of that day, when at fun-fet they were difclofed
to me §. [At midnight] on a fudden the pa-

* Through Paris. Julian honeftly and judicioufly fuggefted the danger and temptation of a laft interview of the
foldiers with their wives and children.   GIBBON.

† Even the Emperors themfelves ufed to meet the legions
by way of honour.   VALOIS.

‡ Such an oath would be decifive in the mouth of a
Pagan, convinced of his falfe religion even to fanaticifm
and enthufiafm, as Julian was, if Julian had not given
fome proofs of duplicity. But when a man is capable of
being of two religions at the fame time, of believing one
and profeffing the other, he may well allow himfelf in per-
jury. Be that as it may, it muft be owned, that if that
prince moved the fprings which raifed him to the fupreme
power, he concealed his play fo well, as to feem to owe all
to chance, and nothing to intrigue.   LA BLETERIE.

It may feem ungenerous to diftruft the honour of a
hero, and the truth of a philofopher. The devout Abbé
de la Bleterie is almoft inclined to refpect the devout pro-
teftations of a Pagan.   GIBBON.

§ He then refigned himfelf to a fhort flumber; and
afterwards related to his friends, that he had feen the Genius of the empire waiting with fome impatience at his
door, preffing for admittance, and reproaching his want
of fpirit and ambition.   Ibid.

lace

lace * was invested, and an universal shout was raised, while in the mean time. I was deliberating what measures to pursue, but without forming any determination. Though my wife was then living †, I happened to sleep alone, in an adjoining upper chamber ‡, from which, there being an opening in the wall, I paid my adoration to Jupiter. The clamour increasing, and a general tumult prevailing throughout the palace, I intreated that God to ... give

* Most probably the palace of the baths (*thermarum*), of which a solid and lofty hall still subsists in the *rue de la Harpe*. The buildings covered a considerable space of the modern quarter of the university; and the gardens, under the Merovingian kings, communicated with the abbey of St. Germain des Prez. By the injuries of time and the Normans, this ancient palace was reduced, in the twelfth century, to a maze of ruins, whose dark recesses were the scene of licentious love.   GIBBON.

.. These remains, which have all the marks of antiquity, are the greatest curiosity in Paris. They are inclosed in a house, whose sign is the iron cross. Our kings of the first race resided in that palace. The daughters of Charlemagne were confined there after his death, when Lewis the Debonnair, a friend to full chant, but an enemy to gallantry, had caused their lovers to be put to death. " He " thought, without doubt," says F. Daniel, with great simplicity, " that the example would intimidate, and that " they would have no more. He was, it seems, mistaken; " they were never without them." *Tableau de Paris*, ch. Antiquities.

† Helena died soon after, at Vienne, says Ammianus, (l. xxi.); others say, in the palace of Julian, and was buried near her sister Constantina, at Rome. Her pregnancy had been several times fruitless, and was at last fatal to herself.   GIBBON.

‡ From Mr. King's very ingenious " Observations on " Ancient Castles," p. 5, &c. we learn, that " the state-" apartments (which Julian, no doubt, then occupied) were

give me a sign. This he immediately shewed me, commanding me firmly to confide in it, and not oppose the resolution of the army *. Though I had received these omens, I did not, however, yield without reluctance, but resisted as much as possible, nor would I admit of the salutation, or the diadem. But not being able singly to oppose so many, and the Gods, whose will it was, strongly animating them, and at the same time, composing my spirits, at length, about the third hour, some soldier, I know not whom, giving me a collar †, I put it on, and then re-entered the palace, groaning, as the Gods can witness, from the bottom of my heart; for though the confidence which the former sign had given me in God could not but

infpire

" always in the third story, an habitation both stately and " airy, free from the annoyance of the enemy's inftruments " of war."

The windows alfo of thefe rooms, even in our cold climate, though highly ornamented, " appear to have had " no glafs, and to have been fenced only with iron bars " and wooden fhutters, as is known to have been the " ufage in early times." *Sequel to the Obfervations on Ancient Caftles*, p. 108.

That the Jews, as well as Pagans, prayed " with their " windows open," appears from this paffage of Daniel, vi. 10. *He went into his houfe, and his windows being open in his chamber toward Jerufalem, he kneeled upon his knees*, &c.

* The conduct, which difclaims the ordinary maxims of reafon, excites fufpicion, and eludes our enquiry. Whenever the fpirit of fanaticifm, at once fo credulous and fo crafty, has infinuated itfelf into a noble mind, it infenfibly corrodes the vital principles of virtue and veracity.

GIBBON.

† Even in this tumultuous moment, Julian attended to the forms of fuperftitious ceremony, and obftinately refufed

the

inspire me with fortitude, I was ashamed and abashed at not seeming to obey Conftantius faithfully to the laft.

A great dejection prevailing in the palace, the friends of Conftantius endeavoured to improve that opportunity of forming a confpiracy againft me, and diftributed money among the foldiers, hoping to alienate fome of them, fo at leaft as to make a divifion between us, if not to perfuade them openly to attack me. One of the officers who attended my wife in public *, hearing what they were clandeftinely tranfacting, difclofed it to me. But finding that I difregarded it, with the frenzy of an enthufiaft, he loudly exclaimed in the marketplace, " Soldiers, foreigners, and natives, do not " betray the Emperor." The minds of the troops being thus inflamed, they all ran armed to the palace. Finding me there alive and unhurt, and rejoicing like friends who meet unexpectedly, they embraced me, clafped me in their arms, and bore me on their fhoulders. It was indeed a moft pleafing fight, feeming like infpiration. Surrounding me on all fides, they then infifted that every friend of Conftantius fhould be put to death. The ftrenu-

the inaufpicious ufe of a female necklace, or a horfe's collar (*equi phaleræ*), which the impatient foldiers would have employed inftead of a diadem.   GIBBON.

The collar which he put on, enriched with jewels, belonged, fays Ammianus, to " one Maurus, afterwards a ". Count, then a fpearman of the Petulants." This event happened in April, 360.

* Ammianus ftyles him *aliquis palatii decurio*, a kind of lictor.

ous

ous endeavours that I used to save them, all the
Gods know. After this, what was my conduct towards Conſtantius? In my letters * to him, even
to the preſent hour, I have never aſſumed the title
which the Gods have given me, only ſtyling myſelf Cæſar; and I prevailed on the ſoldiers to ſwear
to me, that they would attempt nothing farther, if
he would ſuffer me to dwell peaceably in the
Gauls, and ratify all that had been done. Add
to this, the legions that were with me ſent him an
united letter, urging a reconciliation between us.
In return, he ſpirited the Barbarians againſt us,
proclaimed me to them as a public enemy, and
bribed them to ravage the Gallic provinces. He
wrote alſo to them who were in Italy, and warned
them to guard againſt thoſe who came from the
Gauls. In the towns bordering on the Gallic frontier,
he ordered magazines to be formed; in particular,
one of ſix hundred thouſand quarters † of flour at
Brigantia ‡, and another of as many more at the foot
of the Cottïan Alps §; that he might be enabled to
march an army againſt me. All theſe things were
not only ſaid but done. For the letters which he
ſent ‖ to ſpirit the Barbarians I intercepted, and all

* The Epiſtle to which Julian principally alludes has
been inſerted, p. 54.

† Three hundred myriads, or three millions of *medimni*,
a corn meaſure familiar to the Athenians, and which contained ſix Roman *modii*.   GIBBON.

‡ Now Bregentz, on the banks of the Lake of Conſtance.
§ The mountains that divide Dauphiny from Piedmont.
‖ Meaning the letters which Ammianus mentions in his
xxiſt book. Yet he expreſſes himſelf with cool and can-
did heſitation, *ſi famæ ſoli admittenda eſt fides.*   GIBBON.

the

the provifions, which he had ordered to be collected, I feized, and alfo the letters of Taurus *.
Befides this, he addreffed me ftill as Cæfar, and
declared, that he would never be reconciled to me.
He fent, however, one Epictetus †, a Gallic bifhop,
to affure me of my fafety ; and in all his letters he
intimates, that he will fpare my life; but as to
my honour, he is filent. In regard to his oaths, I
think, as the proverb fays, they fhould be written
in afhes, fo little do they deferve belief. My
own honour, not only for the fake of what is
juft and right, but for that of the fafety of my
friends, I am determined to maintain; not to
mention the cruelties exercifed throughout all the
world.

Thefe arguments are to me conclufive ; thefe
meafures appear to me juft; and I adopted them
at firft in the fight and hearing of the Gods. Afterwards, on the very day in which I was going to

* Præfect of Italy, and Conful, with Florentius, in 361,
when this Epiftle was written. He was banifhed by Julian,
foon after, during his præfecture and confulfhip, to Ver-
cellæ, in Italy.

† There was a bifhop of that name, a remarkable favourer of the Arian fect, who, to gratify Conftantius, ufed
great feverity towards the Catholics. But he was bifhop
of Centum-cellæ [now Civita-Vecchia] in Thufcia [Tuf-
cany] not in Gaul. Perhaps Julian wrote Κιντεμκελλων (" of
" Centum-cellæ,") inftead of των Γαλλιων (" of the Gauls".)
Yet Ammianus relates, that the perfon, who was fent into
the Gauls with thefe orders to Julian, was the quæftor
Leonas.   PETAU.

                    harangue

harangue the army concerning our march hither *,
facrificing for the event, for my own fafety, and
much more for the public welfare, and the general
freedom of the world, efpecially of the Gallic nation,
whom he has twice abandoned to her enemies, not
fparing the fepulchres of their anceftors, though he
pays the utmoft attention to thofe of foreigners †, the
omens were aufpicious. I thought it therefore neceffary to reduce our formidable enemies ‡, and to coin
lawful money of gold and filver; and if even now he
fhould be difpofed to treat with me, will be fatisfied
with what I at prefent poffefs. But if he fhould pre-

* Illyricum, where this Epiftle was written.

+ The primitive Chriftians called the temples of the
Heathens " fepulchres," in contempt, becaufe temples
began to be built where their Gods were buried. But this the
Gentiles afterwards retorted on the Chriftians, on account
of the relics of the martyrs, preferved and worfhiped
in the churches. And hence they ftyled the Chriftian
churches nothing but ταφυς (" tombs.")   VALOIS.

‡ After Julian had difmiffed Leonas, and fent a new embaffy to the Eaftern court, that he might keep his troops
in exercife, and preferve the reputation they had gained,
he paffed the Rhine for the fourth time, fubdued the
Attuarii, a nation of the Franks, who ftill made incurfions
into Gaul; and, repaffing the Rhine, reviewed and ftrength-
ened all the garrifons in the frontier towns, as far as the
country of the Rauraci (now the canton of Bafil); from
whence he repaired to Befançon, and then to Vienne,
where he kept his winter-quarters. Before the conclufion
of the winter, the Germans under king Vadomar, having
revolted and pillaged Rhœtia (now the country of the
Grifons), he feized and banifhed that prince, and paffing
the Rhine for the fifth and laft time, furprifed the Barbarians, and forced them to fwear to a peace, which they
never prefumed to violate again during his life.

                                        LA BLETERIE.

                                              fer

fer engaging in a war, and will in no refpect recede from his former determination, I am ready to do or fuffer whatever the Gods may decree. It is more difgraceful to be conquered by ignorance and pufil-lanimity, than by ftrength and numbers. If he excells me in numbers, that is owing, not to him-felf, but to his armies. If he had furprifed me ftill loitering in the Gauls, and tenacious of life, and had furrounded me, declining danger, on the flanks and in the rear by the Barbarians, and in front by his own troops, I muft have fubmitted, not only to the utmoft extremity, but, which to the wife is the greateft of evils, to difgrace *.

Such are the reflections, men of Athens, which I have communicated to my fellow-foldiers, and now tranfmit to you and the other cities of Grece †. May the Gods, the Lords of all, afford me the affiftance, which they have promifed, to the laft, and grant to Athens, that I may, as much as poffible, deferve her favour, and that fhe may for ever have fuch Emperors as may intimately

---

* Julian explains, like a foldier and a ftatefman, the danger of his fituation, and the neceffity and advantages of an offenfive war. GIBBON.

† Lacedæmon and Corinth, Zofimus fays, were two of the other cities that Julian addreffed, but all that remains of either, or any, of thofe Epiftles, is two fhort paragraphs of that to the Corinthians, preferved by Sozomen; in one of which he fays, " Having reluctantly commenced this " war, but having now, in great meafure, fucceeded, " though not yet arrived at the conclufion;" and in the other, he claims their favour, " on account of the friend-" fhip of his father, who had dwelt among them."

H 4

know,

know, and with a distinguished preference esteem,
her * !

* The humanity of Julian was preserved from the cruel
alternative, which he pathetically laments, of destroying,
or of being himself destroyed; and the seasonable death of
Constantius delivered the Roman empire from the calamities of civil war.   The approach of winter could not
detain the monarch at Antioch ; and his favourites durst
not oppose his impatient desire of revenge.   A slight fever,
which was perhaps occasioned by the agitation of his
spirits, was increased by the fatigues of the journey ; and
Constantius was obliged to halt at the little town of Mop-
sucrene, twelve miles beyond Tarsus, where he expired,
after a short illness, in the forty-fifth year of his age, and
the twenty-fourth of his reign.   GIBBON.
This event happened on Sept. 3, 361.   It is pretended
that, upon his death-bed, he named Julian his successor,
willing, no doubt, to make a merit of what he could no
longer with-hold from him, and by that to engage him to
protect Faustina, whom he had married after the death of
Eusebia, and whom he left pregnant of a princess [Con-
stantia], who was afterwards married to the Emperor Gratian.   Julian immediately hastened towards Constantinople,
which he entered, accompanied by the senate, soldiers,
and people, on Dec. 11.   LA BLETERIE.

AN

AN ALLEGORICAL FABLE *.

A CERTAIN rich man † had numerous flocks and herds, and many horses ‡, grazing in his meadows. He had alfo many fhepherds, as well flaves as freed-men, and hired fervants, herdfmen, goat-herds, grooms, with many eftates, fome of which were bequeathed to him by his father § ; but moft of them he had acquired, being defirous to enrich himfelf by right or wrong, and having little regard for the Gods. He had feveral wives, by whom he had fons and daughters ‖,

among

---

* Julian has worked the crimes and misfortunes of the family of Conftantine into an allegorical Fable, which is happily conceived and agreeably related. It forms the conclufion of the VIIth Oration. GIBBON.

See a farther account of it in the Preface.

† This rich man is Conftantine, that eternal object of the hatred and malignity of Julian. LA BLETERIE.

The beginning of this Fable is remarkably fimilar to that of Nathan's Parable, in 2 Sam. xii. 2. which Julian had read in the Septuagint. Πλυσιω ανδρι προβατα ην πολλα, και αγελαι βοων, fays the Emperor. Τω πλυσιω ανδρι ην ποιμνια και βυκολια πολλα σφοδρα, fays the Prophet.

‡ In the original, ιπποι μυριαι (" many mares.")

§ Conftantius Chlorus reigned only over the Gauls, Spain, and Great-Britain. Conftantine, with much good fortune, and perhaps too much addrefs, made himfelf mafter of the whole empire. LA BLETERIE.

‖ Conftantine left three fons, between whom he divided the empire. Conftantine, known in hiftory by the name of the younger Conftantine, had the Gauls, Spain, and Great-Britain. Conftantius had the Eaft. Conftans, Italy,

Illyricum,

among whom he divided his wealth *, before he died, but without instructing them how to manage it, how to acquire more, if it should fail, or, when it was acquired, how to preserve it. So gross was

Illyricum, and Africa. We are acquainted only with two daughters of Constantine the Great; Constantina and Helena. He married the former to Flavius Claudius Hannibalianus, his nephew, son of his brother Dalmatius the Censor. This princess afterwards married the Cæsar Gallus. Helena was married to Julian. It is not at first easy to conceive how he can say, that " the father of the " family divided his estate between his sons and *his daugh-* " *ters*;" as, among the Romans, the daughters were excluded from the empire. But this passage of Julian informs us of two things; 1. That if Constantine gave his nephew Hannibalianus the title of King, with Armenia the Less, Pontus, and Cappadocia, it was on account of his marriage with Constantina, on whom, besides, he conferred the title of Augusta, and a right to wear the diadem. 2. That if he raised Dalmatius, the brother of Hannibalianus, to the dignity of Cæsar, and gave him Thrace, Macedonia, and Achaia, it was because Dalmatius was to espouse Helena, who was then a child. Hannibalianus and Dalmatius were included in the massacre which followed the death of Constantine. One fault of that able politician, a fault much more real than that with which Julian here reproaches him, is that of having raised his brothers and his nephews to such a height as to make them formidable to his children. If he could imagine that he should have authority enough over both to prevent the usual effects of jealousy and ambition during his life, should he have flattered himself that they would have such respect to his memory as to remain within the limits which he had prescribed them? The greatest princes ought always to think that they will not reign after their deaths.

La Bleterie.

* Whether, after the death of Fausta, the mother of Constantius and his brothers, Constantine contracted any other marriage does not appear from the memorials, still remaining, of those times; except that in general Julian here says, that " he had many wives," ἐγένοντο δὲ αὐτῷ γυναῖκες πολλαί, though without naming them. Spanheim.

his

his ignorance, that he thought nothing neceſſary
but riches; nor in that art had he much experience, having acquired it, not by any fixed principle, but rather by uſe and habit, like empirics,
who by practice only cure diſeaſes, and conſequently muſt be ignorant of many. Thus thinking that the number of his ſons would ſufficiently
ſecure the continuance of his family, he uſed no
endeavour to make them virtuous *.

This was the firſt origin of their diſſenſions.
For each of them deſiring, like his father, to have
great riches, and ſingly to poſſeſs all, attacked his
brother. The calamities occaſioned by their folly
and ignorance extended alſo to their neareſt relations, who had had no better education. A general ſlaughter enſued, ſo as to realiſe by divine
vengeance the moſt tragical cataſtrophe. They
divided their patrimony by the ſword, and every
thing was thrown into confuſion. The ſons deſtroyed the temples of their anceſtors, which before indeed had been deſpiſed by their father, and
ſtripped of their offerings, dedicated by many, but
chiefly by his forefathers. But when they deſtroyed
the temples, they repaired the old and erected new
ſepulchres †, as if they had foreſeen, that for their

---

* Julian, in his firſt panegyric on Conſtantius, ſays, that
the children of Conſtantine had the moſt excellent education
that could be given to princes. He then perhaps flattered.
Now perhaps he ſlanders. LA BLETERIE.

† By "ſepulchres" he muſt mean churches. So they
were called by the Pagans, becauſe they were built over the
tombs of the martyrs   *Ibid.* See p. 102, note †.

contempt of the Gods they would ere long want many sepulchres themselves.

Amidst these disorders, marriages also being contracted which were no marriages *, and the laws both of Gods and men being thus alike infringed, Jupiter was moved with compassion, and addressing himself to the Sun †, he said to him,

---

* Constantius first married the daughter of Julius Constantius, his uncle. Though history does not inform us who were the wives of Constantine the younger and Constans, it may be presumed that they also married their cousin-germans. Such marriages were not forbidden among the Romans till Theodosius, whose law was afterwards repealed by Justinian. However, even before the prohibition of Theodosius, they were unusual, because they were odious. It was thought that they bordered upon incest. This we learn from St. Augustine, *de civitate Dei*, *l. xv. c. 16. Raro per mores fiebat quod fieri per leges licebat. . . Factum etiam licitum propter vicinitatem horrebatur illiciti ; et quod fiebat cum consobrinâ penè cum sorore fieri videbatur, quia et ipsi inter se propter tam propinquam consanguinitatem fratres vocantur, et pene germani sunt.* Allowing this, it will be easy to conceive how a passionate enemy, like Julian, may so severely reprobate the marriages of the children of Constantine. This key, I think, may serve for want of better historical light. La Bleterie.

Julian, whose mind was biassed by superstition and resentment, stigmatises these unnatural alliances between his own cousins with the opprobrious name of γαμων τι ου γαμων. The jurisprudence of the canons has since revived and enforced this prohibition, without being able to introduce it either into the civil or the common law of Europe.
La Bleterie.
Gibbon.

One of these " no marriages" was that of Julian himself with his cousin Helena. Another, that of Gallus and Constantina.

† After what has been said before, it is needless here to observe, that Julian means by the Sun that intelligence produced from all eternity by the supreme God, &c. in a word, the Logos of Plato. La Bleterie.

" Of

" Of all the Gods my most ancient off-spring,
" being born before heaven and earth, doft thou
" still retain the memory of the infults thou haft
" received from that difdainful and arrogant man;
" who, by forfaking thee *, entailed fo many
" calamities on himfelf, his family, and his children?
" Though you have not perfonally wreaked your
" vengeance on him, nor have launched your ar-
" rows againft his children, are you lefs the author
" of that deftruction which has defolated his
" family? But let us fummon the Fates, and en-
" quire of them whether any affiftance can be
" given it."

The Fates inftantly attended; but the Sun, as if
abforbed in contemplation, continued to fix his
eyes on Jupiter. The eldeft of the Fates thus replied: ' Juftice and Sanctity, O Father, forbid
' it. But it depends on yourfelf, fince you have
' ordered us to be fubfervient to them, to prevail
' on them alfo.' " True," anfwered Jupiter,
" they are my daughters, and therefore I may
" interrogate them.—Venerable Goddeffes, what
" do you advife?" ' That, Father,' they replied,
' is as you direct; but be careful left that work

* The devotion of Conftantine was peculiarly directed
to the Genius of the Sun, the Apollo of Greek and Roman
mythology; and he was pleafed to be reprefented with the
fymbols of the God of light and poetry. GIBBON.

Among the many coins of this Emperor, found at Re-
culver, in Kent (the Roman Regulbium), fome have, on
their reverfe, the figure of Apollo, with a ftar, and *Soli
invicto comiti.* This device would have ferved equally well
for Julian.

' of

" of all crimes, a zeal for impiety, should univer-
" sally prevail in the world.' " To that," said Jupiter, " I will certainly attend." The Fates then
approached, and spun as the Father directed. Afterwards Jupiter thus addressed the Sun : " You
" see this infant *, the nephew of that rich man,
" and the cousin of his heirs. Though destitute
" and despised, he is your off-spring. Swear,
" therefore, to me, by my sceptre and your own,
" that you will take especial care of him, that you
" will be his guide, and secure him from evil.
" You see he is enveloped, as it were, with smoke,
" and filth, and darkness, and that the flame which
" you have kindled in him is in danger of being
" stifled:

  " And owns no help but from thy saving hands †.
" Take him therefore, and superintend his edu-
" cation. This I and the Fates allow." At
this the Sun much rejoiced, and was pleased with
the child, perceiving in him a small spark of
himself still remaining. From that time he educated the boy, withdrawing him

    Far from alarms, and dust and blood ‡.
But Jupiter ordered the motherless and chaste
Minerva to have a share also in his education.

    Thus instructed, when the youth had attained
that age,

  * Julian himself.
  † Iliad IX. 231. Pope, 304. Part of the speech of
Ulysses to Achilles, requesting him to assist the Greeks.
  ‡ Iliad XI. 164. Pope, 216. applied to Hector, when
protected by Jupiter and Fate.

When

When fprings the down, when youth has all its
    charms *,

Being apprifed of the numerous calamities which
had befallen his relations and coufins, he was
fo terrified, that he would have rufhed headlong into Tartarus, had he not been prevented
by the benevolent Sun and provident Minerva †,
who threw him into a flumber, which banifhed
that idea. Awaking from this, he returned to
his folitude, and there, fitting on a ftone, he confidered with himfelf how he fhould efcape fuch
a variety of evils; for now every thing appeared
adverfe, and he was abandoned even by hope.

Mercury then, who had an affection for him,
affuming the appearance of one of his young
companions, thus kindly accofted him : " Follow
" me, and I will fhew you a fmoother and eafier
" way, as foon as you have gone through this
" winding and rugged path, which obliges, as
" you fee, all who enter it to turn back." The

* Iliad XXIV. 348.

† In the original, της Προνοιας Αθηνας. In his IVth Oration, Julian confiders Pronœa as another name for Minerva.

After the example of Plato, whofe philofophy he adopted,
Julian, like other Heathens, acknowledged God's Providence. Not to mention his mafter Jamblichus (*de Myfter.*
l. 1. *c.* 9.) " the Providence of God" is mentioned by
Euripides, in his Oreftes, ver. 1181. On fome excellent
coins of Commodus it appears under the fymbol of a
woman extending her right hand, and holding a fpear in
her left, or before an altar, with another figure of a
man ftanding, and on each fide a tree, with the infcription
ΠΡΟΝΟΙΑ. And on the Roman coins is fometimes feen a
temple, and fometimes a radiated figure of the fun, with
PROVIDENTIA infcribed, &c.   SPANHEIM.

youth

youth then proceeded cautiously, with his fword, his fhield, and fpear, but with his head unarmed. Relying on his guide, he came to a road, though unfrequented, highly pleafant, and embroidered with fruit-trees and flowers innumerable, fuch as are pleafing to the Gods, and alfo with ivy, laurel, and myrtle.

When they arrived at the foot of a high mountain, "On the fummit of that," faid Mercury, " dwells the Father of the Gods; be careful " therefore, for great is your danger, to worfhip " him in the moft religious manner. Afk of him " whatever you pleafe. You will wifh, my child, " for what is beft." So faying, Mercury difappeared, though the youth was very defirous of being informed by him what petition he fhould prefer to the Father of the Gods. Thus deferted, he could only advife with himfelf, and he could not have been advifed better. " Though I do not " yet fee," faid he, " the Father of the Gods, " let me folicit him for his beft gifts. O Father " Jupiter, or by whatever other name thou pleafeft " to be called, for that to me is indifferent, teach " me the way that leads to thee. For the region " of thy refidence is incomparably beautiful, if I " may judge of its excellence by the pleafantnefs " of the path through which I have been con- " ducted hither." After having thus prayed, he fell faft afleep. During this flumber, or trance, Jupiter fhewed him the Sun in perfon. Aftonifhed at this fight, the youth exclaimed, " For this and

" all thy other favours, O Father of the Gods, I
" offer and dedicate myself to thee." Then embracing the knees of the Sun, he intreated his
protection. But he, calling Minerva, bade her
first observe what arms he had brought. Seeing
only a sword, a shield, and a spear, " Where, my
" son," said she, " are your ægis and helmet ?"
He answered, " I could scarce provide even these;
" neglected and despised, I had no friend in the
" family of my relations." " What then," replied the Sun, " will you say, when I tell you,
" that you must necessarily return to it ?" Hearing this, the youth intreated him, with many tears,
not to send him thither again, as, in that case, he
should never see him more, but should certainly
perish there, overwhelmed with misfortunes. " You
" are young," said the Sun, " and have not yet been
" initiated. Return therefore to earth, and when you
" are initiated *, dwell in safety ; return and pu-
                                        " rify

* By the hands of Maximus [See the first note on Epistle
XV.] Julian was secretly initiated at Ephesus, in the twen-
tieth year of his age. His residence at Athens confirmed
this unnatural alliance of philosophy and superstition. He obtained the privilege of a solemn initiation into the mysteries
of Eleusis, which, amidst the general decay of the Grecian worship, still retained some vestiges of their primæval
sanctity; and such was the zeal of Julian, that he afterwards invited the Eleusinian pontiff to the court of Gaul,
for the sole purpose of consummating, by mystic rites and
sacrifices, the great work of his sanctification. As these
ceremonies were performed in the depth of caverns, and in
the silence of the night; and as the inviolable secret of the
mysteries was preserved by the discretion of the initiated;
I shall not presume to describe the horrid sounds, and fiery

" rify yourfelf from all impiety. You muft
" then invoke me, and Minerva, and the other
" Gods."

The youth, at thefe words, remained filent.
The Sun then conducting him to a mountain, (whofe
fummit fhone with light, but whofe lower parts
were covered with thick darknefs, through which,
however, as through a mift, the rays of the Sun
appeared dim and faint), thus addreffed him :
' You fee your coufin the heir * : Do you fee
' alfo thofe herdfmen and fhepherds ?' He replied
in the affirmative. ' How is he,' faid the Sun,
' and how are his fhepherds and herdfmen, em-
' ployed ?' " He," faid the youth, " feems to me
" afleep ; he lives in retirement, and devotes him-
" felf to pleafure. Few of his fhepherds are well-
" difpofed ; moft of them are wicked, and cruel ;
" for they either devour or fell his fheep, and thus
" doubly injure their mafter ; they ruin his flocks,
" and, though they receive much and return him
" but little, they complain that they are defrauded
" of their wages ; but it were better that they
" fhould be paid the whole, than the fheep be
" deftroyed." ' But fuppofe,' faid the Sun, ' I
' and Minerva, by the command of Jupiter,
' fhould appoint you guardian of all thefe flocks,
' in the room of this heir ?' This the youth again

apparitions, which were prefented to the fenfes, or the
imagination, of the credulous afpirant, till the vifions of
comfort and knowledge broke upon him in a blaze of
celeftial light.   GIBBON.

    * Conftantius.

oppofed,

oppofed, and earneftly intreated to remain there.
The Sun replied, " Be not obftinately difobedient,
" left my hatred fhould be equal to the love that
" .I have borne you." The youth then anfwered,
' O moft excellent Sun and Minerva, and thee
' too I atteft, O Father Jupiter, difpofe of me
' abfolutely as you pleafe.' After this, Mercury, again appearing, infpired him with ad-
ditional courage. For now he thought he had
found a guide in his return, and during the time
that he was to pafs on earth.

Minerva then thus accofted him: " Good fon
" of this excellent and divine father and of me,
" attend! The beft fhepherds, you obferve, do
" not pleafe this heir; but profligates and flatterers
" have enflaved him. Confequently he is not
" beloved by the good and virtuous, and by thofe
" who feem his friends he is injured and dif-
" honoured. Be careful therefore, when you re-
" turn, never to prefer a flatterer to a friend.
" Take another advice, my fon. That man fleeps,
" and of courfe is often deceived; but be you
" fober and vigilant *., A flatterer often affumes
" the confidence of a friend; juft as if a fmith,
" covered with fmoke and afhes, fhould, by a
" painted face and a white garment, induce you to

* Συ δε νηφε, και γρηγορη.
The fame words as thofe of the Apoftle, Νηψατε, γρηγο-
ρησατε, 1 Pet. v. 8.
This is not the firft paffage in which we have feen our
author availing himfelf of his Chriftian erudition.

" give

" give him one of your daughters in marriage.
" Thirdly, let me exhort you to have a particular
" regard to yourself. Refpect us in the firft place;
" among men, thofe who refemble us moft, and
" no one befides. You fee how much this poor
" wretch has fuffered from a falfe fhame and a
" foolifh timidity."

To this the Sun added, ' Thofe whom you felect
' for your friends treat as friends, not as fervants
' and domeftics. Behave to them with freedom,
' candour, and generofity, not thinking of them
' one thing, and faying another. What was fo
' deftructive to this young heir as unfaithfulnefs
' to his friends? Love your fubjects, as you are
' loved by us. Whatever relates to our worfhip
' prefer to all other virtues. For we are your
' benefactors, and friends, and prefervers.'

Delighted at thefe words, the youth clearly
fhewed his defire to obey the Gods implicitly in
all things. "Depart now," faid the Sun, " with
" joyful hopes, for I, and Minerva, and Mer-
" cury will every where be with you, and alfo
" all the Gods who dwell on Olympus, or in the
" air, or on earth, and all the other deities ; fo
" you fhall be pious to us, faithful to your friends,
" and humane to your fubjects, teaching them to
" excell by your example, and never being en-
" flaved by their paffions or your own. Retain
" the armour that you brought hither, and receive
" from me this torch, which will afford you fuch
" light on earth, that you will not need that of
" heaven.

" heaven. Accept alfo from good Minerva an
" ægis and a helmet, for fhe has many, as you
" fee, which fhe beftows on whom fhe pleafes.
" Mercury, befides, will give you a golden wand.
" Depart therefore, relying on this armour, and
" traverfe earth and fea, inviolably obeying our
" laws. Let neither man, nor woman, your
" own countrymen, nor foreigners, perfuade you
" to neglect our precepts. While you obferve
" them, you will be loved and efteemed by us,
" and alfo refpected by our good fervants, and
" formidable both to wicked men and evil dæ-
" mons *. Know that you were invefted with a
" mortal body in order to difcharge thefe duties.
" For the fake of your anceftors, we wifh to
" purify your family from every ftain. Remember,
" therefore, that your foul is immortal, and fprung
" from us; and that, if you follow us, you will be
" a God, and with us will behold our Father."

Whether this be a fable, or a true narrative, I
cannot tell †.

* It is well known that the Platonifts admitted of good
and evil Genii, and that they included both under the
name of dæmons. La Bleterie.

† Thus St. Paul, *Whether in the body, or out of the body,
I cannot tell; God knoweth.* 2 Cor. xii. 3.

The

The Duties of a Priest.

Extracted from the Fragment of an Oration, or Epiſtle *.

A. D. 362 or 3.

*** IF any are detected misbehaving to their prince, they are immediately puniſhed; but thoſe who refuſe to approach the Gods, are poſſeſſed by a tribe of evil dæmons, who, driving many

* This Fragment was interwoven with the Epiſtle to Themiſtius, as has been obſerved in the notes on that Epiſtle. We have therefore publiſhed it ſeparately. It is part of an epiſtle which Julian wrote to ſome High Prieſt, teaching him the example which he ought to ſet to thoſe of his own order both at home and abroad. And there are many things in this Fragment which he wiſhes his people to practiſe in imitation of the Chriſtians.　　PETAU.

Mr. Gibbon ſtyles this " a long and curious Fragment " without beginning or end;" and adds, " The Supreme " Pontiff derides the Moſaic hiſtory, and the Chriſtian " diſcipline; prefers the Greek poets to the Jewiſh pro" phets; and palliates, with the ſkill of a Jeſuit, the *re-* " *lative* worſhip of images."

A more full account of it has been given in the Preface by the Abbé de la Bleterie, whoſe reaſons for not tranſlating the whole I deem concluſive. But, omitting the offenſive parts, the extracts which I have ſelected ſhew the great uſe which Julian made of that *ſound form of doctrine which was once delivered to* him by tranſplanting into his own religious code, but without acknowledgment, many of the moral

many of the atheists * to distraction, make them think death desirable †, that they may fly up into heaven, after having forcibly dislodged their souls. Some of them prefer deserts to towns; but, man being by nature a gentle and social animal, they also are abandoned to evil dæmons, who urge them to this misanthropy; and many of them have had recourse to chains and collars ‡. Thus, on all sides, they are impelled by an evil dæmon, to whom they have voluntarily surrendered themselves by forsaking the immortal and tutelar Gods. But enough of these. I now return to the subject from which I have digressed.

The practice of virtue, in obedience to the laws of their country, should certainly be enforced by the governors of states; but it is also your duty to exhort the people by no means to

moral precepts of the gospel, particularly that *new commandment; Love your enemies, do good to them that hate you,* &c. And, on the whole, if great part of the charge (as it may be called) which he here delivers to his Pagan priesthood, was observed by our Christian clergy, they would be more respectable, and more respected, than they are.

* The usual elogium of the Christians with this apostate.
SPANHEIM.

† Julian seems here to allude to the religious frenzy, the horror of life, and the desire of martyrdom, which possessed the enthusiastic Donatists.

‡ The solitary fanatics, whose iron chains, &c. the philosopher here ridicules, were the monks and hermits who had introduced into Cappadocia the voluntary hardships of the ascetic life. See Tillemont, *Mem. Ecclef. tom. ix. p.* 661, 662.
GIBBON.

These solitary ascetics then abounded in Ægypt, Palestine, and Mesopotamia, as is evident from other remainss of that age.
SPANHEIM.

I 4

transgress

tranfgrefs the facred laws of the Gods. The office
of a prieft being neceffarily more refpectable than
that of any other citizen, it may be proper for
me now to confider that, and to teach you its obligations. Some perhaps may be better informed :
I wifh I could fay all; but I hope it of thofe who
are naturally temperate and virtuous. Such will
own this difcourfe to be adapted to them.

In the firft place, above all things cultivate philanthropy; as this is attended by many other
bleffings, and particularly by that, which is the
greateft and moft excellent of all, the favour of the
Gods. For as thofe who kindly participate in the
concerns of their mafters, in their friendfhips,
their ftudies, and amours, are more beloved than
their fellow-fervants; fo it muft be fuppofed
that the Divine Being, who, by his nature, is a
lover of mankind *, is delighted with thofe who
love each other. Of philanthropy there are various kinds; one is the punifhing offenders fpa-
ringly, and that for the good of the punifhed, as
mafters correct their fcholars; another is the relieving the wants of the poor, as the Gods relieve
ours. Obferve the many bleffings with which
they fupply us from the earth; food efpecially,
of every kind, and that more in quantity than they
have afforded to all other animals united. As we
are born naked, they cloath us with the hair of
beafts, and with fuch raiment alfo as is furnifhed

---

* Φιλανθρωπον. Φιλανθρωπια, in like manner, is afcribed to
God by St. Paul (Tit. iii. 4.), from whom Julian probably
borrowed it.

by

by the earth and trees. And not contented merely with rudenefs and fimplicity, with fuch coats, as, Mofes fays, they made of fkins * ; confider alfo how many gifts we enjoy of induftrious Minerva. What other animal is indulged with wine ? what other with oil ? unlefs we impart to them what we refufe to men. What fifhes feed on corn ? or what beafts on marine productions ? I do not mention gold, brafs, and iron, with all which the Gods have enriched us ; not to incur their refentment by overlooking the vagrant poor, efpecially when any of them are in morals irreproachable, but, having inherited nothing from their parents, are reduced to poverty by a noblenefs of mind which defpifes wealth. On feeing thefe, the generality of mankind are apt to arraign the Gods. Indigence, however, is by no means chargeable to the Gods, but to the infatiable avarice of us who are rich, to which are owing the falfe ideas which men form of the Gods, and the calumnies with which they reproach them. Do we defire that God would rain down gold on the poor, as he did formerly on the Rhodians †? Were this to be granted, immediately fending out our fervants, and every where placing veffels, we fhould drive away all

* Gen. iii. 21.—*the Lord God made coats of fkins, and cloathed them.*

† Jupiter is faid to have rained gold on the Rhodians at the time when Vulcan, cleaving his fkull with a hatchet, delivered him of Minerva. See Pindar. Olymp. VII. and Homer. Il. II. 670.

With joy they faw the growing empire rife,
And fhowers of wealth defcending from the fkies.
POPE 813.
others,

others, that we alone might fnatch the common bleffings of the Gods. Some perhaps may wonder at our wifhing for what cannot poffibly happen, and would be utterly ufelefs; fince what is abfolutely in our power we do not practife. Who was ever impoverifhed by what he gave to others? I, for my part, as often as I have been liberal to the poor, have in return been abundantly rewarded by the Gods; though I have never been a vile hoarder, nor have I ever repented of my generofity. I fay nothing of the prefent time (as it would be abfurd to compare private generofity with Imperial munificence), but, when I was a fub-ject *, I remember that this often happened †. Thus when the eftate of my grandmother ‡, which had been forcibly with-held, at length devolved to me entire; of the little which I then had I ex-pended and beftowed on the poor. We ought therefore of our abundance to be communicative to all men, but efpecially to the virtuous; and to

* Confequently, while he yet frequented the churches of the Chriftians.   SPANHEIM.

† This had of old been divinely faid by another, the wifeft of princes: *He that hath pity upon the poor*, (or, which, is the fame thing, *who giveth to the poor*), *lendeth unto the Lord, and that which he hath given, will he pay him again.* PROV. xix. 17. And in another place, *The liberal foul fhall be made fat; and he that watereth, fhall be watered alfo him-felf.* xi. 25. *Ibid.*

‡ The name of Julian's maternal grand-mother is un-known. She efpoufed Apicius Julianus, who was a præ-fect, and from this marriage fprung Bafilina (the mother of Julian), and the famous Count Julian. LA BLETERIE. See Epiftle xlvi.

the

the indigent, as far as will relieve their neceffities. I will add, though it may feem paradoxical, that it is a duty to give cloathing and food to our ene-mies * ; for we give it to their nature, and not to their conduct. And, therefore, I think that thofe who are imprifoned in dungeons, are alfo worthy of this attention, as fuch humanity by no means interferes with juftice. For as many are imprifon-ed for trial, of whom fome are to be condemned, and others acquitted, it would be much too fevere to refufe compaffion even to the guilty for the fake of the innocent, and rather to treat the innocent with cruelty and inhumanity on account of the guilty. The more I confider this, the more unjuft I think it. We ftyle Jupiter the Hofpi-table, yet we ourfelves are more inhofpitable than the Scythians. How, or with what confcience, can one, who would facrifice to Jupiter the Hof-pitable, approach his fhrine, when he forgets, that

By Jove the ftranger and the poor are fent,

And what to thofe we give, to Jove is lent † ?

---

* Can there be a doubt of the fountain from which Julian drew this living water, fo different from the muddy ftreams of his favourite philofophers ? *If thine enemy hunger, feed him ; if he thirft, give him drink.* Rom. xii. 20. *Inafmuch as ye have done it unto one of the leaft of thefe my brethren, ye have done it unto me.* Matth. xxv. 40.

† Odyff. VI. 207. Broome 247. Part of the fpeech of Nauficaa to Ulyffes on finding him fhipwrecked on Phæacia. The fame lines occur again in Odyf. xiv. 56. and are alfo quoted by Julian in Epiftle xlix. They are there differently tranflated by Pope. Thus alfo Odyff. ix. 270.

——— the Gods revere ;

The poor and ftranger are their conftant care. Pope 301.

And

And how can a worſhipper of ſocial Jupiter, if he ſees any one in diſtreſs, and does not give him part of a drachm, think that he worſhips Jupiter as he ought? When I reflect on theſe things, I am quite aſtoniſhed, ſeeing the ſurnames of the Gods, coeval with the world, conſidered as ſo many painted images, but in fact by no means treated by us as ſuch. The Gods are ſtyled by us Houſhold Gods, and Jupiter the Domeſtic Deity; but we behave to our relations as if they were ſtrangers. For man is related, with or without his conſent, to every other man; whether, as is ſaid by ſome, we all proceed from one man and one woman; or whether the Gods produced not one man and one woman only, but many at once, in great numbers, together with the world. For they who could create one man and one woman, were alſo able to create many, and in the ſame manner that they produced them, they might alſo produce theſe. Conſider not only the variety of cuſtoms and of laws, but, which is more important, more excellent, and more prevalent, that tradition of the Gods which has been tranſmitted to us by the moſt ancient miniſters in things ſacred; namely, that, when Jupiter formed the world, ſome drops of ſacred blood were ſpilled on the earth, from which ſprung mankind. Thus we are all relations; ſince from one man and one woman, or from two perſons, many men and women have ſprung, as the Gods declare, and we muſt neceſſarily believe on the teſtimony of the facts them-

ſelves,

felves, as we all derive our origin from the Gods. That many men were produced at once is teftified by facts, but will be more clearly fhewn in another place. * * * * *.

It is proper alfo to obferve, as has been faid by thofe who have preceded us, that man is by nature a focial animal. Shall we then, who deliver and eftablifh thefe maxims, act unfocially towards our neighbours? Urged by fuch cuftoms and inclinations, let every one of us difcharge the duties of piety towards the Gods, of benevolence towards men, of chaftity in regard to the body, and all the offices of religion. Let us endeavour always to retain in our minds fome religious idea of the Gods, and viewing their temples and images with honour and veneration, let us revere them as much as if we faw the Gods themfelves there prefent. For the images, and altars, the cuftody of the facred fire, and all other things of that kind, were eftablifhed by our anceftors as fymbols of the prefence of the Gods; not that we fuppofe them to be Gods, but that we may worfhip the Gods by them *. . . . .

Befides the images of the Gods, their temples, their fhrines, and their altars are to be reverenced. It is alfo reafonable that the priefts fhould be honoured, as the minifters and fervants of the

---

* This plea in defence of image-worfhip has been fince adopted, as is well known, by the Romifh Church. Other arguments equally futile and jefuitical follow. But the above may fuffice.

Gods,

Gods, who difpenfe to us what relates to them, and contribute much towards procuring us their favours. For they celebrate facrifices, and offer up prayers, for all. And therefore it is juft to pay them not lefs but rather more honour than to the civil magiftrates. But if any one fhould think that the civil magiftrates are entitled to equal honour, as they difcharge a kind of prieftly function, by being guardians of the laws; yet no lefs refpect is due to the others. The Greeks advifed their king to reverence a prieft *, though an enemy; and fhall we not reverence thofe who are our friends, and who pray and facrifice for us?

As my difcourfe has returned to the point from which it digreffed, it is proper for me now to ex- plain how a prieft ought to act in order to be juftly efteemed. As to what relates to ourfelves, that need not here be difcuffed or examined.

As long as a prieft retains his rank, he fhould be honoured and refpected; when he is wicked, let him be degraded from the priefthood, and when he is unworthy, defpifed. But as long as he facri- fices, and makes libations, and attends on the Gods, we fhould behold him, as we do their moft valu- able poffeffions, with regard and veneration. For it is abfurd to love the ftones of which altars are formed, on account of their being confecrated to the Gods, and becaufe they are of fuch a fhape

---

* Hom. Il. I. 23. Speaking of Chryfes. Αιδεισθαι θ' ιερηα, &c. The prieft to reverence, &c.

                                        and

and figure as are suitable to the holy office for
which they are intended; and not to think a man,
who is dedicated to the Gods, worthy of honour.
Some perhaps may think that the same honour is
also due to one who acts unjustly, and is guilty
of many transgressions in his holy office. Such a
one, I say, should be censured, lest by his wickednefs he should offend the Gods; but till he has
been censured, let him not be despised. Nor is it
reasonable, having this opportunity, to deny not
such only, but those who deserve it, the honour
that is their due. Like a magistrate, therefore, let
every priest be respected, as this is the oracle of
the Didymæan God * :

They whom depravity and folly lead
To scorn the priests of heaven's immortal powers,
And to the wise intentions of the Gods
Their own vain thoughts contemptuously oppose,
In safety live not half their days, condemn'd
To perish by th' eternal Gods, who deem
Their servants honour sacred as their own †.

And again, in another place, the God says,

For all my servants by destructive vice, &c.

and declares, that for that he will inflict punish-
ments upon them. As there are many such sayings

* Didymæan Apollo. This title was given to Apollo,
or the Sun, by reason of his own light, and that which
he communicates to the Moon. Macrob. Sat. I. 17.
Others derive the name from a temple and oracle of
Apollo at Didyma in Miletus. See Strabo, *Geog.* l. xiv.
Pliny, and Lucian *de Aſtrologiâ.*
† Julian quotes this oracle again in his lxiid Epiſtle.

of the God, which may inſtruct us how much we
ought to honour and venerate the prieſthood, I will
diſcuſs them more fully on ſome other occaſion.
It may be ſufficient at preſent, as I would ſay nothing inconſiderately, to quote this prophecy and
mandate of the God in his own words. If any one
therefore thinks me in theſe matters, an inſtructor
worthy of credit, let him revere and obey the God,
and pay diſtinguiſhed honour to the prieſts.

What a prieſt ought to be, I will now endeavour
to explain; not on your account (for had I not
been firmly perſuaded, not only by the teſtimony
of our chief *, but by that of the ſupreme Gods,
that you would ably diſcharge this office, as far as
your will and inclination are concerned, I ſhould
not have ventured to entruſt to you a work of ſuch
importance) but that you may inſtruct others in
your neighbourhood, both in town and country,
by ſtronger arguments, and with ſuperior authority, as not being merely your private ſentiments,
or your own practice only, but as being alſo my
opinion, who, in what relates to the Gods, ſeem to
be Supreme Pontiff †, and though by no means
                                    worthy

---

* Καθηγεμονος. Probably Maximus, the perverter of Julian
to Paganiſm (ſee p. 113. note *) whom, writing to
another prieſt (Epiſtle LXIII.) he calls by the ſame
name, " Κοινος καθηγεμων, their common maſter;" and on
whoſe advice, in theſe eccleſiaſtical arrangements, it appears that he chiefly relied.

† It is remarkable, that Julian here does not expreſsly
ſtyle himſelf Sovereign Pontiff, but that " he ſeemed to be"
ſo, δοκεϊλα εναι, though Conſtantine and the ſucceeding Emperor

worthy of fo high an office, yet ftudy to be fo, and for that purpofe conftantly fupplicate the Gods. Be affured, that they have given us great hopes after death, and on them we may with confidence* rely, as they are incapable of deceiving, not only in fuch matters, but in any of the concerns of human life. If, by their excellent power, they can correct all the difturbances and monftrous abufes that happen in this life, how much more in the other (where the contending parts are dif-united, the immortal foul being feparated, and the body dead), will they be able to perform all the promifes that they have made to mankind? Knowing therefore that the Gods have affigned to their priefts great rewards, let us make thofe whofe lives are conformable to their examples, which ought to fpeak to the vulgar, fponfors in every thing for their dignity. This we muft begin with piety towards the Gods. Thus it becomes us to minifter to them as fuppofing them prefent and feeing us (though we fee not them), and, with a fight fuperior to every kind of fplendor, pene-

perors (as has been obferved by Spanheim, from ancient marbles, coins, &c. *Obf. ad Jul. Orat.* 1. p. 278.) retained this dignity till the reign of Gratian.

Neither was Gallienus, as Spanheim afferts, nor Claudius, as others, the laft on whofe coins the titles of Pontifex Maximus, and the tribunitial power, are recorded.
CLARKE.

* This is not fo much a Chaldæan, or an Hermetic, or even a Platonic, as a Chriftian confidence. SPANHEIM.

VOL. I. K trating

trating our moſt ſecret thoughts *. That this is
not my ſentiment, but that of God, expreſſed in
ſeveral paſſages, it may be ſufficient to ſhew by one
inſtance, which will eſtabliſh theſe two points,
that the Gods ſee all things, and that they delight
in the pious:

Nothing eſcapes the wide-extended beam
Of Phœbus; ſolid rocks it penetrates,
And ſeas cœrulean; nor the ſtarry hoſt
Eludes it, through the firmament, untir'd,
Revolving, by neceſſity's wiſe law;
Nor all the nations of the dead, beneath
Immers'd by Tartarus in ſhades of night.
But not high Heaven delights me more than
    goodneſs.

Therefore as every ſoul, eſpecially the human †,
is more nearly connected with and allied to the
Gods than ſtones or rocks, it is probable that the
eyes of the Gods can penetrate them with much
more eaſe and efficacy. Obſerve too the philanthropy of God, in ſaying, that he is " as much
" delighted with the thoughts of religious men,
" as with the purity of Olympus." Will he not
therefore raiſe the ſouls of us all, who piouſly
approach him, from darkneſs and from Tartarus?

* Thus the Pſalmiſt, *Thou underſtandeſt my thought afar
off. Thou art acquainted with all my ways*, &c. Pſ. cxxxix.
2, 3.

† By this diſtinction, or preference, Julian ſeems to ſuppoſe that beaſts alſo have ſouls, as he muſt allude to ſome
beings inferior to the human.

For

For he knows even thofe who are confined in Tartarus, that not being exempted from the divine power. But to the pious, inftead of Tartarus, he promifes Olympus *.

Above all, therefore, it is indifpenfibly neceffary for the priefts to be active ih works of piety, that they may approach the Gods with religious awe +, and not fay or hear any thing that is fhameful. For priefts ought not only to abftain from all impure and immodeft practices, but alfo from all fuch words and fights. Far, therefore, from us be all licentious jefts, and all fcurrilous difcourfe ‡. That you may more clearly underftand my meaning, let no prieft read Archilochus ‖,

nor

* It is curious to hear a heathen philofopher thus inculcating the immortality, or future exiftence, of the foul, the refurrection, &c. But, as the woman of Samaria faid to our Lord, *the well is deep*; and Julian, like her, *had nothing to draw with* but what he borrowed from Chriftianity. Where, for inftance, did he learn, that " the pious are " promifed Olympus?" Virgil, improving on Homer, fpeaks only of Elyfian fields, or pleafant earthly manfions, *locos lætos, et amœna vireta*, &c. in which fages and heroes were placed after death. But that the juft fhall be *caught up into heaven*, or are promifed Olympus, that where God himfelf is, *there they fhall be alfo*, *was brought to light by the gofpel*.

+ Thus the Pfalmift, *Serve the Lord with fear, and rejoice with trembling*. Pfalm ii. 11.

‡ Thus St. Paul, *Neither filthinefs, nor foolifh talking, nor jefting, which are not convenient*, &c. Eph. v. 4.

‖ Julian characterifes the poetry of Archilochus in his viith oration. He was the firft inventor of Iambics.

Archilochum proprio rabies armavit Iambo,

—— —— Archilochus by rage
Was with his own Iambic arm'd,

as Horace expreffes it, in which he wrote fo feverely againft

 Lycamb. s

nor Hipponax *, nor any other writer of that clafs:
let him alfo avoid every thing that has the fame
tendency in the old Comedy †. Much preferable
and more fuitable to us is the ftudy of philofophy

Lycambes; who had promifed him his daughter in marriage,
but gave her to another, that he hanged himfelf. His
poems are now loft.

* A witty poet of Ephefus, whofe Iambics are faid to
have had the fame tragical effect as thofe of Archilochus.
They are alfo loft.

How little Julian obferved this rule himfelf will be evident to any one from feveral of his works, in which he
more than once alludes to the fayings both of Archilochus
and the old comic poets, but particularly from the Cæfars
and the Mifopogon, which are not only feafoned with farcafms and jokes, but alfo abound with fcoffs more cutting
and fevere than any of the Iambics of Archilochus or Hipponax. So that what Cyril faid, in his books againft him,
was not undeferved, that " he ftudioufly covets the reputa-
"'tion of great and various erudition." SPANHEIM.

† The old Comedy was fo called on account of the
alterations that happened afterwards, and which occafioned
three forts of comedy; the old, the middle, and the new.
The old, in which there was nothing fictitious, either in
the fubject, or in the names of the actors: The middle,
where the fubjects were not fictitious; they were true hiftories, but the names were invented: And the new, in
which every thing was feigned; the poets invented not
only the fubjects, but alfo the names. Eupolis, Cratinus,
and Ariftophanes, [all mentioned by Horace, l. 1. fat. 4. 1.]
are the three greateft poets of the old comedy, and were
contemporary, about 400 years before our Saviour. The
liberty which they took of naming notorious offenders,
fuch as Cleon, Hyperbolus, Cleophantes, &c. they often
abufed; Cratinus did not fpare even the great Pericles, and
Ariftophanes refpected not the wifdom of Socrates. Not
contented with making men's actions the fubjects of their
pieces, they reprefented their faces to the life by means of
masks, which were made to refemble them. DACIER.

How clofely Foote, the modern Ariftophanes, trod in the
fteps of thefe ancients is notorious.

alone,

alone, of thofe fects efpecially which boaft the Gods as the firft promulgers of their doctrine, fuch as thofe of Pythagoras *, Plato, and Ariftotle, and alfo thofe who follow Chryfippus † and Zeno ‡. Not that we fhould liften to all, or to the tenets of them all, but to thofe tenets only which are productive of piety: and as to the Gods, thefe teach us, firft, that they are; fecondly, that they regard things below § ; and laftly, that they do not the leaft evil to men or others, or are envious, flanderous, or contentious, as has been related by our poets, but for which they are defpifed, while the Jewifh prophets, for ftrongly afferting the fame, are admired by thofe wretches who adhere to the Galileans ‖. To us thofe hiftories are moft fuitable which relate real facts ; but let thofe fictions, which the ancients have compofed in the form of hiftories, be avoided ; fuch as love-tales,

---

* See p. 21.   † See p. 8.   ‡ See p. 39.
§ Thus St. Paul—*he that cometh to God muft believe that he is, and that he is a rewarder of them that diligently feek him.*
Heb. xi. 6.

‖ The fentiments of Julian were expreffed in a ftyle of farcaftic wit, which inflicts a deep and deadly wound whenever it iffues from the mouth of a fovereign. As he was fenfible that the Chriftians gloried in the name of their Redeemer, he countenanced, and perhaps enjoined, the ufe of the lefs honourable appellation of *Galileans*. GIBBON.

There might be a mixture of policy in it too, as knowing the efficacy of a nick-name to render a profeffion ridiculous.   LA BLETERIE.

This nick-name, however, did not originate with Julian. Epictetus gave the Chriftians the fame appellation near 300 years before. See his Difcourfes IV. § 2. &c.

K 3   and

and every thing in that ſtrain. As all ways * are not proper for a prieſt †, but require being pointed out to him, neither does every kind of reading ſuit him. For the mind is affected by books, and the paſſions, being ſoon raiſed, on a ſudden burſt forth into a dreadful flame. Againſt this, I think, we ſhould watchfully guard long before.

Let no admittance be given to the doctrine of Epicurus ‡, nor to that of Pyrrho §. The Gods indeed

* This refers to the " Sacred Way," a ſtreet in Rome, ſo called, becauſe the prieſts went that way on the ides of each month to ſacrifice. Horace met his Impertinent in it. *Ibam forte viâ ſacrâ*, &c. *l. 1. Sat.* 9.

† As to this inſtitution there is a remarkable paſſage of Athenæus, at the end of his ſixth book, where he treats of the remains of ancient frugality and parſimony, which were ſtill retained in the offices of religion : " We walk in " ſome preſcribed and appointed ways ; we carry [in our " proceſſions] and repeat in our prayers what we are en- " joined, and in our ſacrifices we act with ſimplicity and " œconomy. For we wear nothing more than nature re- " quires, either next to our bodies, or in our outward " garments ; our cloaths and our ſhoes are cheap, and the " veſſels with which we miniſter are of earth or braſs."
PETAU.

‡ Epicurus, the diſciple of Xenocrates and Ariſtotle, ſuppoſed the world to be formed by chance, or a fortuitous concourſe of atoms. He maintained alſo that pleaſure was the end of man, of which he conſtituted ſenſe the judge. He denied the natural relation of mankind to each other, taught irreligion and injuſtice, and his principles led to oppreſſion, adultery, and murder, in the opinion of Epictetus and others.

§ Pyrrho, the founder of the ſect of the Pyrrhoniſts [or Sceptics], was born at Elis, and flouriſhed about the time of Alexander. [He was contemporary alſo with Epicurus and Theophraſtus.] He held, that there is no difference between juſt and unjuſt, good and evil ; that all things are equally

indeed have wifely abolifhed them, many of their writings being loft *; but it cannot be improper to mention them, for the fake of example, to fhew what kind of books the priefts ought principally to fhun. And if books, much rather fhould thoughts, be avoided. For the guilt of the mind, and that of

equally indifferent, uncertain, and undiftinguifhable; that neither our fenfes nor underftanding give us either a true or a falfe information: therefore, that we ought to give them no credit, but to remain without opinion, without motion, without inclination; and to fay of every thing, that it no more is than it is not; that it is no more one thing than another; and that againft one reafon, there is always an equal reafon to be oppofed. His life is faid to have been conformable to his principles; for that he never avoided any thing; and his friends were obliged to follow him, to prevent his running under the wheels of a coach, or walking down a precipice. But thefe ftories perhaps are nothing but mere invention, formed to expofe the abfur-dities of his fyftem. Once, when he faw his mafter An-axarchus fallen into a ditch, he paffed by him, without offering him any affiftance. Anaxarchus was confiftent enough with his principles not to fuffer Pyrrho to be blamed for this tranquil behaviour; which he juftified, as a laudable inftance of indifference, and want of affection. A fine picture this of fceptical friendfhip!

For a more complete account of the fyftem of Pyrrho, fee Diogenes Laertius, in his life; and Lipfius *Manuduct. ad Stoic. Philofoph.* l. II. dif. 3.   Mrs. CARTER.

* The exultation of Julian that thefe impious fects, and even their writings, are extinguifhed, may be confiftent enough with the facerdotal character; but it is unworthy of a philofopher to wifh that any opinions, and arguments the moft repugnant to his own, fhould be concealed from the knowledge of mankind.   GIBBON.

" With the facerdotal character, of a Pagan or a Papift, " fuch exultation may be confiftent;" but furely not with that of a Proteftant, who is taught to " prove all things," and whofe feceffion from the church of Rome was grounded on freedom of enquiry, and juftified by reafon.

K 4

the

the tongue, are not, in my opinion, of an equal
dye; but the mind should in the first place be
guarded, as by it the tongue is taught to offend.
The hymns therefore of the Gods should be
learned, which are many and beautiful, compofed
both by ancients and moderns; and chiefly thofe
which are fung in the temples. For moft of them
the Gods have by fupplications been induced to
deliver; though fome, the effufions of divine infpiration, and of fouls inacceffible to evil, have been
made by men in honour of the Gods. Thefe deferve to be ftudied; and the Gods fhould frequently be addreffed, in private as well as in
public; generally three times a day; or, at leaft,
at the dawn, and in the evening. Nor is it proper
for a prieft to pafs a whole day and night without
a facrifice; for as the dawn is the beginning of
the day, fo is the evening of the night; and
therefore it is reafonable to offer the firft-fruits, as
it were, of both thefe intervals to the Gods when
we reft from our prieftly function. The rites that
are performed in the temples are performed in
obedience to the laws of our country, and neither
more nor lefs is required than they prefcribe.
Thefe are the property of the Gods. Therefore to
render them the more propitious, we fhould
imitate their nature: And indeed if we confifted
of fouls only, as the body would then be no ob-
ftruction to us, it might be proper to prefcribe a
particular mode of life to the priefts. But fince
                                                    the

the priests do not merely confist of souls *, that which they are to study in the time of their miniftration is not the whole of their employment. What then is allowable to one who is appointed to the prieftly office at the feafons when he is not engaged in his facred vocation ? I am of opinion that a prieft fhould in every refpect be immaculate, both by night and day; that he fhould purify himfelf every night with thofe luftrations that our ordinances require; and that he fhould confine himfelf within the precincts of the temple as many days as the laws enjoin. To us at Rome thirty days † are commanded; other places differ. All thofe days he fhould refide, I think, and philofophife in the temple; and not go either home, or to the forum; nor fee even a magiftrate, except in the temple; but take upon himfelf the fuperintendence of divine worfhip, and infpect and regulate the whole. Thofe days being completed, when another has fucceeded to his office, and he returns to the ordinary bufinefs of life, let him freely refort

---

* Something here is wanting; I have fupplied it by conjecture.

† It is remarkable that the leaft refidence enjoined by their local ftatutes to the prebendaries in moft of our cathedrals confifts of exactly the fame number of days, viz. thirty. But their " ftrict refidence," as it is called, being in general indifpenfible, of twenty-one days *in continuum,* is much lefs ftrict than that of thefe Pagan priefts, as it is fatisfied by their appearing in their ftalls once every day, and fleeping in their houfes every night. Thirty days refidence being enjoined (as above) at Rome to every prieft, the number allotted to each temple muft have been twelve at leaft.

to the houses of his friends, and, when he is invited, to the entertainments, not indeed of all, but
of persons whose characters are respectable. At
such times also there is no indecorum in his going,
but rarely, to the forum; or in visiting the duke *
and præfect * of the province, and, to the utmost
of his power relieving the indigent.

Let me add, that I think it becoming for the
priests to wear in the temple, during their mini-
stration, a most magnificent habit, but out of it a
common plain dress. For it is absurd to pervert
what is given us in honour of the Gods to the pur-
poses of pride and vanity. And therefore in the
forum we should renounce our costly vestments,
and totally relinquish all ostentation. The Gods,
admiring the modesty of Amphiaraus, though they
had doomed that army to destruction; in which,
apprised of this decree, he served, and therefore
his fate was inevitable, removed him from this life
to another, and gave him a divine inheritance. For
when all the chiefs who besieged Thebes inscribed
devices on their shields † before they were forged,
and thus erected trophies, as it were, on the calamities of the Cadmeans ‡, this converser with the
Gods went on that expedition with armour unin-

---

* The military and civil commanders, the general and
the governor. The former was styled ηγεμων, or dux.

† The ostentatious devices, or armorial bearings of these
chiefs, may be seen in Æschylus.

‡ The Thebans, so called from Cadmus, the supposed
founder of their city.

            scribed,

ſcribed *, ſo that even his enemies atteſted his clemency and moderation. Prieſts therefore, I think, ſhould [imitate his example †], in order to inſure the favour of the Gods. For we offend them not a little by expoſing to the populace the ſacred veſtments, and improperly divulging them to the public view as a wonderful ſight. From whence it happens, as we are approached by many who are impure, that the ſymbols of the Gods are defiled. But for us to wear the habit, and not to lead the lives, of prieſts, is in itſelf a ſummary

---

* Thus Æſchylus, in his Seven Chiefs againſt Thebes,

———————— with awful port the prophet
Advanc'd his maſſy ſhield, the ſhining orb,
Bearing no impreſs ; for his generous ſoul
Wiſhes to be, not to appear, the beſt § ;
And from the culture of his modeſt worth
Bears the rich fruit of great and glorious deeds. POTTER.

As this modeſt and amiable augur was fighting bravely, the earth opened beneath him, and he deſcended alive to the infernal regions, with all his arms, and in his chariot. Statius has exerted the utmoſt force of his genius in deſcribing this righteous hero.   *Ibid.*

Amphiaraus wearing his ſhield entirely plain is accounted for in the ſame manner by Euripides, who has imitated the above, in his Phœnician Virgins:

——————— no unſeemly pride
In his armorial bearings was expreſs'd,
But on his modeſt buckler there appear'd
A vacant field.   WODHULL.
Homer ſtyles him, Odyſſ. xv. 245.
The people's ſaviour, and divinely wiſe,
Belov'd by Jove and him who gilds the ſkies. POPE, 274.
" By Jove," ſays Euſtathius, " becauſe he was a king, and by Apollo, becauſe he was a prophet."

† Some ſuch words are wanting here in the original.
           § *Eſſe quam videri.*

of

of every tranfgreffion, and the greateft contempt of the Gods. On that therefore I will be more particular.

I addrefs you on this fubject, as I deem you a model. At obfcene theatrical entertainments let not a prieft by any means be prefent; nor admit them in his own houfe; as nothing can be more unbecoming. And if fuch exhibitions could he totally banifhed from the ftage, and if all houfes could be kept pure from Bacchus *, I would ufe my utmoft endeavours to effect fuch a reform. But as I think this fcarce poffible, and, if it were, that it might not be expedient, I have abandoned that vain purfuit. I think it, however, highly proper for priefts to abfent themfelves from theatres, and to leave their lafcivioufnefs to the people. Let no prieft therefore enter the theatre, nor form a friendly connection with any actor, or charioteer †,

and

---

* That his own " cup" was " temperate" we have not only his own word (Epift. xlvi.) but that of his con-temporaries. What he practifed he had therefore a right to preach. St. Paul, in like manner, teaches his bifhops and deacons to be *not given to wine, to be lovers of hofpitality, lovers of good men, juft, holy, temperate,* &c. And, though omitted here, Julian directs his priefts alfo to be *no ftrikers,* in a particular Epiftle (the lxiid) on that fubject.

† Thofe who drove the chariots in the Circenfian or public games, whofe company, like that of our *black legs,* was fhunned by all who had a regard for their own repu-tation. Nero therefore could not more effectually degrade his own character than by affuming that. Had he been a Britifh prince, he would have rid his own horfes at New-market, or driven a ftage-coach on the road. Actors were viewed by Julian, and the lovers of decorum, in the famo

difgrace-

and let no dancer or mimic approach his door. I allow the priests to go only, if they please, to the sacred games; provided they are those at which women are forbidden not only to enter the lists *, but to be present. As to the hunting-matches which are exhibited in some cities within the theatres †, need I say, that from them not merely the priests, but even their sons, should be excluded?

disgraceful light. Though Æsopus in extravagance might rival Cleopatra, neither he nor Roscius was deemed, like our Garrick, a companion for priests and senators.

* Juvenal (Sat. I.) mentions the women in his time as ambitious of shewing their courage in encountering wild beasts, though with the forfeiture of their modesty.

> Cum ——————— Mævia Tuscum
> Figat aprum, &c.

When —— the mannish whore
Shakes her broad spear against the Tuscan boar.

DRYDEN.

Martial compliments the emperor Domitian on the same account; and the women are exposed by Juvenal (Sat. VI.) for engaging even as gladiators.　　　KENNET.

† The *Venatio direptionis* seems to have been an institution of the later Emperors. The middle part of the *Circus* being set all over with trees, removed thither by main force, and fastened to huge planks, which were laid on the ground; these, being covered with earth and turf, represented a natural forest, into which the beasts being let from the *cavea*, or dens under ground, the people at a sign given by the Emperor fell to hunting them, and carried away what they killed to regale upon at home. The beasts usually given were boars, deer, oxen, and sheep. Ibid.

The amphitheatral beasts sometimes broke loose from their dens, and made great havock in the city, as is mentioned by Pliny, Ammianus, and others.

For similar hunting-matches in the Greek amphitheatres bears and panthers were provided, as Julian mentions in his xxxvth Epistle, for the Argives.

I should

I should perhaps have previously mentioned from whence, and how, the priests should be chosen. But there is no impropriety in making this the close of my discourse. Let them consist of persons of the best characters in every city. In the first place, they should be ardent lovers of the Gods; and, secondly, of mankind also *; of the poor as well as the rich. As to that, let no distinction be made between the noble and the mean. For he whom his modesty sequesters is by no means to be rejected on account of the obscurity of his merit. Therefore, though a man be poor, or a Plebeian, if he have these two endowments, love towards the Gods, and love towards men *, let him be elected into the priesthood. His love towards the Gods will appear by his instructing his family in religious duties; and his love towards men by his distributing from a little liberally † to the necessitous, by giving with a willing mind, and endeavouring to do as much good as possible. But this part requires the utmost attention, as some preventive remedy must be provided.

* What are these but the two Christian commandments, the love of God and of our neighbour, on which, says our Saviour, *hang all the law and the prophets?*

† Thus Tobit, IV. 8. *If thou hast abundance, give alms accordingly: if thou have but a little, be not afraid to give according to that little.*

Observing,

Obferving, I fuppofe, that our priefts neglect the poor *, the impious Galileans have adopted this philanthropy, and on the femblance of this duty have founded a moft enormous crime; like thofe who allure children with cakes, which having given them twice or thrice, they inveigle them from their parents, and, conveying them on fhip-board, fell them in diftant countries; and thus for a tranfient fweet the remainder of their lives, is imbittered †. In the fame manner, they, be-

* The author muft have known, from the facred books which he read as lecturer in the church of Nicomedia, that this was an unfair reprefentation, and that the Chriftians had a prior and much more cogent obligation in their divine law, whofe characteriftic is philanthropy and univerfal benevolence. But he is not afhamed firft to plunder and then to revile it.

† He infinuates, that the Chriftians, under the pretence of charity, inveigled children from their religion and parents, conveyed them on fhip-board, and devoted thofe victims to a life of poverty or fervitude, in a remote country. Had this charge been proved, it was his duty not to complain but to punifh. GIBBON.

Though I have tranfcribed this note, I cannot affent to the conftruction which the ingenious writer has put upon the fentiments of Julian in the firft part of it. The " inveigling of children," (above-mentioned) I apprehend to be only (as I have tranflated it) " by way of fimile;" nor is it faid or implied that Chriftians only were the inveiglers. The fimile, as ufual, begins with Ωσπερ (" As") and the application is made by Τον αυτον και αυτον τοπον (" They, in " like manner") fo that the charge againft the Chriftians is confined to their charity and miniftration to the poor (*Forgive* them *this wrong!*) for which indeed (as above remarked) Julian affigns an unworthy and difingenuous motive, qualified by a " fuppofe" (οιμαι) which he could not really " fuppofe" to be true. But ready as he was to calumniate the faithful, let us not impute to him charges which he never brought.

ginning

ginning with what they call a love-feast, and a hospital *, and the ministry of tables † (for, as the work, so also is the word, frequent among them), pervert the faithful to impiety ‡.   * * * * * *

* " Hospital" (υποδοχη) I have here restored to its original sense, as derived from *hospitium*, a sense which, from the disuse of such charitable foundations for age and want, independently of accidents and diseases, seems almost lost amongst us, the term being now generally confined to receptacles for casualty and sickness. But the hospitals established by our ancestors, in the true primitive spirit of the gospel, at and near Canterbury, at Guildford, Croydon, &c. which are still in being, were appropriated, in the former sense, to the lodging and relief of the old and necessitous.

† Διακονιας τραπεζων. The same expression is used by St. Luke, in Acts vi. 2.

From hence it appears, as has been related by Tertullian and others, that, on account chiefly of the poor, those common tables, common banquets, κοιναι τραπιζαι, κοιναι ευωχιαι, as the ancient teachers of the Christians afterwards called them, [misprinted ευχωχιαι. See Athenæus, *l.* viii. *c.* 16.] were furnished by the rich. And also, as is mentioned by Theophanes, that *xenodochia*, or receptacles, were built for receiving any foreign poor, whether Gentiles or Christians; and in the same place he informs us of the certain quantity of corn which was distributed in the province of Galatia for the relief of strangers and the poor.

Spanheim.

‡ The Fragment here ends abruptly. Other charges, equally absurd, might perhaps follow; though, as this is styled the " close" of it (τας λογας λεξαι), it could not be much longer.

T H E

THE CÆSARS *.

JULIAN. IT is the season of the Saturnalia †; the God therefore allows us to be merry; but as I have no talent for the ludicrous, I am inclined, my friend, to blend wisdom with mirth.

FRIEND.

Dec.
361.

* Julian composed this satire after he was Emperor. I would say, that the friend with whom he converses was either Sallust the Second, or Sallust præfect of Gaul, if the satire of the Cæsars were the same as the work, entitled, The Saturnalia, as he seems to say himself (Orat. IV.) that he had addressed that to Sallust. But a passage in the Saturnalia, quoted by Suidas, and which is not in the Cæsars, proves that they were different works. [That passage is as follows: " But we believe Empedotimus ‡ " and Pythagoras, and what, derived from them, has been " delivered by Heraclides, § of Pontus, and was lately " communicated to us by that excellent hierophant " Jamblichus."] It is needless to add that the word *Cæsar* here means *Emperor*. Even after that name had been appropriated to a new dignity, the Augusti still retained it, though those who were only Cæsars never bore the name of Emperors or Augusti. LA BLETERIE.

Julian composed this satire in the winter that he spent at Constantinople. SUIDAS.

‡ He wrote on Natural History.
Julian mentions him also in the Fragment, by the name of " the great Empedotimus," and classes him with Socrates and Dion, as being unustly put to death.

§ A native of Heraclea in Pontus, a hearer of Plato and Aristotle. He left several works, enumerated by Diogenes Laërtius, but all now lost. A little treatise " on Commonwealths" however ascribed to him.

FRIEND. Can any one, Cæsar, be so absurd as to joke seriously? I always thought that this was intended only for relaxation, and to alleviate care.

JUL.

The book of Henry Stephens, preserved in the London library, mentions, in the Catalogue of his books, Συμποσιον, η Κρονια, (" The Banquet, or Saturnalia,") and does not name the Cæsars. PETAU.

' The philosophical fable, which Julian composed under the name of the Cæsars, is one of the most agreeable and instructive productions of ancient wit. Spanheim, in his preface, has most learnedly discussed the etymology, origin, resemblance, and disagreement of the Greek *Satyrs*, a dramatic piece, which was acted after the tragedy, and the Latin *Satires* (from *Satura)*, a miscellaneous composition, either in prose or verse. But the Cæsars of Julian are of such an original cast, that the critic is perplexed to which class he should ascribe them. The value of this agreeable composition is enhanced by the rank of the author. A prince who delineates with freedom the vices and virtues of his predecessors, subscribes, in every line, the censure, or approbation, of his own conduct. GIBBON.

Thus agreeable, and thus instructive, it seems extraordinary that this should be the first attempt (at least I know of no other) to translate the Cæsars into English.

† The festivals of Saturn were instituted in the consulship of Sempronius Atratinus, and Minucius ; or, according to others, in that of Titus Lartius. Others make them commence in the time of Janus, king of the Aborigines, who received Saturn in Italy, survived him, and placed him among the Gods. The better to represent that peace and abundance which were enjoyed in the reign of that God, these festivals passed in entertainments and rejoicings. The Romans quitted the *toga*, and appeared in public in an undress. They sent presents to each other as on new-year's day. Games of chance, forbidden at other times, were then allowed, the senate adjourned, the business of the bar ceased, and the schools were shut. The children proclaimed the festival by running through the streets, and crying *Io Saturnalia.* In ancient times it was held on the 17th of December, according to the year of

Numa,

JUL. You are in the right; but that is by no means my disposition; as I have never been addicted to scoffs, satire, or ridicule. In order, however, to comply with the ordinance of the God, shall I, by way of amusement, repeat to you a fable, which you will not perhaps be displeased to hear?

FRIEND. You will oblige me. For I am so far from despising fables, that I value those which have a moral tendency, being of the same opinion with you, and your, or rather our, Plato, who has discussed many serious subjects in fictions.

JUL. True.

FRIEND. But what, and whose, shall it be?

JUL. Not an ancient one, like those of Æsop, but a fiction from Mercury. This I will repeat to you as I received it from that God, and whether it contain truth, or falshood blended with truth, I will leave you to judge when you have heard it.

FRIEND. Enough, and more than enough, of preface. One would think you were going to deliver an oration rather than a fable. Now then proceed to the discourse itself.

Numa, and continued only one day. Julius Cæsar, when he reformed the calendar, added two days to that month, which were inserted before the Saturnalia, and given to that festival. Augustus afterwards added to it a fourth day, and the Emperor Caius a fifth, named *Juvenalia*. In these five days was included that which was appropriated to the worship of Rhea, called *Opalia*. There was afterwards celebrated for two days the festival in honour of Pluto, called *Sigillaria* (or feast of statues) from some small images that were offered to that God. All these festivals were appendages to the Saturnalia, which thus lasted seven whole days, from the 15th to the 21st of December. SANADON.

JUL.

JUL. Attend.

Romulus, facrificing at the Saturnalia, invited all the Gods, and Cæfars alfo, to a banquet. Couches were prepared for the reception of the Gods on the fummit of heaven, on

Olympus, the firm manfion of th' Immortals *.

Thither, it is faid, like Hercules, Quirinus afcended. For thus, in compliance with the rumour of his divinity, we muft ftyle Romulus. Below the moon, in the higheft region of the air, a repaft was given to the Cæfars. Thither they were wafted, and there they were buoyed up, by the lightnefs of the bodies with which they were invefted, and the revolution of the moon. Four couches †, of exquifite workmanfhip, were fpread for the fuperior Deities. That of Saturn was formed of polifhed ebony, which reflected fuch a divine luftre as was infupportable. For on viewing this ebony the eye was as much dazzled by the excefs of light, as it is by gazing ftedfaftly on the fun. That of Jupiter was more fplendid than filver, and too white to be gold, but whether this fhould be called *electrum* ‡, or what other name fhould

---

* Odyff. vi. 42.

† The Roman mode of reclining, at their meals, on beds or couches, is too well known to need explanation. Every couch held three.

‡ Pure gold was in ufe to the days of Alexander Severus, who permitted a fifth part of filver to be mixed with four parts of gold. This they called *electrum*; and, in confequence of his regulations, medals were confecrated to him as the reftorer of the coin: a compliment due with equal

justice

ſhould be given it, Mercury, though he had enquired of the metalliſts, could not preciſely inform me.

On each ſide of them ſat on golden thrones the
mother and the daughter, Juno near Jupiter, Rhea
near Saturn. On the beauty of the Gods Mercury
did not deſcant; as that, he ſaid, tranſcended my
faculties, and was impoſſible for him to expreſs.
For no terms level to my comprehenſion, however
eloquent, could ſufficiently extol or do juſtice to
the inimitable beauty of the Gods.

Thrones, or couches, were prepared for all the
other Deities, according to their ſeniority. As to
this, there was no diſagreement; for, as Homer,
inſtructed, no doubt, by the Muſes themſelves,
obſerves, " each God has his own throne aſſigned
" him, where he is firmly and immoveably fixed *."
When therefore they riſe at the entrance of their
Father, they never confound or change their
ſeats, or infringe on thoſe of others. Every one
knows his proper ſtation.

Thus all the Gods being ſeated in a circle,
Silenus † fondly placed himſelf near young and
beautiful

juſtice to the providence of the preſent moſt auguſt Sovereign of Great Britain; who, in this and many other reſpects, may be compared to that moſt excellent and virtuous
Emperor. CLARKE.

Julian (as will be obſerved in the ſequel) has not done
juſtice to this prince.

* I do not recollect this paſſage in Homer, nor has the
Index of Seberus enabled me to find it.

† The mixed character of Silenus is finely painted in the
ſixth eclogue of Virgil. GIBBON.

L 3

Servius

beautiful Bacchus (who was clofe to his father
Jupiter), as his fofter-father and governor, di-
verting the God, who is a lover of mirth and
laughter, with his facetious and farcaftic fayings.

As foon as the table was fpread for the Cæfars,
the firft who appeared was JULIUS CÆSAR. Such
was his paffion for glory, that he feemed willing
to contend for dominion with Jupiter himfelf. Silenus, obferving him, faid, " Behold, Jupiter, one
" who has ambition enough to endeavour to de-
" throne you : He is, you fee, ftrong and hand-
" fome, and, if he refembles me in nothing elfe,
" his head, at leaft, is certainly the fellow of
" mine *."

Amidft thefe jokes of Silenus, to which the
Gods paid little attention, OCTAVIANUS entered.
He affumed, like a camelion, various colours, at
firft appearing pale, then black, dark, and cloudy †,
and,

Servius remarks that Virgil took the hint of his Silenus
from Theopompus. According to our ideas of the Heathen
Gods, the part affigned to him by Julian feems rather
more fuitable to Momus.

* It fhould be remembered that Silenus was reprefented
very fhort, flat-nofed, with large eyes, and a fat paunch.
Cæfar, on the contrary, was tall, well-made, and of a
genteel fhape. His aquiline nofe, his piercing eyes, and
his noble air feemed to announce the mafter of the world.
But he was bald, like Silenus, which fo much concerned
him, that of all the diftinctions that were lavifhed upon him
by the Roman fenate and people, none, it is faid, gave him
more pleafure than that of always wearing a crown of
laurel.　　　　　　　　　　　　　　　LE BLETERIE.

† This marks the various characters which the policy of
Auguftus knew how to affume, as occafion required ; the
fupple-

and, at laſt, exhibiting the charms of Venus and the Graces. In the luſtre of his eyes he ſeemed willing to rival the ſun *; nor could any one encounter his looks. " Strange !" cried Silenus ; " what a changeable creature is this ! what miſ- " chief will he do us!" ' Ceaſe trifling,' ſaid Apollo, ' after I have conſigned him to Zeno, I will ex- ' hibit him to you pure as gold. Hark ye,' added he to that philoſopher ; ' Zeno, undertake the care ' of my pupil †.' He, in obedience, ſuggeſting to

ſuppleneſs with which he cringed at firſt to the republican party, his cruelty in the proſcription, &c. his conduct compounded both of good and evil till he had deſtroyed the Triumvirs his collegues ; and, laſtly, the gentleneſs and equity of his government when he was abſolute maſter. On his death-bed he aſked his friends, whether he had performed his part well in the world ; *ecquid iis videretur mimum vitæ commode tranſegiſſe ?* He might have been anſwered, that the actor was inimitable, and that the piece would have been applauded without exception, if its beginning had been leſs tragical, *Ibid.*

* Theſe particulars are found in Suetonius: " His " eyes were bright and lively, and he affected to have it " thought there was a certain divine vigour in them, and " was wonderfully pleaſed, if any one, when he looked " earneſtly upon him, turned down his eyes to the ground, " as at the luſtre of the ſun." *Suet. Aug. c.* 79. *Ibid.*

This image employed by Julian, in his ingenious fiction, is juſt and elegant ; but when he conſiders this change of character as real, and aſcribes it to the power of philoſophy, he does too much honour to the power of philoſophy and to Octavius. GIBBON.

† It is pretended that the converſation of the philoſophers, in particular that of Athenodorus the Stoic, contributed greatly to correct the faults of Auguſtus, Athenodorus ſhall be mentioned in the cloſe of theſe remarks. Let it be obſerved, by the way, that Julian places the philoſophers in heaven, with the exception, no doubt, of Epicurus and Pyrrho, whoſe tenets he deteſted. LA BLETERIE.

L 4

him

him a very few precepts, as if he had muttered
the incantations of Zamolxis, foon rendered him
wife and virtuous.

The third who approached was TIBERIUS, with
a grave but fierce afpect, appearing at once both
wife and martial. As he turned to fit down, his
back difplayed feveral fcars, fome cauteries and
fores, fevere ftripes and bruifes, fcabs and tumours,
imprinted by luft and intemperance. Silenus then
faying,

" Far diff'rent now thou feemeft than before *",
in a much more ferious tone, ' Why fo grave, my
' dear ?' faid Bacchus. " That old fatyr, " replied
" he, has terrified me, and made me inadvertently
" quote a line of Homer." ' Take care that he
' does not alfo pull your ears,' faid Bacchus ; ' for
' thus, it is faid, he treated a certain grammarian †.'

" He

---

* Αλλοιος μοι, ξεινε, φανης νιον η.το παροιθεν.

This is what Telemachus fays, in the xvith book of the
Odyffey, to his father Ulyffes, whom he did not yet
know, and in whofe outward appearance Minerva had juft
wrought a metamorphofis.   LA BLETERIE.

" Before," in Englifh, is as equivocal as παροιθεν, in
Greek. This the French tranflator, as he obferves, could
not retain, auparavant not fignifying the fame as par
devant.

† This fact is unknown. But we know that Tiberius had
at his table fome men of learning (they were at that time
diftinguifhed by the name of grammarians), whom he
delighted to embarrafs by frivolous and abfurd queftions.
He afked them, for inftance, who was the mother of He-
cuba ; what name Achilles bore at the court of Lyco-
medes ; what the Sirens fung, &c. Thofe who had the
misfortune to difpleafe this tyrant did not always efcape fo
well as he whom Julian mentions. As the queftions of
Tiberius

" He had better," returned Silenus, " bemoan
" himſelf in his ſolitary iſland (meaning Capreæ)
" and tear the face of ſome miſerable fiſherman *."

While they were thus joking, a dreadful
monſter [CALIGULA] appeared. The Gods averting their eyes, Nemeſis delivered him to the avenging Furies, who immediately threw him into
Tartarus, without allowing Silenus to accoſt him.
But on the approach of CLAUDIUS, Silenus began
to ſing the beginning of the part of Demoſthenes in the Knights of Ariſtophanes †, cajoling

CLAU-

Tiberius often related to what he had read, the grammarian Seleucus took care to learn what books the Emperor was reading. Tiberius being appriſed of it, not
contented with baniſhing him from the palace, forced him
to deſtroy himſelf. *Suet. Tiber.* 70 and 56. LA BLETERIE.

* A few days after Tiberius had retired into the iſland
of Capreæ, a fiſherman came over the rocks; and preſented him with a barbel of an extraordinary ſize. Tiberius,
who thought himſelf in this retreat inacceſſible, being terrified at the boldneſs of this fiſherman, ordered his face
to be ſcratched with his fiſh. And the poor man rejoicing
that he had not alſo preſented him with a monſtrous crab
that he had caught, Tiberius commanded his face to be
torn with the crab. *Suet. Tib.* 60. *Ibid.*

† In the firſt ſcene of that comedy, whoſe object is to
depreciate in the eyes of the people one Cleon, who had
gained their entire confidence, Demoſthenes and Nicias,
two Athenian generals, complain bitterly of the tyranny
which this new-comer exerciſes in the houſe, meaning the
ſtate, over the other ſlaves, that is, thoſe who had a ſhare
in the government. " Alas! alas!" ſays Demoſthenes,
" how much reaſon we have to complain! May the juſt
" Gods confound that wicked Paphlagonian, both him and
" his projects! That ſlave, lately purchaſed, ſince he has
" been introduced into the family, inceſſantly beats the
" ſervants."

CLAUDIUS. Then turning to Quirinus, " You
" are unjuft," faid he, " to invite your defcendant
" without his freed-men, Narciffus and Pallas.
" But, befides them, you fhould alfo fend for his
" wife Meffalina, for without them, he appears
" like guards in a tragedy, mute and inanimate."
    While Silenus was fpeaking, NERO entered,
playing on his harp, and crowned with laurel. Silenus then turned to Apollo, and faid, " This man
" makes you his model."   ' I fhall foon uncrown
' him,' replied Apollo : ' he did not imitate me in
' every thing, and when he did, he was a bad imi-
' tator.'   Cocytus therefore inftantly fwept him
away, divefted of his crown.

" fervants." Among the Greeks, the term *Paphlagonian*
was an affront; it meant a Barbarian, a blockhead, a
ftammerer. In every fenfe it fuited the Emperor Claudius,
who was born in the Gauls; who, with fome learning and
genius, never reafoned when he was in fear, and he was in
fear during his whole life, even on the throne; and his
words were fo badly articulated, that he could fcarce be
underftood. But the Paphlagonian of Ariftophanes ill-
treated the flaves; while the Paphlagonian of Silenus was
governed and ill-treated by the flaves. Claudius was always the fervant of his freed-men. He only complained
of it, and that even in the fenate. He faid there one day,
fpeaking of a certain freed-woman of his mother, " She
" has always confidered me as her mafter. I fay it to her
" commendation, becaufe there are at this time fome in
" my own family who do not think me their mafter." *Suet.*
Claud. 39. The mixture of truth and irony, in the verfes
of Ariftophanes applied to Claudius, throws, I think, more
humour into the pleafantry of Silenus. M. Spanheim has
but half underftood it,   LA BLETERIE.

                                                After

After him, seeing many come crowding together, VINDEX *, OTHO, GALBA, VITELLIUS, Silenus exclaimed; " Where, ye Gods, have you found " such a multitude of monarchs? We are suffocated " with smoke; for beasts of this kind spare not " even the temples of the Gods †."   Jupiter then looked at his brother Serapis ‡, and said, pointing to VESPASIAN, ' Send this miser, as soon as possible, ' out of Ægypt, to extinguish these flames.   Bid ' his eldest son [TITUS] solace himself with a prosti-

* C. Julius Vindex, governor of Celtic Gaul, descended from the ancient kings of Aquitaine, was the first who revolted from Nero.   Virginius Rufus, governor of Upper Germany, marched against him; but the two generals had a conference, in which they agreed against the tyrant: this, however, did not prevent the two armies from engaging, in spite of Virginius and Vindex, who could not restrain them.   The latter was defeated, and killed himself in despair.   Julian thinks that he designed to make himself Emperor.   Yet he had written to Galba to offer him his forces and allegiance, if the latter would accept the empire.   LA BLETERIE.

† Silenus has here chiefly in view the burning of the famous temple of Jupiter Capitolinus, which was perpetrated under Vitellius, and by those of his party.   This passage, which throws light on what Vespasian says afterwards, and to which the Latin translators, not even F. Petau, have attended, I have corrected from an excellent Greek MS. of the works of Julian.   SPANHEIM.

‡ Julian (*Orat.* iv.) says, that " Serapis is the same " as Pluto," to whom he assigns some functions very different from those which are ascribed to him by the poets. Here Jupiter addresses himself to Serapis, because Vespasian was first acknowledged by the legions that were in Ægypt, and proclaimed in Alexandria, July 1, 69.   The years of his reign are reckoned from this day.   Besides, it is pretended that this prince had received several striking marks of the protection of Serapis. *Tacit. Ann.* IV. 81.   LA BLETERIE.

' tute *, but chain his younger son [DOMITIAN †],
' near the Sicilian tyger ‡.'

Then

* Μετα της Αφροδιτης της πανδημε, *cum Venere publicâ.* The manners of Titus, before he was Emperor, were far from irreproachable. See *Suet. Tit.* 7. His passion for Berenice was very scandalous. The tragedy of Racine has long accustomed the French to consider her as a virtuous princess, worthy to ascend the throne of the Cæsars. Great poets sometimes determine reputations unjustly. Virgil and Racine have made two celebrated queens what they were not. The prudence of Berenice was always very equivocal, at least. She became a widow very young; and her zeal for the Jewish religion, which she professed, did not prevent her being accused of entertaining more than friendship for her brother Herod Agrippa. In order to put a stop to a report so injurious to her honour, she married Polemon, king of Cilicia, after having obliged him to embrace Judaism; but she did not live long with him, and left him, it is said, through libertinism. This account, taken from Josephus, makes me suspect that she is principally alluded to by Silenus, under the name of *Venus publica.* If the colours seem too strong, let it be remembered, that those of satire in general, and of this in particular, are not always exact. Is Julian, for instance, excusable in saying nothing of the good qualities of Titus, and in characterising him only by one vice, which ought scarce to be admitted into his portrait, even by way of shade, as he was divested of it when he was Emperor? " This report," says Suetonius, " turned to his advantage, and was afterwards changed into the highest praises; when there was " found in him no one vice, but, on the contrary, the most " consummate virtues. . . . . He immediately dismissed " Berenice from the city, with the utmost reluctance " on both sides." All that can be said in excuse of Julian is, that the reign of Titus was so short, that one cannot venture to affirm, that his manners were really changed. This was probably the idea of the poet Ausonius, when he styled him " happy in not having reigned " long:" *Felix brevitate regendi.*   LA BLETERIE.

The reverse of this. *Infelix brevitate regendi,* M. de la Bleterie applies to Jovian, as a motto to his History of that prince.

The

Then came an old man [NERVA §], of a beautiful aspect (for even old age is sometimes beautiful),
in his manners most gentle, and in his adminis-
tration mild.   With him Silenus was so delighted,
that he remained silent.   'What!' said Mercury,
'have you nothing to say of this man?' "Yes,
" by Jupiter," he replied ; " for I charge you all
" with partiality, in suffering that blood-thirsty
" monster to reign fifteen years, but this man
" scarce a whole year." 'Do not complain,'
answered Jupiter; ' many good princes shall suc-
' ceed him.'

TRAJAN immediately entered, bearing on his
shoulders the Getic || and Parthian trophies. Silenus,
observing him, said, in a low voice, but loud
enough to be heard, "Our lord Jupiter must
" now be careful, or he will not be able to keep
" Ganymede to himself."   After him advanced a

† The cruelties of Domitian are well known.

‡ Phalaris.

§ Nerva, when he was raised to the empire, was sixty-
three years old, at least. LA BLETERIE.

|| Though the name of Getes was given more peculiarly
to the nations beyond the Danube, who bordered on the
mouths of that river, the Greeks gave the same name
also to the Dacians, that is, the Transylvanians, the Wal-
lachians, and the Moldavians. Trajan subdued them. In
his reign the power of the Romans was at the greatest
height it had ever attained. In the North, he reduced
Dacia to a province. In the East, he made himself master
of Armenia, Mesopotamia, and Assyria. The Parthians,
to whom he had given a king, were in some sort become
subject to the Romans. That

venerable

venerable sage [HADRIAN], with a long beard *;
an adept in music, gazing frequently on the heavens,
. . . .   and

* Hadrian was the first of the Emperors who wore a
beard. "He let his grow," says Spartianus, " in order to
" conceal some natural deformity;" *ut vulnera, quæ in facie
naturalia erant, tegeret.* In reading the history of Hadrian,
and even the little which Julian says of him in this satire,
I am struck with some marks of resemblance between these
two Emperors. They had both as much genius as it was
possible to have, and of the same kind. They were greedy
of glory, jocose, and sarcastic, fond to extravagance of
the Greeks and the Grecian literature, both friends of
the arts and sciences, both authors, both full of zeal for
idolatry, superstitious, persecutors, astrologers, desirous of
knowing every thing, perpetually inquisitive, so as to be
accused of magic, fickle, obstinate, singular, and vain of
being so. They both made very wise laws, and performed
many acts of mercy. Hadrian sometimes seemed cruel,
and it is said that Julian was humane only through vanity.
Julian had not the infamous vices of Hadrian, and was not
even suspected of them; but he had almost all his faults
and absurdities.   LA BLETERIE.

More striking to me are some marks of resemblance
which may be traced between this Imperial sophist and the
royal philosopher of Sans-souci. Both are authors of no
small repute in various branches of literature. The Memoirs of himself and his family, which Julian has inserted
in his Epistle to the Athenians, may be compared with
those of the House of Brandenburgh, and the History of
his Gallic campaigns, now lost, but mentioned by Libanius,
with the Commentaries, yet unpublished, of the Prussian
monarch. That Julian was a poet as well as Frederick, appears
from a collection of his verses mentioned also by Libanius
(*Orat. parent.* p. 161.) though two small pieces (which I
have quoted and translated in the notes on the Misopogon),
are all that now remain. Both solaced their leisure with
the charms of music. The epistles of both have an air of
familiar elegance. If the Cæsar lamented the loss of his
friend Sallust, recalled by his jealous cousin, the prince
deplored the fate of his favourite Kat, condemned to
death by his cruel father. Both were married, early in
life,

and curiously investigating the abstrusest subjects *.
" What," said Silenus, think you of this Sophist ?
" Is he looking for Antinous † ? If so, one of
" you may tell him that the youth is not here,

life, by their predecessors, to princesses not of their own
choice, yet neither of them was ever charged with any
illicit amour. " The chastity of Julian," says Mr.
Gibbon, " is confirmed by the impartial testimony of
" Ammianus, and by the partial silence of the Christians."
" Fortune," said the Prussian hero, after his defeat at
Kolin, " is a female, and I am no gallant." The Roman
carried the simplicity of his dress to an indecent extravagance; his beard and its inhabitants, his inky nails, &c.
are recorded by himself. The German, by the scantiness
of his wardrobe, his boots, and his snuff, as Dr. Moore
informs us, is almost as singular in these more polished
times. Early attached to Grecian literature, Julian neglected and despised the language and writers of Italy.
Equally enamoured of the French language, Frederick has
always professed a kind of aversion for those of Germany.
If the Emperor invited Maximus, Priscus, and other Platonists from Greece, the King sent for Voltaire, Mauper-
tuis, and other academicians from France. In war too, as
well as in literature, these heroes have acted a distinguished
but not always a successful part. In two particulars, however, they materially differ: Julian was a superstitious Pagan: Of Paganism or superstition Frederick has never been
suspected; yet the former believed the immortality of the
soul, which, it appears from his Epistle to Marshal Keith,
&c. the latter does not.

 * It is said, that Julian here meant to describe himself.
He informs us (*Orat.* iv.) that " from his infancy, he
" stopped to contemplate the stars with so much pleasure,
" that he was even then deemed an astrologer (αϛϛομαϰΐης)
" though he did not yet know what astrology was." Is the
title of *curiositatis omnis explorator*, which Hadrian so justly
deserved, and that of " Sophist," less applicable to the
censor of Hadrian ? La Bleterie.

 † The deification of Antinous, his medals, statues,
temples, city, oracles, and constellation, are well known,
and still dishonour the memory of Hadrian. Gibbon.

" and

" and thus check his madness and folly." To
these succeeded a man of moderation, not in ve-
nereal * but political pursuits [ANTONINUS PIUS.]
Silenus, on seeing him, exclaimed, " Strange!
" how important is he in trifles.! This old man
" seems to me one of those who would harangue
" about a pin's point †.

At the entrance of two brothers, MARCUS AU-
RELIUS and LUCIUS VERUS, Silenus contracted his
brow, as he could by no means jeer or deride them ‡.

                             MARCUS,

* Our satyr here obliquely charges Antoninus Pius with
lasciviousness; an imputation which was not true, it being
certain that that Emperor was temperate and chaste. But
he seems to have been accused, though not justly, of avarice, for adopting, when he was Emperor, the simple diet
and parsimony of a private subject.   PETAU.

Titus Antoninus, surnamed *Pius,* that is, " the good,"
was one of the greatest and best princes that the Romans
had. Pausanias justly says, that " he deserved not only
" the name of Pius, but also that of Father of Mankind,
" which was formerly given to Cyrus." Antoninus had
in fact the frailties with which Silenus reproaches him; but
he early corrected them.   LA BLETERIE.

† Εἰς τῶν διαπριοντὰ τὸν κυμινον. " One that cuts cumin;"
which seems analogous to our English phrase of " skinning
" a flint.' This we apply, however, only to misers; but,
as M. de la Bleterie observes, " that of the Greeks refers
" not only to avarice, but a littleness of mind. Anto-
" ninus was generous, but not at the expence of any other
" person; *largus sui, alieni abstinens.*" Our " splitting a
" hair" may perhaps come nearer to it.

‡ They were brothers only by adoption. Silenus had
too much to say of Lucius Verus: Indeed he was a good-
natured prince, a sincere friend, and incapable of disguise.
He always considered himself as the lieutenant rather than
the collegue of his brother. But he indulged himself,
without moderation, in all kinds of debaucheries, and was

        X   a slave

MARCUS, in particular, though he strictly scru-tinised his conduct with regard to his son and his wife *; as to her, in his immoderate grief for her death, though she little deserved it; as to him, in hazarding the ruin of the empire by preferring him to a discreet son-in-law †, who would have made a better prince, and studied the advantage of his son more than he did himself. Notwithstand-ing these failings, Silenus could not but admire his exalted virtue. Thinking his son ‡ [COM-MODUS] unworthy of any stroke of wit, he silently dismissed him. And he, not being able to support himself, or associate with the heroes, fell down to the earth.

a slave to the ministers of his pleasures. Excepting that he was not cruel, that he did not drive chariots in the circus, nor act on the stage, he much resembled Nero.
- LA BLETERIE.

* The greatest and perhaps the only fault of Marcus Aurelius was his excessive good-nature, which made him blind or too indulgent as to his brother, Lucius Verus, his wife, the too famous Faustina, and his son, Commodus. We shall mention him more than once in the sequel. *Ibid.*

† Claudius Pompeianus, originally of Antioch, and son only of a Roman knight, but a man of extraordinary merit. Marcus Aurelius caused him twice to be nominated consul, and gave him in marriage his daughter Lucilla, the relict of Lucius Verus. *Ibid.*

‡ One of the most wicked princes that ever reigned. "The " enemy of the Gods and of his country, the parricide, the " executioner of the senate, the gladiator, more cruel than " Domitian, more infamous than Nero," is part of the funeral elogium which the senate made on Commodus. This assembly, which thought it had always a right to sit in judgment on the Emperors, would have ordered his body to be thrown into the Tiber, had not Pertinax pre-vented it. *Ibid.*

PERTINAX then approached, still lamenting the mortal wound that he received at a banquet *. This excited the compassion of Nemesis, who said, " The authors of this deed shall not long exult; " but, PERTINAX, you were culpable † in being " privy to the conspiracy that destroyed the son " of MARCUS." He was succeeded by SEVERUS ‡, a prince inexorable in punishing. ' Of him,' said Silenus, ' I have nothing to say; for I am terrified ' by his stern and implacable looks.' His sons would have accompanied him, but Minos prevented them, and kept them at a distance. With a prudent distinction, however, he dismissed the youngest

---

* The senate and people flattered themselves with having again found Marcus Aurelius in Pertinax; but he only reigned eighty-seven days. The Prætorian guards, who could not bear an Emperor so different from Commodus, massacred him in the palace.   LA BLETERIE.

† The reproof given him by Silenus [rather Nemesis] for being concerned in the conspiracy of Letus and Marcia seems not well founded; but Julian perhaps follows some historian unknown to us. The death of Pertinax was revenged by Didius Julianus, who put Letus and Marcia to death; and by Severus, who cashiered the Prætorians. Julian is right in not naming among the Emperors Didius Julianus, worthy of eternal oblivion, for buying the empire which the Prætorian guards had put up to auction.
Ibid.

‡ Severus was perhaps the most warlike of all the Emperors. Like Hannibal an African, he had all his virtues; but he had also all the vices which the Romans ascribe to the Carthaginian general. What Sylla said of himself may be said of Severus; " no one was a better friend or a worse enemy."
Ibid.

[GETA],

[GETA], and ordered the eldeſt [CARACALLA] to be puniſhed for his crimes *.

That crafty murderer MACRINUS †, and the youth of Emeſa ‡ [ELAGABALUS], were driven from the ſacred incloſure. But ALEXANDER THE SYRIAN §, being placed in the hinder ranks, be-
wailed

* The antipathy of Caracalla and Geta is well known: The latter ſeemed to have ſome good qualities. The former ſtabbed his brother in the arms of Julia, their common mother, who herſelf received a wound in the hand: He was as wicked, and almoſt as ſtupid, as Caligula. He was a profeſſed enemy to men of learning. LA BLETERIE:

† Macrinus, Prætorian præfect, knowing that Caracalla intended to kill him, cauſed that prince to be aſſaſſinated, on the road from Edeſſa to Carræ. The army, who did not think him guilty of that murder, choſe him Emperor ; and their choice was confirmed by the Senate. But fourteen months after, Varius Avitus Baſſianus, afterwards known by the name of Elagabalus, having aſſumed the title of Auguſtus, marched againſt him, and attacked him on the borders of Syria and Phœnicia. Macrinus ſhamefully fled, while the event of the battle was yet undetermined. Endeavouring to eſcape into Europe, he was overtaken by his purſuers, and put to death. Ibid.

‡ Elagabalus was of Emeſa in Syria, the ſon of Varius Marcellus, a Roman ſenator, by Soëmia, the daughter of Mæſa, ſiſter to the Empreſs Julia. He may in ſome manner be conſidered as the nephew of Caracalla. He pretended even to be his ſon. All the infamous, extravagant, and cruel practices that can be committed by a young man without genius, taſte, or the leaſt ſpark of virtue or ſentiment, who, to indulge his caprice, endeavours to exhauſt the power and wealth of a Roman Emperor ; this is an abſtract of the reign of that prince, or, to ſpeak more properly, that monſter. Ibid.

§ Alexander Severus is conſidered by many, even at preſent, as a moderate-prince, *magis extra vitia quàm cum virtutibus*, of a narrow genius, timid, the ſlave of an imperious mother, &c. He owes this reputation to the hiſtory

 of

wailed his misfortune: Silenus added, " O thou
" fool and madman! highly exalted as thou wert,
" thou didſt not govern for thyſelf, but gaveſt

of Herodian, an author by no means exact, but agreeable and intereſting, whom two tranſlations, one in Latin,
the other in French, as good at leaſt as the original, have
put within the reach of every one. Herodian diſcovers an
extravagant prejudice againſt the Emperor Alexander, for
which we might perhaps be able to account, if the hiſtorian
were known to us otherwiſe than by his work. It were to
be wiſhed that a pen as brilliant as his would endeavour to
re-eſtabliſh the memory of a prince in all reſpects the moſt
amiable and accompliſhed that is mentioned in ancient hiſtory. He wanted neither courage nor firmneſs. If he
had a great deference for his mother Mamméa, it was as
much owing to his diſcernment as to his gratitude and
tenderneſs for her. The œconomy with which they are
reproached was a virtue more neceſſary than ever in the
ſtate to which the ſenſeleſs prodigality of Elagabaſus had
reduced the finances. Alexander died at twenty-nine years
of age, and conſequently was younger than Trajan, T.
Antoninus, and Marcus Aurelius were when they aſcended
the throne; and yet he deſerves at leaſt to be compared
with them. Julian has followed the Memoirs of Herodian;
and, beſides, it ſhould not be forgotten, that Mamméa
was probably a Chriſtian; that Alexander, inſtead of per-
ſecuting the Chriſtians, worſhipped Jeſus Chriſt, whoſe
ſtatue he honoured, in his oratory, with thoſe of Apollo-
nius Tyanæus, Abraham, and Orpheus; that he had a
deſign of building a temple to Jeſus Chriſt, and of cauſing
him to be received among the deities adored by the Romans. This was more than ſufficient to make Alexander
deſpiſed by Julian. Among the ſtrokes of ſatire which
are couched under the name of *Syrian*, which he gives to
the ſon of Mamméa, and which, however, he did not deſerve, except by his birth, I have no doubt that Julian includes the character of a worſhipper of Jeſus Chriſt. We
know that Judea, where the Chriſtian religion had its riſe,
was an appendage of Syria, and that the diſciples of Jeſus
Chriſt were firſt ſtyled Chriſtians at Antioch.

LA BLETERIE.

" thy

" thy wealth to thy mother, and could'ft not be
" perfuaded that it was much better to beftow it
" on thy friends than to hoard it *."   ' All, how-

                                                   ' ever,'

* MAXIMIN, of the Gothic nation, the firft of the Barbarians of the North, whom I find invefted with the
Roman dignities, made a fenator by Alexander, and commanding fome troops, confpired againft his benefactor,
caufed him to be affaffinated near Mentz, and ufurped the
fupreme power. This Maximin was a kind of giant, being
eight feet high, and with ftrength proportioned to his ftature; he was a great warrior, but fo cruel and blood-thirfty,
that he was named Cyclops and Phalaris. He obliged the
whole empire to revolt againft him, and, with his fon, was
at length flain by the foldiers, who thus revenged the
death of Alexander.

It is furprifing that Julian fays not a fingle word of any
of the Emperors who reigned from Alexander to Valerian;
namely, PUPIENUS and BALBINUS, GORDIAN the younger,
the two PHILIPS, TRAJAN-DECIUS, and Æmilian. If he had
omitted only the two firft Gordians, and fome others,
Æmilian, for inftance, it might be fuppofed that he confidered them only as the phantoms of Emperors. Yet ftill
they deferved to be named as much as Galba, Otho, and
Vitellius, and more fo than Vindex. Will it be faid, that
fome of them were unworthy to reign? Yet others were
worthy; and, befides, Julian has juft mentioned Elagabalus.
Will it be faid, that all thofe princes had a tragical end?
But he prefently introduces Valerian. It may alfo be obferved, that Julian appears to have efteemed the younger
Gordian by offering facrifices and libations on his tomb,
while he was marching againft the Perfians.

In the IVth century, at lateft, it was faid, that the Emperor Philip the father had been a Chriftian, and that he
had fubmitted to public penance; a tradition the more
ftriking, as the Chriftians had little intereft in claiming
the murderer of Gordian. The Chriftianity of Philip, real
or pretended, and the manner fo unchriftian in which he
arrived at the throne, might have fupplied the Silenus of
Julian with fome fingular ftrokes. Trajan-Decius would
have been reckoned among the good princes, if he had

‘ ever,’ said Nemesis, ‘ who were acceſſary to his
‘ death, I will deliver to the tormentors.’   And
thus the youth was diſmiſſed.

GALLIENUS then entered, with his father [VA-
LERIAN], the latter dragging the chain of his captivity, the other effeminate both in his dreſs and
behaviour.   Silenus thus ridiculed the father :

   " ———— By thoſe ſnowy plumes diſtinguiſh’d,
   " Before the ranks who marches in the van *."
                                                    And

not been a perſecutor of the Chriſtians ; and doubtleſs it
is not on that account that Julian eraſes him from the liſt
of Emperors.   Certain it is that no ſatisfactory reaſon can
be aſſigned for all theſe omiſſions.   It ſeems therefore very
probable to me that the text is here mutilated.   It is not
the only chaſm that I think I perceive in the ſatire of the
Cæſars.   LA BLETERIE.

   * Wodhull’s tranſlation.

   Theſe two verſes are taken from the Phœnician Virgins
of Euripides.   By ο λευκολοφας, " with the white plume,"
I imagine that Silenus alludes to the age and white hairs
of Valerian.   No one is unacquainted with his captivity,
any more than the barbarity with which he was treated by
Sapor I.   Upon a falſe report of the death of Valerian, the
Romans placed him among the Gods.   Thus this unfortunate prince had altars in Rome, while in Perſia he was
trodden under foot.   He was perhaps flead alive.   Certain
it is, that the Perſians tanned his ſkin, dyed it red, and
covered it with ſtraw, in order to preſerve it in a temple.
Valerian had ſome excellent qualities ; and his fate would
perhaps have had more claim to pity, if he had not deſerved it by ſhedding the blood of the Chriſtians.   The
moſt dreadful circumſtance of his misfortune was, the
having on the throne a ſon who did not ſend even to
demand his releaſe.   " He would have been revenged,"
ſays M. de Tillemont, " if he had not had a ſon."   When
Gallienus was informed of the impriſonment of his father,
he anſwered by an apophthegm ; " I knew that my father
" was liable to the misfortunes of human nature."   How
                                                    much

And to the fon he faid,

" Him gold adorns, all dainty as a bride *,"

Jupiter ordered them both to depart from the
banquet †.

They were fucceeded by Claudius ‡, on whom
all the Gods fixed their eyes, admiring his magnanimity,

much are princes to be pitied ! The flatterers of Gallienus
difcovered philofophy, and even heroifm, in the indifference
of this unnatural fon.   La Bleterie.

*, This is an imitation of a line of Ariftophanes, in his
comedy of The Birds. Gallienus was a cowardly, flothful, effeminate prince, a good orator, a good poet, but
a very bad emperor. While he was engaged in his debaucheries, and amufing himfelf in fome mifplaced ftudies,
in fome effufion of wit, in making fome pretty verfes, or
uttering fome good jokes on the lofs of provinces, Italy
itfelf was ravaged by the Barbarians. Without reckoning
Zenobia and Odenathus, eighteen ufurpers affumed the
purple. Gallienus, to prevent fuch revolts, excluded the
fenators from all military employments; a fatal policy,
which, in the fequel, contributed to raife to the throne
mere cyphers, men who had nothing Roman but the name.
In fhort, the reign of Gallienus is the æra of the fall of
the empire, which never perfectly recovered the violent
fhocks which it then received.   *Ibid.*

† Gallienus deferved to be excluded. But Julian feems
to reprefent the Gods as ungrateful. Ought they thus to
treat the fate of the unfortunate Valerian, who was fo
zealous for their worfhip ? Misfortune, after all, is not a
crime. But it fhould be remembered that Valerian was
taken by his own fault, and that, according to the Pagan
ideas, being a prifoner, he ought to have fhortened his difgrace, and not have furvived his liberty. When Perfeus,
king of Macedonia, applied to Paulus Æmilius not to
lead him in triumph, the Roman confidered him as a
coward, and anfwered, " That depended, and ftill depends,
on himfelf."   *Ibid.*

‡ Claudius II. had every civil virtue and military talent.
His reign lafted only two years ; but he fignalifed it by a
M 4   great

nanimity, and granted the empire to his descendants, thinking it juft that the pofterity of fuch a
lover of his country fhould enjoy the fovereignty
as long as poffible *.

After him entered AURELIUS †, as if to efcape
thofe who were accufing him before Minos. For
many

great victory gained over the Germans, and by the defeat of
320,000 Goths. It is faid, that he devoted himfelf for the
fafety of his country. This devotement (if we underftand by it a folemn devotement, like that which the Decii
made of their perfons in the time of the republic) is a fiction, contrary to the relation of the beft hiftorians, who
fay, that Claudius died of a peftilential fever at Sirmium.
Julian, however, manifeftly alludes to it. He believed, or
was willing to believe, an incident fo honourable to the
memory of Claudius, whom he confidered as the founder
of his family. Conftantius-Chlorus, the grandfather of
Julian, was the fon of Claudia, the daughter of Crifpus,
one of the brothers of Claudius II. The furname of Conftantine came from the family of Claudius, as he had a
fifter named Conftantina. Julian paffes over Quintillus,
the brother and fucceffor of Claudius, becaufe he reigned
only twenty days at moft.   LA BLETERIE.

In his firft oration in praife of Conftantius, Julian celebrates alfo " the eminent virtues" of their common anceftor
the Emperor Claudius ; " the battles which he fought with
" the Barbarians beyond the Danube, his condefcending
" manners, and that modefty of drefs which was ftill ob-
" fervable on his ftatues."

* In Julian this was not adulation, but fuperftition and
vanity.   GIBBON.

† Aurelian, the conqueror of the Barbarians, of Zenobia,
and of Tetricus, completed the recovery of what Gallienus
had loft. If he did the ftate too many fervices to be placed
in the rank of bad princes, he was too fevere and too cruel
to be reckoned among the good. He was born in Pannonia, or Dacia, of a very obfcure family. The mother
of Aurelian, prieftefs of the Sun in her village, infpired
her fon, no doubt, with the zeal which he always profeffed

many charges of murder, which he could not palliate or excuse, were brought against him. But my Lord the Sun *, who had patronised him on other occasions, assisted him also on this, by informing the Gods, that the Delphic oracle

" That he who evil does, should evil suffer,

" Is righteous judgment,"

had been fulfilled.

The next was PROBUS, who in less than seven years re-built seventy cities, and also enacted many wise laws. Having suffered unjustly, he was honoured by the Gods, and his death was revenged by the punishment of his murderers. Silenus, nevertheless, endeavoured, in like manner, to ridicule him; and many of the Gods urging him to be silent, " Let those who shall follow," said he, " the oracle of Delphi. Also tossed for that God. He chose him for his tutelar deity, as Julian did afterwards.

TACITUS, a prince truly respectable, and worthy of the senate who chose him, ought to have been placed at the feast of the Cæsars. Nevertheless, he is not even named. Is the omission owing to Julian, or the transcribers? As Tacitus reigned only six months, I will not venture to determine. As to his brother, Florian, who reigned only three, or perhaps two, and who, besides, took possession of the empire, as of an inheritance, without being chosen by the senate, or even proposed by the army, he deserved to be omitted.   LA BLETERIE.

* Aurelian adored that Deity as the parent of his life and fortunes. His mother had been an inferior priestess in a chapel of the Sun: a peculiar devotion to the God of light was a sentiment which the fortunate peasant imbibed in his infancy, and every step of his elevation, every victory of his reign, fortified superstition by gratitude. GIBBON.

he

he, " grow wiser by his example. Dost thou
" not know, O Probus, that physicians make bitter
" potions palatable, by infusing them in mead?
" But thou, who wert always so severe and cruel
" that none could equal thee *, hast suffered, how-
" ever unjustly, in like manner. For no one can
" govern brutes, much less men, but by sometimes
" gratifying and indulging them ; as physicians
" humour their patients in trifles, that they may
" insure their compliance in things essential."
' What! dear father,' said Bacchus ; ' do you now
' play the philosopher upon us?' " Why not?"
replied Silenus. " Were not you too, my son,
" instructed by me in philosophy? Know you not
" that Socrates also held, like me, the first rank
" in philosophy among his contemporaries, if you
" credit the oracle of Delphi? Allow me therefore
" to speak not always jocosely, but sometimes
" seriously."

While they were thus talking, CARUS with his
sons [CARINUS and NUMERIAN] would have

* This censure of Silenus is extravagant. Probus can
only be reproached for having enforced military discipline
with a strictness of which the Roman armies were no longer
capable. In time of peace he employed them in useful
labours. One day happening to say inadvertently, that
" there should soon be no more need of soldiers," this expression cost him his life. The same army, however, who
had murdered him, erected a monument to him, with this
inscription : *Hic Probus Imperator et verè Probus situs est,
victor omnium gentium barbararum, etiam tyrannorum.*

LA BLETERIE.

entered,

entered, had not Nemefis repulfed them *. Diocletian †, accompanied by the two Maxi-

---

* Hiftory reprefents Carus as a prince above mediocrity : *virum medium, inter bonos, magis quàm inter malos, collocandum.* But he had the misfortune to fucceed Probus, and to have Carinus for his fon. On the other hand, he defeated the Perfians, and took Seleucia and Ctefiphon, when a flafh of lightning terminated his conquefts and his life. It muft not, however, be faid that the fentence of Julian is too fevere, as Carus dared to affume, or fuffered flattery to give him, the title of " Lord and God." Befides, Julian thought perhaps that Carus was guilty of the death of his predeceffor Probus; but the fact is at leaft doubtful. His fecond fon, Numerian, was not unworthy of a place at the banquet. Hiftory fpeaks of him advantageoufly. As to what is faid of Carinus, the juftice of Nemefis cannot but be applauded.   LA BLETERIE.

† Diocletian reigned for twenty years with great profperity and addrefs; but he difgraced the latter part of his reign by the moft barbarous of all perfecutions. He was a foldier of fortune, and having learned nothing but the art of war, he was a profound politician, and had a fubtle genius that penetrated every thing, but was itfelf impenetrable. He always attended to what was folid. His projects, though grand and vaft, were never chimerical, unlefs it were that of extinguifhing the Chriftian name; yet of that he was not the author. He had the art of doing good himfelf, and of employing others to do evil. Being mafter of his paffions, he could difguife all his vices, except pride, which made him introduce into the court of the emperors the ceremonial of the court of Perfia. He fhould be confidered as the founder of a new empire, which had not, it may be faid, any thing in common with that which was founded by Auguftus, but the name. The effective partition of the provinces fubject to the Romans annihilated the ancient plan, and gave the finifhing ftroke to the fenate, which till then had always had an influence in public affairs, and whofe authority was much reftored after the death of Aurelian. The averfion of Diocletian to the city of Rome prepared the great event of the foundation of Conftantinople.   *Ibid.*

MIANS,

MIANS, and my grandfather Constantius *, then approached, magnificently dreſſed. Theſe, though they held each other by the hand, did not walk on a line with Diocletian. Three others † also

                                               ſur-

* Conſtantius-Chlorus.

† Diocletian, firſt divided the empire with Maximian, afterwards ſurnamed Herculius, his old friend, a great general, very liberal, and not deficient in genius; but un-poliſhed and cruel, without education, and without manners. They gave in conjunction the title of Cæſar to Conſtantius-Chlorus and Maximian-Galerius, and divided the Roman empire, which was governed by two Emperors and two Cæſars, into four parts.

Conſtantius Chlorus was the only one of the four who was of high birth. With all the talents of his collegues, he had none of their faults. His ſole ambition was to make his people happy. No prince ever loved money ſo little, or was ſo much lov'd by his ſubjects. — Through fear of oppreſſing them, he denied himſelf neceſſaries. Such is the picture that is drawn of him even by the authors who have written ſince his family has been extinct.

As for Maximian-Galerius, ſurnamed *Armentarius*, or "the Herdſman," he was rather a Barbarian than a Roman. He had great talents for war, and all imaginable vices, which he nevertheleſs concealed a little; ſo much was he affraid of Diocletian. He had almoſt an equal hatred to the Chriſtian religion and to learning, and forced Dio-cletian to become a perſecutor. Theſe four princes go-verned with a perfect union, whoſe tie was the reſpect which Maximian-Herculius, and the two Cæſars, had for Diocletian, whom they regarded as their father, and almoſt as their God. Diocletian, on his ſide, did not exalt him-ſelf above them; and, in particular, he took care to ſtifle bad reports. What Julian here ſays of the modeſty of that prince and his collegues adinits, however, of ſome exception. Diocletian ſometimes treated Galerius with great haughtineſs; and Galerius, tired of trembling before him, made him tremble in his turn, and forced him to abdicate the empire. Diocletian and Herculius quitted the purple on the ſame day; the firſt at Nicomedia, and the

furrounded him, in the manner of a chorus; but when, like harbingers, they would have preceded him, he forbade them, not thinking himfelf entitled to any diftinction. Transferring only to them a burthen which he had borne on his own fhoulders, he walked with much greater eafe. Admiring their union, the Gods affigned them a feat fuperior to many. But MAXIMIAN * behaving with imprudence and haughtinefs, Silenus, though he did not think him worthy of ridicule, would not admit him into the fociety of the Emperors. And, befides, he was not only addicted to all kinds of lafcivioufnefs, but by his impertinent officioufnefs and perfidy often interrupted the harmonious concert. Nemefis therefore foon banifhed him, and whither he went I know not, as I forgot to afk Mercury.

other at Milan. The abdication of Diocletian has been confidered as the greateft effort of human virtue; neverthelefs, it was not fo voluntary as is generally fuppofed. But he made it honeftly, and without return; wifer than Herculius, who, after refuming the purple, and occafioning many difturbances, was obliged to deftroy himfelf.

LA BLETERIE.

* I know not why Julian excludes only one of the two Maximians. As a proof that neither of them deferved to be admitted, we do not immediately difcover which he means. However, as this Maximian alone difturbed the concert formed by the union of Diocletian and his collegues, Julian muft neceffarily fpeak of Maximian Galerius. He died at Sardis, of a dreadful diforder, confidering his death as a punifhment of the cruelties which he had exercifed againft the Chriftians. *Ibid.*

To this moft melodious tetrachord a harfh, dif-
agreeable, and difcordant found fucceeded *. Two
of the candidates Nemefis would not fuffer to approach even the door of the affembly. LICINIUS
came thus far, but having been guilty of many
crimes, he was repulfed by Minos. CONSTANTINE
entered, and fat fome time; and near him fat his

* Diocletian had flattered himfelf that the partition of
the empire between two Emperors and two Cæfars would
fubfift in future; but one of the chagrins which he felt in
his retirement was the ambition and mifunderftanding of
his fucceffors, each of whom thought only of making himfelf mafter of the whole empire. Thofe whom Julian has
here in view are Maxentius, Maximin-Daïa, Licinius, and
Conftantine.

Maxentius, the fon, or fuppofed fon, of Maximian-Herculius, was a prince ill-made, without genius, cowardly;
flothful, cruel, debauched. When he harangued his
foldiers, it was to exhort them to make good cheer, to
fpend money, to enjoy life; *fruimini*. He obliged Sophronia,
daughter of the governor of Rome, to renew the tragical
hiftory of Lucretia. It is well known that he perifhed in
the Tiber, in his endeavour to deftroy Conftantine.

Maximin-Daïa, as defpicable as Maxentius, and a ftill
more cruel perfecutor than his uncle Maximian-Galerius;
being vanquifhed by Licinius, efcaped to the city of
Tarfus, and took poifon at the end of a great entertainment. This poifon, failing of its entire effect, occafioned
him a horrible and long malady. I do not find in all antiquity a death more fhocking than his.

Though Licinius had courage and fuccefs in war, he was
ftill more wicked than Maximin. He confidered literature
as the peft of a ftate. Conftantine vanquifhed him, obliged him to quit the purple, and, foon after, deprived
him of life. Of Conftantine and his fons more in the
fequel.   LA BLETERIE.

fons. As for MAGNENTIUS *, he was refufed admittance, becaufe he had never done any thing laudable, though many of his actions might appear brilliant. But the Gods, perceiving that they did not flow from a good principle, difmiffed him much afflicted.

* Magnentius, who derived his origin from the Franks and the Saxons, ferved with reputation in the Roman troops, when he affumed the purple at Autun, and caufed the Emperor Conftans to be put to death. He was vanquifhed by Conftantius in the battle of Murfa in 352, and in the following year, through fear of falling into the hands of the conqueror, he killed himfelf in the Gauls, after having killed all his family. He had profeffed Chriftianity, though he was perhaps a Pagan in his heart. Courage is afcribed to him, or that which often produces the fame effect, the art of concealing his timidity, with a tafte for books, learning, a lively and animated eloquence, and refpect and zeal for the laws, when they were no obftacle to his ambitious projects. No writer charges him with debauchery, and this filence expreffes much. Such vices, however, are given him as are always given to unfuccefsful ufurpers. Julian, in particular, elfewhere paints Magnentius in the moft hideous colours; but it is in his panegyrics of Conftantius. The opinion which he forms here feems much more credible, and fufficiently agrees with that of Zofimus. " Magnentius," fays that hiftorian (*l. ii.*) " was bold in " profperity, and timid in adverfity. He knew fo well " how to difguife his natural perverfenefs, that thofe " who did not know him took him for a man of fim- " plicity and of an excellent character. I think myfelf " obliged to make this remark," continues Zofimus, " becaufe fome have thought that he governed the ftate " well. Let them be no longer deceived in him. Magnentius " did nothing from good motives, from a principle of " virtue." Let us obferve, by the way, that the true or falfe idea which Julian gives of Magnentius is exactly the fame which we ought to have of Julian.

LA BLETERIE.

In

In this manner was the banquet prepared. At the table of the Gods nothing was wanting, for all things are theirs. But that of the heroes Mercury thought imperfect, and Jupiter was of the same opinion. Quirinus had long requested to introduce another of his descendants. But Hercules said, "I will not suffer it, Quirinus. For "why have you not invited my ALEXANDER also "to the feast? If therefore, Jupiter, you intend "to enroll any of the heroes among us, send, "I intreat you, for ALEXANDER. When we "are canvassing the merits of men, why should "the bravest be omitted?" What the son of Alcmena proposed was approved by Jupiter. ALEXANDER therefore entered the assembly of heroes; but neither CÆSAR, nor any one else, rose up to him; so that he was obliged to take the seat which the eldest son of SEVERUS had left vacant *, he, for his fratricide, having been expelled.

* What is the reason that Alexander takes the seat intended for Caracalla, when there are so many others vacant? This is one of those little circumstances that give narrations a greater air of truth. Besides, this recalls some facts. Caracalla was inflamed with a foolish passion for Alexander. Not contented with filling the cities, the temples, Rome, and the capitol with the statues of that prince, with having a phalanx whose officers bore the names of the generals of Alexander, and dressing in the Macedonian manner, he endeavoured to identify himself with his hero in some fantastic pictures, where the face was composed of half that of Alexander and half that of his own. He persecuted the Peripatetic philosophers, because Aristotle was suspected of being concerned in the death of that conqueror.   LA BLETERIE.

Silenus

Silenus then scoffing at Quirinus, said, ' Take care,
' or this one Greek will 'excell all your Romans.'
" By Jove," replied Quirinus, " I think that many
" of them are, in every respect, his equals. My
" posterity indeed have so much admired him, that
" of foreign generals they style and think him
" only great; not that they deem him superior to
" their countrymen, or are void of national preju-
" dice. But that we shall soon determine when we
" have brought their merits to the test !" Saying
this, Quirinus blushed *, and seemed evidently
anxious for his descendants.

After this, Jupiter asked the Gods, whether all
should enter the lists, or whether they should adopt
the practice observed in wrestling, where whoever
conquers him who has gained the most victories is
deemed the only victor, even of those who have
been vanquished by his antagonist, though they
have not been his competitors ? This was generally
approved, as a just determination. Mercury then
proclaimed that CÆSAR should advance first, OCTA-
VIANUS next, and TRAJAN third, those being the
greatest warriors. Silence being commanded, Saturn, turning to Jupiter, expressed his surprise at
seeing martial Emperors summoned to this contest,

* We must not forget that Julian is a Greek to the
bottom of his soul. His only comfort in being a Roman
was his having been born at Byzantium, and his considering
Rome as a colony of Greeks.   LA BLETERIE.

but no philofophers *.   " Thefe," he faid, " are
" equally dear to me. Call therefore, and intro-
" duce MARCUS [AURELIUS]." He being fum-
moned, advanced with a ferious afpect †, occafioned by the labours of his mind. His eyes were
hollow, his brow was contracted ‡, and his whole
form difplayed unftudied beauty ; for his hair was
uncombed, his beard was long, his drefs fimple
and œconomical, and by fcanty nourifhment § his

body

* It is right for Saturn, a pacific God, and the father
of the golden age, to be interefted for philofophical princes,
and for Marcus Aurelius in particular, the greateft philofopher of them all ; who, in fpite of the various fcourges
with which the empire was afflicted in his time, promoted
the happinefs of the Romans. It is faid of this Emperor,
that Providence gave him to mankind in mercy, to temper
the feverity of the chaftifements which it had inflicted upon
them in juftice.   LA BLETERIE.

† It is pretended, that, even in his childhood, neither
joy nor forrow ever made him change countenance : but his
gravity had nothing in it fad or auftere. *Sine triftitiâ gravis.*
Ibid.

‡ He is thus reprefented on his medals, efpecially thofe
which were ftruck in the latter years of his life.   *Ibid.*

§ At the age of twelve years, Marcus Aurelius took the
habit of a philofopher, and foon after he was defirous of
practifing all the aufterities of the Stoic philofophy, even
to the lying on the ground under his cloak. His mother
ufed her utmoft endeavours to perfuade him to lie on a
wooden bedfted covered with a fingle fkin. A life fo
hardy made no abatement in the fweetnefs of his temper,
but it impaired his health. Neverthelefs, his habitual in-
firmities never prevented him from fulfilling all his duties,
and from finding time befides for ftudy. His foul appeared
to have gained what his body had loft.

Julian piqued himfelf on being an imitator of Marcus
Aurelius, flept hardly, and lived on vegetables. Some of
the

body was transparent and splendid, like the pureſt
and cleareſt light. When he was admitted within
the ſacred incloſure, Bacchus ſaid, " King Saturn
" and Father Jupiter, can any thing imperfect be
" allowed among the Gods?" No anſwer being
returned, " Let us ſend then," proceeded he,
" for ſome lover of pleaſure." ' But,' replied Jupiter, ' it is not lawful for any one to be admitted
' here who does not worſhip us *.' " Let judgment
" therefore," ſaid Bacchus, " be pronounced on
" him in the veſtibule. We will call, with your
" leave, a prince, not indeed unwarlike †, but
                                        " ſoftened

the Epiſtles of Julian give us reaſon to think, that he was
frequently ill. But it is more eaſy to wear the beard of
Marcus Aurelius, to copy his auſterities, and to ruin one's
health, like him, than to acquire his ſolidity of genius,
his love of virtue for virtue's ſake, his contempt of glory;
and, if I may venture ſo to expreſs myſelf, that ſobriety
of wiſdom, which was the foundation of his character.
                                        LA BLETERIE.

* Ου Θεμίιον ειςω Φοιλαν ανδρι, μη τα ημίιερα ζηλευῆι. M. de la
Bleterie tranſlates this, " Whoever does not take us for
" his model cannot ſet foot here;" but I underſtand it,
" Whoever is not a worſhipper of us," &c. in alluſion to
Conſtantine, who was a Chriſtian. It is obſervable, however, that Conſtantine and his ſons are before mentioned as
entering the aſſembly and ſitting ſome time.

† If Conſtantine had been a ſlave to his pleaſures, ſo far
as to deſerve, though he had declared for Chriſtianity, the
protection of Bacchus, he would not have been ſo diſtinguiſhed in war and in peace ; he would not have reigned
ſo glorioully for more than thirty years, that is, much
longer than any Emperor had reigned ſince Auguſtus.
This general reflection may be ſufficient to ſhew the injuſtice
of Julian. Hiſtory repreſents Conſtantine to us as a prince
always engaged in ſome uſeful project, giving frequent au-

" foftened by pleafure and enjoyment. Let Con-
" STANTINE come as far as the veftibule."

This ……… diences, drawing up his laws and difpatches himfelf, borrowing from his fleep time to read the holy fcriptures, and
to compofe fome religious difcourfes, which he pronounced
in public, endeavouring to obtain the affiftance of Heaven
by prayer, fafting, and abftinence from lawful pleafures.

If we deduct from thefe elogiums whatever may be taken
from panegyrics, if we fet afide the good that is faid of him
by Chriftian writers, and even the praifes that are given him
by fuch of the Pagans as may be fufpected of flattery, having
written in his reign, or in that of his fons, I mean Libanius,
and the hiftorian Praxagoras; in a word, if Conftantine be
judged by the teftimony of Eutropius, who dedicates his
work to Valens, and by what is faid of him by that Victor
who wrote in the reign of the fons of Theodofius I. the
refult will be, that Conftantine was a prince of an elevated
genius, active, vigilant, laborious, and, even independently of
what he did for the Chriftian religion, and notwithftanding
the blemifhes that are found in his life, that he deferved
the title of Great. The teftimony of thofe authors is
the more important, as they fpare neither his faults nor
failings.

Zofimus, a partial writer, and the declared enemy of
the Chriftian Emperors, is the only one, befides Julian,
who accufes him of being devoted to pleafures. Yet Zofimus throws this reproach only on the latter years of his
reign. In fact Conftantine could have given no pretext
for that accufation till after the foundation of New
Rome. Tired of wars, and even of victories, he thought
that he had acquired a right to tafte the fruit of his
labours. Without remaining in inactivity, or living in
voluptuoufnefs (for, to the end of his life, he employed
himfelf in affairs of ftate, and in thofe of the church),
he gave fome brilliant entertainments. His court was
magnificent; he procured himfelf fome amufements that
had nothing criminal in the eyes of the world, and which
perhaps he thought were allowed him becaufe he had
not yet been baptifed.

It

This being allowed (the mode of their contention having been previously settled) Mercury advifed, that every one fhould feverally fpeak for
himfelf, and that the Gods fhould then give their
votes. But of this Apollo difapproved, infifting,
that truth only, and not eloquence, or the charms
of oratory, ought to be difcuffed and examined
by the Gods. Jupiter, wifhing to oblige all, and,
at the fame time, defirous to prolong the affembly,
replied, " There can be no inconvenience in di-
" recting each of them to fpeak by a certain
" meafure of water *, and afterwards we may
" interrogate them and fcrutinife their thoughts."
Silenus jocofely added, ' Take care, Neptune, or
' TRAJAN and ALEXANDER †, miftaking the water

' for

It is fuppofed that the imagination and malignity of
Julian working on this canvas might make Conftantine a
flave to pleafure. Let us never forget that Julian detefted
his uncle as the deftroyer of Paganifm; and that he was
by tafte, by principle, by vanity, an enemy to all pleafures.
How much muft the magnificence of Conftantine have
wounded a man who gave into the oppofite extreme, who
carried philofophy to fuch an excefs, as to defpife decorum,
and who, by the manners which he afcribes to himfelf in
the Mifopogon, feems to have been defirous that his picture fhould be the companion of that of Diogenes !
                                                LA BLETERIE.

* When the Greeks and Romans would give orators a
certain fixed time, they employed hour-glaffes of water,
to which they gave the name of *clepfydra*, which the modern
Latinifts apply very improperly to our fands.   *Ibid.*

† It is well known that Alexander was very fond of
wine, and that in drunkennefs he was capable of the
                    N 3   greateft

' for nectar, will fwallow it all, and fo leave none
' for the reft.'   Neptune anfwered, " They were
" much more fond of your draughts, Silenus,
" than of mine.   It behoves you therefore to be
" rather afraid of your own vines than of my
" fprings:"   Silenus was chagrined, and made no
reply, but afterwards attended folely to the dif-
putants.   Mercury then proclaimed,

     * ' The arbiter of prizes due
        ' To fignal merit now begins.
        ' Delay no longer, Time exhorts,
        ' But lend your ears to what the voice
        ' Of herald Mercury proclaims.
        ' Ye kings, to whofe fuperior fway
        ' Of old fubmiffive nations bow'd,
        ' Who launch'd in fight the hoftile fpear,

greateft exceffes. His laft debauch coft him his life. As
for Trajan, he was obliged to forbid the execution of any
orders which he might give at coming from a great entertainment. One of the methods of which Hadrian availed
himfelf to gain his friendfhip was to caroufe with him at
table.   La Bleterie.

  * See Lucian, at the end of his Demoniacs.   Petau.
The three firft lines only (in the original) are quoted
from that work.

This proclamation, in the tafte of thofe which were
made in Greece at the opening of the games, confifts of
forms ufed on thofe occafions, and of ends of verfes taken
from the Greek poets that we have, and thofe whom we
have not. This kind of cento has in the original,
or rather had, a merit which we may imagine, but
which it is impoffible to transfufe into another language.
                                          La Bleterie.
  M. de la Bleterie has only given the fenfe. The Englifh
is almoft literal.

                      ' Advance,

‘ Advance, contend, with prudent minds
‘ Oppofe your rivals, and await
‘ The juft, th’ impartial will of Heaven !
‘ Wifdom thefe think the end of life,
‘ Thofe, vengeance on their foes to wreak,
‘ And ferve their friends : of life, of toil,
‘ Pleafure fome make the fingle view,
‘ Feafts, nuptials, all that feeds their eyes :
‘ From dainty ornaments of drefs,
‘ Or rings, with precious gems adorn’d,
‘ Others fuperior blifs derive.
‘ Jove will the victory decree.’

Mercury having made this proclamation, the combatants drew lots : and the lot happened to concur with the love of pre-eminence habitual to CÆSAR. This augmented his pride and arrogance ; fo that ALEXANDER would have declined the conteft, had he not been encouraged and perfuaded by Hercules. ALEXANDER obtained the next turn of fpeaking after CÆSAR. When all the reft had had their proper turns affigned them, CÆSAR thus began :

“ It was my good fortune, O Jupiter and ye “ Gods, to be born, after many heroes, in that “ illuftrious city, which has extended her do- “ minion farther than any other ; fo that they all “ may be fatisfied, if they obtain the fecond place. “ For what other city, deducing its origin from “ three thoufand men, has, in lefs than fix hun- “ dred years, carried its conquefts to the utmoft

N 4   “ extremities

" extremities of the earth? What other nation has
" produced so many diftinguifhed warriors and
" legiflators, or fuch devout worfhippers of the
" Gods? Born in a city fo renowned, I furpaffed,
" by my actions, not only my contemporaries, but
" all the heroes that ever lived. Of my own
" countrymen I know not one that will deny me
" the fuperiority. But as this Grecian is fo pre-
" fumptuous, which of his actions will he pretend
" to put in competition with mine? His Perfian
" trophies perhaps, as if he knew not how many
" I won from Pompey. And who was the moft ex-
" perienced general, Pompey or Darius? Which of
" them commanded the braveft troops? Inftead of
" the refufe of mankind, Pompey had in his army
" more warlike nations than were ever fubject to
" Darius; of Europeans, thofe who had often
" routed the hoftile Afiatics, and of them the
" moft valiant; Italians, Illyrians, and Gauls.
" Having mentioned the Gauls, can the Getic
" exploits of ALEXANDER be compared with my
" conqueft of Gaul? He paffed the Danube once;
" I twice paffed the Rhine; and of my German
" victories no one can difpute the glory. I fought
" with Arioviftus *.

" I was the firft Roman who dared to crofs the
" German ocean †. Though this was a wonder-.

* The antithefis is this : " Alexander met with no op-
" pofition in his Getic expedition, and therefore he
" marched with impunity. But I was refifted by Arioviftus."
PETAU.

† In the original, της εκτος θαλασσης, " the outward fea."
The inner was the Mediterranean.

" ful

" ful atchievement, however it may be admired,
" more glorious was my intrepidity in being the
" firſt who leaped on ſhore *. Of the Helvetic
" and Iberian nations I ſay nothing; nor have I
" mentioned my actions in Gaul, where I took
" above three hundred towns †, and defeated two
" millions of men. Great as thefe actions were,
" that which followed was greater and more il-
" luſtrious. Being obliged to wage war with my
" fellow-citizens, I vanquiſhed the unconquered
" and invincible Romans. If we ſhould be judged
" by the number of our battles, I fought thrice
" as many as are aſcribed to ALEXANDER by his
" greateſt panegyriſts; if by the number of towns
" taken, not in Aſia only, but alſo in Europe, I
" reduced more. ALEXANDER ſaw and rav'rſed
" Ægypt; I, while I feaſted there, ſubdued it.
" Will you alſo compare the clemency of each of
" us, when victorious? I pardoned my enemies,

* He alludes here to the deſcent which Cæſar made on
Britain. But the memory of Julian deceives him. He at-
tributes to Cæſar what Cæſar himſelf ſays (*l. v. de bello
Gallico*) of the eagle-bearer of the tenth legion. " He
" who bore the eagle of the tenth legion, after beſeeching
" the Gods, that the event might be proſperous to the
" legion, ſaid, ' Leap aſhore, ſoldiers, unleſs you would
' betray the eagle-to the enemy.' " Saying this, with a
" loud voice, he threw himſelf out of the ſhip, and ad-
" vanced with the eagle towards the enemy, &c." It was
Alexander, who, after paſſing the Helleſpont, firſt leaped
aſhore completely armed. Such a proceeding is more ſuit-
able to the impetuous valour of Alexander than to the
phlegmatic and ſedate courage of Cæſar. LA BLETERIE.
† See Plutarch.

" and

" and received from them such a return as Nemesis
" has revenged. He never spared his enemies, nor
" even his friends. In particular, as you dispute
" the pre-eminence, and will not immediately yield
" to me, like the rest, you compel me to mention
" your cruel behaviour to the Thebans *. On
" the contrary, how great was my humanity to
" the Helvetii! The cities of the former were
" burnt by you; the cities of the latter, burnt by
" their own inhabitants, were rebuilt by me †.
" Which, in short, was most illustrious; your
" defeating ten thousand Greeks, or my repulsing
" the attacks of a hundred and fifty thousand Ro-
" mans? Much more could I add, both of ALEX-
" ANDER and myself; but as I never had leisure
" to study the art of oratory ‡, you must excuse
" me, and, forming a just and impartial judge-
" ment both from what I have said, and what I
" have omitted, will, I doubt not, give me the
" superiority."

* When Alexander took Thebes by storm, the inhabitants were slain and destroyed for several hours without
regard to sex or age; and the city was afterwards razed,
the house of Pindar only excepted.

† The Helvetii having abandoned their country, and
burnt their towns, as they were preparing to enter Gaul,
were defeated by Cæsar, sent back to their country, and
ordered to re-build their houses.

‡ In the original, το λεγειν εξεμελετησα, or εξεμελησα. Perhaps he does not mean to say, that Cæsar had no excellence in speaking; for he was reckoned among the
orators of his time; witness Cicero, in his Brutus; but
that he was not used to speak without premeditation.

CANTOCLARUS.

CÆSAR

CÆSAR thus concluded, but feeming defirous of faying ftill more; ALEXANDER, who before had with difficulty reftrained himfelf, could refrain no longer, but, with much anxiety and emotion, thus began :

"How long, O Jupiter and ye Gods, fhall I
" filently bear the infolence of this boafter *! He
" fets no bounds, you fee, to his praife of himfelf,
" or to his abufe of me. Much better would it
" have become him to have abftained equally from
" both, as both are alike intolerable, but chiefly
" that of depreciating my conduct, which he made
" the example of his own. Such is his affurance,
" that he has dared to ridicule his own model.
" You fhould have recollected, CÆSAR, the tears
" which you fhed on hearing of the memorials
" that were raifed in honour of my deeds †. But
" you afterwards owed your elevation to Pompey,
" who, though he was really infignificant ‡, was
" idolifed by his countrymen. As to his African

* This is not unlike the beginning of Cicero's Oration againft Catiline, *Quoufque tandem abutére, Catilina, patientiâ noftrâ?*

† At Gades, obferving in the temple of Hercules a ftatue of Alexander the Great, he fighed, and, as if afhamed of his own fupinenefs in having done nothing memorable at an age when Alexander had conquered the world, he importunately urged to be recalled to Rome, that he might be ready on the fpot to embrace any occafion that might offer for more important undertakings. *Sueton. Jul. Cæfar. c. 7.* See alfo Plutarch.

‡ It is plain that Julian had read the Epiftles of Cicero to Atticus. LA BLETERIE.

" triumph,

" triumph *, no great exploit, his fame was owing
" to the weaknefs and inactivity of the confuls †.
" The fervile war ‡ was not waged with men, but
" with the moft abandoned flaves, and it was con-
" ducted by Craffus and Lucius §, though Pompey
" had the name and the reputation. Armenia and
" the neighbouring provinces were conquered by
" Lucullus; yet for thefe alfo Pompey triumphed.
" He was then flattered by his fellow-citizens,
" and named the Great. But than whom of his
" predeceffors was he greater? Which of his
" actions is comparable to thofe of Marius, or of
" the two Scipios? or of Camillus, who was almoft
" as much the founder of Rome as this Quirinus,
" having rebuilt his city when it was almoft falling?
" For they did not arrogate to themfelves the
" works of others, as is ufual in buildings founded
" and finifhed at the public expence, where the
" magiftrate, who has only plaiftered the walls,
" on completing the edifice, infcribes the foun-
" dation-ftone. But thefe heroes, as public ar-
" tificers and architects, have juftly immortalifed
" their own names. It is no wonder therefore,
" that you vanquifhed Pompey, fcratching his

* Pompey, at the age of twenty-nine, when he was only
a knight, was fent into Africa to encounter the party of
Marius.   LA BLETERIE.

† M. Tullius Decula and Cn. Cornelius Dolabella.

‡ The war of Spartacus.

§ Lucius Gellius. See Plutarch's Life of Craffus, and
Appian, *Bell. Civil.* I.

" head,

" head *, and more refembling a fox than a lion.
" When he was deferted by Fortune, who had
" long favoured him, you eafily conquered him
" fingle. But that your fuccefs was owing to no
" fuperior abilities is evident; for being in want
" of provifions (which, you know, is no fmall fault
" of a general †), you fought, and were defeated.‡.
" And if Pompey, by his imprudence, or folly, or
" becaufe he could not govern his army, when he
" fhould have protracted the war, gave battle §,
" and did not purfue his victory, his failure was
" the confequence of his own mifconduct, not of
" your military fkill. The Perfians, on the con-
" trary, though in every refpect well prepared and
" amply provided, fubmitted to my dominion.
" And as it becomes a good man and a wife

* In the original, δακτυλω κινωμενε, which the French
tranflator has paraphrafed, " who, for fear of difarranging
" his hair, did not venture to touch his head but with his
" finger's end." Yet Ammianus (xvii. 11.) mentioning
two ludicrous faults that the envious imputed to Pompey,
fays that this was one, quod genuino quodam more caput uno
digito fcalpebat; " that he fcratched his head, in a par-
" ticular manner, with one of his fingers."

† Julian himfelf committed the fame fault in his Perfian
expedition.

‡ At the battle of Dyrrhacium.

§ This interpretation agrees better with the fenfe, and
with hiftory, than the proper fignification of the Greek
words, [which is, " when he fhould have declined to give
" battle."] For certain it is, from Appian, Plutarch, and
other writers, that Pompey did not act like a prudent general in offering battle to Cæfar at Pharfalia, when Cæfar
was in fuch a fituation, that he muft eafily have been reduced by his want of neceffaries. CANTOCLARUS.

" prince

" prince to act not only with moderation, but with
" juftice, I took arms to revenge the Greeks on
" the Perfians, and to free Greece from civil war.
" Nor was it ever my intention to ravage Greece,
" but thofe only, who would have prevented my
" march againft Perfia, I chaftifed. You, after
" fubduing the Gauls and Germans, turned your
" arms againft your own country. What can be
" worfe, what more infamous ?

" You have mentioned, with a fneer, ' my de-
' feating ten thoufand Greeks.' " That you your-
" felves fprung from the Greeks, and that the
" Greeks inhabited the greateft part of Italy, I
" well know; but on this I will not infift. With
" a fmall nation of them, the Ætolians, your
" neighbours, you thought it of great confequence
" to make an alliance ; but after they had fought
" for you, why did you reduce them, and that
" not eafily, to fubjection? If then, in the old age,
" as it has been called, of Greece, you could
" fcarce reduce, not the whole, but one fmall
" nation, which was fcarce known when Greece
" was in her vigour, what would have been the
" event, if you had been obliged to contend with
" the Greeks when flourifhing and united ? How
" much you were alarmed by the invafion of
" Pyrrhus you need not be reminded. As you
" think the conqueft of Perfia fuch a trifle, and
" depreciate an enterprife fo glorious, tell me
" why, after a war of above two thoufand years,
" you have never fubdued a fmall province be-
                                        " yond

" yond the Tigris *, fubject to the Parthians?
" Shall I inform you? The darts of the Perfians
" prevented you. Antony, who ferved under
" your command, can give you an account of
" them †. But in lefs than ten years I conquered
" both Perfia and India. After this, do you dare
" to contend with me, who, trained to war from
" my childhood, performed fuch deeds, that the
" remembrance of them, though they have not
" been fufficiently celebrated by hiftorians, will
" live for ever, like thofe of the invincible Her-
" cules, of whom I was the follower and imitator?
" I rivalled, in fhort, my anceftor Achilles, and,
" admiring Hercules, I trod in his fteps as nearly
" as a mortal can follow a God. Thus much, O
" ye Gods, it was neceffary for me to fay in my
" own defence againft an opponent, whom per-
" haps it might have been better to have filently
" defpifed. If I was guilty of any cruelties, the

* Meaning Babylonia, where the Romans never made any folid conqueft. It was the northern part of Mefopo-tamia.　　　　　　　　　　　　　　　LA BLETERIE.

† Antony, having entered Media, thought himfelf happy to efcape with the remains of his army, after lofing twenty thoufand men, and all his baggage. Julian might have quoted many other Roman generals and Emperors [Craffus in particular], who were worfe treated even than Antony, in their expeditions againft the Parthians, or Perfians. But he did not forefee that he himfelf would foon add to the number of thofe unfortunate heroes. *Ibid.*

It is impoffible to read the interefting narrative of Plutarch (tom. v. p. 102 — 116.) without perceiving that Mark Antony and Julian were purfued by the fame enemies, and involved in the fame diftrefs.　　　　GIBBON.

" innocent

" innocent were not the objects, but such as had
" frequently and notoriously offended, and had
" made no proper use of their opportunities.
" And my offences even against them were fol-
" lowed by Repentance *, a very wise Goddess,
" and the preserver of those who have erred. As
" for my chastising the ambitious, who always
" hated and had often injured me, in that I
" thought myself excusable."

This military harangue being concluded, the attendant of Neptune gave the hour-glass to OCTAVI-
ANUS, measuring to him a very small quantity of
water, and at the same time, reminding him of his
insolence to that Deity †. On which having reflected with his usual sagacity, omitting to say any
thing of others, he thus began :

" Instead of depreciating the actions of others,
" O Jupiter and ye Gods, I will confine my whole
" speech to what concerns myself. In my youth

* Μεταμέλεια. This Goddess, thus deified by Julian,
seems rather taken from the Christian scriptures, than the
Heathen mythology. The French translator styles her
Métanée, from Μετάνοια, and " a celebrated retreat for pe-
" nitents, known in Ecclesiastical history by the name of
" *la Métanée*."

† In the war which Octavius waged against Sextus
Pompey, many reproach him as well for some of his ex-
pressions, as for his conduct, having said, when his fleet
was lost in a storm, that " he would gain the victory even
" in spite of Neptune." And accordingly, when the Cir-
censian games were next performed, he excluded the image
of that God from the solemnity. *Suet. Aug. c.* XVI.

Julian himself, in like manner, swore afterwards, in a
passion, that he would never sacrifice again to Mars. See
Ammianus, XXIV. 6.

" I had

" I had the government of my native city, like
" this illuftrious ALEXANDER. The German wars,
" like my father CÆSAR, I happily concluded.
" Involved in civil diffenfions, I fubdued Ægypt
" at Actium in a fea-fight. I defeated Brutus and
" Caffius at Philippi, and I made the fon of Pom-
" pey contribute to my glory. Such, however,
" was my attachment to philofophy, that, inftead
" of being difgufted at the freedom affumed by
" Athenodorus *, I was pleafed with it, and re-
" vered him as a preceptor, or rather as a parent.
" Areus † alfo was my friend and confident. And,
" upon the whole, I was never guilty of the leaft

---

* A very bold action is related of this philofopher: Auguftus, whofe behaviour was never very guarded, fometimes made fome private affignations which might have
been fatal to him. One day, when a Roman lady was to
go to the palace incognito, Athenodorus got into a clofe
chair, and ordered himfelf to be carried to the apartment
of the Emperor. Then, ftepping out, with a fword in
his hand, " See," faid he, " to what you expofe yourfelf!
" Are you not afraid that fome republican, or an enraged
" hufband, fhould take fuch an opportunity of putting
" you to death?" Auguftus thanked the philofopher for
his leffon, and promifed to reform. He took greater precautions, no doubt, for the future, but his reformation
went no farther. Livia, it is well known, to maintain her
afcendant over him, was obliged to connive at his infidelities.
LA BLETERIE.

† Julian in his Epiftles mentions more than once the
philofopher Areus, and the efteem which Auguftus had
for him. Certainly if by philofophy are meant the philofophers, fhe cannot but be well fatisfied with Auguftus.
Such equivocal expreffions are too common. *Ibid.*

Areus is mentioned in the Epiftle to Themiftius, (fee p.
25. and note *) and in Epiftle LI.

VOL. I.   O   " offence

" offence againſt philoſophy. As Rome, I ſaw, had
" been frequently reduced to the laſt extremity by
" inteſtine diviſions, I ſo re-eſtabliſhed her affairs,
" as to render them, by your aſſiſtance, O ye
" Gods, firm and adamantine. Without indulg-
" ing an inſatiable ambition, I ſtudiouſly endeav-
" oured to enlarge her dominions; but I concurred
" with nature in fixing the rivers Danube and
" Euphrates as their boundaries. After having ſub-
" dued the Scythians and Thracians, I did not
" employ the long reign with which you indulged
" me in meditating war after war, but devoted my
" leiſure to the correction of the evils which war
" had occaſioned, and to legiſlation; in which, I
" apprehend, I did not conſult the public wel-
" fare leſs than my predeceſſors; nay, if I muſt
" boldly ſpeak the truth, I conſulted it more than
" any who have governed ſuch an empire. For
" ſome who have commanded armies, when they
" might at length have reſted in peace, have made
" one war the pretence for another, as the litigious
" contrive law-ſuits. Others, when forced into a
" war, have been immerſed in pleaſure *, and have
" preferred the moſt infamous purſuits, not only
" to their glory, but even to their lives. Well
" weighing all theſe things, I do not think myſelf
" entitled to the loweſt place. But it becomes
" me to acquieſce in whatever you, O ye Gods,
" may pleaſe to determine."

* Alluding to Antony.

T R A-

Trajan was appointed to harangue next. Though he had a talent for speaking *, such was his indolence, that he usually employed Sura to compose his orations. Bawling, rather than speaking, he displayed to the Gods his Getic and Parthian trophies. He then lamented his old age, as if that had prevented him from extending his Parthian conquests. ' You fool,' said Silenus, ' you ' reigned twenty years, and this ALEXANDER only ' twelve. Why, then, do you not condemn your ' own indolence, instead of throwing the blame on ' want of time?' Provoked at this taunt, for he was not deficient in eloquence, though it was often blunted by intemperance, TRAJAN added,

" O Jupiter, and ye Gods, when I assumed the " reins of government, I found the empire in a " torpid and divided state, occasioned partly by

---

* Trajan, it is said, had written the history of his wars with the Dacians. There is a short Greek epigram by him in the Anthologia. He was not learned ; but he esteemed and favoured men of letters. When he triumphed over the Dacians, he had in his car the sophist Dion, Chrysostom, and, during the procession, he frequently turned to speak to him. L. Licinius Sura was the confident of Trajan, who loaded him with riches, and raised him thrice to the consulship. The enemies of Sura accused him of a design against the life of the Emperor. Trajan, by way of answer, went to sup with Sura, had his eyes examined by the surgeon, and was shaved by the barber, of Sura, and supped with great gaiety. On the next day he said to the accusers, " Confess that, if Sura wanted to dis- " patch me, he yesterday missed a fine opportunity." After the death of Sura, Trajan borrowed the pen of Hadrian.

LA BLETERIE.

O 2

" the

" the tyranny which had long prevailed at home,
" and partly by the insults of the Getes abroad *.
" I did not hesitate, however, singly to attack the
" nations beyond the Danube.   That of the Getes
" I subdued and extirpated; of all the most war-
" like, not only by their bodily strength, but by
" the courage with which they are inspired by the
" doctrine of their renowned Zamolxis †.   For the
                                                 " firm

* By the Getes may be understood the Dacians.   Decebalus, king of the Dacians, had obliged Domitian to purchase a peace, of which he endeavoured to cover the difgrace by a magnificent triumph.   ". The poets of the
" time," says M. de Tillemont, " equalled his pretended
" victory to those of Alexander and Cæsar."   For that
they were paid, or expected to be paid;. but the Romans
did not give them credit.   Trajan, who was not disposed
to be tributary to the Barbarians, availing himself of the
first infraction which Decebalus made, or seemed to make,
of the treaty, marched against the Dacians.   They de-
fended themselves with much courage, and even conduct.
But at length Decebalus, being reduced to the last extremities, destroyed himself, and Dacia was made a province.   La Bleterie.

† Zamolxis was the lawgiver of the Getes. [See p. 152.]
Some Greeks pretend that he had been the slave of Pythagoras; but Herodotus thinks Zamolxis much more
ancient.   The opinion of the Getes as to the immortality of
the soul had an affinity to the metempsychosis : They said
that the dead went to find Zamolxis, and every five years
they sent an express to represent to him the exigencies of
the nation.   See Herod. *l.* iv. 49.

It must not be supposed, that, before Zamolxis, those
people believed that the soul perished with the body.   Zamolxis only published his own private ideas concerning the
state of separate souls.   No nation is or ever was persuaded
that all ends with death.   No nation has received from its
lawgivers the belief of another life ; the lawgivers have
                                                  every

" firm perfuafion that they fhall not perifh, but
" only change their place of abode, makes them
" always prepared as for a journey. This enter-
" prife I completed in lefs than five years. Of
" all the Emperors who preceded me * not one
" was fo mild to his fubjects, nor can that be
" contefted with me even with this CÆSAR, be-
" fore unrivalled in clemency, nor by any other.
" The Parthians, till they infulted me, I thought it
" unjuft to attack ; but after they had infulted me,
" neither my age, nor the laws which allowed me
" to quit the fervice †, prevented my invading

every where found it. Some have not mentioned this
doctrine, becaufe it was fufficiently eftablifhed. Others
have mentioned it, not in order to prove it, which was by
no means neceffary, but to particularife it, and to difplay its confequences. The perfuafion of the immortality of the foul, as well as that of the exiftence of God,
is the tenet of mankind; and the faith of nature.
The contrary error is either the frenzy of a philofopher
who choofes to be fingular, or the interefted wifh of a li-
bertine.   · LA BLETERIE.

   * In the original, Παντων των προ εμε γεγονοτων αυτοκρατορων
ωφθην τοις υπηκοοις πραοτατος, " Of all the Emperors who pre-
" ceded me I was the mildeft to my fubjects." This paffage, by which Trajan confounds himfelf with his predeceffors, is fimilar to that of Milton (noticed by Addifon in
the Spectator, N° 285.) in which Adam and Eve are ranked
among their pofterity.
      Adam, the goodlieft man of men fince born
      His fons, the faireft of her daughters Eve.
   † Regularly, every Roman, after twenty years fervice,
was exempted from bearing arms. Trajan had ferved from
his earlieft youth. He was fifty-five years old, at leaft,
perhaps fifty-feven, when he made war with Cofroes, king
of Parthia.   LA BLETERIE.

                              " them.

" them. Thus circumstanced, am not I, who was
" eminently mild to my subjects and formidable
" to my enemies, and who revered your divine
" daughter, Philosophy, justly entitled to superior
" honours, and even to the first rank ?"

Trajan having concluded, it was allowed that
he excelled all in clemency, a virtue particularly
pleasing to the Gods.

Marcus Aurelius then beginning to speak, Silenus said, in a low voice, to Bacchus, ' Let us
' hear which of his wonderful paradoxes and
' aphorisms this Stoic will produce.' But he,
fixing his eyes on Jupiter and the other Gods, thus
addressed them :

" I have no occasion, O Jupiter and ye Gods,
" to harangue or dispute. If you were ignorant
" of my actions, it would be proper for me to ac-
" quaint you with them ; but as you are privy to
" them, and nothing is concealed from you, you
" will honour me as I deserve."

Thus Marcus, as in every thing else, seemed
worthy of admiration for his extraordinary prudence in knowing when to speak, and when to be
silent *.

* This is an imitation of a verse of Æschylus, quoted
by Aulus Gellius. In this particular, the pretended copy
of Marcus Aurelius did not resemble his original. Julian
spoke much and often. *Linguæ fusioris et admodùm raro
silentis,* says Ammianus.   La Bleterie.

Con-

CONSTANTINE * was then summoned to speak. He entered the lists with confidence; but when he reflected on the actions of his competitors, his own seemed trivial and inconsiderable. He defeated, it is true, two tyrants †; one of them unwarlike and pusil-

* Every impartial reader must perceive and condemn the partiality of Julian against his uncle and the Christian religion. On this occasion the interpreters are compelled, by a more sacred interest, to renounce their allegiance, and desert the cause of their author.　　　GIBBON.

The reflections, or sarcasms, on the other candidates are confined to Silenus, or their antagonists. On this occasion Julian is betrayed by his prejudice into a breach of the unity of character before observed, by taking, or rather making Mercury, his informant, take a decided part against Constantine.

† Julian uses his utmost endeavours to depreciate the exploits of his uncle. Constantine was a great general; and perhaps his most substantial fault is his having been too warlike. If he had good fortune, he deserved it; and the Pagans themselves acknowledged that his talents were equal to his good fortune. *Innumeræ in eo animi corporisque virtutes claruerunt*, says Eutropius. *Militaris gloriæ appetentissimus, fortunâ in bellis prosperâ fuit; verùm ita ut non superaret industriam.* I know that Maxentius was a kind of Sardanapalus, who, remaining at Rome, while his collegue made war, said, that he alone was Emperor, and that the others were his lieutenants; that he considered the going from his palace to the gardens of Sallust as a long journey, &c. But he had 200,000 troops, a great deal of money, and good officers. " To dethrone him, Constantine," says a contemporary author, " with an army less numerous " than that of Alexander when he marched against Darius," that is, with no more than 40,000 men, " must have forced " the pass of Succi, and have gained the battles of Turin, " Brescia, Verona, and Rome, of which the three first, " at least, must have been very obstinate and bloody."

With regard to Licinius, he was not above fifty years old when he was defeated at the battle of Cibal, and about

sixty

pufillanimous, the other unfortunate and advanced in years, and both of them odious to Gods and men. As for his exploits againſt the Barbarians, they were ridiculous. For he, in a manner, paid them tribute, to indulge his love of pleaſure. He ſtood therefore at a diſtance from the Gods, near the entrance of the moon, of whom he was enamoured *, and, gazing only on her, was regardleſs of the victory.

How-

ſixty when he loſt the battles of Adrianople and Chryſopolis, which rendered Conſtantine maſter of the empire. Licinius, with all his vices, was brave and ſkilful in the conduct of war. He made his troops obſerve the ancient diſcipline with extreme ſeverity. Whatever Julian may ſay of him, his age had not at all abated his courage, any more than the vigour of his conſtitution. He was always proſperous when he had not Conſtantine to encounter. Add, that the reproach with which ſome writers have branded Conſtantine of breaking his word with Licinius, by putting him to death after having promiſed him life, ſeems removed by the ſilence of Julian. As to the victories which he gained over the Barbarians, that is, over the Franks, the Germans, the Sarmatians, and the Goths, Julian is the only one who deſpiſes thoſe " exploits." It is well known that Conſtantine, far from " paying tribute" to the Barbarians, freed the Romans from that which they paid to the Goths under the honourable name of penſion. But as he took into the ſervice of the empire 40,000 men of that nation, the pay which he gave them is probably that which Julian calls " tribute."   LA BLETERIE.

   * Why does Julian make Conſtantine " enamoured of " the moon ?" This is an ænigma which I have endeavoured to ſolve. Am I ſo fortunate as to have at laſt ſucceeded ? The reader ſhall determine. Antiquaries agree, that, from the earlieſt times, the creſcent was the diſtinction, or, as we ſhould now expreſs it, the arms of Byzantium, as it ſtill continues to be of Conſtantinople. Thus,
when

However, as it was neceſſary for him to ſpeak,
"In theſe particulars," ſaid he, "I am ſuperior
"to my opponents; to the Macedonian, in having
"fought againſt the Romans, Germans, and Scy-
".thians, inſtead of Aſiatic Barbarians; to CÆSAR
"and OCTAVIANUS, in not having vanquiſhed,
"like them,. good and virtuous citizens, but the
"moſt cruel and wicked tyrants. : To TRAJAN'
"alſo, for my ſtrenuous exertions againſt tyrants,
"I deſerve no leſs to be preferred. To recover
"the province * which he conquered ſeems to me
"equally

when Julian reproaches his uncle with being enamoured of
the moon, and attending ſolely to her, inſtead of thinking
of the victory, the author, without detriment to the other
ideas to which this reproach may give riſe, principally
means, that Conſtantine, wholly devoted to the care of
founding and embelliſhing his new city, had neglected the
affairs of ſtate, and ſuffered his laurels to wither. This is
exactly what Zoſimus, the copyer of Eunapius and the
echo of Julian, imputes to him, by ſaying, that " Con-
" ſtantine, after the foundation of Conſtantinople, had no
" ſucceſs in war; διέλεισι πολεμον εδενα καλορβωρκως, and that
" he ſuffered the Barbarians to inſult him in his new ca-
" pital." LA BLETERIE.
The above ingenious ſolution of a difficulty, before inſu-
perable, will, I doubt not, be approved by every reader,
and adopted by all future commentators on the Cæſars.
* Meaning Dacia, which Trajan had reduced to a province. Aurelian having abandoned it, it was uſurped by
the Goths. There can be no doubt of Conſtantine having
carried his arms beyond the Danube. The two Victors
enumerate, among his great actions, his having made a
bridge over that river. But it is certain, that he did
not conquer the country of the Dacians. I am convinced
that Julian, in order to render him ridiculous, repreſents
him as affecting the importance of a conqueror on account
of

" equally meritorious: perhaps to regain is more
" laudable than to gain.   As to this MARCUS, he,
" by saying nothing for himself, yields us all the
" precedency."

'But, CONSTANTINE,' said Silenus, 'why do
' you not mention, among your great works, the
' gardens of Adonis *? " What mean you, " replied
CONSTANTINE, " by the gardens of Adonis † ?"

of some advantages which he had gained over the Goths
settled in Dacia; and perhaps for some forts which he had
erected on the left of the Danube.   With the same view,
Julian makes him draw, from the silence of Marcus
Aurelius, the most absurd, and, I may venture to say,
the most foolish conclusion that can be imagined.

LA BLETERIE.

* Thus Suidas: " The gardens of Adonis consisted of
" lettuce and fennel, which were sown in pots.   It is used
" as a proverb of things immature, or, when in season,
" slight, and not rooted, not lasting, but adhering only
" to the surface."   See Athen. l. IV. c. 8. and Arrian's
Epictetus.   CANTOCLARUS.

Thus Shakspeare says,
Thy promises are like Adonis' gardens,
That one day bloom'd, and fruitful were the next.

1 Hen. IV. Act. I. Sc. II.

And Mr. Bramstone, in his Man of Taste.   (Dodsley's
Poems, Vol. I.) says,
Pots o'er the door I'll place, like cits balconies,
Which Bentley calls the gardens of Adonis;
and refers to Bentley's Milton, b. IX. ver. 439.

———————— those gardens feign'd
Or of reviv'd Adonis.

He might have referred to much more ancient writers
than Milton or his commentator, whom one would not
have expected to have been ridiculed for this expression by
a scholar.

† Could Constantine, though a Christian, be ignorant
of the rites of a religion which he had long practised?   If
I mistake not, he is here meant to be accused on the most
common subjects.   LA BLETERIE.

' Pots,'

' Pots,' anfwered Silenus, ' filled with earth, in which
' women fow herbs in honour of that lover * of
' Venus. They flourifh for a fhort time, but foon
' fade.' At this CONSTANTINE blufhed, knowing
it to be intended as a farcafm on his own actions.

Silence being proclaimed, it was expected that
the Gods would immediately have determined the
pre-eminence by their votes. But they thought it
proper firft to examine the intentions of the candidates, and not merely to collect them from their
actions, in which Fortune had the greateft fhare;
and that Goddefs, being prefent, loudly reproached
them all, OCTAVIANUS alone excepted, who, fhe
faid, had always been grateful to her. Of this the
Gods apprifed Mercury, and commanded him to
begin with afking ALEXANDER " what he
" thought the higheft excellence, and what
" was his principal view in all the great actions
" and labours of his life?" He replied, ' Univerfal
' conqueft.' " And in this," faid Mercury, " did
" you think you fucceeded?" ' Certainly,' anfwered ALEXANDER. Silenus added, with a fneering laugh, " You forget that you were often con-
" quered by my daughters," meaning vines; and
ridiculing ALEXANDER for his intemperance.
ALEXANDER, well verfed in the Peripatetic apho-
rifms, replied, ' Things inanimate cannot conquer.
' There can be no contention with them, but only
' with men or animals.' At this, Silenus ironically

* Ἀνέρι (" hufband") in the original.

expreffing

expreſſing his admiration, exclaimed, "Alas! alas!
" how great are the ſubterfuges of logicians! But
" in what claſs will you rank yourſelf; among
" things inanimate, or among the animate and
" living?" ALEXANDER, with ſome diſpleaſure,
replied, ' Be leſs ſevere; ſuch was my mag-
' nimity, that I was convinced that I ſhould be,
' nay that I was, a God.' " You allow then,"
ſaid Silenus, "' that you were often conquered by
" yourſelf, when anger, grief, or ſome other paſſion
" debaſed and debilitated your mind." ' But,'
anſwered ALEXANDER, ' for any one to conquer
' himſelf, and to be conquered by himſelf, are ſy-
' nonymous. I am talking of my victories over
' others.' " Fie upon your logic!" returned Silenus; " how it detects my ſophiſtry! But when
" you were wounded in India *, and Peuceſtes lay
" near you, and you, almoſt breathleſs, were car-
" ried out of the city, were you conquered by him
" who wounded you, or did you conquer him?"
' I not only conquered him,' replied ALEXANDER,
' but I alſo deſtroyed the city.' " Not you, indeed,
" you Immortal," ſaid Silenus; " you lay like Homer's

---

* Alexander, when he was beſieging the capital of the
Oxydracæ, according to Quintus Curtius, but, as others
ſay, of the Mallians, was ſo raſh as to leap alone into
the city, where he was dangerouſly wounded with an
arrow by an Indian, who, believing him dead, then advanced to ſtrip him. Alexander, however, recovering,
killed him with his dagger, and was ſoon after reſcued by
his ſoldiers, and carried off to his tent almoſt dead.

LA BLETERIE.

" Hector,

" Hector *, languid, and almoſt expiring ; others
" fought ;and conquered." ' True, anſwered
ALEXANDER, ' but under my command.' " How
" could they obey you," ſaid Silenus, " who were
" carried out almoſt dead ?"

He then ſung theſe verſes of Euripides † :

" Unjuſt the cuſtom of the Greeks; the troops

" The battle gain, their leaders gain the glory."

' Say no more, my dear father,' ſaid Bacchus,
' leſt he ſhould treat you as he treated Clitus.'
At this ALEXANDER bluſhed, wept, and was
ſilent.

This diſcourſe ended, Mercury thus interrogated
CÆSAR : " What, CÆSAR, was the principal view
" of your life ?" ' To excell my contemporaries,'
he replied, ' and neither to be, nor to be thought,
' ſecond to any." " This," ſaid Mercury, " is
" not quite clear. In what did you particularly
" wiſh to excell, in wiſdom or eloquence, in mili-
" tary skill, or political abilities?" ' In every
' thing,' anſwered CÆSAR. ' I was deſirous of be-
' ing the firſt of men ; but, as that was impoſſible,
' I endeavoured to be the moſt powerful of my
' fellow-citizens.' " And had you much power
" among them?" ſaid Silenus. ' Certainly,' re-

---

* When he was wounded by Ajax: Il. XIV. 432. and
XV. 246.

† In his Andromache. Clitus is ſaid to have repeated
theſe verſes at a banquet of Alexander, in order to depreciate his exploits, by which he provoked Alexander to
kill him, as Quintus Curtius informs us, in his eighth book,
and Plutarch, in his Life of Alexander.   BARNES.

                              plied

plied CÆSAR, for I became their governor."
" That," returned Silenus, " you might be; but
" you could never gain their love, though, for
" that purpose, you diffembled much humanity,
" acting a part like a player, and meanly flatter-
" ing all men." ' What!' faid CÆSAR; ' was I
' not loved by the people who perfecuted Brutus
' and Caffius?' " That," replied Silenus, " was
" not becaufe they had murdered you; for on that
" account the people made them confuls *; but
" for the fake of your money, as foon as they had
" heard your will, and found that no fmall reward
" was given to thofe who fhould be their enemies."

This difcourfe alfo being concluded, Mercury
thus accofted OCTAVIANUS: ' Will you alfo tell us
' what was your principal view?' He replied,
" To reign well." " What means that?" faid

---

* This is contrary to hiftory. Brutus and Caffius were
not nominated to the confulfhip by the people. The
former was to have filled that place four years after, but
that was an arrangement made by Cæfar. Though, inftead of υπατυς, " confuls," we fhould read ανθυπατυς,
" pro-confuls," Julian would ftill be miftaken. It was
not the people, but the fenate, that invefted Brutus and
Caffius with pro-confular power in the provinces of which
thofe two republicans had taken poffeffion. LA BLETERIE.

M. de la Bleterie has altered this paffage, in his tranflation, to " they thought them worthy of the confulfhip
" for having killed you." I cannot allow myfelf fuch a
liberty, remembering the rule of Rofcommon,

Your author always will the beft advife,
Fall when he falls ————

A tranflator may correct his author in the notes, but
in the text he fhould let him fpeak his own language.

Silenus,

Silenus. " Explain, AUGUSTUS, as this is pretended
" even by the wicked. Even Dionyſius * thought
" that he reigned well; and ſo did the ſtill more
" abandoned Agathocles *."   ' You know then,'
replied OCTAVIANUS, ' ye Gods, that when I
' parted with my grandſon †, I prayed you to
' give him the courage of CÆSAR, the conduct of
' Pompey, and my good fortune.'   " Many ſtatues
" of Gods," ſaid Silenus, " moſt curiouſly carved,
" of Gods of great merit, have been ſent us by
" this ſtatuary."   ' Why,' anſwered OCTAVIANUS,
' do you give me that ridiculous appellation?'
" As Nymphs are carved," he replied, " have not
" you formed Gods, one of whom, and the prin-
" cipal, is this CÆSAR?"   OCTAVIANUS bluſhed ‡,
and ſaid-no more.

Mercury then, addreſſing himſelf to TRAJAN,
aſked, ' what end his actions had in view?' " The
" ſame," he replied, " as thoſe of ALEXANDER,
" but with more moderation."   ' So you were
' conquered,' ſaid Silenus, ' by more ignoble paſ-
' ſions. He was frequently ſubdued by anger,
' you by the vileſt and moſt diſgraceful plea-

* Tyrants of Syracuſe well known.

† Auguſtus wiſhed this to C. Cæſar, the eldeſt ſon of
Agrippa and Julia, when he ſent him to wage war in the
eaſt.   LA BLETERIE.

‡ Auguſtus had reaſon to bluſh at thoſe extravagant
apotheoſes ; and Julian was in the right to ridicule them.
But ſhould he not have reflected that many of th. Gods
whom he worſhipped were no more than images a little
older ? *Magis è longinquo reverentia.*   Ibid.

' ſures.

' fures *, " Plague on you!" faid Bacchus. " Your
" farcafms prevent their fpeaking for themfelves.
" A truce with your jokes, and confider now what
" you can find reprehenfible in MARCUS; for he
" feems to me, in the fenfe of Simonides †, per-
" fect and faultlefs ‡." Then Mercury, turning
towards MARCUS, faid, ' And what, O fage, did
' you think the greateft happinefs?' With a low
voice, and with great diffidence, he replied, " To
" imitate the Gods." This anfwer was immediately deemed highly noble and praife-worthy.
Nor would Mercury queftion him any farther,
convinced that MARCUS would always anfwer with
equal propriety. In this opinion all the other
Gods concurred. Silenus only exclaimed, ' By
' Bacchus, I will not fpare this fophift §. Why
' did you formerly eat bread and drink wine, and
' not nectar and ambrofia, like us?' " Not in
" order to imitate the Gods," replied he, " but
" to nourifh my body, from a perfuafion, whether
" true or falfe, that your bodies alfo require

---

* Yet Pliny the younger makes an admirable elogium on
the chaftity of Trajan. Rely on panegyrifts. LA BLETERIE.

† A native of Ceos, one of the Cyclades, diftinguifhed
by his elegiac verfes. His anfwer to Hiero's queftion,
" What is God?" is well known.

‡ In the original, τετράγωνος, " four - cornered," or
" fquare." This expreffion occurs in one of the fragments
of this poet ftill preferved.

§ No one lefs deferves the name of fophift than Marcus
Aurelius. " A great proof of the regard of the Gods for
" me," fays he, . . . " is that having a very great love
" for philofophy, I have never fallen into the hands of any
" fophift; that I have not amufed myfelf with reading
" their books, or unravelling their vain fubtleties, &c."
Meditations of Marcus Antoninus.   LA BLETERIE.

being

" being nourished by the fumes of sacrifices *. I
" did not, however, think that you were to be imi-
" tated in this, but in your minds." Silenus, as
much stunned at this as if he had been struck by a
skilful boxer, replied, ' This is somewhat plau-
' sible †; but tell me now, in what did you for-
' merly think, that the imitation of the Gods con-
' sisted ?' Marcus answered, " In having as few
" wants, and doing as much good, as possible."
' What! had you no wants ?' said Silenus. " As
" to myself," replied Marcus, " I had none; but
" my body perhaps had a few." Marcus seeming in this also to have answered wisely, Silenus at
last insisted on what he thought improper and
unjust in the conduct of Marcus towards his
wife and son, his enrolling her among the God-
desses, and entrusting the empire to him. ' In
' this also,' said Marcus, ' I imitated the Gods.
' For I practised that maxim of Homer,

* Julian adopts this gross conception by ascribing it to
his favourite Marcus Antoninus. The Stoics and Platonists
hesitated between the analogy of bodies and the purity of
spirits; yet the gravest philosophers inclined to the
whimsical fancy of Aristophanes and Julian, that an un-
believing age might starve the immortal Gods. GIBBON.
 † The Gods of Julian are not jealous Gods. On the contrary, they are of a good composition, according to the arrogant philosophy of the Stoics, who were so chimerical as to
imagine, that man has no need of any inward support, and
that he may become like to God without any other strength
than that of nature. " In which man," said they, " has
" the advantage of Jupiter himself. Jupiter is good by
" nature, but the wise man is good by his own choice."
                                        LA BLETERIE.

‘ The wife whom choice and paffion both approve,
‘ Sure every wife and worthy man will love *.
‘ And as to my fon, I am juftified in my behaviour
‘ by that of Jupiter himfelf. “ I fhould long ago,”
‘ faid he to Mars, “ have transfixed thee with a
“ thunder-bolt, if I had not loved thee, becaufe thou
“ art my fon †.” ‘ Befides, I never imagined that
‘ Commodus would have proved fo profligate. And
‘ though his youth, affailed on all fides by ftrong
‘ temptations, was hurried away by the worft, I
‘ entrufted the government to one not yet cor-
‘ rupted. Afterwards, indeed, he became wicked.
‘ My tendernefs therefore to my wife was copied
‘ from the example of the divine Achilles ‡, and
                                              ‘ that

* Pope, 450. This is faid by Achilles, on the fubject
of Brifeis, whom he confiders as his wife, and whom Agamemnon had taken from him. Il. IX. 343. La Bleterie.

Julian, after Homer, ftyles Brifeis “ the wife” ($\gamma\alpha\mu\epsilon\tau\eta\varsigma$)
of Achilles, as he had before ftyled Adonis “ the husband”
($\alpha\nu\eta\rho$) of Venus. One would think he had read Thelyphthora.

† This is the fubftance of what Jupiter fays to Mars.
Il. V. 896, &c.

‡ It is impoffible fully to juftify the weaknefs of Marcus
Aurelius in regard to his wife. Julian, however, might
have made him offer a more plaufible excufe than a maxim
true in general, but liable to fome exceptions; and which,
for having come from the mouth of the divine Achilles, an
authority very weak in point of conduct, was not the more
applicable to the cafe of Marcus Aurelius. He might
have alleged, not in his juftification, but as an excufe,
that, never fufpecting evil, and judging of others by himfelf, he had thought that his wife was what fhe ought to
have been. Whatever fome hiftorians may fay, Marcus
Aurelius was ignorant of the irregularities of Fauftina, as
he thanks the Gods “ for having given him a wife fo good-
                                            “ natured

‘ that to my fon * was in imitation of the fupreme
‘ Jupiter ; and, befides, in both thefe I was guilty

‘ of

“ natured and obliging, full of tendernefs for her husband,
“ and of a wonderful fimplicity of manners.” *Meditations
of Marcus Antoninus*, l. i. XVII.

“ This ought not to feem very furprifing,” fays Madam
Dacier, “ if we confider, on one fide, the fimplicity of
“ Antoninus,” (fo fhe always calls Marcus Aurelius) “ and,
“ on the other, the genius of Fauftina, who had no lefs
“ art than beauty, and who had captivated the emperor
“ by all the external demonftrations of a tendernefs, which
“ appeared great in proportion to its falfhood. Half as
“ much would have been fufficient to deceive a man much
“ more diftruftful and fufpicious than Antoninus. If, after
“ this, any are obftinately aftonifhed at his ignorance,”
continues Madam Dacier, “ I have no objection, perfuaded,
“ that thofe who are fo aftonifhed are in the fame fituation ;
“ for the world abounds with fuch examples, and there is
“ nothing of which women are more capable than fuch
“ diffimulation.”

Madam Dacier adds, that, “ if, in the fatire of the
“ Cæfars, this prince, inftead of excufing himfelf on ac-
“ count of his ignorance, alleges the maxim of Achilles,
“ and the example of other emperors, who have paid the
“ fame honours to their wives, though they were no more
“ worthy than Fauftina, the reafon probably was, that
“ Julian meant to include in this fatire the wives of Ha-
“ drian, Vefpafian, and Auguftus.” That may be. But
I rather think that Julian imagined he had anfwered every
thing when he had quoted fome verfe of Homer.

LA BLETERIE.

The deification of Fauftina is the only defect which
Julian’s criticifm is able to difcover in the all-accomplifhed
Marcus Aurelius.

GIBBON.

Another “ defect,” obferved by Julian in Marcus Aurelius, was the entrufting the empire to his fon. See p. 209.

* We will not fay, with the Emperor Severus, that
Marcus Aurelius ought to have put his fon Commodus to
death. But the faults, which paternal tendernefs made that
philofophical Emperor commit, are utterly inexcufable in fo

P 2

great

‘ of no innovation. It is the general cuſtom for
‘ ſons to ſucceed to the inheritance of their fathers,
‘ and this is alſo the wiſh of all. Nor was I
‘ the firſt who decreed divine honours to a wife,
‘ there being many precedents. To have intro-
‘ duced it might perhaps have been unreaſonable;
‘ but to prevent the neareſt relations from fol-
‘ lowing a cuſtom eſtabliſhed by others, would be
‘ unjuſt. But I forget myſelf, and have been too
‘ prolix in my apology to you, O Jupiter and ye

great a man. I know that he at firſt took all poſſible
methods to give his ſon an excellent education. But ſome
corrupters inſinuated themſelves into the favour of that
prince. It is ſaid, that, when Marcus Aurelius removed
them, Commodus was ſo chagrined as to be ill, and that
his father had the weakneſs to reſtore them to him.

Be that as it may, one of theſe three things muſt be
allowed; either Marcus Aurelius was appriſed of the bad
inclinations of his ſon; or he conſidered him as a young
man wavering between good and evil; or, laſtly, he thought
him ſolidly virtuous. In the firſt caſe, the empire not being
hereditary, Marcus Aurelius ſhould have cauſed the ſenate
to name him another ſucceſſor, and not have falſified the
fair ſpeeches which he himſelf had made: “ May my
“ children periſh, if they leſs deſerve to be loved than
“ thoſe of Caſſius, and if their lives are not uſeful to the
“ republic!” In the ſecond caſe, was the love of his
country diſplayed by expoſing it to the riſk of having a vicious
Emperor? On the third ſuppoſition, how can this prince
be exculpated for having depended too much on the virtues
which he thought he ſaw in a child? He made the ſenate
confer on him, at the age of fifteen or ſixteen at moſt, both
the conſulſhip, and the tribunitial power, and even the title
of Auguſtus; and by that in a manner diveſted himſelf of
paternal authority. Antoninus had not done ſo much in
favour of Marcus Aurelius himſelf, though he was ſo early
attached to virtue.   -   LA BLETERIE.

‘ Gods,

' Gods, who know all things. Pardon me this
' indiſcretion.'

When Marcus had finiſhed his ſpeech, Mercury interrogated Constantine, and aſked him,
" What good end he had in view?" ' Having
' amaſſed great riches *,' he replied, ' to disburſe
' them liberally in the gratification of my own de-
' ſires, and thoſe of my friends.' At this, Silenus
burſt into a fit of loud langhter, and ſaid, " You
" now wiſh to paſs for a banker †; but how can
" you

* It is difficult to conceive that Conſtantine did not op-
preſs his ſubjects. I mean, that he did not lay ſome new
burthen upon them, and even that he granted ſome dimi-
nution of the old ones, according to M. de Tillemont.
However, if we conſider the ſtate in which the empire muſt
be, after ſo many civil wars, after having ſuffered the reigns
of that crowd of Emperors and Cæfars, or rather tyrants,
each of whom expended as much as a ſingle ſovereign, we
ſhall allow that, in ſuch circumſtances, the deſign of founding a new capital, and of making Conſtantinople at once
equal to Rome, the work of ſo many ages, was not that
of a prince ſufficiently intent on the welfare of his ſubjects.
But to ſay that, in amaſſing wealth, his object was to
ſatisfy the paſſions of others, is unjuſtly to render him reſponſible for the abuſes which were made of his liberality
by ſome of his friends, whom perhaps he had not choſen
with ſufficient diſcernment. To pretend that his view was
to ſatisfy his own paſſions is a calumny, unleſs it means his
paſſion for New Rome: that paſſion, however, did not ſo
exhauſt his treaſures as to leave him nothing to diſtribute
in immenſe charities, in building and endowing churches,
and in magnificently rewarding men of letters and artiſts.
                                        La Bleterie.

† To underſtand this ſarcaſtic pleaſantry of Silenus, we
muſt ſuppoſe that the bankers at that time lived and dreſſed
very penuriouſly. " As by your own confeſſion," ſays
                        Silenus,

" you forget your living like a cook, or a hair-
" dreffer? This your hair and looks formerly

Silenus, " you employed yourfelf in receiving and counting
" money, like a banker, you ought to have lived and
" dreffed like one. You ought not to have indulged your-
" felf in good cheer, in inventing new ragoûts, in paying
" fo much attention to your hair." The table of Conftantine was ferved with magnificence. By his medals it is
thought that he was perhaps too curious in drefs. Eufebius mentions fome white hair that was among the prefents which were fent him by Barbarian kings *. He wore
gold-flowered ftuffs, and a diadem adorned with jewels and
pearls. What a fcandal to Julian, who banifhed from his
palace all the cooks, who lived on vegetables, who neglected his hair and his perfon, on whom the diadem fat
fo heavy that he retained it only through policy! He muft
have been enraged at him who had made the ufe of it
common, and by that means laid his fucceffors under the
neceffity of wearing it.   LA BLETERIE.

The drefs and manners, which, towards the decline of
life, he chofe to affect, ferved only to degrade him in the
eyes of mankind. The Afiatic pomp, which had been
adopted by the pride of Diocletian, affumed an air of
foftnefs and effeminancy in the perfon of Conftantine. He
is reprefented with falfe hair of various colours, laborioufly
arranged by the fkilful artifts of the times, a diadem of a
new and more expenfive fafhion, a profufion of gems and
pearls, of collars and bracelets, and a variegated flowing
robe of filk, moft curioufly embroidered with flowers of
gold. In fuch apparel, fcarcely to be excufed in the youth
and folly of Elagabalus, we are at a lofs to difcover the
wifdom of an aged monarch, and the fimplicity of a Roman
veteran. Julian, in the Cæfars, attempts to ridicule his
uncle. His fufpicious teftimony is confirmed, however,
by the learned Spanheim, with the authority of medals.
Eufebius alleges, that " Conftantine dreffed for the public,
" not for himfelf." Were this admitted, the vaineft coxcomb could never want an excufe.   GIBBON.

---

* See Eufebius's Life of Conftantine IV.

" proved, but now your words demonstrate."
Thus severely sarcastic was Silenus.

Silence being proclaimed, the Gods gave their
votes privately. Most were in favour of MARCUS *,
but Jupiter, after discoursing apart with his father,
ordered Mercury to make the following proclamation : ' All you who have engaged in this con-
' test, know, that, by our laws and decrees, the
' victor is allowed to rejoice, but not to insult the
' vanquished. Depart then wherever you please,
' under the patronage of the Gods, and, for the
' future, residing here, let every one choose some
' guardian and protector.'

ALEXANDER immediately hastened to Hercules,
and OCTAVIANUS to Apollo; but MARCUS attached himself closely both to Jupiter and Saturn.
CÆSAR wandered about, and ran here and there,
'till Mars and Venus, moved with compassion,
called him to them. TRAJAN joined ALEXANDER,
as if he would seat himself in the same place.
But CONSTANTINE not finding among the Gods
the model of his actions, and perceiving the Goddess of Pleasure, repaired to her. She received
him very courteously, embraced him, and then
dressing him in a woman's variegated gown, and

---

* Julian was secretly inclined to prefer a Greek to a
Roman. But when he seriously compared a hero with a
philosopher, he was sensible that mankind had much greater
obligations to Socrates than to Alexander.   GIBBON.
See his Epistle to Themistius, p. 24.

P 4

nicely

nicely curling his hair, led him away to Luxury *.
With her he found one of his sons †, who loudly
proclaimed,

---

* Ασωλια, Julian here perfonifies Luxury, or (as M. de
la Bleterie tranflates it) Debauchery, and places her among
the Gods, in the fame manner as he had before deified
Pleafure (Τρυφη), and Repentance (Μίλαμελεια.)

† This fon, whom Conftantine finds with Debauchery, is
not one of the three who had followed him to the banquet,
and whom, Julian fays a little lower, their father " led
" out of the affembly of the Gods." He here means
Crifpus, the eldeft of all, a pupil of the celebrated Lac-
tantius, and known by his tragical death ftill more than
by his victories. But why does Julian place near Debauchery that prince whom hiftory mentions as an unfortunate hero? Is it becaufe he thought him guilty of the
crime of which his ftep-mother accufed him? No; that
would tend to the exculpation of Conftantine. It is rather
owing to Julian's continuing to treat a manner of living
lefs fingular than his own as effeminacy and debauchery.
Crifpus was charged by the Emprefs Faufta with the fame
crime of which Phædra had formerly accufed Hippolytus,
and of intending to dethrone his father. Conftantine, too
credulous, put his fon to death, and foon after, having
difcovered the innocence of Crifpus, he punifhed the falfe
accufer with a rigour that was confidered as a new crime.
Thefe two deaths, and that of his nephew, young
Licinius, are indeed enormous crimes, which might have
been expiated by the baptifm which Conftantine received
before he died. But we may judge of the effect which
they produced on fuch fuperficial and corrupt minds as
imputed to religion the faults of its profeffors, both by the
blafphemies of Julian and of modern infidels. Without
pretending to penetrate into the judgments of God, we
may confider, with M. de Tillemont, as the chaftifement of
thefe cruel actions of Conftantine, both the faults which
the Arians made him commit, and the extinction of his
family, which feemed likely to continue for many ages; yet,
numerous as it was, perifhed in lefs than forty years, by
fuch a variety of bloody and untimely deaths, as excites
horror. *Now therefore the fword fhall not depart from
thine*

proclaimed, " Let all, whether they be libertines,
" or murderers, or whatever be their crimes*;
" boldly

*thine houfe . . . becaufe thou haft given great occafion to the
enemies of the Lord to blafpheme.*   LA BLETERIE.

Such haughty contempt for the opinion of mankind,
whilft it imprints an indelible difgrace on the memory of
Conftantine, muft remind us of the very different behaviour
of one of the greateft monarchs of the prefent age. The
Czar Peter, in the full poffeffion of defpotic power, fubmitted to the judgment of Ruffia, of Europe, and of pofterity, the reafons which had compelled him to fubfcribe
the condemnation of a criminal, or, at leaft, a degenerate
fon.   GIBBON.

* One would think, at firft, that Julian alludes to the
ftory which the Pagans of the fifth century circulated
on the fubject of the converfion of Conftantine. They
faid, that that prince, ftruck with remorfe for having put
his fon and his wife to death, having afked Sopater, chief
of the Platonic fchool, and the Pagan pontiffs, whether
the religion of the Gentiles had any expiation to efface
fuch crimes, anfwered him, that it had not; that, in confequence, Conftantine had a conference with a certain
Ægyptian, who had come from Spain to Rome, and was well
known to the women of the palace; that this Ægyptian and
fome bifhops affured him that the Chriftian religion would
give him what the Pagans refufed him; and that there was
no kind of wickednefs which could not be wafhed in the
blood of Jefus Chrift; and that, upon their anfwer, he
embraced Chriftianity, and declared himfelf its protector.
This relation proves that the Pagans did not confider
Conftantine as a man without confcience; and that, more
equitable than our free-thinkers, they afcribed his change,
not to policy, but to conviction. If the ftory were true,
there would be no more pretence to infult us for the faults
of Conftantine, as he muft have committed them in the
darknefs of idolatry. But truth obliges me to fay, that the
fact cannot be fupported. For, 1. as Sozomen remarks,
the philofopher Sopater, being well verfed in the religion
of the Gentiles, could not be ignorant that it had fome
pretended expiations for fuch cafes as that of Conftantine.

4.   2. It

"‛ boldly advance, for by fprinkling them with
" water, I will immediately make them pure. And
                                                    " if

2. It is not credible that the pontiffs of the idols fhould
have been fo filly as to lay him under an abfolute neceffity
of providing himfelf elfewhere. If they had not had expiations, they would have invented them, to quiet the confcience of an Emperor whom they faw on the eve of deferting them, and throwing himfelf into the arms of the
Chriftians. 3. Crifpus, Faufta, and young Licinius died
in 326; and in the year 312 Conftantine acknowledged the
Chriftian religion as the only true one.

Julian was too well acquainted with the hiftory of his
family, and the æra of the converfion of Conftantine, to
have had in view a fable, which he confidered as a fable,
fuppofing that in his time it had been yet invented. I
imagine therefore that this apoftate introduces Crifpus
vaunting the efficacy of baptifm and repentance, in order
to infinuate, by that profane irony, that the profpect of the
refources offered to finners by the Chriftian religion had
emboldened Conftantine to fhed the blood of his relations.
It was a common calumny with the Pagans to fay, that
Chriftianity favoured the corruption of men by promifing
pardon to the greateft crimes; as if the gofpel promifes any
thing to incorrigible finners, or affures them that they fhall
have time and the will to reform.

This calumny is the more atrocious in the mouth of
Julian, as, having been of the clergy, he muft be better
acquainted with the fpirit of the church, with the wife
precautions and long probations that fhe employs to be
affured of the converfion both of catechumens and of
penitents. A religion, which did not offer to the moft mife-
rable man a method of recovering the favour of God, would
be an ineffectual religion, and little worthy of the goodnefs
of God who would have all men faved. It would indeed
favour corruption by plunging or leaving the guilty in defpair. A religion, which fhould pretend to efface crimes by
mere ceremonies, without reforming the criminal, would be
no more than a farce, a defpicable palliative, likely to ex-
afperate the difeafe, but not to cure it. Chriftianity obferves the juft mean. Adapted to the wants of mankind,
                                                    and

" if they should relapse, they need only smite
" their breasts and beat their heads, and they will
" again be purified."

To

and worthy of the sanctity of its author, it presents men,
to whatever abyss of degradation and misery vice may have
reduced them, with a line which conducts them strait to
God, provided, and not else, that they become new men
in and by Jesus Christ. In all times, some, separating the
promise from the condition, have assumed, by a deplorable
abuse, a kind of title to sin more boldly. But God forbid, that, on the word of an accuser, who guesses and cannot prove, we should think that Constantine was of that
number, and that the expectation of baptism should have
influenced him to actions for which he is justly reproached!
After all, it is not the fault of physic, if, from the uncertain hope of the assistance that it offers, some are so extravagant as to aggravate their diseases.

Besides the slanderous imputation just mentioned, I perceive in the words of Crispus a satirical stroke which is not
undeserved. By the confession of Eusebius (which is saying
every thing) Constantine did not enough distinguish from
true Christians those who embraced Christianity only to
make their fortunes. " By their hypocrisy and artifice,"
says Eusebius, " they insinuated themselves into the favour
" of the Emperor, and much injured his reputation." Julian
therefore here means to reproach Constantine for having
over-looked every thing, and pardoned every thing, provided
his religion was professed. But why did not the censor
perceive, that he himself is more justly entitled to the like
censure ? Neither the uncle nor the nephew had sufficient
delicacy as to their proselytes. Yet they must have been
well acquainted with a memorable story of Constantius.
Chlorus. That prince, at the time when his collegues
were persecuting Christianity with fire and sword, as-
sembled such officers of his palace, and governors of his
provinces, as were Christians, and gave them the alternative, either of retaining their places, by sacrificing to the
Gods, or of losing them by adhering to their religion.
When they had all made their options, he said to the pre-

varicators,

To this Goddefs Constantine gladly devoted himfelf, and with her conducted his fons out of the affembly of the Gods. But the Deities who punifh atheifm * and bloodfhed avenged on him and them the murder of their relations †, till Jupiter, in favour of Claudius ‡ and Constantius, gave them fome refpite.

varicators, " You have bafe and venal minds. I cafhier " you, and banifh you for ever from my palace. He who " betrays his confcience is capable of betraying me. As " for you," faid he to the others, " I give you my efteem " and confidence. A man is faithful to his prince and " the community when he is faithful to his God." He retained them in his fervice, and entrufted them with the guard of his perfon, and the principal affairs of ftate; confidering them as his fureft friends and real treafures. I fhall conclude this long note, or rather differtation, with obferving that M. de Tillemont queftions whether Crifpus had received baptifm. The fpeech which Julian affigns to him leaves no room to doubt it. But it was not before perceived that it is Crifpus who fpeaks in this paffage.
La Bleterie.

Dr. Bentley, under the borrowed name of Phileleutherus Lipfienfis, ftyles this " a ridiculous and ftale banter, ufed " by Celfus and others, before Julian, upon the Chriftian " doctrines of baptifm, and repentance, and remiffion of " fins," and has refuted it at large in his Remarks on a late difcourfe of Free-thinking, § xlii.

* Julian treats the Chriftians as atheifts, becaufe they reject the plurality of Gods, and acknowledge one only.
La Bleterie.

† After the death of Conftantine, the foldiers laid violent hands on his three brothers, and five of his nephews. Conftantius was confidered as guilty of this maffacre, and Julian probably means to charge with it Conftantine the younger alfo, and Conftans. Be that as it may, the two latter made war on each other, and Conftantine the younger was killed near Aquileia by the troops of Conftans. That Conftantius put Gallus to death is well known.　　*Ibid.*

‡ Claudius II. mentioned p. 167.

" As

" As for you," said Mercury, addressing himself to me, " I have introduced you to the know-
" ledge of your father the Sun *; obey then his
" dictates, making him your guide and secure
" refuge, while you live; and when you leave
" the world, adopt him, with good hopes, for
" your tutelar God."

* Julian, as soon as he rose, always addressed a prayer
to Mercury. He thought himself under the protection of
that God. We have said in the preface, and shall again
observe in another place, that by the Sun he understands
the Demiurgus, or Logos. La Bleterie.

The

The following Lift of the Roman Emperors, from
Julius Cæsar to Julian, will give a fuccinct
view of all that are mentioned, and all that are
omitted, in the foregoing Satire.

Before Xt.		A. D.	
1 Julius Cæsar, died 44		26 * Maximin, died	238
	A. D.	and	
2 Augustus	14	Maximus	238
3 Tiberius	37	27 Pupienus	238
4 * Caligula	41	and	
5 Claudius I.	54	Balbinus	238
6 * Nero	68	28 Gordian	243
[Vindex]	68	29 Philip	249
7 Galba	68	30 Decius	251
8 Otho	69	31 Gallus	252
9 Vitellius	69	32 † Valerian	260
10 Vefpafian	79	33 † Gallienus	268
11 Titus	81	34 Claudius II.	270
12 * Domitian	96	35 Aurelian	275
13 Nerva	98	36 Tacitus	276
14 Trajan	117	37 Probus	282
15 Hadrian	137	38 † Carus	284
16 Antoninus Pius	161	† Carinus	285
17 Marcus Aurelius	180	and	
and		† Numerian	284
Lucius Verus	169	39 Diocletian	
18 † Commodus	193	and resigned	305
19 Pertinax	193	Maximian	
20 Julian I.	193	40 Conftantius-Chlorus d.	306
21 Severus	211	and	
22 * Caracalla	217	† Galerius	311
and		41 † Constantine the	
Geta	212	Great	337
23 † Macrinus	218	and	
and		† Licinius	323
Diadumenus	218	42 † Conftantine II.	340
24 † Eliagabalus	222	† Conftantius	361
25 Alexander Severus	235	and	
		† Conftans	350
		43 Julian II.	363

N. B. Thofe marked † were excluded the affembly; thofe *
were thrown into Tartarus; and thofe in Italicks are not mentioned.
Vindex, though mentioned, was not Emperor. And Tiberius,
Commodus, and Elagabalus, though they efcaped Tartarus, deferved it.

The

The MISOPOGON, or the ANTIOCHIAN *.

ANACREON † compofed many ludicrous poems ‡, the Fates having endowed him with a fportive vein. But neither Alcæus §, nor Archi-

A. D. 363.

---

* Being jeered by the Antiochians, and feveral afperfions having been thrown on his beard in particular, Julian took his revenge in this fatire, in which, by a figurative reprehenfion of himfelf, he drew his keen pen againft the manners and luxury of the people of Antioch. This work, and its fubject, are mentioned by Ammianus, *l.* xxii. Zofimus, *l.* iii. Gregory Nazianzen, *Orat.* ii. on Julian, and Socrates, *l.* iii. *c.* 17. PETAU.

It feems as if Julian meant in fome fort to confound himfelf with his beard, which was fo dear to him that it difpleafed the inhabitants of Antioch. After all, the title of a book frequently refers to fome paffage only in the work. LA BLETERIE.

Inftead of abufing, or exerting, the authority of the ftate, to revenge his perfonal injuries, Julian contented himfelf with an inoffenfive mode of retaliation which it would be in the power of few princes to employ. He had been infulted by fatires and libels; in his turn, he compofed, under the title of " The Enemy of the Beard," an ironical confeffion of his own faults, and a fevere fatire on the licentious and effeminate manners of Antioch. This imperial reply was publickly expofed before the gates of the palace, and the Mifopogon ftill remains a fingular monument of the refentment, the wit, the humanity, and the indifcretion of Julian. GIBBON.

The fatire of Julian, and the homilies of St. Chryfoftom, exhibit the fame picture of Antioch. *Ibid.*

In like manner, Hadrian, it is obfervable, was alfo much offended with the levity and petulance of the Antiochians, and had thoughts of disjoining Phœnicia from Syria, that their city might not continue the metropolis of fo many others.

A Lyric

Archilochus * of Paros, were favoured by the
Gods with a Muse who had a talent for mirth and
pleasantry ; for when they were oppressed with
misfortunes, they had recourse to the Muses, and
alleviated the weight of their cares by railing at
their enemies. The law, however, forbids me, as
well as every one else, to accuse any by name ‖,

even

† A Lyric poet of Teos, a city in Ionia, who wrote
many more odes than are transmitted to us, as Horace
says,—*persæpe cavâ testudine flevit amorem.* Epod. XIV. 4.

‡ We read in the editions, " Anacreon made many
" serious and ludicrous poems," χμελη σιμνα και χαριεντα.
Whether this poet wrote any thing but songs, is the question. By saying, that " Anacreon made some serious verses,"
Julian would say the direct contrary of what he meant. I
think therefore that the text shoul be corrected, and the
word τερπνα substituted, or that we should only read χαριεντα.
In one of the MSS. of the King's library, which has been
lent me, the words σιμνα και are not to be found ; and the
other informs the reader, that there are some MSS. in
which those words do not occur.   LA BLETERIE.

§ A native of Mitylene. From him the Alcaïc verses
derive their name. His pieces were severe satires against
the tyrants of Lesbos, Pittacus in particular. His style,
according to Quintilian, was lofty, and much resembled
that of Homer.

* See p. 131.

‖ The Roman laws, beginning with those subsequent
to the XII tables, condemn severely the authors of defa-
matory libels. Julian, though in joke, is glad to shew that
he has a republican spirit. He considered the Emperors, as
justly subject to all the laws, except those with which they
had specifically dispensed.   LA BLETERIE.

Personal satire was condemned by the law of the twelve
tables.

*Si mala condiderit in quem quis carmina, jus est
Judiciumque.*   Hor.

Julian owns himself subject to the law, and the Abbè
de la Bleterie has eagerly embraced a declaration so agreeable

even of thofe, who, as I have in no refpect injured them, are hoftile aggreffors. And, befides,
the mode of education, which is at prefent purfued
by perfons of fafhion *, deprives me of the har-
mony

able to his own fyftem, and indeed to the true fpirit of the
Imperial conftitution. GIBBON.

* I do not remember elfewhere to have read that poetry
was then fo much decried. However that might be, in
Greece the age of verfe was not then over: witnefs St.
Gregory Nazienzen, whofe fublime and truly Homeric
poems prove that genius and enthufiafm require not the
affiftance of fable. Julian himfelf was a poet; and Libanius informs us, that there was a collection of verfes
made by that prince to celebrate the arrival of fome men
of learning at his court. Two fmall pieces of his writing
are all that now remain. In one of them, he elegantly
and forcibly defcribes an organ, confifting, like ours, of
pipes, bellows, and ftops. The other is an epigram
" againft beer." It muft have been made in the Gauls.
LA BLETERIE.

Of the latter, M. de la Bleterie has given a paraphrafe,
or imitation, in French. The following are clofe tranflations of them both. The originals, as literary curiofities, are annexed.

The Emperor Julian on an Organ.

Reeds ftrike my wond'ring eyes, unknown before;
Sprung from fome brazen foil, fome foreign fhore;
Fruitlefs our efforts, for in vain we blow,
Till, from a cave of leather, winds below
To hollow pipes harmonious powers impart:
Then, if fome mafter, in th' Orphéan art
Experienc'd, touch the well-according keys,
Inftant they warble, and refponfive pleafe.

Ιȣλιανȣ Βασιλεως εις το οργανον.

Αλλοιην οροω δονακων φυσιν· ητε απ' αλλης
Χαλκειης ταχα μαλλον ανεβλαστησαν αρȣρης.
Αργιοι, ȣδ' ανεμοισιν υφ' ημετερης δονεονται,
Αλλ' ȣπο ταυρειης προϊοραι σπη'υγγος αυλης

mony of numbers. For it feems now as difhonourable to cultivate poetry, as it was in former
times to be unjuftly rich.

I will

Νερθεν ευτρηΐων καλαμων υπο ριζαν οδευει.
Και τις ανηρ αγερωχος *, εχων θοα δακΐυλα χειρος,
Ιϛαΐαι αμφαφοων κανονας συμφραδμονας αυλων †·
Οι δ' απαλοι σκιρΐωνΐες αποθλιβυσιν αοιδην.

Merfennus has inferted a Latin tranflation of this epigram, in his lib. III. *De Organis*, p. 113. and Zarlino,
who wrote in 1571, is of opinion, that the organ here
mentioned was effentially the fame with the organ of his
time. But the introduction of it into churches is generally
afcribed to Pope Vitellianus, who was advanced to the Pon-
tificate, A. D. 663. Dr. Prieftley indeed (Hiftory of the
Corruptions of Chriftianity, vol. II. p. 122.) by fome miftake, fuppofes it to be introduced into churches by Marinus
Sanutus fo late as 1312. An organ is mentioned by
Gervafe the monk, who wrote in 1200, as having been
fometime erected in Canterbury Cathedral, over St.
Michael's chapel (*ubi organa folent effe*), and the foundation
of its loft remains to this day. An hydraulic organ (of
which Sir John Hawkins has given a fketch from Kircher)
is defcribed by Vitruvius, who lived in the reign of Auguftus. The following note is from Dr. Burney.

The moft ancient proof of an inftrument refembling a
modern organ blown by bellows, and played by keys, very
different from the *Hydraulicon* (or water-organ) which is of
much higher antiquity, is a Greek epigram in the *Antha-
logia*, attributed to the Emperor Julian the Apoftate, who
flourifhed about 364 ‡.

I fhall here give a literal tranflation of this epigram,
which, though it contain no very beautiful or poetical
images, will anfwer the hiftorical purpofe of afcertaining

---

* A tall fturdy fellow, " alluding to the force neceffary to beat
down that kind of clumfy carillon keys of this rude inftrument
of new invention.   BURNEY.

† The rulers of the pipes, literally *keys*.   *Ibid.*

‡ This is a fmall chronological miftake, as Julian died in June,
363.

the

I will not, however, totally difclaim the affiftance of the Mufes. I have feen the barbarous
nations beyond the Rhine delighted with the
melody of favage mufic, whofe notes refemble the
diffonant fcreams of birds. Bad muficians difguft

the exiftence of an inftrument in the fourth century, which
in many particulars refembled a modern organ.

" I fee reeds of a new fpecies, the growth of another
" and a brazen foil; fuch as are not agitated by our winds,
" but by a blaft that rufhes from a leathern cavern be-
" neath their roots; while a robuft mortal, running with
" fwift fingers over the concordant keys, makes them, as
" they fmoothly dance, utter concordant founds."

Nothing material is omitted in the verfion of this epigram, or rather enigma, upon the organ, though not a
very ingenious one; for the word αυλων, *the pipes*, difcovers
the whole myftery.   BURNEY.

The Emperor Julian on Barley-wine.

Who, what art thou? thy name, thy birth declare:
Thou art no Bacchus, I by Bacchus fwear.
Jove's fon alone I know, I know not thee;
Thou fmell'ft like goats, but fweet as nectar he.
In Gallia, thirfty Gallia, thou wert born,
Scanty of grapes, but prodigal of corn.
Bromus, not Bremius, ftyl'd, thy brows with corn,
As fprung from Ceres, not from Jove, adorn.

The turn, or pun, at the conclufion, cannot be preferved
in Englifh. *Bromius* was one name of Bacchus, from Βρεμω,
" to rave," like the Bacchanals. And Julian gives the
name of *Bromus* to beer, from Βρομος, " oats." Such, however,
is the improvement of climates, that modern Gaul produces as much and as good wines as Italy; and Britain more
and better beer than ancient Gaul.

Ἰουλιανου Βασιλεω; εἰς οἰνον απο κριθης.

Τις; ποθεν εἰς, Διονυσε; μα γαρ τον αληθεα Βαχχον,
Οὐ σ'επιγιγνωσκω· τον Διος οἰδα μονον.
Κεινος νεκταρ ὀδωδε· συ δὲ τραγον. η ρα σε Κελλοι
Τη πενιη βοτρυων τευξαν απ' ασταχυων.
Τῳ σε χρη καλεειν Δημητριον, ου Διονυσον,
Πυρογενη μαλλον, και Βρομον, ου Βρομιον.

their

their hearers, but they are naturally pleasing to themselves. Reflecting on this, I have been wont to whisper to myself, not indeed with equal address, but, I am certain, with equal magnanimity, what Ismenias * said of old, " I will sing for the Muses " and myself." But my song is in prose, and will contain many bitter sarcasms, not on others, by Jupiter, (for how can that be, as they are illegal?) but on the author himself. For no law forbids my writing a panegyrick or satire on myself; though if I were desirous of praising myself, I could not, but blame I can in many instances.

And, first, I will begin with my face. To this, formed by nature not over beautiful, graceful, or becoming, my own perverseness and singularity have added this long beard †, to punish it, as it

were,

---

* Ismenias was a very skilful player on the flute. Julian is the only one who ascribes to him this expression. Cicero, [in his Brutus, c. 50.] puts one very like it in the mouth of Antigenidas, another player on the flute, who, in order to encourage one of his scholars, whom the public did not relish, said to him, " Play for the Muses, and for me."

LA BLETERIE.

† Some friends, for whose understanding and taste I have the highest respect, supposing themselves to speak in the name of the nation, requested me to suppress entirely the idea which Julian here conveys. It is only by sufferance that they have allowed me to intimate it by one rapid word. For my own part, I was afraid of giving a handle to infidelity...Will the French delicacy go so far as to falsify authors? The more disgusting this passage of Julian is, the more it characterises him; and every thing that characterises, when it does not offend good manners or religion,

· should

were, for no other reason but because Nature has not made it handsome. Therefore I suffer lice to scamper about it, like beasts through a thicket : I cannot indulge myself in eating voraciously, and must be cautious of opening my mouth wide when I drink, lest I swallow as many hairs as crumbs. As for kissing, and being kissed, they give me not the least trouble.

Yet amongst other inconveniences of my beard, this is one, that it prevents my joining pure lips to smooth, and, I think, much sweeter lips, as was formerly observed * by one, who, inspired by Pan

should be sacred to a translator. As the notes admit any thing, here follows a faithful translation of the passage in question ; excepting that the original calls the things by their name. [In the French translation therefore φθειρων, " lice," are rendered by *de petits animaux incommodes*, " some " little troublesome animals," which might as well be fleas. And why not *des insectes*, or *de la vermine ?*] That a Roman emperor should boast of such a circumstance, and that he should boast of it falsely, as I suppose, is, literally speaking, a singular stroke, which paints Julian better than a thousand volumes. LA BLETERIE.

The friends of the Abbè de la Bleterie adjured him, in the name of the French nation, not to translate this passage so offensive to their delicacy. Like him, I have contented myself with a transient allusion ; but the little animal, which Julian names, " is a beast familiar to man, " and signifies love." [Shakspeare, 2 Hen. IV.] GIBBON.

Mr. Gibbon's " transient allusion" is " the shaggy and " populous beard," and " *la barbe longue et peuplée*" is the " rapid word" of M. de la Bleterie.

* Theocritus, Idyll. XII. 32.

Ὃς δὲ κε προσμάξῃ γλυκερώτερα χείλεσι χείλη, κ. τ. λ.

He who shall lips to lips most sweetly join, &c. speaking of a garland that was presented at the tomb of Diocles to the youth who gave the sweetest kiss,

and Calliope, made some verses on Daphnis *. You say, that " it is only fit to twist into ropes." That I would readily allow, provided you could so artfully extract the bristles, as to prevent their hurting your soft and tender fingers. Think not that this offends me; for I will give you a reason why I wear a chin like a goat, instead of making it smooth and bare like those of beautiful boys, and of all women by nature lovely. You, such is the delicacy, and perhaps simplicity, of your manners, even when old, imitate your sons and daughters by studiously shaving your chins, thus displaying the man by the forehead only, and not, like me, by the cheeks. But not contented with this length of beard, my head is also nasty and seldom combed, my nails are unpared, and my fingers are usually black with ink. And, to tell you a secret, my bosom too is rough and hairy, like the mane of the lion, king of beasts, nor have I ever made it smooth, such is my meanness and illiberality. If I had any warts, I would readily disclose it, as Cimon did, but at present in truth I have none.

* The son of Mercury, whose story is sung in the first Idyllium. Diodorus Siculus supposes him to have been the first author of bucolic poetry; and, agreeably to this, Theon, an old scholiast on Theocritus, in his note on the first Idyllium, ver. 141. mentioning Daphnis, says, " he " was the inventor of bucolics." Be that as it may, this Daphnis was probably the first subject of bucolic songs.

FAWKES.

Theocritus has also an epigram " to Daphnis sleeping." The above is a note of the translator.

Another

Another circumstance, well known to you, I will also mention. Not satisfied with such an uncomely person, I lead a very rigid life. I absent myself from the theatres, through mere stupidity; nor do I allow a play at court, such a dolt am I, except on the calends of the year *, when I resemble a poor farmer bringing his rent, or taxes, to a rapacious landlord; and when I am there, I seem as solemn as at a sacrifice †. As it is not long since you saw him, you may recollect the youth, the genius, and understanding of my predecessor ‡; my way of life, so different from his, is a sufficient proof of my frowardness.

But to add something farther; I have always hated horse-races as much as a debtor hates the forum. Therefore I seldom resort to them, except on the festivals of the Gods, nor do I ever pass

---

* The calends of January were celebrated by the ancient Heathens with all kinds of public mirth and lasciviousness, and for a long time were devoted by the Christians to no very different amusements. PETAU.

† There is in the original a sentence which I omit. The passage is certainly faulty, and so it is thought to be by F. Petau. Literally translated it would be thus: " I " have no possessions; and though I am styled the great king, " like a præfect or duke, I am in fact a king, or general, of " players and charioteers." But this sense does not connect with that which precedes and follows it. The MSS. have here given me no assistance. LA BLETERIE.

For the same reason it is also omitted here.

‡ Constantius. It is needless to say, this is ironical. The " genius and understanding" of Constantius Julian despised; and as to his " youth," he was 44 years old when he died.

Q 4

the whole day there, as was the practice of my
cousin *, my uncle †, and my brother ‡; but after
seeing six races §, and that not with the keenness
of a sportsman, but, by Jupiter, with disgust and
aversion, I depart with joy. But enough of my
public conduct. And yet how few of my offences
against you have I mentioned!

As to domestic affairs, sleepless nights on straw,
and food less than enough, give a severity to my
manners, totally repugnant to a luxurious city ||.
Be not offended with me for this **. A great and

foolish

* Constantius.

† Count Julian. See Epistle xiii.

‡ Gallus. Julian styles him (as he was) "his half-
brother."

§ Out of four and twenty, which was the usual number.
A twenty-fifth race, or *missus*, was added, to complete the
number of one hundred chariots, four of which, the four
colours, started each heat.

> *Centum quadrijugos agitabo ad flumina cursus.*

It appears that they ran five or seven times round the
meta, and (from the measure of the *Circus Maximus* at Rome,
the Hippodrome at Constantinople, &c.) it might be about
a four-mile course.   GIBBON.

|| The private life of Julian in Gaul, and the severe dis-
cipline which he embraced, are displayed by Ammianus.
(xvi. 5.) who professes to praise, and by Julian himself,
who affects to ridicule, a conduct which in a prince of the
family of Constantine might justly excite the surprise of
mankind.   *Ibid.*

** It may not be improper to add here the picture which
Libanius draws of Julian's manner of life. "Always ab-
"stemious, and never oppressed by food, he applied him-
"self to business with the activity of a bird, and dispatched
"it with infinite ease. In one and the same day he gave
"several audiences; he wrote to cities, to magistrates, to
"generals of armies, to his absent friends, to those who
"were

foolish mistake has from my childhood induced me
to wage war with my stomach. I therefore never
allow it to be filled with food. Consequently, to
nothing am I so little addicted as to vomiting : and
this, I remember, befell me once only since I became
Cæsar; and that by accident, not repletion. It
may not be amiss to relate the story, not that I
think it entertaining, but as it was to me of the
utmost consequence.

I happened to be in winter quarters at my dear
Lutetia #; for so the Gauls call the town of the
Parisians.

" were on the spot; hearing letters read that were addressed
" to him, examining petitions, and dictating with such ra-
" pidity, that the short-hand writers could not keep pace
" with him. He alone had the secret of hearing, speaking,
" and writing at the same time; and in this multitude of
" complicated operations he never mistook. After having
" dispatched business, and dined merely through urgent ne-
" cessity, shutting himself up in his library, he read and com-
" posed till the instant when affairs of state summoned him
" to other labours. A supper still more sparing than the
" dinner was followed by a sleep as light as his meals.
" He awaked in order to labour with other secretaries
" whom he had allowed to sleep on the preceding day.
" His ministers were obliged to relieve each other; but, as
" for himself, he knew no repose but the change of em-
" ployment. He alone was always labouring, he multi-
" plied himself, and assumed as many forms as Proteus.
" Julian was pontiff, author, diviner, judge, general of
" the army, and, in all these characters, the father of his
" country." *Liban. Orat. Parent.*   LA BLETERIE.

* Leucetia, or Lutetia, was the ancient name of the
city, which, according to the fashion of the ivth century,
assumed the territorial appellation of *Parisii.*

The licentiousness and corruption of Antioch recalled to
the memory of Julian the severe and simple manners of his
" beloved

Parisians. It is situated in a small island; two wooden bridges lead to it, and the river seldom rises or falls, but is generally of the same depth both in summer and winter. The water is very clear to the eye, and pure to the taste *. This is of great

importance

"beloved Lutetia;" where the amusements of the theatre were unknown or despised. He indignantly contrasted the effeminate Syrians with the brave and honest simplicity of the Gauls, and almost forgave the intemperance which was the only stain of the Celtic character. If Julian could now revisit the capital of France, he might converse with men of science and genius, capable of understanding and of instructing a disciple of the Greeks; he might excuse the lively and graceful follies of a nation, whose martial spirit has never been enervated by the indulgence of luxury, and he must applaud the perfection of that inestimable art which softens, and refines, and embellishes the intercourse of social life. Gibbon.

Worthy patriot! Enlightened philosopher!

Whatever "softens, refines, and embellishes," human life, in a proper degree, is certainly desirable. But why must France be commended with such warmth of approbation, as if she possessed this " inestimable art" exclusively? I think, in this polished and enlightened age, the art is known and practised in England, as much as is consistent with the national character, and the preservation of that manly spirit, which is necessary to the existence of civil liberty; an " inestimable" blessing, which enlarges, and ennobles, and secures all the natural rights and enjoyments of human nature.

I cannot think it consistent with a good citizen, and a lover of one's country, to admire and extol the " martial " spirit" of that nation, which is at this moment most hostile to all we hold dear, and which in the present war has behaved with such perfidy as would stigmatise an individual in private life with perpetual disgrace.

Knox.

* Julian gives the water of this river a better character than is usually allowed it, in modern times at least,

and

importance to the inhabitants, as they are iflanders. The winter there is extremely mild, which is attributed to the warmth of the fea, it not being above ninety ftadia diftant * ; fo that wholefome exhalations from the ocean are perhaps wafted thither, falt-water being warmer than frefh. Whether this be the reafon, or fome other unknown to me, fuch is the fact, the inhabitants of that country have mild winters ; good wines therefore are produced there, and fome have even raifed figs by covering them with mats by way of cloathing, and other fuch prefervatives from the inclemency of the weather.

The winter was then uncommonly fevere, and the river fupported blocks, as it were, of marble, (you know, without doubt, the Phrygian quarries, which large flakes of ice †, floating on each other, greatly refemble) forming a kind of continual paffage and a ftream of bridges. Being, on this occafion, more boorifh than ufual, I would not fuffer my fervants to warm the chamber in which I

and efpecially by foreigners. A late writer, a Frenchman too, expreffes himfelf thus : " The Seine-water relaxes " the ftomach of thofe who are not ufed to it. Foreigners " generally fuffer the inconvenience of a flight diarrhœa ; " but they might avoid it if they had the precaution of " putting a fpoonful of white vinegar into every pint of " water." *Tableau de Paris.*

* The calculation is juft ; but I will not be anfwerable for the natural philofophy of the Parifians of thofe times. *The philosophy is good.* LA BLETERIE.

† The inhabitants of Antioch had never feen the river bear. *Ibid.*

flept,

flept, though the cold increafed and grew every
day more intenfe, left it fhould draw the damp
out of the walls. I only ordered fome lighted
brands, and a few live coals, to be carried in and
placed there. Thefe exhaled fo much vapour
from the walls, that, my head being oppreffed, I
fell afleep, and narrowly efcaped fuffocation. But
being carried into the air, and, by the advice of my
phyficians, difgorging the food that I had juft
fwallowed, though I did not difcharge much, I
was immediately relieved, fo as to pafs an eafy
night, and on the next day I was again fit for
bufinefs.

Thus, while I refided among the Gauls, like the
Humourift * of Menander, I led an auftere life.
This, however, gave no offence to that ruftic nation †. But fuch a rich, flourifhing, and populous
city as yours is juftly difpleafed; a city, in which
are many dancers, many pipers, more players than

---

* Δυσκολος, the title of a comedy of Menander.

† Though the Gauls had long become Romans, foreign
manners had not yet penetrated into the northern parts of
Gaul. Politenefs, with its advantages and inconveniences,
makes the tour of the world. If Julian were now to re-
vifit his " dear Lutetia," would he take it for Antioch?
No. He would find there fo much love and refpect for
the fovereign, that he would be foon undeceived.

                                               La Bleterie.

Spoken like a Frenchman! Julian would never have
thought highly of the fenfe, or fincerity, of a people who
could " love and refpect" fuch a fovereign as Louis XV.
in whofe reign the above note was written.

citizens,

citizens, and no refpect for fovereigns.　A blufh
befits only the pufillanimous ; but fuch heroes as
you fhould revel in the morning, purfue pleafure
at night, and not only teach by words, but fhew
by deeds, your utter contempt of the laws. Thofe
therefore, who, like you, infult the prince, offer
a ftill greater infult to the laws. That fuch is your
delight you frequently and clearly demonftrate,
particularly in the forum and the theatre ; the
people by fhouts and clamour ; the magiftrates by
their extravagance, which gains them more diftinction and applaufe, from all to whom they have
given thefe expenfive entertainments, than Solon,
the Athenian, obtained from his converfation with
Crœfus, king of Lydia *.　All there are hand-
fome, fmooth and beardlefs ; all, both young and
old, imitate alike the happinefs of the Phæäcians †, and

 Variety of dreffes, baths, amours,
they prefer, without hefitation, to what is juft and
right.

 ANTIOCHIAN.　And do you think, Julian, that
your rufticity, favagenefs, and morofenefs are fuit-

---

 * Every one knows the journey which Solon took to the
court of king Crœfus, and the truths which he dared
utter to that prince, intoxicated, as he was, with opu-
lence and grandeur.　 LA BLETERIE.

 † The ifland of Phæäcia is now the ifland of Corfu.
Homer, (Odyff. VIII. 249.) reprefents the Phæäcians as a
nation given up to good cheer, luxury, mufic, dancing,
and all kinds of pleafure.　 *Ibid.*

     able·

able to us? O thou moſt ignorant and odious * of all men, is your temperate, little animal, as ſome mean mortals have ſtyled your ſoul, ſo mad and fooliſh, that you think it requires the ornaments and trappings of wiſdom? In this you are miſtaken; for, firſt, tell us, as we know not, what wiſdom is? With the name only we are acquainted, but of the meaning we are ignorant. If it be that which you now practiſe, it conſiſts in enforcing ſubordination to the Gods and the laws, in teaching equals to bear with equals, in obſerving moderation, in preventing the poor from being oppreſſed by the rich, and, for theſe purpoſes, ſtifling reſentment, encountering enmity, anger, reproaches; in ſhort, ſupporting all theſe with firmneſs, without being provoked, or giving way to paſſion, but keeping it, as much as poſſible, in proper bounds, and under due ſubjection. And if it ſhould alſo be deemed a branch of wiſdom to renounce even thoſe pleaſures which are not unbecoming, nor ſeem diſhonourable, from a perſuaſion that it is impoſſible for any one to be temperate at home, and in private, who is diſſolute abroad, and in public, and enamoured of the theatre; if this too be wiſdom, you ruin yourſelf, and you would alſo ruin us. The very name of

---

* Φιλαπεχθημονεστατε, " who art moſt fond of being hated." This is one of the many Greek words which can only be rendered by a periphraſis. M. de la Bleterie has tranſlated it *le plus haïſſable*. It occurs again in the cloſe of this ſatire.

I   ſervitude

fervitude either to the Gods or the laws difgufts us. Liberty is fweet in all things.

Of what prevarication are you guilty? You fay, you are not Lord *, nor can you endure the name.

You

* The word *dominus*, which the Greeks tranflated by κυριος and δεσποτης [or "lord"] properly fignified the power of mafters over their flaves. Under Auguftus, children already gave that name to their father, fometimes brothers gave it to their brothers, and wives to their hufbands, who returned them that of *domina*. Auguftus fuffered none but his flaves to give him that title, nor even his children and grand-children to treat him as " lord" by way of joke. *Dominum appellari fe nec a liberis quidem aut nepotibus fuis vel feriò vel joco paffus eft, atque hujufmodi blanditias inter ipfos prohibuit.* Suet. Aug. Satisfied with having deftroyed liberty, he fcrupuloufly banifhed every thing that could induce a thought of flavery. Some one having called Tiberius " Lord," he faid, with an angry look, that he did not like to be affronted. " I am," added he, " the prince of the fenate, and the general of the " army; but I am lord only of my flaves." Caligula took the name of Lord, and even that of God. But none of the emperors who fucceeded him, not even Nero, followed his example, till Domitian, who exprefsly commanded himfelf to be called Lord and God, both in letters and in fpeech. One day, dictating an edict, he began it with thefe words, " Our Lord and our God ordains what fol-" lows." It appears, by the letters of Pliny the younger, that Trajan, averfe as he was to that impious pride, fuffered himfelf, neverthelefs, to be called Lord; but at that we muft not be furprifed. The more flavery augmented, the more complimentary the nation became. In the time of Seneca they gave each other the title of " Lord," almoft as commonly as we give one another the appellation of " Sir," which is much lefs fignificant. *Obvios, fi nomen non fuccurrit, dominos appellamus.* Men gave women that of *domina* as foon as they were fourteen years old. How it was ufed by the fucceffors of Trajan is not known. Certain it is, that Alexander, the fon of Mammea, rejected the title of Lord as too oftentatious.

You refent it fo much, that you have induced many, who were formerly accuftomed to it, to banifh it from the empire, as invidious; yet you oblige us to obey the magiftrates, and the laws. How much better would it be for us to call you Lord, but in fact to be allowed freedom! O mild in appearance *, but in deeds moft cruel! How unmerciful

tatious. At laft this name made part of the ceremonial of the court, and was inferted even in the public monuments. It is affirmed, that it is not found on any medal till thofe of Aurelian, and even on them it is rare: it is more common on thofe of Carus', and frequent on thofe of Diocletian, his collegues, and his fucceffors. Julian had not time to abolifh it. It is read on many of his.
LA BLETERIE.

As Julian never abolifhed, by any public-law, the proud appellations of *Defpot*, or *Dominus*, they are ftill extant on his medals, (*Ducange, Fam. Byzantin. pp.* 38, 39.) and the private difpleafure which he affected to exprefs only gave a different tone to the fervility of the court. The Abbé de la Bleterie has curioufly traced the origin and progrefs of the word *dominus* under the Imperial government.   GIBBON.

In the Hippolytus of Euripides, an officer fays to that prince,
My royal Mafter, (for the Gods alone
Challenge the name of Lord,) &c.

on which Mr. Wodhull obferves, after mentioning the practice of Auguftus and Tiberius, that " we find, by the " Mifopogon of Julian, that he followed their example at " Conftantinople" [rather Antioch] " in much later times, " furrounded, as he was, by Afiatic flaves, inured to the " yoke, men to whom the fight of a philofopher on the " throne was fo ftrange, that they ridiculed that moderation " in the conduct of their fovereign, which they felt them- " felves incapable of imitating."

* In the original, ομματα (" eyes") perhaps for ονοματα (" names") for Julian was called by his friends πραοίατος και φιλοσοφωτατος, " the mildeft and moft philofophical." Theod. l. III. c. 15.   PETAU.

He

merciful is it to require moderation from the rich in the courts of juftice, and to reftrain the poor from flander! By abolifhing the ftage, the players, and the dancers, you have ruined our city, fo that we have no confolation left, except, after having groaned under your oppreffions for feven months *, that of referring our prayers for a deliverance from fo great an evil to the old women † who conftantly frequent the tombs of the dead. But we have fucceeded by our fcurrility, transfixing you with farcafms as with arrows. If you are thus intimidated by our taunts, how, noble Sir, will you be able to fuftain the darts of the Perfians?

But we will now exhibit another charge. You refort frequently to the temples, perverfe, morofe, and abandoned as you are. On your account, the populace, and even many of the magiftrates, flock thither, and welcome you with fhouts, acclamations, and all the fplendid applaufes of the theatre. Why then are you not pleafed? But, in-

He had probably in his view that line of Homer's Achilles,

—— Κυνος ομματ' εχων, κραδιη δ'ελαφοιο.

Thou dog in forehead, but in heart a deer,

as Pope tranflates it.

* Julian arrived at Antioch in the month of July, 362. He therefore compofed the Mifopogon in the month of January, or of February, 363. —— LA BLETERIE.

† The churches were generally built over the tomb of fome martyr. Julian fuppofes that the women, more affiduous at the churches than the men, requefted God by the interceffion of the martyrs to deliver them from him. In that there might be fome truth. *Ibid.*

stead of approving, you endeavour, in this respect, to be wiser even than the Pythian *, by haranguing the people, and severely reproving those who clamour †; thus addressing the most active: "You "seldom enter the temples, through reverence to "the Gods, but when you resort to them on my ac- "count, you fill their sanctuaries with disturbance. "Men of sound minds should pray, and ask bles- "sings of the Gods in silence, observing this rule "of Homer,

"Silently pray ‡.

"Remember too that Ulysses checked Euryclea ||,

* The priestess of Apollo, who delivered his oracles standing on a tripod called Cortina, which was placed on the mouth of a hollow in Mount Parnassus, whence proceeded a vapour that affected the head; and round this hollow was built the temple of Delphi.

† In his LXIVth Epistle Julian reproves the people of Constantinople on the same account.

‡ In the VIIth book of the Iliad, ver. 193, &c. Ajax, ready to fight with Hector, says,

Now while my brightest arms my limbs invest,
To Saturn's son be all your vows addrest.
But *pray in secret*, lest the foes should hear,
And deem your prayers the mean effect of fear.
Said I in secret? No, your vows declare,
In such a voice as fills the earth and air. Pope, 229.

How could Julian find, in these words of Ajax, a law which enjoins to "pray in silence?" All the Greeks had the practice of quoting Homer at random. It is vexatious to see authors, infinitely more respectable than Homer, sometimes quoted with as little propriety. LA BLETERIE.

|| Euryclea was the nurse of Ulysses. See Odyss. XXII. 411.

"when

" when she loudly expressed her astonishment at
" the greatness of the deed ;

" Woman, experienc'd as thou art, controul
" Indecent joy, and feast thy secret soul *.

" None of the Trojans in the Iliad, neither
" men nor women, are made suppliant to Priam,
" or to any one of his daughters, or sons, not
" even to Hector, though it is said they extolled
" him as a God : but to Minerva all the women,
" he says,

" With hands uplifted, and imploring eyes,
" Fill all the dome with supplicating cries †.

" This, indeed, was suitable to Barbarians and
" women, but was no impiety towards the Gods;
" such as you commit by praising mortals like
" Gods, or rather flattering us more than Gods ;
" when, instead of flattering even them, you had
" much better worship them wisely."

JULIAN. I repeat, you see, one of those re-
monstrances which I have been accustomed to make,
and, instead of speaking boldly and freely, with
my usual absurdity, I bear false witness against
myself. Are these, and the like, proper lessons for
those who would treat with freedom not only
princes, but also the Gods? Can they deem any
one a mild and benevolent parent, who is naturally wicked like me?

* Pope, 448.
† Iliad. VI: 301. Pope, 374.

ART.

ANT. It is plain then, Julian, that they hate you, and that they jeer you both in public and private, since those who see and applaud you in the temples you deem flatterers. You have not studied how to accommodate yourself to their ideas, lives, and manners. Well, but who can excuse this? You sleep almost every night alone *, nor

can

* Καθευδεις ως επιπαν νυκτωρ μονος. " You sleep *almost always* " alone." How is this " *almost always*" to be reconciled with the perfect continence which the Pagan authors ascribe to Julian, and which none of the Christian writers, not even St. Gregory Nazianzen himself, deny? Mamertinus scruples not to say that " the bed of that prince was " purer than that of the Vestals." If we believe Libanius, Julian never had the least frailty, either before his marriage, or after the death of his wife Helena. What that orator says is susceptible of no ambiguity or exception. I will content myself with quoting the Latin translation of Fabricius : *Nisi conjugii vinculis à Junone fuisset innexus, de mutuis hominum amplexibus, non aliâ ratione quam ex libris sermonibusque edoctus, moriturus fuisset* .... *Legitimam quidem luxit uxorem ; aliam vero nullam, sive antea, sive post fœminam attigit*, &c.

It may be replied, that Mamertinus and Libanius are panegyrists. But what shall we say of Ammianus, whose testimony is as positive as that of Libanius? Ammianus is a most judicious historian, and does not spare Julian for any of his faults. He knew him perfectly, and seems even to have interrogated, on the point in dispute, those domestics of Julian to whom his frailties, supposing he had any, could not but be known. *Ita inviolatâ castitate enituit, ut post amissam conjugem, nihil unquam venereum agitaret* ... *ut ne suspicione quidem tenùs libidinis ullius vel citerioris vitæ ministris incusaretur.* Ammianus was of Antioch. Though he wrote in Latin, he was better acquainted with Greek. He had read the Misopogon. Perhaps then Martimius, the Latin translator of this satire, M. de Fleury, M. de Tillemont,

5

mont,

can any thing soften your savage and brutal dif-
position. You have closed up all the avenues of
                                            pleasure,

mont, and myself translate this passage of Julian improperly, and the Greek words ως επιπαν do not signify here
" almost always," but " always," absolutely. At least,
it is certain that επιπαν occurs in both significations. In
this case, I ought to have translated it, " You never share
" your bed with any one." I think, however, that it ought
to be translated, as I have done, " You share scarce ever."
This restriction seems to me a refined but severe raillery
against the inhabitants of Antioch, from which nothing
can be inferred against the chastity of Julian. It is
in their name that he abuses himself. He must therefore
speak their language. Throughout the whole satire he
represents them as persons immersed in debauchery, and
abandoned to the most infamous pleasures. People of
this character do not believe in virtue. They suppose all
men to be vicious, and that they only differ in vice as to
the more and the less. On the part of Julian, whose morals
were superior to all suspicion, it is a stroke of pleasantry
to represent his enemies as persuaded that his wisdom suffered eclipses, and making, nevertheless, his excess of
wisdom a crime in him. M. de Tillemont, who understands the text in question literally, and considers it as a
confession, which Julian himself makes, of his incontinence,
observes, in order to strengthen this pretended avowal, that
Julian, in an Epistle to the philosopher Jamblicus [the
XLth] speaks of the man " who nursed his children."
This learned writer adds, that Codin, in his Antiquities
of Constantinople, mentions some statues of Julian, and
his children. " Now," says M. de Tillemont, " he never
" had any legitimate, excepting a son, who was destroyed
" by the midwife that was suborned by the empress Eusebia:
" the fact is certain; he therefore had some illegitimate."
  Let us briefly examine these two difficulties, always remembering that the Pagans, on the one side, pass an elogium on the chastity of Julian, the completest, the most
forcible, and the most exclusive of the least restriction; and
that, on the other side, the Christians, far from controvert-
R 3   ing

pleafure, and, which is the greateſt of evils, you delight in leading ſuch a rigid life, and make pleafure
the ſubject of your deteſtation.   In ſhort, you are
angry at the mention of this, though you ought
rather to thank thoſe who have kindly and har-
moniouſly admoniſhed you in anapæſts, firſt, to
ſhave thoſe cheeks, and then, having begun with
yourſelf, to exhibit all pleaſurable entertainments
to this laughter-loving people, ſuch as players,
dancers, and, in particular, lewd women, public
aſſemblies, and feſtivals, not ſacred indeed, in
which wiſdom and temperance muſt be obſerved *,
for theſe are as abundant as acorns, ſo as to occaſion a general diſguſt.

'Julian. The Emperor, I allow, ſacrificed once
in the temple of Jupiter, and afterwards in that of

ing thoſe elogiums, have not ſaid a word that can render
them ſuſpected. This eſtabliſhed, what ſtreſs ought to be
laid on the mere indication of a modern Greek, ſuch as
George Codin, who is known to have ſurvived the taking
of Conſtantinople by Mahomet II. ?"If Julian had had
baſtards, would he have erected ſtatues to them ? Would
he, who ſaid, that " incontinence is ſufficient to tarniſh
" the beſt life," have publiſhed his own ſhame, and that
of his children, in tender age ? &c.   La Bleterie.
  For what is ſaid on the paſſage above-mentioned in the
XLth Epiſtle, ſee the notes on that Epiſtle.
  This ſuſpicious expreſſion (ὡς ιππικαν) is explained by the
Abbé de la Bleterie, with candour and ingenuity.
                                                          Gibbon.
  * This is not abſolutely contrary to what is related of
the extravagant proceſſions of Julian on the feſtivals of
Venus and others. All the Pagan feſtivals were not ſo li-
centious as thoſe of Venus.   La Bleterie.
                                                       Fortune.

Fortune *. He also went thrice to that of Ceres. I forget how often I went to the temple of Daphne, that august fabrick which was betrayed by the treachery of the keepers, and by the presumption of the impious †. On the Syrian calends ‡, Cæsar

goes

* Genius and Fortune were *Dii Contubernales*, and had temples dedicated to them jointly. See *Pausan. Bœotic.* p. 313. Hence what Ammianus calls *Genii templum* (XXIII. 1.) Julian here styles τυχης, the one a male, the other a female, deity, the images of both being set up together. Modern antiquaries, as well as artists, by a kind of mythological solecism, have confounded that distinction, who call a female deity the Genius of a city. BOWYER.

† After Babylas (a bishop of Antioch, who died in prison in the persecution of Decius) had rested near a century in his grave, his body, by the order of the Cæsar Gallus, was transported into the midst of the grove of Daphne. A magnificent church was erected over his remains; a portion of the sacred lands was usurped for the maintenance of the clergy, and for the burial of the Christians of Antioch, who were ambitious of lying at the feet of their bishop; and the priests of Apollo retired, with their affrighted and indignant votaries. As soon as another revolution seemed to restore the fortune of Paganism, the church of St. Babylas was demolished, and new buildings were added to the mouldering edifice which had been raised by the piety of Syrian kings. But the first and most serious care of Julian was to deliver his oppressed deity from the odious presence of the dead and living Christians, who had so effectually suppressed the voice of fraud or enthusiasm. The scene of infection was purified, according to the forms of ancient rituals; the bodies were decently removed; and the ministers of the church were permitted to convey the remains of St. Babylas to their former habitation within the walls of Antioch. The modest behaviour, which might have assuaged the jealousy of an hostile government, was, on this occasion, neglected by the zeal of the Christians. The lofty car, that transported the relics

of Babylas, was followed, and accompanied, and received by an innumerable multitude; who chanted with thundering acclamations, the Psalms of David, the most expressive of their contempt for idols and idolaters. The return of the saint was a triumph; and the triumph was an insult on the religion of the Emperor, who exerted his pride to dissemble his resentment.—During the night which terminated this indiscreet procession [22 Oct. 362.] the temple of Daphne was in flames, the statue of Apollo was consumed, and the walls of the edifice were left a naked and awful monument of ruin.—The Christians of Antioch asserted, with religious confidence, that the powerful intercession of St. Babylas had pointed the lightnings of heaven against the devoted roof;—but as Julian was reduced to the alternative of believing either a crime or a miracle, he chose, without hesitation, without evidence, but with some colour of probability, to impute the fire of Daphne to the revenge of the Galileans.   GIBBON.

Julian (in Misopogon) rather insinuates, than affirms, their guilt.—Ammianus (XXII. 13.) treats the imputation as *levissimus rumor*, and relates the story with extraordinary candour.   *Ibid.*

I do not find that Ammianus treats this report in the manner here affirmed. All that he says of it is this, *Suspicabatur enim id Christianos egisse, stimulatos invidiâ, quòd idem templum inviti videbant ambitiosâ circumdari peristylio.* For " he suspected the Christians to have been the perpetrators, " urged to it by envy, on seeing reluctantly that temple " surrounded by a spacious peristyle." Then follows, *Ferebatur autem, licet rumore levissimo, hâc ex causâ conflagrasse delubrum,* &c. " But it was reported, though on the slightest " grounds, that this was the cause of the fire. The phi- " losopher Asclepiades, being on a visit to Julian, and " going to that suburb, as he was used to carry with him, " wherever he went, a small silver image of Juno, placed " it at the feet of the great image, and lighting wax tapers, " as usual, departed; from which, in the middle of the " night, when no one could attend or assist, sparks flying " adhered to the very ancient materials," &c. To this story therefore, and not that of the Christians, the *levissimus rumor* is applied.

‡ As in the conclusion of the Misopogon, Julian reckons the Macedonian month *Lous* the tenth of the Syrian year,

this

goes again to the temple of Jupiter Philius *. Then comes the general festival †, and Cæsar goes to the temple of Fortune. Omitting an inauspicious

this year began with the month *Dius*. In the Syrian year, which is used by Eusebius, St. Epiphanius, Evagrius, Malela, &c. the month Dius answers to the month of November. But perhaps the city of Antioch had a Syrian year that was peculiar to it. In different Macedonian cities, the month Dius answered to different Roman months. It is certain that the Syrian year of Antioch began in autumn. We cannot, however, positively assert in which of the Roman months, September, October, or November. This is the result of some learned and judicious observations communicated to me by a friend to whom I owe several of my remarks.　　　　　　　　　　　　La Bleterie.

* The patron of friendship, the same with *Hospitalis*, "a bearded face, with a placid look, to denote," says Tristan, " that true friendship is the result of age." He had a temple at Antioch, where Julian sacrificed to him more than once, during his residence there; pleased, no doubt, to have so good an authority for his beard, which, as the inhabitants little regarded in Jupiter, no wonder they ridiculed in the Emperor.　　　　　　　　　Bowyer.

† The calends of January [mentioned above, p. 231] when the consuls entered on their office, and the priests in a solemn procession, offered vows for the public safety of the empire, or of the Roman senate and people.

This therefore Libanius, in like manner, (in his description of the calends), styles " a general festival to all who " live under the Roman government."　　　　Spanheim.

This day was deemed a festival throughout all the Roman world, though all did not begin the year with it. For instance, the Romans then commenced the year with Dius, which answers to the Julian November: Therefore, in the above passage of Julian ἡ Σύρων Νεομηνία, (" the Syrian " calends,) are the first day of the month Dius. This passage has been misunderstood by Martinius, the [Latin] translator.　　　　　　　　　　　　　Valois.

day

day *, he again pays his vows in the temple of Jupiter Philius, after the manner of his ancestors †. Who can endure Cæsar's going so frequently to the temples, when the Gods should be troubled only once or twice to celebrate those festivals which are common to all the people, and of which not only they who honour the Gods, but they also with whom the city is filled, participate ‡? What an exquisite pleasure and delight does every one constantly enjoy in the sight of a number of dancing men, dancing women, and dancing boys!

Reflecting on these things, I cannot but think you happy in such diversions, and yet I am by no means dissatisfied with myself; for the life I lead, by the influence perhaps of some God, is to me agreeable. Believe me, therefore, far from being offended with those who reprobate my life and manners, I even add to their sarcasms as many as possible, and accumulate on myself more reproaches for being such a fool as not to perceive at first what were the manners of this city, especially as none of my contemporaries, I am certain, are more conversant with books than myself.

* Jan. 2. The days immediately following the calends, nones, and ides, were reckoned inauspicious. *Ovid Trist.* I. 55 *et seq.*

† On Jan. 3, when solemn vows were offered for the safety of the prince.

‡ He means the games and shews at which the Christians, as well as the Gentiles, were present, to the great offence of the most holy prelates; which St. Chrysostom, among others, frequently mentions. PETAU.

It is related that the king who was namesake to this city, or rather, to whom it owes its name (for it was built by Seleucus *; but takes its name from his son), Antiochus I mean, from an exceſſive indulgence in luxurious delights, always loving and being loved, was at length illegally enamoured of his mother-in-law †. He wiſhed to conceal his paſſion, but could not; his body being emaciated, and secretly decaying, his ſtrength failing, and his mind being languid. His caſe ſeemed myſterious, the diſorder having no apparent cauſe, and the nature of it not being known. The young man's illneſs, however, being certain; the great difficulty propoſed to a Samian phyſician ‡ was, to diſcover what the diſtemper was. He, ſuſpecting from Homer what are "the limbs-conſuming cares §", and that anxiety of mind, not weakneſs of body, is often the cauſe of bodily decay, and obſerving the youth, as well by years as conſtitution, to be not averſe to love, took this method to diſcover the diſeaſe. He ſat down by the bed-ſide, and looking the young man ſtedfaſtly in the face, he deſired ſome beautiful women to be introduced, beginning

* Seleucus Nicator.

† Stratonice, the daughter of Demetrius Poliorcetes, and wife of Seleucus.

‡ Eraſiſtratus.

§ Γυιοϐοροι μελιδωνες, "the anxieties that devour the body." I do not find the word γυιοϐοροι in the Index of Homer, made by Wolfgangus Seberus. If the Index be not faulty, Julian is miſtaken, or quotes ſome work of Homer which we do not poſſeſs. LA BLETERIE.

with

with the queen. As foon as fhe appeared, or as foon as he faw her, the youth betrayed fome fymptoms of his diforder: he breathed fhort, as if he had been afthmatic; with his utmoft endeavours he could not avoid trembling, great was the evident agitation of his mind, and his face was covered with blufhes. The phyfician, obferving this, applied his hand to his patient's breaft, and found his heart beat violently, as if it would burft forth. Such were his fenfations while the queen was prefent. But when fhe had withdrawn, while the others were paffing by, he remained tranquil, and feemed in perfect health. Having thus difcovered his malady, Erafiftratus communicated it to the king, and he, being an affectionate father, faid, he would refign his wife to his fon. He then refufed it; but his father dying not long after, the prefent, which, when offered him before, he nobly declined, he then very eagerly feized *. Such was the conduct of Antiochus.

That his defcendants therefore fhould imitate their founder, or, at leaft, their namefake, is not blameable. For, as in plants, it is probable that the qualities are widely diffufed, and perhaps thofe which are produced altogether refemble thofe

---

* Plutarch relates the ftory differently in his life of Demetrius. For he fays, that Antiochus, the fon of Demetrius Poliorcetes, married his mother-in-law in the life-time of his father.　　　　　　　　　　　　PETAU.

which produce them; so, among men *, the manners of the descendants are likely to be similar to those of their ancestors. Of the Greeks I think the Athenians the most liberal and humane; though all the Greeks, I have observed, are the same, and I can truly affirm of them, that of all men they are the greatest lovers of the Gods, and most hospitable to strangers; but of the Greeks, I give this testimony chiefly to the Athenians. And if they retain in their manners the resemblance of ancient virtue, why may not the same similitude be traced in the Syrians, the Arabians, the Gauls, the Thracians, the Pannonians, and that nation which is situated between the two latter on the banks of the Danube? I mean the Mysians, the stock from which I am descended †, who are absolutely inelegant, boorish, austere, uncivilised, and obstinately tenacious of their opinions, all which are proofs of lamentable rusticity.

First, therefore, I ask pardon for myself, for imitating the manners of my ancestors, and then I grant it to you for the same offence; nor do I mention, as a reproach, your being

In lying and in wanton dances skill'd ‡.

* The inhabitants of Antioch were nothing to Antiochus. The kind of argument which Julian here employs must not be understood seriously. It is a mere joke. LA BLETERIE.

† Eutropius, the great grandfather of Julian, and the father of Constantius-Chlorus, was of the province of Mysia. *Ibid.*

‡ Iliad. xxiv. 261. Priam's reproach of his nine surviving sons.

On

On the contrary, your following the examples and
ſtudies of your fathers I think much to your honour. Thus Homer alſo, praiſing Autolycus, ſays,
that he excelled all men

    In thieving and in ſwearing *.

* Homer, in the xixth book of the Odyſſey, v. 396,
ſays, that Autolycus, the maternal grandfather of Ulyſſes,
excelled other men, κλεπτοσυνη θ'ορκωſι, " in theft and oaths."
Mad. Dacier, on this paſſage, ſays, in effect, that the word
κλεπτοσυνη may ſignify not only " theft," but alſo " cunning,
" addreſs, ſtratagem, ſkill to conceal the knowledge of
" his ſchemes, to penetrate the ſecrets of others, &c."
" and that Homer meant to ſay that Autolycus was a very
" acute politician, an artful prince, an able negociator, who
" knew how to make treaties to his advantage, but, on the
" whole, was faithful to his word, and one who reſpected
" his oaths." Admitting the charitable explanation of Mad.
Dacier, it is unfortunate for him to have been praiſed by
Homer in equivocal terms; for the knavery of Autolycus
has grown proverbial. Martial, ſpeaking of a thief, ſays,
Non fuit Autolyci tam piceata manus.   LA BLETERIE.
  Dr. Clarke (on the above line in the Odyſſey) un-
derſtands it, however, as a commendation; and Fenton,
agreeably to the ſame interpretation, has, in his tranſlation, aſcribed to Autolycus

    ——————— a mighty name
For ſpotleſs faith, and deeds of martial fame. 456.
  Shakſpeare, on the contrary, has given his name
to a roguiſh pedlar: " My father," ſays he, " named me
" Autolycus, who being, as I am, littered under Mercury,
" was likewiſe a ſnapper-up of unconſidered trifles."
               Winter's Tale, Act IV. Sc. II.
  Euripides had two dramas (now loſt) named Autolycus;
the firſt ſatyric (as we learn from Julius Pollux) of which
a fragment is preſerved by Galen and Athenæus. Barnes
and Dr. Muſgrave ſuppoſe that it derives its name from
this Autolycus; but from what is tranſmitted to us, Mr.
Wodhull, who has tranſlated it, thinks, with more probability, that another Autolycus, a champion in the public games, was its hero.

                         And

And so, you say, do I in rusticity, obstinacy, morosenefs, in not being easily softened by supplications, or induced by intreaties or clamours, to mind my bufinefs. With thefe reproaches I am not in the leaft offended. Which of us is the moft excufable is known to the Gods, but no man can determine between us, fuch is our felf-love, every one admiring his own endowments, and defpifing thofe of others. But he, who bears with indulgence a courfe of life the reverfe of his own, feems to me the moft benevolent.

[On reflection, I find that, in fome other particulars, I have been much my own enemy. For when I came to a free city, which could not endure the naftinefs of my hair, I came to it uncombed and bearded, as if barbers had been wanting *. You would have taken me for Smicrines or Thrafyleon †, a morofe old man, or a

frantic

* Soon after his entrance into the palace of Conftantinople, Julian had occafion for the fervice of a barber. An officer, magnificently dreffed, immediately prefented himfelf. " It is a barber," exclaimed the prince, " that " I want, and not a receiver-general of the finances." He queftioned the man concerning the profits of his employment; and was informed, that, befides a large falary, and fome valuable perquifites, he enjoyed a daily allowance of twenty fervants, and as many horfes.. GIBBON.

Libanius fays, that a thoufand cooks, as many barbers (κεμαρς εκ ελατω), more cup-bearers, &c. were diftributed in the feveral offices of luxury which Julian abolifhed or retrenched.

† Thefe were probably two comic characters of Menander, as Cafaubon (*Animadv. in Athenæum, l. vi. c. 12.*)

mentions

frantic soldier, when I might have appeared, by the ornamental advantages of dress, a handsome boy, or, at least, a youth, if not in years *, in effeminacy and features †.]

ANT. You know not how to associate with men; you adopt not the maxims of Theognis ‡, nor imitate (as he recommends) the changeful polypus §,

mentions a comedy by that poet named Thrasyleon. He adds, that there was one of the same name in Latin by Turpilius, a translation, he supposes, from Menander, which is often quoted by Nonius.

* When Julian first came to Antioch, he was thirty-one years old.

† The paragraphs between [ ] are omitted here, and removed lower, by the French translator. They seem indeed a repetition of what was said at the beginning, yet I do not think myself warranted to transpose them, though I thoroughly assent to the propriety of the following remark of M. de la Bleterie, as an excuse for the incorrectness of the author, but not for the corrections of his translator : " In general, the Misopogon is a little unsewed, " and the repetitions in it are too frequent. It was com- " posed perhaps in the space of one or two nights. Julian " was too much employed to be an author by premedi- " tation. When an author scarce reads what he writes, " we cannot wonder at tautology."

‡ Theognis, a poet of Megara, lived about 550 years before the Christian æra. We have some sentences, or maxims, by him, in elegiac verse.   LA BLETERIE.

§ Ulysses, clinging to a cliff, is compared to this fish by Homer, Odyss. V. 432. Aristotle, and others, suppose, that it changes its colour, in order more easily to catch its prey, or from fear. St. Paul, who, for good reasons *became all things to all men*, is on that account, compared to a polypus by Julian in his work against the Christian religion, preserved and confuted by Cyril. But its more extraordinary power of re-production was reserved for the speculation of modern naturalists.

which

which affumes the colour of rocks, but, on the contrary, you behave to all with the proverbial rufticity, folly, and morofenefs of a Myconian *. Know you not, that we are widely different from the Gauls, the Thracians, and the Illyrians? This city, you fee, abounds with fhops. But you provoke the retailers by not fuffering them to extort, both from natives and foreigners, what price they pleafe for provifions. They complain of the landholders † ; but thefe alfo you make your enemies,

* Archilochus of Paros writes, that Pericles ufed to come uninvited to the entertainments of others, after the manner of the Myconians, who inhabiting a barren ifland [in the Archipelago] were notorious for their avarice and rufticity.   ATHENÆUS.

On this proverb fee Euftathius (*in Odyff.* XVII.) Suidas, and Zenobius.   PÉTAU.

† This paffage is obfcure. What follows may explain it. Ammianus fays (*l.* XXII.) that Julian, " with no " apparent reafon, for the fake of popularity, endea-" voured to make all commodities cheap, which fome-" times, by improper management, occafions dearth and " famine." Nor could the magiftrates of Antioch diffuade him. By fixing therefore a lower price on things that were to be fold, he made the retailers his enemies. And when thofe retailers, being charged with the unreafonablenefs of their demands, complained that they bought corn and provifions dearer of the landholder, he compelled them alfo, by the fame edict, to make abatements. This feverity and rigour, exercifed againft thefe two ranks, extended to the chief men of the city and the magiftrates, who fupplied the markets, and owned the lands. And thus they were doubly mulcted.   *Ibid.*

The magiftrates of Antioch perhaps condefcended to fell wine themfelves by retail, like fome of the prefent nobility of Florence, as mentioned by Lord Corke, Dr. Smollett, and other travellers.

by obliging them to be juft. The magiftrates, who, availing themfelves of both thefe diftreffes, rejoiced before at receiving double profits, both as landholders and as retailers, now, on being deprived of both thefe advantages, are equally exafperated. The Syrians too, at being precluded both from drinking immoderately and dancing lafcivioufly, are no lefs enraged; but by giving them bread in plenty, you think they are fufficiently regaled. And fo gracious are you, that you are not contented with procuring them oyfters only.

When a complaint was lately made, that no fifh, and fcarce any poultry, could be procured in the markets, you faid, with a fneering laugh, that " a frugal city ought to be fatisfied with bread, " wine, and oil; that meat was a dainty; but " fifh and poultry were more than dainties, and " would not have been indulged even to the fuitors " in Ithaca." Thus you would have us deem pork and mutton luxuries, and fubfift, like you, on vegetables *, thinking that in this you govern well,

and

* In the time of Julian, the philofophers of the reigning fect, who had blended the Ægyptian and Chaldean tenets with Platonifm and the ruins of the doctrine of Pythagoras, tranfmitted by a very uncertain tradition, thofe philofophers, I fay, or rather the moft perfect among them, adopted a very auftere mode of life, which made part of the doctrine which was revealed, in the myfteries, to the initiated. As Orpheus paffed for the firft inftitutor of the myfteries, it was pretended that this kind of life was that

which

and are giving laws to your Thracian countrymen,
or to those ſtupid Gauls, who, by their education,
have made you a mere block of holm or maple,
not a Marathonian but half an Acharnian * warrior,

                                        one

which Plato and ſome other ancients have mentioned under
the name of " Orphic life," Ορφικος Βιος: This life, which
Porphyry preaches in his book, *De abſtinentiâ animalium,*
conſiſted in the practice of moral virtues, added to the pri-
vation of things allowed in common life. The Orphics
muſt have reſembled the Ægyptian prieſts and the Bramins.
Julian had not embraced the Orphic life, but he endeavoured to approach near it. To what I have elſewhere
ſaid of his extreme frugality, I will add here what I find
in his funeral oration. See the *Bibliotheca Græca* of Fabricius, *vol.* VII. *p.* 309, 310. " What private philoſopher
" in his cottage," ſays Libanius, " ever practiſed an ab-
" ſtinence ſo rigorous as that of this Emperor? Who de-
" prived himſelf more often than he, ſometimes of one
" food, ſometimes of another, in honour of Pan, of Mer-
" cury, of Hecate, of Iſis, of all the deities? Who, like
" him, ever took delight in abſtaining frequently from all
" nouriſhment? Thus he lived in an intimate connection
" with the Gods . . . his body not allowing him to raiſe
" himſelf to heaven, they deſcended on earth to converſe
" with him. They came to inſtruct him in what he ſhould
" do or forbear. . . . He had no occaſion for human
" wiſdom or underſtanding. The immortal beings, who
" know every thing, were both his council and his guard.
" By them he was almoſt always ſurrounded." After this
quotation, to which I could add many ſimilar, no one, I
fancy, will have the leaſt doubt of the fanaticiſm of Julian
any more than of that of his panegyriſt. LA BLETERIE.

    * The Acharnians (ſo one of the tribes of Athens was
called) were valiant, but rough and hardy. In the comedy
of Ariſtophanes, entitled the Acharnian, ſome old men
of that tribe are ſtyled " men of oak and maple, ſoldiers
" of Marathon;" meaning invincible warriors. The inhabitants of Antioch, in alluſion to this paſſage of the
comic poet, reproach Julian for having the hardineſs, the

unpolite-

one generally odious and disguftful. Was it not
better for you to walk the forum, fcented with
perfumes, and preceded by beautiful boys, and
thus to attract the eyes of the citizens, and bands
of women, fuch as you fee affembled every day *?

Jul. But to look wantonly, cafting my eyes on
all fides, and to appear beautiful to you in perfon,
not in mind, my principles will not allow me.
" The true beauty of the mind confifts," you fay,
" in the enjoyment of life." But my governor
taught me, when I attended mafters, to behold the
ground, not the ftage, and to cherifh the hairs of
my chin more than thofe of my head. And even

unpolitenefs, the roughnefs, of the Acharnians, without
the courage of thofe brave Attic peafants. To thefe ideas,
which are purely Greek, I have fubftituted fome that are
equivalent.   La Bleterie.

In this tranflation the Greek ideas are retained. As
Julian is the fpeaker, let him fpeak as a Greek or Roman,
and not like a Londoner or Parifian. Though it is not uncommon with us to fay, in like manner, of thofe who are
hardy, that they are " made of iron and fteel;" and thus
Charles XII. was ftyled by the Turks, " iron-head," and
by Dr. Johnfon, " a frame of adamant, a foul of fire."

* Nothing could equal the feftivals of Venus, and other
fuch folemnities, when, refufing to give audience to the
officers and magiftrates, Julian conducted through the city
the female proftitutes, and the other victims of the public
incontinence. The women walked firft; after them came
the effeminate youths. Between thefe two infamous troops,
who burft into loud fhouts of laughter, and uttered all that
debauchery could dictate, marched the reformer of Paganifm, with a burlefque gravity, heightening as much as
poffible his puny ftature, extending a pointed beard, and
affecting the ftep of a giant. His horfe followed at a diftance, and his guards clofed this extravagant pomp.
                                              La Bleterie.

at that age I never went to the theatre privately
and voluntarily, but twice or thrice only,

To pleafe Patroclus, by the prince commanded *,
my intimate friend and kinfman. I was then a
fubject.

Pardon me therefore, and rather turn your refentment againft that wicked governor, who was
then fo troublefome to me by inculcating thofe
moral leffons. He has occafioned all your diflike
to me by fixing, and, as it were, carving on
my mind what I ought to fhun. And, as if he
meant to pleafe me, he exerted himfelf with the
utmoft earneftnefs, calling rufticity gravity, and ftu-
pidity temperance, faying, that to refift the paffions
was fortitude, and that the gratification of them
does not conftitute happinefs. My governor often
faid to me, when I was quite a boy, as Jove and the
Mufes can witnefs, " Do not fuffer yourfelf to be
" feduced to the theatre by the crowd of your
" companions, nor be enamoured of fuch enter-
" tainments. Do you wifh to fee a chariot-race?
" It is elegantly defcribed in Homer † : open the
" book, and read. Do you hear of pantomime

---

* Πατροκλω επινεα φερων, αρχων επελατλεν.
This, though not printed as fuch in the editions, or obferved by the commentators, is an heroic verfe; but
it does not occur in Homer, nor is it clear whom Julian here means by " Patroclus." The prince (αρχων)
muft probably be his brother, Cæfar Gallus.

† In the xxiiid book of the Iliad, Achilles caufes fome
games to be celebrated in honour of the funeral of Patroclus. Among them is a defcription of a chariot-race.
LA BLETERIE.

" dancers?

" dancers? Away with them! The Phæäcian
" youths are less effeminate *. You have there
" the harper Phemius †, and the singer Demo-
" docus ‡. His trees too are more delightful to
" the ear than ours are to the eye,

    " Thus, seems the palm §, with stately honours
      " crown'd,
    " By Phœbus' altar ‖ ; thus o'erlooks the ground,
    " The pride of Delos.

* See the dances of the Phæïcians in the viiith book of
the Odyssey.   LA BLETERIE.

† Phemius was a musician of the island of Ithaca, whom
the suitors of Penelope forced to play on the harp during
their banquets.   Ibid.

‡ The Greeks must certainly have been very fond of
their Homer, as a governor so grave as that of Julian ad-
vises a child to read the scandalous romance of Mars taken
in the nets of Vulcan, which Demodocus sings at the feast
of Alcinöus. See Odyss. viii.   Ibid.

Another grave and intelligent tutor, himself a proficient
in music, (who has lately given excellent " Advice to his
" pupils,") was also inattentive to these *furia Deorum*, as
Virgil modestly styles them, when he said, " The wise men
" of Heathen antiquity reserved the powers of music for
" the instilling moral instruction into youth." *Jones's Phy-
siological Disquisitions*, p. 354.

§ Odyss. vi. 162. Broome, 193. Nausicaa is compared
to this palm-tree by Ulysses.

Because the Ulysses of Homer said, that he " saw a tall
and tender palm-tree at Delos," the same is still shewn at
this day. *Cicero de Legibus*, I, 1.

The palm also of Delos is visible from the time of that
God [Apollo.] *Plin. Nat. Hist. l.* xvi. 44.

‖ In the original it is παρα βωμω. Casaubon, in his notes
on Athenæus, xvi. 9. quotes it περι βωμω. But Julian, in
the passage above, reads it, or quotes it by memory, παρα
βωμον.   CLARKE.

                      " And

" And the woody ifland of Calypfo, and the
" groves of Circe, and the garden of Alcinöus,
" be affured you will fee nothing more enchant-
" ing."

Would you know the name of this governor,
and his family? By all the Gods and Goddeffes,
he was a Barbarian, a Scythian, and name-fake to
him *, who perfuaded Xerxes to wage war againft
Greece and the renowned Argives. He was an
eunuch, a title, which twenty months ago † was
revered, but is now the fubject of fhame and reproach. He was educated by my grandfather ‡,

¿ that

---

* It is well known that it was Mardonius, the fon of
Gobryas, who, in the council of Xerxes, gave his opinion
for making war with the Greeks, and whofe advice prevailed. Herod. VII. The governor of Julian had the fame
name. La Bleterie.

† He principally means Eufebius, the chamberlain of
Conftantius, [fee the Epiftle to the Athenians, p. 68.] who,
in his reign, had the management of public affairs. Ammianus, (xxi. 15.) relates, that " Conftantius died Oct. 5.
" in the confulfhip of Taurus and Florentius," which was
A. D. 361. He alfo fays, in the next book, that " Julian
" compofed his Mifopogon towards the end of the year 362,
" and that he marched from Antioch againft the Perfians,
" March 1, 363." So that from the death of Conftantius to the time of his writing the Mifopogon there was
an interval of not quite fifteen months. But Julian reckons
twenty. Whether it is a miftake, or not, I cannot tell.
Petau.

Julian probably fixes the epocha of the difgrace of the
eunuchs to the time of his declaring war againft Conftantius.
La Bleterie.

‡ The præfect Julian (probably Anicius Julianus, who was
conful in 322) the moft illuftrious private perfon of his age

by

that he might inſtruct my mother * in the poems of
Homer and Heſiod. I was her firſt and only ſon †,
and a few months after my birth ſhe died, leaving
me an orphan, and oppreſſed with many misfortunes. Young and tender, at ſeven years of age I
was entruſted to his care. From that time, conducting me to proper maſters, he perſuaded me
that this was the only right way; and as he himſelf would not know, nor would ſuffer me to pur-
ſue, any other, he has expoſed me to your reſentment.

But, if you pleaſe, we will now make peace,
and terminate our animoſity. For he had no idea
of my coming hither, far from expecting that I

by his birth, his riches, and his reputation; and perhaps the
firſt Roman ſenator who made a public profeſſion of Chriſtianity. He had been engaged in the party of Maxentius;
but Conſtantine, after the victory, revered the ſuperior
talents of this great man, and a virtue ſtill ſuperior to
them. He made him conſul, præfect, and at length his
brother-in-law. La Bleterie.

*, Baſilina. It is ſaid, that, when ſhe was ready to lie
in, ſhe dreamed that ſhe brought Achilles into the world;
and that, upon her waking, while ſhe related this dream,
ſhe was delivered of Julian, almoſt without pain. This
princeſs died in the flower of her age. She appears to have
been an Arian and a perſecutreſs, which is not ſurpriſing,
if ſhe was related to Euſebius of Nicomedia. " It is certain that Julian was a diſtant relation of this biſhop," ſays
Ammianus: probably by the ſide of Baſilina, whoſe mother,
the maternal grandmother of Julian, might be of Ionia or
Bithynia. *Ibid.*

† Gallus (as above-mentioned) was by another mother.

ſhould

should govern' such an empire * as the Gods have beſtowed, much againſt the will, believe me, both of the giver and receiver. For he who conferred † this honour, or favour, or whatever elſe you may pleaſe to call it, conferred it with reluctance, and by him who accepted it, the Gods well know, it was ſincerely rejected. But their will is and muſt be obeyed. If my governor could have foreſeen this, he would, without doubt, have endeavoured to make me acceptable to you. But now, whatever manners I may have previouſly contracted, whether gentle or booriſh, it is impoſſible for me to alter or unlearn. Habit is ſaid to be a ſecond nature; to oppoſe it is irkſome; but to counteract the ſtudy of more than thirty years is extremely difficult, eſpecially when it has been imbibed with ſo much attention.

Ant. Allowing this, what induced you to inveſtigate and determine matters of traffick ? This, I imagine, was not taught you by your governor, as he did not foreſee your reigning.

Jul. This alſo was owing to that wicked old man, whom, as the principal director of my ſtudies, you ſo juſtly reproach as well as me; but know, that he was deceived by others. You have often

---

* Conſtantius, by the courſe of nature, might have had children, and Gallus was the elder brother of Julian, who was intended for the eccleſiaſtical ſtate. La Bleterie.

† It is pretended that Conſtantius, on his death-bed, named Julian his ſucceſſor. Julian believes, or affects to believe, it. *Ibid.*

heard,

heard, I fuppofe, the names of Plato, Socrates, Ariftotle, and Theophraftus *, mentioned with derifion. On thefe that old man had the folly to rely, and afterwards finding me young and capable of improvement, he told me, that, if in every thing I would make them my models, I fhould excell, he would not fay all other men (for with them there was no competition), but myfelf. Thus guided by him, how could I act otherwife? Were it ever fo defirable, I can now make no alteration, and when I reproach myfelf for not indulging every vice, I recollect what the Athenian ftranger fays in Plato +: " He is to be honoured who commits
" no crime; he who prevents others from being
" criminal is worthy of more than double honour:
" the former is equal in dignity to a man; the
" latter, who difcovers to the magiftrates the crimes
" of others, is equal to many. But he, who, in
" punifhing, affociates himfelf in authority with
" the magiftrates, is a great and perfect citizen,
" and fhall be deemed victor in the lifts of virtue:
" the fame praife is due to temperance and pru-
" dence, and to all thofe other good qualities
" which are not only ufeful to the poffeffors, but
" are alfo imparted to others."

* A Peripatetic philofopher, who fucceeded Ariftotle in his fchool. *Cic. in Orat.* xix. His books of plants and moral characters are all that remain of his compofition; the reft of his works are enumerated by Diogenes Laërtius in his life. His name was changed by Ariftotle, for his eloquence, from Tyrtamus.

+ *De Legibus*, l. v.

I

Such

Such were the inſtructions that I received from one who thought that he was forming a private individual, not foreſeeing the rank in which Jupiter has placed me. I ſhould be aſhamed of appearing worſe as a prince than as a ſubject. I have indeed ſo far forgotten myſelf as to acquaint you with my ruſticity. Another law of Plato, which has made me recollect myſelf; and be your enemy, ſays, that " the magiſtrates and elders ſhould prac- " tiſe modeſty and temperance, that their lives " may be leſſons to the people." Singly, therefore, or rather with a few, I obſerve theſe rules ; but the event has been different from what I expected, and has juſtly involved me in diſgrace. Seven of us foreigners *, who have lately arrived among you, (but one, who has ſince joined us, is your own fellow-citizen †, dear to Mercury and to me, an excellent maſter of oratory,) have no connection with the reſt of the world ; we go out but ſeldom, and that only to the temples of the Gods. To the theatres we never reſort, thinking them of all places the moſt ignoble, of all purſuits the moſt inglorious. If the Grecian

---

* In the number of the ſix friends, whom the Emperor had with him, muſt certainly be placed the philoſophers Maximus of Epheſus, Priſcus of Epirus, the ſophiſt Himerius of Bithynia, and the phyſician Oribaſius of Pergamus. It may be ſurmiſed that the two others were Salluſt the ſecond and Anatolius. But I do not think that Julian here ſpeaks of any officer of the empire. LA BLETERIE.

† It is needleſs to obſerve that Libanius is here meant.
Ibid.

ſages

ſages will allow me to diſtinguiſh our ſociety by
the moſt remarkable circumſtance that attends it,
nothing ſeems ſo peculiarly our characteriſtic as
an averſion to public entertainments *. Thus we
ſolicit your hatred and reſentment, inſtead of cajoling and endeavouring to pleaſe you.

ANT. Suppoſe a man is guilty of injuſtice. What
folly is it in you to interfere ! You might not only
have ingratiated yourſelf with him, but have
ſhared the emoluments of his injuſtice. Yet you
prefer his enmity. You ſhould have conſidered
that one who is injured never complains of the
magiſtrates, but only of the perſon who has injured him. But, when he has been puniſhed, inſtead of blaming his accuſer, he turns his reſentment
againſt the magiſtrates. With your uſual wiſdom
therefore you ſhould have refrained from compel-
ling others to be juſt by force, and have allowed
them all full liberty to act as they pleaſed, the
manners of this city being remarkably free. Not
attending to this, how can you think they will
obey the dictates of prudence, or renounce that
freedom which even the aſſes and the camels here
enjoy ? The drivers lead their camels through the
porticoes, like ſo many brides, magnificently
dreſſed †. As if the wide ſtreets and narrow lanes

* There being no ſenſe to be collected from the original,
as it appears in the editions, both printed and MS. I have
adopted that which M. de la Bleterie has ſubſtituted.

† A ſatirical ſtroke on the bad police of Antioch.

4

were

were not intended for their ufe, they freely range the porticoes, and no one interferes, left he fhould be thought to abridge their liberty. Such is the freedom of this city; and yet you would have the young men here live peaceably, and think, or, at leaft fpeak, what it may give you pleafure to hear. But they are accuftomed to banquet freely every day, efpecially on feftivals.

Jul. The Romans formerly took vengeance on the Tarentines for affronting their ambaffadors at a Bacchanalian debauch *. But you, much happier than the Tarentines, inftead of a few days, revel the whole year †, and inftead of foreign ambaffadors,

you

---

* In the year of Rome 473, the Romans fent an embaffy to the city of Tarentum to demand fatisfaction for an act of hoftility committed againft their fhips. Their ambaffadors had an audience in the theatre, which was the ufual place of affembly in all the Greek cities. The Roman ambaffadors defiring to fpeak in Greek were treated as Barbarians, infulted for their foreign accent and drefs, and at length driven out of the affembly. A buffoon, with beaftly impudence, foiled their robes, to the diverfion of every one, and was unanimoufly applauded. "Laugh now," faid Pofthumus, the chief of the embaffy; "you fhall weep "hereafter. This habit fhall be wafhed with ftreams of "blood." The Romans declared war againft the inhabitants of Tarentum. They called Pyrrhus to their affiftance; but Pyrrhus being forced to abandon Italy, the Tarentines furrendered at difcretion. The Romans defpoiled them of a confiderable part of their territory, obliged them to deliver up their arms and their fhips, deftroyed the walls of the city, and made it tributary. LA BLETERIE.

† Let Julian fay what he will, I do not imagine that the inhabitants of Tarentum were at all inferior to thofe

of

you infult your own princes, and, in particular, deride their beards, and the devices of their coin *. I congratulate you, moft modeft citizens, fome for indulging thefe fportive conceits, and others for applauding and admiring them. Thofe, it is certain, are not more delighted with uttering, than thefe are with hearing, fuch ribaldry. Such a harmonious concurrence is wonderfully pleafing to me, and happy is this one city in being actuated only by one mind.

To check and reftrain the petulance and licentioufnefs of youth is by no means right or laudable. For to deprive men of the power of faying and doing whatever they pleafe is an offence againft liberty of the deepeft die. Thoroughly convinced that you ought in all refpects to be free, firft, you allow your wives to be their own rulers, that they may be as licentious as poffible; and, next, you devolve upon them the education of your children, left by our laying reftraints upon you, they alfo fhould at length be enflaved; or, when they advance to maturity, they fhould be taught to refpect their elders, and then by degrees fhould reverence their princes; and, laftly, fhould thus be claffed, not among men, but flaves, and by becoming temperate, juft, and honeft, fhould be corrupted and

of Antioch. It is faid of the former, that they had more feafts and public feftivals than there were days in a year.
LA BLETERIE.

* The inhabitants of Antioch ridiculed the marks of idolatry that appeared on the coins of Julian. *Ibid.*

ruined.

ruined. As to the women, they seduce their children to their religion by the charms of pleasure *, which is deemed the greatest good not only by men, but brutes. In consequence of this, you are most happy when you renounce all subjection; first, to the Gods, secondly to the laws, and, lastly, to us, the guardians of the laws. And if the Gods thus connive at this licentious city, and make no vengeance on its crimes, for us to be indignant and enraged would be folly in the extreme.

Neither the *Chi* nor the *Kappa*, you say, have hurt your city. This ænigma of your wisdom it is difficult to understand. But from some interpreters, of your city, I have learned, that these letters are the initials of certain names, the one of Constantius, the other of Christ †. Allow me, on this subject, to deliver my sentiments with freedom. The only instance, in which you were injured by Constantius, was his not putting me to death when he made me Cæsar. Would to heaven, that you alone, of all the Romans, had many Constantii, or rather might experience the rapine of his favourites! As for him, he was my relation

---

* It is an accuser who speaks. However, it is easy to suppose, that, in the reign of a prince so eager, as Julian was, to make proselytes, fathers and mothers were extremely indulgent to their children, lest they should embrace the religion of their sovereign. It is said, that, among the modern Greeks, the children of the lowest of the people, when they are ill-treated by their parents, threaten to turn Turks, and sometimes keep their word. LA BLETERIE.

† Χριϛος and Κωνϛαντιος.

and friend; but after he converted his friendship to enmity, and the Gods had terminated our dispute by gentle means *, I became a more sincere friend to him than, before our rupture, he could have expected. Why then should you think me displeased with those who praise him? On the contrary, I am offended with those who disparage him.

But you love Christ, and adore him as a tutelar deity, in the room of Jupiter, Daphnæan Apollo, and Calliope, who has detected your imposture †. . . . Did the Emesenians ‡ shew their love of Christ by burning the sepulchres of the Galileans? But have I ever offended the Emesenians? On the contrary, whom have I not offended of you? Most, if not all, of you, the senate, the rich, the populace? Or, rather, all the people, being attached to impiety, are displeased with me

* There was no blood shed in the war. Constantius died of a fever, (see p. 104, note.) while he was marching against Julian.   LA BLETERIE.

† Though neither the printed editions, nor the MSS. take notice here of any chasm, the passage seems to me defective. I suspect that there were some blasphemies here, which the transcribers have retrenched.   Ibid.

‡ The inhabitants of Antioch placed to the account of the other people of Syria, and in particular of the city of Emesa, the songs and satires which they composed against the Emperor. But Julian was not duped by them: the other cities of Syria testified a zeal for Paganism, which would not admit a suspicion that they wished to dishonour the restorer of their religion. The inhabitants of Emesa had set fire to the churches built over the tombs of the martyrs, and had spared only the principal, which they converted into a temple of Bacchus.   Ibid.

for

for adhering to the laws and ceremonies of my anceſtors; the rich, becauſe I prevent their exacting unreaſonable prices; and all on account of the dancers and players, not becauſe I aboliſh them, but becauſe I regard them no more than the frogs of the lakes *. After having excited ſo much hatred, may I not be allowed to accuſe myſelf?

The Roman Cato (what kind of beard he wore I know not †, but of this I am certain) excelled all who were moſt renowned for temperance, magnanimity, and, which is the greateſt of all, bravery. When, therefore, he viſited this populous, luxurious, and wealthy city, ſeeing in the ſuburbs the young men under arms, and the magiſtrates in their robes, he thought all this parade was exhibited by your anceſtors in compliment to him; and alighting immediately from his horſe ‡, he haſtened forward, and blamed his friends, who had entered the city before him, for appriſing the

* A proverbial hyperbole, meaning that the buſineſs is nothing to us §. And it is juſtly alſo applied to detractors, when we mean to ſay we hold their calumnies in contempt. As though frogs croak continually, and bark at the paſſers-by, repeating inceſſantly that odious ditty, Βρεκεκεκεξ κοαξ κοαξ, yet no one is offended.　ERASMUS.

† Julian muſt ſurely have known that, in the time of Cato of Utica, the Romans wore no beards. It may be ſaid that he is ſorry that Cato had not one as long as his own.　LA BLETERIE.

‡ Plutarch ſays, that "Cato was on foot, as was his "uſual cuſtom, and his friends, who accompanied him, on "horſeback. On this occaſion, he made them diſmount."

§ Rather that we totally diſregard it; as many do not regard what greatly concerns them; and, on the contrary, pay great attention to matters with which they have no concern. STEPHENS.

citizens of his approach, and perfuading them to go and meet him. While Cato thus hefitated, and feemed abafhed, the mafter of the ceremonies coming up to him, faid, " Stranger, how far off " is Demetrius ?" He was a freed-man of Pompey, and was poffeffed of much wealth. You will afk me how much *, as I know nothing more likely to excite your curiofity. For this I muft refer you to my author, Damophilus † of Bithynia, who collected many fuch ftories from various writers, which are very entertaining both to young and old who have a tafte for fuch fubjects. For old age feems to renew the curiofity of youth in the moft incurious; to which, I imagine, it is owing, that both old and young are equally fond of ftories. But to return. Would you know what anfwer Cato gave? Sufpect not that I traduce the city. The ftory is not mine. If the name of a certain native of Chæronea ‡ has reached your ears, of that vile fect, as it is called, of infolent philofophers, into which I have not indeed yet been admitted, though fuch is my folly, I have

* Bifhop Warburton, in a note on ver. 390, of Pope's Epiftle to Arbuthnot, " What fortune, pray," [had your parents] where " his friend's perfonating the town, and " affuming its impertinent curiofity, gives great fpirit to " the ridicule of the queftion," quotes this paffage of Julian as " a parallel ftroke."

† Damophilus lived, it is faid, in the reign of Marcus Aurelius. Julian gives us no high idea of this compiler, and ridicules him by the way.   LA BLETERIE.

‡ Every one knows that Plutarch was of Chæronea in Bœotia. He relates this ftory in the Life of Pompey. *Ibid.* He relates it alfo in the Life of Cato.

wifhed

wished it; he, I say, relates that Cato made no answer, but only exclaimed, like a madman, "O " miserable city!" and departed.

Wonder not therefore at my behaving to you in the same manner, especially as I am more savage, and as much bolder and prouder, than Cato as the Gauls are than the Romans. He lived almost all his life in his native country. But I was scarce arrived at manhood when I was sent among the Gauls and Germans, and into the Hercynian forest * ; and having spent much time there, fighting with savages, like a hunter chasing wild beasts, I contracted such a disposition as cannot fawn nor flatter, but can live on terms of simplicity and equality with all men. As in the days of my early youth I travelled through the works of Plato and Aristotle †, I had no talents for this civil life, and no taste for pleasure. When I became a man, and my own master, I lived among the most fierce and warlike nations, who had no connection with Venus, the Goddess of love, but in the way of marriage, and for the sake of an off-spring; nor with Bacchus, the God of wine, but for the sake of drinking as much as they could. In their theatres, they have no obscenity, no insolence, no lascivious dances. It is said, that not long ago a certain Cappadocian fled thither from hence. You know whom I mean ; the same who

* See a Fragment on this forest at the end of the epistles.
† Η τι εν μειρακιοις οδος δια των Πλατωνος και Αριστοτελυς λογων. Literally, " my way lay through the discourses," &c.

was

was educated in your city by a goldfmith. He had imbibed, I know not where, fome diffolute prin- ciples, which, I know not how, he had reduced to practice *. Being introduced to one of their kings †, remembering what he had feen here, he firft entertained them with a number of dancers, and afterwards with many other curiofities of this city. At length, being in want of a cotylift ‡,

(with

---

* In the original, μα'ων οπε και ιμαθεν, ως ὁ διον ομιλειν γυναιξι, μειρακιοι; δ'επιχειρειν, ουκ οιδα οποσα ειθαδι δρασας και παθων. I have fubftituted, with the French tranflator, more decent ge- neral expreffions.

† Παρα τον εκεισι βασιλεα, *ad regem qui illic.* - Muft we un- derftand, by this, a Barbarian king, for inftance, the chief of fome tribe of Franks, who, in the time of Magnentius, fettled themfelves in a diftrict of Gaul? Magnentius, who derived his origin from the Franks, might have called fome of them to his affiftance. Befides, Conftantius had fent word to the people beyond the Rhine, that they might enter into the Gauls, and that he would cede to them all the conquefts that they might make there. The Barbarians feconded his views too well. Julian had much difficulty to make them repafs the Rhine. Perhaps too it may be fuppofed (but this fenfe feems to me lefs natural) that it relates to one of the Emperors, or Cæfars, who refided in the Gauls before Julian. The name of βασιλευς was given to the Emperors and Cæfars. It is fometimes given to them even by Julian, notwithftanding his republican ideas.

LA BLETERIE.

‡ The word *cotyliftes* occurs in no other paffage of Julian. We are totally ignorant of what he means. However, as κόλυλος and κόλυλη fignify a kind of cup, κυλυλιστης, their de- rivative, may fignify perhaps " a player with cups, or " a jugler." Seneca calls thefe goblets *præfligia- torum acetabula.* It is remarkable that κόλυλη and *acetabulum* have another meaning, which is common to them. They both fignify the cavity of the *os ifchion*, in which the head of the thigh is inferted. As *acetabulum* means " a cup to ". play tricks," there is great probability that κόλυλη is ufed

(with this you are well acquainted both in word and deed) he fent for one alfo from hence, fuch was his attachment to your refpectable way of life. Though the Gauls were ftrangers to a cotylift, for this was the firft time that any one had been feen at court, yet, when the dancers exerted their fkill in the theatre, they deferted it, thinking thofe performers fools or mad.

To me a theatre feems no lefs ridiculous. But there, the few were derided by the many; here, I with the few am derided by you all. This, however, does not offend me; for it would be unjuft in me, after concurring with them, not to bear with patience this treatment from you. I was fo beloved by the Gauls, for the fimilitude of my manners, that they not only took up arms for me, but alfo made me many prefents; on my refufing them, they frequently obliged me to accept them, and in every thing readily obeyed me. From thence, which was of the utmoft importance, my name was often tranfmitted to you with glory; and all exclaimed, that I was brave, prudent, juft, equally expert in peace as in war, mild, and courteous.

Of this the manner in which you have treated me has been quite ther everfe. Firft you fay, " I " have fubverted the world *." In anfwer; I know

of

in the fame fenfe. I am indebted for this erudition to the learned M. Falconet.   LA BLETERIE.

  * According to Socrates, (*l.* III. *c.* 17.) the faying, that " Julian had fubverted the world," was owing to a bull and an altar appearing on his coins. F. Petau, M. Fleury,

T 3 and

of nothing that I have subverted, either by design
or inadvertence.   Next, that " my beard should
" be twisted into ropes."   And, lastly, that " I

and M. de Tillemont suppose, that Socrates says, the bull
lay on his back.   But the historian says no such thing. We
know, of no medal of this prince on which is seen a bull
thrown down, or even a bull with an altar. We are acquainted with some on which appears a bull standing, above
which are two stars. At the feet of that animal is an eagle,
who holds a crown in his beak, and seems to present it to
the bull; but there is no altar. Supposing that Socrates is
not mistaken, he alludes to some medal that is unknown to
us.   A victim, ready for sacrifice, stamped on the coins of
the Emperor, shewed that the empire had changed its religion; and that is what the inhabitants of Antioch might
very well call the subversion of the world."   After all,
Julian, by his restless and reforming genius, by the various
changes which he introduced, both in the state and religion,
sufficiently deserved the above reproach, without its being
necessary to think that this reproach was relative to any
one of his coins.   La Bleterie.

One medal of Julian with a bull and an eagle, and another
with a bull and two stars, are described by Occo. Among
the Imperial brass coins belonging to the library of Christ-
Church, Canterbury, are three, which are supposed to
be Julian's. One of them, which seems to have his head, has
this inscription, DN Constanti .... " from which"
(says the expositor) " one would think this coin a Con-
" stantine; but the head does not resemble either of the
" Constantines, and I do not find that Julian took the
" name of Constantinus, or any name like it. His titles
" were Flavius Claudius Julianus.   The reverse is a war-
" rior on foot, directing his javelin against a horseman,
" with his horse falling to the ground. Fel. Temp. ....
" Dufresne describes this reverse on a coin of Julian, as
" doe also Occo, and I find no such of either of the Con-
" stantines. I should think Constanti .... might possibly be
" filled up Constantinopolis, but DN, Dominus noster, shews
" it to be the emperor's name, and not the city's."
Constanti . . . on this coin may perhaps mean Constantius, as a coin of his, described by Occo, has the reverse here mentioned.

" wage

" wage war againſt the *Chi* *, and that you regret
" the *Kappa* †." I wiſh that the guardian-gods of
this city would give you two ſuch *Kappas*, and thus
revenge your ſlanderouſly imputing the libels
againſt me to many of the neighbouring holy cities,
which agree with me in worſhipping the Gods;
cities, which, I am certain, have more affection for
me than for their own children, as they immediately reſtored the temples of the Gods, and, at
a ſignal lately given by me, deſtroyed all the
tombs of the atheiſts ‡, being ſo ardent and zealous

to

* Chriſt.   † Conſtantius.

‡ The cruelties, which were exerciſed againſt the Chriſtians by thoſe " holy cities," may be ſeen in the eccleſiaſtical hiſtory. At Heliopolis, a city ſituated at the foot
of Libanus, men were ſeen to gnaw the entrails of the
ſacred virgins, to tear out the liver of a deacon named
Cyril, and to eat it publickly. The inhabitants of Gaza
in Paleſtine tore ſome of the Chriſtians to pieces, and committed the ſame barbarities on the remains of their bodies
which in other places were practiſed on the relics of the
martyrs. The like enormities happened at Arethuſa, &c.
I know that Julian did not command thoſe barbarities; but
he could not be ignorant of what the populace are capable.
When we looſen the reins, we are reſponſible for their
fury. Julian ſhould at leaſt have puniſhed theſe exceſſes,
inſtead of apologiſing for them.   LA BLETERIE,

This imperfect and reluctant confeſſion may appear to
confirm the eccleſiaſtical narratives, that in the cities of
Gaza, Aſcalon, Cæſarea, Heliopolis, &c. the Pagans
abuſed, without prudence or remorſe, the moment of their
proſperity; that the unhappy objects of their cruelty
were releaſed from torture only by death; that, as their
mangled bodies were dragged through the ſtreets, they were
pierced (ſuch was the univerſal rage) by the ſpits of cooks,
and the diſtaffs of enraged women; and that the entrails of
Chriſtian prieſts and virgins, after they had been taſted

T 4

by

to punish those who had transgressed against the Gods, as even to exceed my wishes.

As to you, many of you, whom my lenity has scarce been able to pacify, have overthrown the altars lately erected. But after we had sent the dead body * back from Daphne †, some of you, who worshipped

by those bloody fanatics, were mixed with barley, and contemptuously thrown to the unclean animals of the city. Such scenes of religious madness exhibit the most contemptible and odious picture of human nature.

GIBBON.

* Of Babylas, a Christian bishop of Antioch, mentioned in a former note, p. 247.

† At the distance of five miles from Antioch the Macedonian kings of Syria had consecrated to Apollo one of the most elegant places of devotion in the Pagan world. A magnificent temple rose in honour of the God of light, and his colossal figure almost filled the capacious sanctuary, which was enriched with gold and gems, and adorned by the skill of the Grecian artists. The deity was represented in a bending attitude, with a golden cup in his hand, pouring out a libation on the earth; as if he supplicated the venerable mother to give to his arms the cold and beauteous DAPHNE; for the spot was ennobled by fiction; and the fancy of the Syrian poets had transported the amorous tale from the banks of the Peneus to those of the Orontes. . . The temple and the village, insensibly formed by the perpetual resort of pilgrims and spectators, were deeply bosomed in a thick grove of laurels and cypresses, which reached as far as a circumference of ten miles, and formed in the most sultry summers a cool and impenetrable shade. . . . . The groves of Daphne continued for many ages to enjoy the veneration of natives and strangers; the privileges of the holy ground were enlarged by the munificence of succeeding Emperors; and every generation added new ornaments to the splendor of the temple.   GIBBON.

The whole of the garden at Rousham [in Oxfordshire] laid out by Kent, for General Dormer, is as elegant and antique,

worſhipped the Gods, by way of expiation, gave up the temple of the Daphnæan God to others who were enraged on account of the relics of the dead. And theſe, by their negligence or connivance, kindled thoſe flames, and exhibited to foreign nations a fight moſt horrid, but to your citizens moſt pleaſing, and by the ſenate hitherto diſregarded. The God indeed ſeems, in my opinion, to have deſerted the temple long before the fire *. This, at my firſt entrance, the ſtatue declared to me; and I appeal to the great Sun, as a witneſs of it againſt unbelievers.

I muſt now remind you of another of my offences, and then, as I have done before, I will cenſure and condemn myſelf. In the tenth month †, accord

antique, as if the Emperor Julian had ſelected the moſt pleaſing ſolitude about Daphne to enjoy a philoſophic retirement. 　　　　　　　　　　　　　　　　　WALPOLE.

* Ecclefiaſtical critics, particularly thoſe who love relics, exult in this confeſſion of Julian, and that of Libanïus, (*Nænia*, p. 185.) that Apollo was diſturbed by the vicinity of one dead man. Yet Ammiänus (XXII. 12.) clears and purifies the whole ground, according to the rites which the Athenians formerly practiſed in the iſle of Delos.
　　　　　　　　　　　　　　　　　　　　GIBBON.

† F. Petau thinks, that we ſhould read " the eleventh " month," and not " the tenth;" ſuppoſing that the month Hyperbereteus was the firſt of the Macedonian year. But Suidas and Zenobius, from a Macedonian proverb, inform us, that this month was the laſt; and conſequently the month Dius was the firſt. The following is the order in which the phyſician Ætius, and all the ephemeriſts, place the Macedonian months. I will annex the Roman months to which they anſwer in the Syrian year, which the ecclefiaſtical writers
　　　　　　　　　　　　　　　　　　　　　　have

according to your reckoning, (you call it, I think, Löus), is the ancient feſtival of this God, when great crowds uſed to aſſemble at Daphne. I therefore haſtened thither from the temple of Jupiter Caſſius *, expecting to ſee a profuſion of wealth and

have adopted ; but, as I have ſaid before, it was not perhaps that of Antioch :

1	*Dius,*	November.	7 *Artemiſius,*	May.
2	*Appellæus,*	December.	8 *Dæſins,*	June.
3	*Audinæus,*	January.	9 *Panemus,*	July.
4	*Perittius,*	February.	10 *Löus,*	Auguſt.
5	*Dyſlrus,*	March.	11 *Gorpiæus,*	September.
6	*Xanthicus,*	April.	12 *Hyperberetæus,*	October.

La Bleterie.

* Jupiter was called Caſius, or Caſſius, from a very high hill of that name in Syria, which bounds Antioch to the ſouth, about fifteen miles diſtant. This was a day's journey; but Julian performed it ſeveral times during his reſidence in that city. Nothing was difficult to him when it was to viſit a place revered by the Pagans. One day, while he was ſacrificing there, he ſaw at his feet a man proſtrate on the ground, who humbly intreated him to geant him his life. He aſked who he was. " Theodotus," he was anſwered, " formerly chief of the council of " Hierapolis, who, when he conducted Conſtantius back, " then preparing to attack you, complimented him be- " fore-hand on his victory, and with ſighs and tears " conjured him to ſend immediately to Hierapolis the " head of that rebellious, that ungrateful wretch ; thus " he ſtyled you." ' I have heard this long ago,' ſaid the Emperor, ' and I have heard it from more than one.' Then addreſſing himſelf to Theodotus, who was half-dead with fear, he added, ' Return home in ſafety, and diſmiſs all ' apprehenſions. You live under a prince, who, accord- ' ing to the maxim of a great philoſopher, ſtudiouſly en- ' deavours to diminiſh the number of his enemies, and to ' increaſe that of his friends.' *Ibid.*

Trajan,

and splendor. Already I feigned to myself, and saw there, as in a dream, the solemn pomp, the victims, the libations, the dances, the incense, and the boys, with minds properly disposed to the God, arrayed in white and elegant garments. But when I entered the temple, I found there neither incense, nor cake, nor victim. This much surprised me, and I concluded that you were waiting without the gate, by way of respect, for a signal from me as sovereign Pontiff *. I therefore asked the priest what offering the city intended to make on that solemn anniversary? He replied, " I have brought " the God a sacred goose from my own house, " but the city has provided nothing." Odious as I am apt to render myself, I expostulated, on this occasion, with the senate in severe terms, which it may not be unseasonable here to repeat: " Shameful," said I, " it is, that so great a city " should contemn the Gods more than any village in " the remotest parts of Pontus, and though posses- " sed of a territory so extensive, on the late annual " festival of your tutelar Deity, the first since the

Trajan, in his progress against the Parthians, made an offering to Jupiter Casius; on which account his temple is represented on several of his coins, and those of other emperors afterwards. He is supposed to be the same with the God Terminus among the Romans.   Bowyer.

Others derive this name of Jupiter from a hill in Palestine near Ægypt, where that God had a temple, and Pompey a tomb. See Luc. vii. 451. and Plin. v. 12.

* Julian discovers his own character with that καιρελῖ, that unconscious simplicity, which always constitutes true humour.   Gibson.

          " Gods

" Gods difpelled the cloud of impiety, fhould not
" have brought him even a fingle bird, when
" every tribe ought to have facrificed an ox ! Or,
" if that had been too expenfive, the whole city
" might have joined to have offered him a bull.
" None of you fcruple being profufe of expence
" on your private entertainments, and many of
" you, I know, lavifh large fums on the feftival of
" the Maïuma * ; but none, either as individuals or a
" community,

* I know not whether we muft believe, on the authority
of Suidas and of fome comments, that the Maïuma was
originally a Roman feftival. Suidas fays, that in the
month of May, the magiftrates of Rome, followed, no
doubt, by all the people, went to celebrate it at Oftia, and
that, amidft diverfions and licentioufnefs, they pufhed one
another into the fea. But we find in no other author
that this feftivity was ever celebrated in Italy, or in any
other part of the Weft. It even feems to have been peculiar
to the Orientals, and particularly to the Syrians. As
places where there was much water were chofen for its
celebration, fuch as the fuburb of Daphne near Antioch,
and we know not that it was celebrated in the month of
May, it is more probable to fuppofe that it was called
Maïuma, becaufe that word in Syriac fignifies " waters."
All that is known of this feftival is, that it lafted feven
days, and that it " was the effence of it not to abftain
" from any kind of infamy." This is the expreffion of
Libanius, who, a thorough Pagan as he is, often mentions
it with horror. Godefroy thinks that the infamous fpec-
tacle againft which St. John Chryfoftom inveighs with fo
much zeal muft refer to the Maïuma. In the middle of an
amphitheatre, in a refervoir filled with water, the common
women fwam and gambolled in the fight of the whole city.
If Godefroy be not miftaken, as we alfo know that the city
of Maïuma in Paleftine, fituated on the fea-fhore, was particularly devoted to the worfhip of Venus, I fhould fufpect that the feftival of the Maïuma had originally for its
object

" community, facrifice for their private or the
" public fafety. The prieft alone has facrificed,
" who, in my opinion, ought rather to have car-
" ried home fome part of your offerings. For
" the Gods require the priefts to honour them
" only by their probity, and attention to virtue,
" and their decent miniftration of the facred duties;
" but the city, I think, fhould facrifice both in
" public and private. Inftead of this, all of you
" fuffer your wives to fquander your fubftance on
" the Galileans, who, by feeding the indigent at

object the celebration of the birth of that Goddefs, who,
according to the fable, fprung from the waves. But it appears that, in the time of Julian, the Maïuma was no longer
confidered as part of the religious worfhip of the Pagans.
However, it is no lefs ftrange to fee the Chriftians of
Antioch partake of this fcandalous feftivity. But, as M.
de Tillemont fays, " a great nation is often more zealous
" to defend the name of Chriftianity than to practife its
" morality." " A wife prince," fays Libanius, (he is
fuppofed to mean Conftantius) " had fuppreffed the feftival
" of the Maïuma." But it was tolerated in the reigns of
Julian and Valens, and till the laft years of Theodofius I. who forbade it fome time before his death. Ar-
cadius, in 396, allowed it to be celebrated on condition
that nothing fhould be done there contrary to decency.
Clementiæ noftræ placuit, ut Maïumæ, *provincialibus lætitia red-
deretur; ita tamen ut fervetur honeftas, et verecundia caftis
moribus perfeveret.* But as it was impoffible to exact this, the
fame emperor forbade it three years after. *Ludicras artes
concedimus agitari, ne ex nimiâ harum reftrictione triftitia ge-
neretur. Illud verò quod fibi nomen procax licentia vindi-
cavit,* Maïumam *fœdum atque indecorum fpectaculum, dene-
gamus.* xv. *Cod. Theod. tit.* vi. *de Maïumâ.* Some remains
of this feftival were found neverthelefs at Conftantinople in
the ixth century, in the reign of Leon the fon of Conftantine Copronymus.   LA BLETERIE.

" your

" your expence, exhibit a wonderful proof of
" impiety to their poor, who feem to abound
" every where. But you, though you contemn
" the worfhip of the Gods, think yourfelves blame-
" lefs. No one fupplies the altar with neceffaries,
" not being able, I fuppofe, to defray the expence.
" Yet when any one of you celebrates his birth-
" day, he provides a fuitable entertainment, and
" magnificently treats his friends. While on a
" folemn feftival no one brings the God a libation,
" nor a victim, nor even oil for his lamp, nor
" incenfe. In what manner this may appear to
" any good man among you, I know not; but
" that it cannot pleafe the God, I am certain."

Such, I remember, were my expoftulations, and
thefe the God, by his teftimony, approved ; which
I wifh he had not, but, inftead of deferting the
fuburb in which he had fo long refided, had in
the late tempeft turned the hearts, and opened the
hands, of the magiftrates *. But I was fo abfurd

as

---

* In the original, των κραλυνίων. Who thefe κραλυνίες are is,
not fufficiently clear to me ; unlefs he means the guardian
genii of the place [Daphne] whofe attention and power
were baffled by a divine interpofition, which, in order to
avenge the people of Antioch, occafioned that conflagra-
tion.   PETAU,

The following is the manner in which the whole paffage
ought, I think, to be tranflated, by repeating a negation -
that occurs a little before. " In that horrible event,
" Apollo would not have diverted the attention of the tutelar
" genii of the place ; he would have ftopped the hands of

" the

as to be angry with you, when I ought rather to have been filent, like many who entered the temple with me, and to have made no inquifitive enquiries nor reproaches. But fuch was my precipitation, and fo ridiculous my flattery, (for it cannot be fuppofed that the fpeech which I addreffed to you was dictated by friendfhip, but by a vain-glorious affectation of reverence to the Gods, and of a fincere regard for you, which of

" the incendiaries." For my part, I am convinced that κρατῦντες fignifies here " the people in power, the magiftrates," and if I thought, that, by " the ftorm," we fhould underftand " the burning of the temple of Apollo," I would tranflate it " he would not have diverted the attention of " the magiftrates." But I think it more natural to underftand by this " ftorm," or " agitation," εν εκεινη τη ζαλη, the commotions and diforders that happened at Antioch on account of the fcarcity which Julian mentions in the fequel. The avarice of the magiftrates, and the moft powerful perfons of the city, was the caufe of that fcarcity. Thus Julian would fay, that Apollo, if he had ftill been in his temple, would have prevented or ftopped the diforders, by touching the hearts of thofe rich mifers, by forcing them to open their hands to diftribute the corn which they locked up in their granaries. This is the explanation which I have adopted. I will not venture, however, to affirm that it is the true one. La Bleterie.

I adopt the fame explanation, though I choofe to tranflate the words literally. M. de la Bleterie renders them, " In the commotions by which it has lately been agitated, " he would have forced the magiftrates to open their " granaries, he would have infpired them with fentiments " more humane." Τρεψας αλλαχου την διανοιαν feems very analogous to our fcripture expreffion, ος αποκαλασησει καρδιαν, κ. τ. λ. he fhall turn the heart, &c. Mal. v. 6.

all

all flatteries is the moſt ridiculous,) that I raſhly inveighed againſt you.

Juſtly therefore you now repay me for thoſe invectives, though not in the ſame place. For I reproached you before the God, at the altar, at the feet of the ſtatue, and in the preſence of few ; but you are thus ſarcaſtic on me in the public markets, before all the people, and by the mouths of ſome of your worthy fellow-citizens. For, be aſſured, all who ſpeak have a communication with their hearers ; but he who eagerly liſtens to calumnies enjoys equal pleaſure, with more ſafety, and is no leſs culpable than he who utters them.

Thus the whole city hears your lampoons on this unfortunate beard, and on its wearer, who has never ſhewn, nor will ever ſhew you, what you call a good example. For he will not lead ſuch a life as you lead yourſelves, and as you ex-pect your princes ſhould lead. As to the aſper-ſions which you have both privately and publickly thrown upon me in ſcurrilous anapæſtic verſes, I alſo condemn myſelf, and very readily allow you ſtill farther liberty. I will never expoſe you, on that account, to the danger of death, ſtripes, bonds, impriſonment, or to any other puniſhment. What purpoſe would that anſwer? But as the temperate life which I here lead with my friends ſeems to you deſpicable and loathſome, and exhibits a ſight by no means agreeable, I have determined to re-

move

move and quit your city *; not from a perfuafion that my perfon and manners will be more acceptable where I am going, but becaufe I think it expedient, fhould I fail of being thought good and virtuous, to give others fome fhare of my difagreeablenefs, and no longer to difguft this happy city with the ftench, as it were, of my moderation, and of the temperance of my friends. For none of us have purchafed fo much as a field or a garden here, or have married, or given in marriage, or have been enchanted with any of your amufements; nor have we coveted the Affyrian wealth, nor been lavifh of our patronages † ; nor have we fuffered any of the magiftrates to fhare with us the dominion over you; nor have we allured the people by the ruinous feftivity of banquets or plays. On the contrary, we have made them fo voluptuous, that, free from any apprehenfions of indigence, they have compofed anapæfts on thofe to whom they are indebted for fo much affluence. No gold have we exacted, no filver have we demanded, nor have we

---

* Julian had refolved to return after the Perfian campaign, and to pafs the winter at Tarfus in Cilicia.

La Bleterie.

This not being permitted, he ordered his corpfe to be interred there, in the fuburbs.

† Ουδ' ιπιμαμιθα τας προφασιας. In the Latin, *Neque præfecturas depafti fumus.* Rather, *Neque patrocinia diftribuimus.* For he means the guardianfhip and protection of certain orders, and bodies, or the negociation of bufinefs with the Emperor, the foliciting which was very lucrative to the great.

Petau.

      U   increafed

increased the taxes; but, besides the arrears now due, we have remitted to all a fifth of what they used to pay.

Not contented with being regular myself, I have also, (by Jupiter and all the Gods, I am firmly persuaded) a most temperate usher *; who has been much censured, however, by you, because though old, and rather bald on the fore part of his head, yet such is his perverseness, that he is not ashamed to wear his hair on the back part, like the Abantes † of Homer. Two or three more, in no respect his inferiors, I may say four, I have also at my house; and if you desire, even a fifth, such was my maternal uncle and namesake ‡, who go-

verned

---

* I know not whom Julian here means. La Bleterie.
Εἰσαγγελευς. One who introduces persons to a king or prince. Robertson.
This answers to the English word and place of gentleman-usher, or master of the ceremonies.

† Among the Greeks who went to the siege of Troy, Homer reckons the Abantes, to whom he gives the epithet of οπιθεν κομοωντες, *retrò comati*, because they threw their hair back. La Bleterie.
Down their broad shoulders flows a length of hair. Pope.

‡ Julian, Count of the East, brother to Basilina. After the profanation and destruction of Daphne, (see p. 248.) being ordered by the Emperor to shut up the cathedral of Antioch, then possessed by the Arians, his zeal induced him to exceed his commission by shutting up all the other churches, and even by beheading a presbyter, named Theodoret. For this rash act being reprimanded by his nephew, he was seized, a few days after, with an inveterate ulcer, of which he languished two months, and then died: " His " seasonable death," says Mr. Gibbon, " is related with

† " much

verned you with the strictest justice, as long as the Gods allowed him to continue and co-operate with us, though he did not manage the affairs of the city with the utmost prudence. For those governors who rule with mildness and moderation seem to me highly laudable, and this, I hoped, would have atoned for my want of beauty. But since the length of my beard, the negligence of my hair, my dislike to the theatres, my gravity in the temples, and, above all, my adherence to equity in the courts of justice, and my earnest endeavours to banish extortion have given you such offence, I shall with pleasure leave your city. If I were to attempt to alter my conduct, I should probably exemplify the old fable of the kite. For the kite, it is said, having originally a voice like other birds, was desirous to neigh like a high-bred horse; but not being able to attain the one, and losing the other, he was afterwards deprived of both, and in voice became inferior to them all. In like manner, I am very apprehensive of being neither rustic nor polite. For, as you yourselves perceive, I am now, by the will of the Gods, on the verge of that age, when, according to the Teian poet,

Grey hairs will mingle with the black *:

But

" much superstitious complacency by the Abbè de la Ble-
" terie." To the above-mentioned indiscretion of his uncle the Emperor probably here alludes. See Epistle xiii. which is addressed to this Count Julian.

* Ευδε μοι λευκαι μελαιναις αναμεμιξονlαι τριχις.

The poems of Anacreon, now preserved, are said to have been first discovered by Henry Stephens; but where or how

But tell me now, I conjure you, by the immortal Gods, and by Jupiter, the guardian of your city, what has occasioned this ingratitude? Has any private or public offence of mine so provoked you, that, not being able openly to revenge it, you lampoon me in the forum, in anapæstic verses, as the comic poets treat and represent Hercules and Bacchus *? Is it because, though I have abstained from injuring you by my deeds, I have offended you by words, that you take your revenge in the same manner? Can this have occasioned your enmity and resentment? But certain I am, that nothing injurious, nothing offensive, has been done, nor any thing reproachful said, by me, either

is scarce known. His first edition of them, which was published at Paris in 1544, was deemed a happy discovery by some of the learned, and suspected by others. Stephens, falling into a kind of distraction in the latter part of his life, suffered his two MSS. which he had carefully collated, to perish, without communicating them even to Casaubon, his son-in-law. This we learn from M. de la Monnoie in Bayle's article Anacreon. And M. de Pauw, who published an edition of that poet at Utrecht in 1732, in 4to, is fully persuaded that the odes were composed by different authors; and, besides, doubts whether Anacreon was really the author of any single ode in the whole collection. Julian has quoted from him one passage (as above), and refers to another in his xviiith Epistle. But neither of them are to be found in Stephens's edition.

* We need only open Aristophanes, and cast an eye, in particular, on his comedies of The Frogs and The Birds, to be convinced of the licentiousness with which the Greek poets treated the Gods. The most abused, and those whom they represented in the most ridiculous characters, were Bacchus and Hercules.   La Bleterie.

privately

privately againſt individuals, or publicly againſt
the community. I have even beſtowed commen-
dations, whenever I thought them due; and I have,
in ſome reſpects, been ſerviceable to you, as became one who was deſirous of being, to the utmoſt of his power, a general benefactor. It was
impoſſible, you may be aſſured, that all the taxes
ſhould be remitted to thoſe who pay them, and
that by thoſe who uſed to receive them all ſhould
be returned. As therefore it appears that I have
not diminiſhed the public largeſſes, which uſed to
be defrayed at the Imperial expence, though I
have remitted you ſeveral taxes, does not this ſeem
myſterious? But it is more proper for me to be ſilent
as to what I have done for all the citizens in
general, that I may not ſeem ſtudiouſly to publiſh
my own panegyric, after declaring that I would
compoſe a bitter ſatire on myſelf. The inſtances
of my raſhneſs and imprudence towards you, though
they ought not to have incurred your diſpleaſure,
it is, I think, incumbent on me to mention, as
they are really diſgraceful to me, and being more
true, and relating wholly to my mind, are much
more important than my perſonal defects, I mean
the roughneſs of my viſage, and my unpoliteneſs *,

* Καὶ τῆς αναφροδισιας. *Veneris odium* in the Latin tranſlation, not properly. To αναφροδιτον is oppoſed to επαφροδιτον.
But this means "agreeable and elegant." That therefore
is "diſagreeable and inelegant;" and αναφροδισια "ruſticity;"
"unpoliteneſs."   PETAU.

U 3   And,

And, firſt, I highly extolled you, before I was acquainted with you, or was appriſed on what terms we ſhould be, on this conſideration only, that you were deſcended from the Greeks, as I, though by birth a Thracian, am in manners and diſpoſition a Greek. I preſumed, therefore, that we ſhould have a mutual regard for each other. In this one inſtance I judged raſhly. Afterwards, though you were the laſt who ſent ambaſſadors to me, not excepting the Alexandrians, who are ſo remote as Ægypt, yet I remitted you much gold and ſilver, and many taxes, in particular, more than to any other city. I alſo augmented the number of your ſenators * to two hundred, and I exempted none †,

my

* Zoſimus, *l.* iii. " The Emperor, indulging the city, as " was juſt, and granting it a large number of ſenators who " were deſcended from parents of that rank, who were born " of the daughters of ſenators, (which, we know, was al- " lowed to few cities.)" But this was not ſo agreeable and honourable to thoſe who were enrolled as to the city itſelf. For it was rather burthenſome to be returned to the ſenate, and generally declined on account of the weight of aſſeſſ- ments. Therefore, ſoon after, he ſays, he enrolled thoſe two hundred in the ſenate, " ſparing no one," φεισαμενος εθνος. For the more powerful and opulent thought it, as has been obſerved, a burthen ; and therefore they were to be compelled.   *Ibid.*

† Every city had a ſenate, which was called in Latin *Curia,* the name of *Senatus* being uſually appropriated to the ſenates of Rome and Conſtantinople. Two annual magiſtrates, named *Duumviri,* were at the head of that aſſembly, whoſe members bore the name of *Curiales* or *Decuriones.* The decurions, among other burthenſome func- tions, were charged with collecting the taxes in the diſtrict

of

my view being to increafe and aggrandife your city,
I allowed you therefore to choofe them from
among the richeft of my treafurers *, and the
officers of the mint. You did not, however, make
choice of thofe who were beft qualified, but, when
an opportunity offered, your conduct was that of an
ill-governed city, and not unlike yourfelves. Shall
I remind you of one inftance ? Having nominated
a certain fenator, before he was enrolled on the
lift, and while the procefs of his election was yet
depending, you dragged him from the ftreets into
the fenate, indigent as he was, and thus admitted
into your fociety one of the loweft of the people,
of thofe who are every where elfe difregarded, but
whom you chofe to purchafe at any price †. Such

is

of their city, and with making good the payments. Individuals therefore avoided thofe places as much as they
could. But it was equally the intereft of the empire, and
of the cities, to have the curiæ numerous and filled with re-
fponfible perfons. *Curiales fervos effe reipublicæ, ac vifcera civi-
tatum, nullus ignorat, quorum cœtum recte appellavit antiquitas
minorem Senatum*, fays the Emperor Majorian. *Novell. Theod.
l.* iv. *tit.* 1. Julian therefore gave a proof of his zeal for the
public good, and of his affection for the city of Antioch, by
allowing it to augment the number of its fenators, and to
choofe them from among the officers of the Emperor, who
pretended that they were exempted.　　　LA BLETERIE.

　* Ἀπο των επιτροπευσαντων τας θησαυρας. He means the Præfects and Counts of the treafuries, of whom the Notitia
treats; who were under the direction of the Counts of the
facred largeffes. Thus οι εργασαμενοι το νομισμα are the
officers of the mint.　　　　　　　　　　　PETAU.

　† Martinius and Spanheim confider this as two inftances
of popular licentioufnefs; the one, that of a man, who

was

is your difcernment. Many of your elections have
been equally irregular, but, as I cannot connive
at them all, the remembrance of my paft favours
is loft ; and for the refufal of what juftice would
not allow me to grant, you are incenfed againft
me. But thefe were of little importance, and by
no means fufficient to irritate the whole city. What
follows was my chief offence, and gave the greateft
provocation *.

When I firft came hither, the people, oppreffed
by the rich, began with exclaiming in the theatre,
" There is plenty of all things, yet all things are
" extravagantly dear." Next day I difcourfed
with your magiftrates, and endeavoured to convince them of the propriety of fpurning unjuft,

was enrolled into the fenate, while he had a fuit depending, whofe iffue ought to have been expected ; the other,
that of a poor man, taken from the dregs of the people.
Their miftake feems to arife from the words μετιωρυ της δικης
ϣσης, which they apply to a law-fuit, and Αλλον, which, as
ufually printed, begins the next fentence. But the former
words may as well refer to the procefs of the fenatorial
election yet undetermined, and accordingly M. de la Bleterie tranflates them, lorfque le procès, dont fa nomination
fut fuivie, étoit encore pendant. And for Αλλον (" Another
" man") I would fubftitute αλλα or αλλ' (" but"), and
clofe the former paragraph with a comma only, or femi-
colon. That Julian meant to produce no more than a
fingle inftance appears from his introductory words, Βελισθε
ινος υμας υπομνησω ; " Will you allow me to remind you of
one of them ?"

* Julian proceeds to make his apology on account of the
kind of famine which Antioch fuffered, while he refided
there. Let him fay what he will, the conduct, which he
then purfued, does lefs honour to his prudence than to his
difintereftednefs and good intentions.   LA BLETERIE.

gain,

gain, and of obliging their fellow-citizens and
foreigners. They promised to attend to what I
said; but after waiting with confidence for three
months, such was their negligence that I despaired
of any good effect. Finding therefore that the
popular clamour was just and reasonable, and that
the markets were straitened not by dearth, but by
the avarice of the rich, I fixed a moderate price
on every commodity, of which I ordered public
notice to be given. And as there was great plenty
of wine, oil, and all other provisions, except
wheat, whose scarcity was owing to the drought
of the preceding year, I determined to supply
that deficiency from Chalcis, Hierapolis, and other
neighbouring cities. From them I imported for
your use four hundred thousand measures; and
when they were consumed, I brought from my own
house, and gave to the city, first, five thousand,
then seven thousand, and now, lastly, ten thousand
modii, as you style them, all which wheat was sent
me from Ægypt, for my own consumption, and
fifteen measures I ordered to be sold at the same
price that used formerly to be given for ten *. If ten

measures

---

* With a salutary view, the Emperor ventured on a
very dangerous and doubtful step, of fixing, by legal authority, the value of corn. . . . The consequences might
have been foreseen, and were soon felt. The Imperial
wheat was purcased by the rich merchants; the proprietors
of land, or of corn, with-held from the city the accustomed supply; and the small quantities that appeared in
the market were secretly sold at an advanced and illegal

price.

meaſures coſt you an *aureus* * in ſummer, what could be expected, when, as the Bœotian poet ſays, ———— cruel famine rages in the houſe † ? Would you not have accepted five meaſures ‡, or leſs, in ſuch a ſevere winter as followed? Why then did your rich merchants clandeſtinely ſell their ſtanding corn for more, and thus take advantage of the public diſtreſs? Notwithſtanding this, beſides the citizens §, numbers alſo from the country

price, Julian ſtill continued to applaud his own policy, treated the complaints of the people as a vain and ungrateful murmur, and convinced Antioch, that he had inherited the obſtinacy, though not the cruelty, of his brother Gallus. The ignorance of the moſt enlightened princes may claim ſome excuſe; but we cannot be ſatisfied with Julian's own defence [as above], or the elaborate apology of Libanius, *Orat. Parent. c.* XCVII. *p.* 321. . GIBBON.

* From Mr. Greaves's elements, in his excellent diſcourſe on the *denarius*, we may fix the currency of the *aureus* at ſomewhat more than eleven ſhillings. *Ibid.*

† Καλιπον γιγνισθαι τον λιμον ιπι δωματι.

" If I have ſearched well," (as M. de la Blèterie ſays of another paſſage), theſe words are not to be found in any of the works of Pindar that have been tranſmitted to us.

‡ Julian ſtates three different proportions of five, ten, or fifteen *modii* of wheat, for one piece of gold, according to the degrees of plenty and ſcarcity. From this fact, and from ſome collateral examples, I conclude, that, under the ſucceſſors of Conſtantine, the moderate price of wheat was about thirty-two ſhillings the Engliſh quarter, which is equal to the average price of the ſixty-four firſt years of the preſent century. GIBBON.

§ Και ux η πολις μοιος. Something, I think, is wanting here. For the ſentence ſeems abrupt, and rather incomplete. Underſtand it thus. Julian made the price of corn only, and the making of bread, cheap; that is, he ſold fifteen *modii* of corn for one *ſolidus*. But the Antiochians,

beſides

country came hither in crowds to purchase bread, the only commodity that is plentiful and cheap. But which of you remembers, even in the most favourable seasons, fifteen measures of corn sold so cheap as for one *aureus?* I was therefore hated by you because I would not suffer wine, vegetables, and fruit to be sold at an exorbitant price; nor corn, which the rich had hoarded in their granaries, to be immediately converted by them into gold and silver. They infamously sold it to foreigners, and, in consequence, exposed you to famine,

—— that cruel scourge of mortals, *

as it is styled by a God, who severely reprobates such transgressors. Thus, by my attention, the

besides corn, wished to have plenty also of wine, vegetables, and fruit. Compare this with another passage (p. 258.) where he mentions their complaints against him for occasioning a plenty of bread only, and not also of wine, fish, and poultry. But here, he says, he was reproached for not suffering garden-stuff and fruit αποδιδοσθαι χρυσυ, " to " be sold for gold." Where χρυσος, that is " gold," not χρυσες, "' a piece of gold so called," I suppose to be meant. For when the common people had hitherto purchased from the rich, at an extravagant price, not only corn but wine, and other articles less necessary to subsistence than corn, Julian, by supplying the people with plenty of corn alone, in this particular alleviated their wants. But when by his edict he had lowered the prices of meat, wine, and other things, they were no longer publickly sold by the rich; which not being regarded by the Emperor occasioned the popular complaints. PETAU.

* Λιμος αλοιηληρα βρολειων. This is the conclusion of an heroic verse, though not so distinguished in the edition. I suppose it to be taken from one of the Didymæan oracles (so called) from which Julian has given another quotation in his Duties of a Priest, p. 150, and in his LXIId Epistle.

city

city abounded in bread, but in nothing elſe. Such conduct, I was well aware, would not be generally pleaſing; but this gave me no concern, as I thought it my duty to relieve an oppreſſed people, and alſo the foreigners who accompanied me hither, and the officers who attended me. But ſince they are now departed, and the whole city has combined againſt me, being hated by ſome, and from others, whom I have ſupported, having no return but ingratitude, relying on divine Nemeſis, I will remove to another nation, another city, without reminding you of your acts of juſtice on yourſelves nine years ago[*], when the populace, with furious clamours, ſet fire to the houſes of the magiſtrates, and maſſacred the governor; and, in return, were puniſhed by a reſentment juſt in the motive, but rigorous in the execution[†].

[*] In 354, when Gallus ſet out for Hierapolis, the people of Antioch begged him to order an importation of corn. Gallus contented himſelf with replying, that " he left them " Theophilus, governor of Syria, who very well knew " how to procure it for them." The people, remembering theſe words, made Theophilus reſponſible for the dearth. On account of a quarrel that happened at the games of the Circus, they attacked and murdered the governor, and diverted themſelves with dragging his body through the ſtreets. Eubulus, one of the principal perſons of the city, and his ſon, narrowly eſcaped the ſame treatment. But the people ſet fire to their houſe. Conſtantius ſent Strategius to puniſh the rioters. Julian hints that it was at the deſire of the magiſtrates.　　　　　LA BLETERIE.

[†] Libanius, however, in his oration on this ſedition, much applauds the clemency of Conſtantius.

In

In fhort, what part of my conduct has given
you fo much offence? Is it my fupporting you,
from my own houfe, at an expence which no other
city has feen equalled? Is it my augmenting the
number of your fenators? Is it my pardoning
the frauds which I have detected? Left this fhould
be deemed a rhetorical fiction, let me fpecify one
or two.   Three thoufand lots of land, you faid,
were vacant *, and defired the grant of them; but
when they were granted, the rich alone divided
them.   This, on enquiry, being clearly proved, I
took them from thofe unjuft poffeffors, and making
no fcrutiny into the former exemption of thofe
who had no right to it, applied them to the principal expences of the city.   Thus thofe of you
who annually breed horfes have about three thoufand exempt portions, owing partly to the prudence and good management of my uncle and
namefake ✝, and partly to my generofity, who,
for thus punifhing thieves and cheats, am juftly
thought by you to have fubverted the world ‡.

---

* He here charges the Antiochians with another inftance
of ingratitude.   For when three thoufand κλῆροι, or lots, of
land, were vacant, having fallen in by the deaths of the
heirs, Julian, at their requeft, gave them to the citizens.
But as the few rich divided them among themfelves, he foon
after refumed them, and reftored them to the public towards
the expence of their games and entertainments, efpecially
thofe of the Circus; which, he fays, was the act of his
uncle Julian.   PETAU.

✝ Count Julian, of whom above, p. 290.

‡ See p. 277.

For,

For, believe me, lenity to such offenders encourages
and hardens the wicked *.

This is the whole of my meaning, and with this
I shall close my discourse. My misfortunes originate
from myself alone. They are owing to the ingratitude of those whom I have obliged, and are therefore the effect, not of your liberty, but of my
folly. This will teach me to act with more discretion for the future, and for the kindness which
you have publicly shewn me, may you be properly
requited by the Gods †!

* Julian, it is observable, is silent as to his sending the
whole body of the senators of Antioch, consisting of two
hundred of the most noble and wealthy citizens, under a
guard, from the palace to the prison, for their disrespectful
and interested boldness. But he suffered them to return to
their respective houses before the close of the evening.
" Their short and easy confinement," says Mr. Gibbon,
" is gently touched by Libanius, (*Orat. Parent.* c. xcviii.
" pp. 332, 333.")

† Though Julian affected to laugh, he could not forgive.
His contempt was expressed, and his revenge might be
gratified, by the nomination of a governor [Alexander, of
Heliopolis] worthy only of such subjects; and the Emperor,
for ever renouncing the ungrateful city, proclaimed his resolution to pass the ensuing winter at Tarsus in Cilicia.
Libanius, in a professed oration, invites him to return to
his loyal and penitent city at Antioch. ·   GIBBON.

Soon after writing this satire, viz. March 5, 363, Julian
began his march towards Persia, of which he has given the
particulars, as far as Hierapolis, in his xxviith Epistle
(the latest extant), to Libanius, " one citizen of Antioch,"
as the above cited historian expresses it, " whose genius and
" virtues might atone, in the opinion of Julian, for the
" vice and folly of his country."

XVI Epistles

XVI Epiftles of LIBANIUS* to JULIAN.

EPISTLE I.†

MAY the prefent health and ftrength, that, you fay, you poffefs, be your conftant portion! For your grief may God fupply a remedy! Or rather your grief requires in part only the assiftance

A. D. 358.

* The fophift Libanius was born in the capital of the Eaft [Antioch]. He publickly profeffed the arts of rhetoric and declamation at Nice, Nicomedia, Conftantinople, Athens, and, during the remainder of his life, at Antioch. The preceptors of Julian had extorted a rafh but folemn affurance, that he would never attend the lectures of their adverfary: the curiofity of the royal youth was checked and inflamed; he fecretly procured the writings of this dangerous fophift, and gradually furpaffed, in the perfect imitation of his ftyle, the moft laborious of his domeftic pupils. When Julian afcended the throne, he declared his impatience to embrace and reward the Syrian fophift, who had preferved, in a degenerate age, the Grecian purity of tafte, of manners, and of religion. The Emperor's prepoffeffion was increafed and juftified by the difcreet pride of his favourite. Inftead of preffing, with the foremoft of the crowd, into the palace of Conftantinople, Libanius calmly expected his arrival at Antioch; withdrew from court, on the firft fymptoms of coldnefs and indifference; required a formal invitation for each vifit; and taught his fovereign an important leffon, that he might command the obedience of a fubject, but that he muft deferve the attachment of a friend. . . The volu-

minous

aſſiſtance of God, for ſome part of it you yourſelf can alleviate. You are able, if you pleaſe,
to re-build the city ‡ ; but for your concern on
account

minous writings of Libanius ſtill exiſt; among them, near
two thouſand of his letters * . . . His birth is aſſigned to
the year 314. [In a letter to Priſcus] he mentions the 76th
year of his age (A. D. 390.) and ſeems to allude to ſome
events of ſtill later date.   GIBBON.

. Libanius was a great admirer of Julian, fond of Gentiliſm,
and averſe to Chriſtianity, but not an enemy to all Chriſtians. He did not embrace Chriſtianity, having been educated in great prejudices againſt it, and having never examined its evidence. Nevertheleſs, I cannot but eſteem
him an uſeful man. For, as Socrates acknowledges, he
was an excellent ſophiſt ; he was continually employed in
teaching polite literature ; and had many ſcholars; ſome
of whom were afterwards men of great eminence. Among
them, Socrates and Sozomen reckon John Chryſoſtom,
Theodore of Mopſoueſtia, and Maximus biſhop of Seleucia
in Iſauria.   LARDNER.

By comparing their works, we find in reality that Julian
reſembles Libanius, but it is with a handſome likeneſs, and
in the ſame manner as a perſon of quality, who ſpeaks
well without affecting to do ſo, may be ſaid to reſemble a
rhetorician who makes it his ſtudy. " Hence, I imagine,"
ſays Libanius, " his ſubſequent writings have ſome affinity
" to our ſtyle, as if he had been one of our ſcholars."
Julian ſubmitted to his criticiſm both his actions and writings. He was thought to have aſſiſted him in the compo-
ſition of the Miſopogon. " Libanius," ſaid he, " loves
" me more than ever my mother did ; he is not attached
" to my fortune, but to my perſon."   LA BLETERIE.

† This Epiſtle is one of the three firſt publiſhed by
Fabricius, with a Latin tranſlation, in his Bibliotheca
Græca, vol. VII. p. 397. In the edition of Wolfius, it is
the xxxIIId.

‡ Nicomedia, the capital of Bythinia, which, from the
beauty of its ſituation, the magnificence of its buildings,

* In his Life, his letters, he ſays, were innumerable.

its

account of the dead, may Heaven afford you confolation ! Nicomedia, ruined as fhe is, I deem
moft happy.   Her fafety indeed would have been
moft defirable ; but even thus fhe is honoured * by
your tears.   Nor are thefe inferior to the lamentations which the Mufes are faid to have uttered
for 'Achilles †, or to the drops of blood which
Jupiter, in honour of his deareft fon, poured down
at the approaching death of Sarpedon ‡.   That
fhe therefore, who was lately a city, may again be
a city, will be your concern.   Elpidius §, always

its grandeur, and its riches, had been looked upon as the
fifth city in the world, was deftroyed by an earthquake,
Aug. 24, 358, followed by a fire which lafted five days.
A monody, by Libanius, on this fubject, I have inferted in
vol. II. Julian was then only Cæfar ; but he vifited the city,
and gave orders for re-building it, in his way from Conftantinople to Antioch, May 15, 362, after his acceffion to the
empire.   Another earthquake, which was alfo felt at Conftantinople and Nice, fwallowed up the remains of Nicomedia, on January 1, 363.

   * Τιμηνται δε ομως I have added, to complete the fenfe,
from the [French] king's largeft MS. where thefe words are
written in the margin, but in a more modern hand.   That
of the Vatican alfo has on the fide τιμηνται δε ομως πεουτα.
For the city might be honoured indeed, but could not be
reftored from its ruins, by the tears of Julian.   Valois
quotes this paffage of Libanius, in his notes on Ammianus,
xxii. 9. p. 319.   WOLFIUS.

   † Alluding to Homer, Odyff. xxiv. 60.
   Round thee the Mufes, with alternate ftrain,
   In ever confecrating verfe, complain.   POPE, 77.
   ‡ Iliad. xvi. 459.
   Then, touch'd with grief, the weeping heavens diftill'd
   A fhower of blood o'er all the fatal field.   POPE, 559.

   § A philofopher, to whom Julian has addreffed his LVIIth
Epiftle.   Libanius alfo has addreffed feveral Epiftles to him,
and has mentioned him in feveral others.

VOL. I.   X   a man a man of diftinguifhed probity, has now made wonderful improvements. Thus it is not only true, as Sophocles fays, that

Wife kings are form'd by converfe with the wife *, but the wifdom of a king improves alfo his friends in virtue. So ferviceable have you been to Elpidius, making him not only richer but better. Though younger than he, you have been his inftructor in thefe laudable purfuits, in equity, in an eager defire to affift his friends, to treat courteoufly thofe whom he knows not, and by fo treating them, always to retain their friendfhip. For all, who have approached and converfed with him, have firft admired and then inftantly loved him, or rather have difcovered your ideas in all that you have entrufted to him. I often difcourfe with him; and all our difcourfes turn on you, on the understanding that you poffefs, and the important affairs in which you are engaged. The manner in which you will complete them, and how you will ward fome impending dangers, we have fagely difcuffed. I feemed, as it were, converfing with yourfelf. With particular pleafure I received the intelligence of your having defeated the Barbarians †, and that you had related your victories in a commentary ‡, thus acting

* Σοφοι τυραννοι των σοφων συνεσια.
I have fearched Sophocles in vain for this verfe. WOLFIUS.
† Probably his victories over the Salian Franks and Chamarians. See the Epiftle to the Athenians, p. 87.
‡ We fhould add him to the number of celebrated hiftorians, if his Memoirs of the Gallic war had been tranfmitted to us.　　　　　　　　　　　　　LA BLETERIE.

at

at once as an orator and a general *. Achilles
required a Homer, and Alexander many such †,
but your trophies, your own voice, which has
erected them, will tranfmit to pofterity. Thus
you furpafs the fophifts, by propofing to them not
only actions for them to celebrate, but the orations, which you have compofed on your actions, for
their emulation.

To thefe your trophies I wifh you to add that
of reftoring Pompeianus ‡ to his rights; and think
not this an unworthy contention. For this is the
man, whom formerly, in Bithynia, when he was
ambaffador from hence, you faw with pleafure, and,
on being informed of what he had been defrauded,
gave him hopes of recovering his property. Of this
promife, O prince §, I intreat you to be mindful.

---

* See the Epiftle to the Athenians, p. 68, note *.

† Τ.Ιανων [the common reading] has no meaning. Spanheim has συγ̄ζαφϣ·ῖων, perhaps for συγζαφϣων, "writers."
M. V. la Croze preferred Σειϱηνων, ("Sirens.") To me it is
not yet clear. Suppofe we fhould read τοιϵ̃ων; ("fuch,")
which I have expreffed in my tranflation? Salvinius has
" Titenibus." WOLFIUS.

‡ Pompeianus, who had been præfect of Bithynia, is
mentioned with elogiums by Libanius in many other Epiftles,
and fome are alfo addreffed to him.

§ Ω Βασιλιυ. Though Julian was then only Cæfar, as
appears from fome paffages above, both Fabricius and Wolfius have tranflated this Imperator. But Βασιλιυς was often
applied to the Cæfars.

EPISTLE

EPISTLE II. *.

A. D.
362.

ARE you then forgetful of us? But Phœnicia does not suffer us to be forgetful of you, as she celebrates your reign in immortal hymns †. From your ‡ Asia also flows the fame of your actions, increasing our expectations. For nothing that we have heard, great as all these actions are, is so great as to exceed the hopes that we have formed. We, on account of our relation to the Ionians §, rejoice, trusting that you will proceed in the right road, and that your authority both over them and us will be more firmly established. But this must be left to the providence of God.

Andragathius, in requesting to be the bearer of this, has rather conferred than asked a favour of me.

* This is another of the Epistles preserved by Fabricius. In the edition of Wolfius it is the ccxxivth.

† Godefroi, in one of the indexes to his edition of the Theodosian Code, quotes this passage; but supposes this letter (then unpublished) to be addressed to Count Julian, Consular of Phœnicia.

‡ Υμέτερας. In the Barocc. MS. Ημέτερας. Our reading is supported by four others; and justly, as Libanius appeals to the accounts sent him, of the actions performed by Julian, from foreign and distant parts. Addressing Julian, he styles Ionia (which is soon after eloquently named) "*Your* Asia," meaning a district of Asia Minor, in which, having left Phœnicia, he then was. WOLFIUS.

§ For this relationship, of which Libanius, an orator of Antioch, here boasts, the scholiast thus accounts: "The " Ionians near Smyrna formerly sent a colony to Antioch, " and therefore he styles them relations." *Ibid.*

For

For he will not be more gratified by the pleafure of feeing you than I am by thus being enabled to accoft you. This youth will have thefe three recommendations to you; an energy of fpeech, which he has difplayed before the præfects; a courtefy of behaviour, which endears him to all with whom he converfes; and fuch an intimacy with me, as, in that refpect, to exceed all the friends that I have had fince my childhood.

EPISTLE III. *

YOU have gained a double victory †, one by your arms, the other by your eloquence. One trophy is erected to you by the Barbarians, and the other by me your friend; a trophy this moft pleafing even to a conqueror. For all parents wifh to be excelled by their children ‡, and you,   A. D. 358.

* The Barocc. MS. to the name Ιυλιανω adds, Καισαρι, ("Cæfar,") but the Medic. B. τω Καταρατω ("the execrable.") Ezech. Spanheim quotes the beginning of this epiftle in his preface to the works of Julian, p. 4.   WOLFIUS.
In the edition of Wolfius, this is the ccclxxiid.

† Thus our author, in his cccxcivth epiftle, a: " The " excellent Anatolius has gained two victories over us."
                                                   Ibid.

‡ A comparifon by no means foreign to this paffage, as the fophifts ufed to ftyle their fcholars their fons. See Eunapius, in Julian, and Damafcius in the Life of Ifidorus in Photius on Zenodotus; " alone thought worthy of " being called the darling child of Proclus." Our author alfo in his epiftles has frequently the fame expreffion. That Julian had been inftructed in the art of fpeaking by the precepts of Libanius, is evident from this as well as from other paffages.   Ibid.

                              who

who by me have been inſtructed in writing, have
in that excelled your inſtructor.   But now for the
brevity * of my epiſtle, I, the orator, muſt account to
you, the general, or rather to one no leſs conſummate
in the art of oratory than in that of war.†.   After
the Emperor ‡ had given you a ſhare in the government, I thought myſelf bound to lay ſome
reſtraint on my freedom, and not to indulge it, as
I had been accuſtomed, to a man ſo exalted.   For
knowing, as we do, in our declamatory ſkirmiſhes,
how to accoſt Pericles, Cimon, and Miltiades, it
would have been ſhameful in real life to neglect
thoſe laws.   And as you yourſelf ſay, that the
letters of generals, on account of their avocations,
ſhould be ſhort, this induced me to contract my

* Julian loved long epiſtles, as appears from his ſecond
to Prohæreſius : " Sages, like you, may make long and
" verboſe orations, but from me to you a little is ſuffi-
" cient."

† This union of war with eloquence and the other arts
is applauded by Libanius in other places, but eſpecially in
his iiid oration to Julian, p. 183.   " You alone com-
" prehend the accompliſhments that are divided among
" others ; and no orator, nor warrior, nor judge, nor
" ſophiſt, nor myſtic, nor philoſopher, nor prophet can
" admire himſelf when compared with you.   For in your
" actions you excell thoſe who act, in your ſpeeches thoſe
" who ſpeak."   WOLFIUS.

‡ That Conſtantius, who, when he was oppreſſed with
the difficulties of the Gallic war, though by no means a
friend to Julian, rather thinking that he had cauſe to fear
him, yet yielded to the exigence of the times, and aſſo-
ciated Julian in the empire. For this reaſon, in the Barocc.
MS. this epiſtle has the addition of " Cæſar."   Ibid.

epiftles, fenfible, that he whofe bufinefs prevents him from writing long letters, by one who fends him long letters muft be much interrupted. But now, as you order me to be diffufe, I will obey.

And, firft, I congratulate you, that, with arms in your hands, you have not fufpended your application to oratory, but wage war, as if war were your only ftudy, and attend to books, as if you were a ftranger to arms. And next, that he *, who has given you a fhare in the empire, has had no caufe to repent of his having given it, but confidering him as your coufin, and collegue, and lord, and mafter, in all your actions you promote his glory, and exclaim to your falling enemies, " what " would be your fare, if the Emperor were pre- " fent?" All this I applaud, and alfo your not having changed your manners with your drefs, nor loft, by gaining power, the remembrance of your friends. Many bleffings attend you for fhewing that, when I celebrated your talents, I was not a liar, or rather for having fhewn that I was a liar in promifing nothing equal to what you have performed! This is all your own, and copied from no model. For though fome, together with the empire, have affumed the love of money, contracting defires to which before they were ftrangers, and others have given more indulgence to their former inclinations, you alone, when raifed to the throne,

* Conftantius. See the laft note, p. 310.

X 4

have

have shared, your fortune * among your friends,
giving one a house, another flaves, land to this,
money to that, and, when a fubject, were more
wealthy than now when you are prince. Nor do
you exclude me from the number of your friends,
though I am not one of thofe who have shared
your favours. For I can affign a reafon of my
alone having received nothing. As you would
have cities abound with every thing that can promote their happinefs, you deem nothing more
effential to this than oratory, knowing that, if that
were extinct, we should refemble the Barbarians.
Apprehending therefore, that, if I abounded with
riches, I should neglect my art, you thought it
right for me to remain poor, that I might not be
tempted to defert my ftation: Such, at leaft, is my
folution. Not that you have faid, " Amphiaraus
" and Capaneus are fomething †; but this man
" has neither name nor place ‡." But your not

having

---

* This may illuftrate what our author, in his Life, p. 42,
relates of Julian, viz. that " Libanius loved himfelf, but
others loved his riches."   WOLSIUS.

† This is a proverbial expreffion, which I do not remember to have read elfewhere. In other paffages of the
ancients, Capaneus is applied to a faithful friend, becaufe
Capaneus, amidft great wealth, living with frugality and
œconomy, was moft attentive to his friends.   *Ibid.*

It is needlefs to add, that Amphiaraus and Capaneus
were two of the feven chiefs againft Thebes.

‡ Ουτ' εν λογω ϖτ ιν αριθμω. This oracle of Apollo, to the
inhabitants of Ægina, is quoted by the fcholiaft on Theocritus: Υμης δ', ω Μεγαρης, ϖτ' εν λογω, κ. τ. λ. Compare the
Chiliades of Erafmus, p. 437.   *Ibid.*

The

having given me any thing is owing to your regard for the public. Therefore though we are indigent of money, we abound with words. This is your concern ; may we not difgrace the part that is allotted to us, nor you your illuftrious rank!

EPISTLE IV. *

I SENT you a fhort oration on an important fubject. You can add to its length, by fupplying what is effential to that purpofe. If you give that, you will fhew that you think I have a talent for encomiums. If you do not give it, I fhall be induced to entertain fome other fufpicions.

EPISTLE V. †

UNLESS you were well apprifed how long ago my friendfhip with the excellent Macedonius ‡ was contracted, and for what reafons it has been fince improved, of thefe I would

The inhabitants of Ægina, fay fome, of Megara, fay others, after gaining a naval victory, enquired of Apollo who was the braveft of the Greeks; to which he gave a depreciating anfwer, concluding as above.

* This, in the edition of Wolfius, is the DXXVth. It is alfo one of thofe preferved in Latin by Zambicari. See a note on Epiftle XV. To what oration Libanius here alludes does not appear.

† This is the DLXXXVith in the edition abovementioned.

‡ The fon of Pelagius, of Cyrus, a city in Syria, an orator, and a philofopher. Libanius mentions him with great encomiums in feveral other epiftles, and has addreffed three to him, one of which is a congratulation on his marriage.

firft

firſt apprife you; but knowing, as you do, its foundation, you will not wonder that I, who would decline no danger for my friends, ſhould devote to his fervice this letter. He has indeed prevailed with me to ask a favour of you, not that you grant favours eafily, or grant all that are afked; but ſuch as are juſt and right you willingly confer. And, in truth, whoever does not oblige his friends, in matters thus irreproachable, blames the daughter * of Jove for retaining the Graces in her veſtibule. But that you favour thofe who ask nothing un-reaſonable is evident to all. Now obſerve whether my requeſt is ſuch as can be cenſured.

Macedonius married a wife who had a fon by a former husband. That fon is now dead. I wiſh therefore that the mother †, in preference to the grandfather, may ſucceed to his eſtate, if a regard to honour can induce the grandfather to wave his right, and to prefer praife to a compliance with the law. Be it therefore your endeavour to con-

---

* The Greek mythologiſts ſtyle her Δικη, (" Juſtice,") whom he virtually condemns, that does not return to a friend the favour which he could and ought. WOLFIUS.

† The mothers, among the Romans, had not, in the beginning, any ſhare in the fucceſſion of their children, whether they were emancipated or not. In procefs of time, the mothers did ſucceed, but differently according to the different times, and the whimfical changes that many laws made in their right of fucceſſion. In England, if, after the death of a father, any of his children die inteſtate, with-out wife or children, in the life-time of the mother, the mother, in that cafe, fucceeds jointly and equally with the brothers and fiſters of the deceafed and their reprefenta-tives. STRAHAN.

vince

vince him, that it is more creditable for him to decline than to take thefe effects. You will be doubly
perfuafive, as, befides the powers of oratory, you
poffefs fupreme dominion. And I hear that this
old man is vain of a good reputation, and had
rather accumulate fame than wealth. Delay not
therefore to fend for and confer with him, and
thus perform an action more humane than any law.
Nor think that we will admit, as an excufe, your
alleging that the difcuffion of fuch matters does
not belong to you, or, by way of fubterfuge, that
you are unable to perfuade him. To be the inftrument of conferring wealth on the mother, and
fame on her father, will do you no difhonour.
Every word from you makes a ftrong impreffion
on the hearers.

⸻

EPISTLE VI. *

THE laws and myfelf will take care that that
moft abandoned fervant fhall be punifhed for
what he has faid and done. But you, together
with the empire, fhew that you poffefs alfo fuch
benevolence as the excellent Prifcian † difplayed
to Seleucus ‡. Acting thus, you will induce the

* This, in the edition of Wolfius, is the DXCIft.

† Prifcian was an excellent orator, and on that account
was invited by Julian to Conftantinople. Libanius has
addreffed feveral Epiftles to him.

‡ Seleucus is alfo mentioned as a friend of Libanius in
many of his Epiftles, and many are addreffed to him.

preceptors

preceptors of Arrhabius, I mean Calliopius *, and his father, to treat him with more indulgence. For Seleucus married the daughter of one, and the fifter of the other. Him therefore, whom in your letters you fo highly honour as to ftyle him your fon, affift, I intreat you, in his literary improvements.

EPISTLE VII. †

WOULD you have me believe that you do not take the leaft concern in the affairs of Ulpian and Palladius ‡, that you neither regard them as friends, nor efteem them as orators, nor recollect that they may affift you with their friendly offices? Such reports, which it does not become me to repeat, are circulated by many. On the contrary, I contend that none of them, as far as you are concerned, are true. Write therefore, and confute them. You will thus confer a favour on yourfelf, as well as on me.

---

* Calliopius, by fome of the Epiftles to him, appears to have been an orator.

† This in the edition of Wolfius is the ꝺcꞁꞁd, a.

‡ Two orators, frequently mentioned by Libanius.

E P I S T L E VIII. *

I HAVE difcharged my obligations to Ariftophanes †; but you, in return, have given me
fuch fplendid tokens of a vehement affection as are
confpicuous both to Gods and men. So that now
I feem almoft to foar into the fky, elevated by your
epiftle, which has infpired me with fuch hopes,
and has fo decorated my oration ‡, that all things
elfe, the wealth of Midas, the beauty of Nireus §,
the fwiftnefs of Crifon ‖, the ftrength of Poly-
damas **, the fword of Peleus ††, feem little in my
fight.

A. D.
362.

---

* This Epiftle is one of the three firft publifhed by Fabricius. In the edition of Wolfius it is the DCLXXth.

†. This oration for Ariftophanes, a Corinthian, the fon
of Menander, who had been feverely fined by the præfect of Ægypt, on account of his confulting aftrologers,
is preferved in the works of Libanius, vol. II. p. 210, &c.
WOLFIUS.
It is faid in this oration, that he had been fined, fcourged,
and imprifoned.

‡ The Epiftle of Julian to Libanius, to which this is an
anfwer, is the LXVIIIth, or laft, in vol. II.

§ See Homer. Iliad. ii. 671.

‖ Crifon was that native of Himera, who gained three
victories in the Olympic games. See the Prolegomena of
Erafmus Schmidius on Pindar, p. 31. Add. Paufan. Eliac.
p. 172. WOLFIUS.
** A famous Theffalian wreftler, who ftrangled a lion
on mount Olympus, tamed a wild bull, and ftopped a
chariot drawn by the ftrongeft horfes. He was crufhed to
death by a rock under which he took fhelter from a ftorm;
and this was owing to his indifcretion in flattering himfelf
that

fight. Even the nectar of the Gods, were I allowed to enjoy it, could not give me greater delight than I now feel, when my prince, such a one as Plato formerly fought and could scarcely find *, has commended my sentiments, admired my oration, and has not only promised that he will give something, but, which is much greater honour, that he will consult with me what to give. They who observe the rising of the celestial goat †, do not always obtain their wishes; but I, though I have not attended to this, have been most successful. And if I want any other favour, the Emperor, imitating the Deity, is ever gracious. Your epistle therefore shall be prefixed to my oration, to inform all the Greeks, that my dart has not been launched in vain, for by what I have written, Aristophanes will be honoured, as I am by what you have returned; or rather both of us shall

that he could support the rock, which was beginning to fall, when his companions fled.　　　　MORERI.

Libanius mentions him also in his xvith Declamation.

†† Peleus received a sword from Vulcan, with which he could defend himself against all attacks, as we learn from the scholiast on the ivth Nemean of Pindar, ver. 88, &c.　　　　WOLFIUS.

* Alluding to the famous saying of Plato, that "governments would be happy, if kings philosophised or philosophers reigned."　　　　Ibid.

† A proverbial expression, often used of those with whom every thing succeeds happily, and as they wish; because it was of old a vulgar opinion that they who saw that goat, who was the nurse of Jupiter, and on that account was made a constellation, obtained whatever they desired.　　　　ERASMUS.

shall

ſhall glory in what has been written and will be given by you, for each of us is honoured by each of theſe.

But now it may divert you to hear how Ariſtophanes has been terrified. One of your uſual evening-attendants informed us that, on coming to your door, he was refuſed admittance, becauſe he was told, you were buſy in compoſing an oration. This immediately occaſioned an apprehenſion that you had determined to controvert my oration *, and confute your preceptor, and would thus over-whelm Ariſtophanes like the Nile †. We haſtened therefore to the excellent Elpidius, who, on hearing the cauſe of our alarm, burſt into a loud laughter. Thus we recovered our ſpirits, and ſoon after I received your elegant epiſtle ‡.

* Libanius means the oration, which he, who had formerly been the preceptor of Julian, had ſpoken for Ariſtophanes.   WOLFIUS.

† Alluding, I imagine, to the inundation of the Nile, and, at the ſame time, to the torrent of Julian's eloquence, which might over-power Ariſtophanes. Thus Suidas aſcribes to Chryſoſtom " cataracts like thoſe of the Nile," and Tzetzes mentions " Nile-like floods," both applied to eloquence. See p. 305.   Ibid.

‡ This Epiſtle of Julian to Libanius is here ſubjoined in a note, by Wolfius, from Fabricius. But I have added my tranſlation of it to his other Epiſtles in Vol. II.

────────

EPISTLE IX. *

HOW much foever I condemned that journey
(fatiguing as it was) †, I no lefs, or rather
more, condemned myfelf for returning fo foon,
inftead of going to the place appointed, and
there indulging my eyes, the next morning, at
fun-rifing, with the fight of his divine vifage.
And fo unfortunate is the city, that fhe cou'd not
afford me the leaft confolation. I ftyle her unfortunate, not on account of the dearth of provifions, but becaufe fhe has been and is adjudged
wicked, invidious, and ungrateful ‡ by him whofe

prudence

────────

* To the name Ιϰλιανω, Αυλοκραλορι (" Emperor,") is prefixed in two MSS. And in another, τω τρισκαλαραλω (" moft
" execrable,") is annexed to it: WOLFIUS.
 In the edition of Wolfius it is the DCCXIIth. It is alfo
one of thofe preferved in Latin by Zambicari.

 † What fatiguing and fruitlefs journey Libanius had
taken, does not appear. Perhaps it was to Mount Caffius,
(fee the Mifopogon, p. 282.) where Jupiter had a temple,
fifteen miles, or a day's journey, from Antioch, which,
however, Julian performed feveral times during his refidence in that city. For " from thence," fays Ammianus, (xxii. 14.) " at the fecond cock-crowing, is firft
" feen the rifing of the fun."

 ‡ Meaning Antioch, at that time not only afflicted with
famine, but expofed to the refentment of the Emperor for
difregarding his edict for lowering the price of provifions,
and not abftaining from farcafms on himfelf. This appears
from the embaffy (πρισβευλικος) our author fent to Julian for

the

prudence furpaffes his dominions, extenfive as they are. While Alcimus * was with me, I had one who would hear with indulgence my felf-reproaches and my boafts of the diftinction fhewn me by you. But after his departure, confidering the cieling as my only friend, I looked up to it, as I lay in my bed, and faid, " Now the Emperor fent for me : " now I entered and fat down (for that he allowed " me); now I pleaded for the city, as I was per- " mitted to intercede with him for thofe who " had offended him. But he prevailed, fo juft " was his charge, and fo powerful his elocution. " And though I oppofed him, I was neither dif- " liked, nor ejected." With this banquet I regale myfelf, and I intreat the Gods, firft, that they will give you the fuperiority over your enemies, and, fecondly, that they will render you as propitious to us as you were formerly. I have alfo a third petition, which they have heard, but I will not here mention. I ought not, however, even to have faid that I will not mention it. For you are ingenious enough to conjecture this third article from my wifhing to conceal what I wifh. And, in-

the Antiochians, which is in the fecond volume of his works, p. 151, and alfo from his oration to the Antiochians *de Imperatoris irâ*, which, before unpublifhed, our learned Fabricius has inferted in his Bibliotheca Græca, vol. VII. p. 207.
WOLFIUS.

See alfo the Mifopogon, p. 296, &c.

* A native of Nicomedia, and a man of learning, as appears from feveral letters addreffed to him by Libani .

VOL. I.   Y   deed,

deed, I apprehend that the contrary will be your choice *.

Now then pass the rivers; rush on the archers † more impetuously than a torrent; and afterwards think on what you said you would think. But fail not to solace me, in your absence, as much as you can. I, for my part, will send epistles to extort your answers from the midst of the battle, as I am convinced that you have a genius that can at once command an army, fight an enemy, and correspond with a friend. I am so infirm, that I am obliged to hear what I ought to see. Happy is Seleucus ‡ in this glorious fight, and in preferring the honour of serving such a prince to that which he derives from a good wife, and a most beloved daughter!

* I should understand this of marriage, to which Julian was averse: WOLFIUS.

† Meaning the Persians, Julian being then engaged in that expedition. Ibid.

‡ Seleucus has been mentioned in Epistle VI. p. 315.

EPISTLE

EPISTLE X. *

THAT Alexander †, was appointed to the government, it firſt, I confeſs, gavė me ſome concern, as the principal perſons among us were diſſatisfied. I thought it diſhonourable, injurious, and unbecoming a prince; and that repeated mulĉts would rather weaken than improve the city. But now the good effeĉts of this ſeverity are ſo manifeſt, that I recant ‡. For théy, who formerly bathed and ſlept at noon, now, imitating the

---

* This, in the edition of Wolfius, is the DCXXIId.

† This is the Alexander of whom Ammianus ſays, (XXIII. 2.) " When Julian was going to leave Antioch, he made " one Alexander, of Heliopolis governor of Syria, a tur- " bulent and ſevere man, ſaying, that ' undeſerving as he ' was, ſuch a ruler ſuited the avaricious and contu- ' melious Antiochians," Conſult Valois on that paſſage, who refers to this Epiſtle, then unpubliſhed. WOLFIUS. See the Miſopogon, p. 302. note †.

‡ Αδω παλινωδιαν. This proverb is taken from a tranſaĉtion of Steſichorus, the Lyric poet, mentioned by Plato in his Phædrus. For having ſlandered Helen, in a poem, he was deprived of his eye-ſight; but Achilles, by her deſire, as Pauſanias relates, in his Laconica, having acquainted him with the cauſe of his blindneſs, he immediately ſung a recantation, by praiſing Helen, whom before he had cenſured; and thus he recovered his ſight. Socrates ſays, in joke, that " he wiſhes to imitate him, and would rather ſing a recan- " tation in favour of love, which he had blamed, than " loſe his eyes." ERASMUS.

Y 2

manners

manners of the Lacedæmonians *, labour indefatigably not only in the day-time, but no small part of the night, nailed, as it were, to the gate of Alexander. And when he clamours from within, every thing is inftantly in motion. Thus the fword will never be wanted, fince his threats alone are fufficient to render the impudent modeft, and the flothful induftrious. Calliope is alfo honoured, agreeably to your wifhes †, not only by horfe-races, but theatrical exhibitions; and facrifices are offered to that Goddefs in the theatre, without our making the leaft alteration. Loud applaufe is given, and amidft this applaufe the Gods are invoked. With this applaufe the governor feems fo delighted, that he urges many more to add to it. Of fuch importance, O prince, to mankind is divination ‡, as it teaches every one the beft manner of governing a family, a city, a nation, and a kingdom.

---

* For the Lacedæmonians were far from being delicate. Hence arofe the proverb, Λακωνικως διπνειν, (" to fup Lacedæmonially,") on which fee Erafmus, p. 268. WOLFIUS.

† This muft probably be ironical, as Julian was far from being a favourer, or frequenter, of the circus, or the theatre. See the Mifopogon, pp. 232, 261, and 268.

‡ Libanius here flatters Julian, as if he had learned by divination that Alexander was fuch a one as ought to govern Syria and the Antiochians. WOLFIUS.

EPISTLE

EPISTLE XI. *.

ON all accounts I was pleased to see Ablavius †, but principally because he brought me a letter from you. For sooner than blame you I should detest myself; such has been your attention to the promotion of my interest, amidst this tedious war, which you could not have been, if any one had spoken to my disadvantage. In seeming to laugh, and in pardoning those who, in order to flatter one, calumniate another, you acted like yourself. Flattery is their trade, and as necessary to their subsistence as rowing is to that of sailors. That sage, with whose morals Ablavius acquainted me, though he would not disclose his name, gave me no concern on any account, this only excepted, that in mentioning me he was guilty of a solecism; and I, though guilty of no offence, was sent by him among the Barbarians ‡. Inform him of this, and caution him to avoid such mistakes for the future; he may then, if he pleases, speak evil of me, for then, at least, he will not speak ill §. But this

* This, in the edition of Wolfius, is the MXXXVth.

† Libanius has two Epistles to Ablavius, by which it appears that he was an orator.

‡ Libanius ridicules the man, by whose speaking barbarously of him, he himself was, as it were, made a Barbarian.　　　　　　　　　　　　WOLFIUS.

§ This play on the words λεγειν κακως, and ερει κακως, I have endeavoured to retain in English, by the equivocal meaning of " evil" and " ill," as applied to slander and to language.

man is unalterable *. If, however, by his calumnies he should still offend you, and you wish
to punish him, you easily may, by confining him
to his house, in an afternoon, and obliging him
to sup at home; and when he again grows
insolent, through repletion, and drinks your own
wine against you †, you need only repeat that
punishment; you cannot inflict a greater. This
will effectually curb his licentious tongue; but,
whatever be his name, let me know it, that, when
I write his elogium, it may not be anonymous.

EPISTLE. XII. ‡

A D.
358.

ALAS! alas! how insatiable is your desire of
farther attainments! You possess the palm
of eloquence, snatched from others, at once
    A matchless prince and a most potent sage §.
                                        Other

* Σταθερος in Greek, usually signifies "firm, immoveable."
I understand, therefore, this passage of a man who cannot
be changed, but always remains the same.   WOLFIUS.

† πινων του σου εαυτον κατα σε. It should seem by this passage,
that it was customary to drink health, or confusion, in
those times as it is in ours.

‡ In the edition of Wolfius this is the MCXXVth.

§ Αρχων τ' αγαθος, κρατερος τε σοφιης.
In allusion to Homer. Iliad III. 178.
    Αμφοτερον βασιλευς τ' αγαθος, κρατερος τ' αιχμητης.
"Great in the war, and great in arts of sway." POPE, 236.
That Libanius here did not flatter Julian, in praising
him for his eloquence, his orations and epistles still extant
attest. To which may be added what Spanheim says in
his preface to the works of Julian, c. 2. "Among the
" Emperors his predecessors, or those who followed him
                                        " in

Other princes have acted, and we applauded; but you excell in both those capacities. For how can we speak so highly in commendation of your actions as you do of that short letter *? Hence I conjecture what you will do, when you have subdued Phœnicia †, as already you administer justice to your subjects, wage war with the Barbarians, and in the composition of orations far exceed the common rank. Though I am not solicitous as to the future, I shall be as much pleased with this slaughter as with a victory. For when the vanquished and the victor are friends, the vanquished has a share in the triumph; as friends, it is said, have all things common ‡.

" in the same exalted station, I cannot see any, who as to the
" extent, or copiousness, of their learning, or the bright-
" ness of their genius, or the power of their eloquence,
" can in those arts, and in the talent of writing, contest
" with him the superiority." Libanius bestows a similar
elogium on Julian in his own Life, p. 41. styling him " the
" most temperate, the most oratorical, and the most war-
" like." WOLFIUS.

* Julian also highly commended other orations of Libanius. See on this subject the remarkable Epistle of Julian, before unpublished, mentioned in p. 317. now the [LXVIIIth.] Ibid.

† I should understand this of the orators of Phœnicia. Ibid.

‡ Κοινα γαρ, φασι, τα των φιλων. This proverb is quoted by Euripides in his Orestes, in the same words. See the Chiliades of Erasmus [p. 13.] and Gregory Nazianz. Ep. LXIV. Ibid.

" No proverb," says Erasmus, " is more salutary, or " more celebrated, than this."

EPISTLE

EPISTLE XIII. *

GEMELLUS † is my relation and my friend, and by his manners is no difgrace to his family. If he had been poffeffed of money and a large eftate, he would long ago have been employed on fome public function. But as his fortune is fmall, he has, by my advice, taken a method which may exempt him from tears and chains, the ufual attendants of thofe whom public employments have reduced to poverty.

Happy he is in difcharging this office under your infpection; as you never fail to reprobate injuftice, and to honour what is juft and equitable. Many there are who look upon juftice and equity as meannefs, and accordingly defpife them. But far different is your conduct; for you were well born, and well inftructed, and therefore glory more in being virtuous than in the numerous nations which you govern. Of this Gemellus has proofs; and, that he may have more, let him be obliged for thofe to you, but for thefe to me. For if he fhould receive any greater favours in confequence of my letter, he will certainly be indebted for them to my advice.

* In the edition of Wolfius this is the Mccccxcivth.
† To this Gemellus Libanius has feveral epiftles.

EPISTLE

EPISTLE XIV. *

WE have made a mutual agreement, that I should write to you in behalf of my friends, and that if their requests are reasonable, you will assist them. Of your assistance let this Hyperechius † first reap the advantage. He has long been harrassed and oppressed by those whose chief study is unjust gain. He was one of my scholars in my former prosperity. Such I deem the time of my residence at Nicomedia ‡ ; not on account of the wealth, but of the excellent friends, that it procured me, many of whom are no more. This man, whose hopes now rest on you, then came from Ancyra §. In eloquence, none excelled him; in manners, none equalled him. I love him therefore with a parental affection. I cannot see him injured without assisting him myself, and urging others to assist him also. And if in this you think that I act no bad part, shew by your deeds that you approve my conduct.

---

* In the edition of Wolfius this is the Mccccxcth.

† An orator, the son of Maximus, a native of Galatia. Libanius has addressed several epistles to him.

‡ Our author affirms, in his Life, p. 21, that he spent five years with pleasure at Nicomedia, and calls that time "the spring of his life." WOLFIUS.

§ The same city which Libanius, in his xxvith oration, p. 599, styles "the principal and largest city in Galatia." *Ibid.*

EPISTLE XV. *

A. D.
363.

THE oration †, which contains some account of your glorious actions, you honour not only with praise, but admiration. And as you are ranked among the learned, you maintain, I am told, that Demosthenes could not have written more forcibly, Socrates more agreeably, or Plato more copiously, on the occasion. You affirm also, that greater glory will redound to you from my writings, than from the fortunate event of your actions. My opinion is far different. For though, with my most studious and elaborate endeavours, I strove to exalt your name; yet, as my strength was unequal to such a weight, what I performed I performed with great pleasure. But so brilliant are your praises, that the rudest genius may seem

---

* This is the iiid of the iid book of the Epistles of Libanius, collected in Greece by Francisco Zambicari of Bologna, and published, in his Latin translation only by John Somerfeld, at Cracow, 1504. It is also inserted by Fabricius, in his Bibliotheca Græca, vol. VII. p. 390.

† His Προσφωνηΐκος, or panegyrical address to Julian, when he was at Antioch, just before he set out on his Persian expedition. It is the Vth in the IId Vol. of the works of this Sophist, published by Morell. How agreeable it was to the Emperor Libanius mentions in an Epistle to Celsus [the DCXLVIIIth], as well as in the above.

FABRICIUS.

-suffi-

sufficiently decorated by the dignity of the subject. Your actions therefore were the nobleſt
ornaments of my oration. And though I attempted
to illuſtrate thoſe actions which in their own nature
were moſt ſplendid, I rather illuſtrated myſelf.
So that you have no cauſe to return me thanks,
or to think that they are due to me. But that I
may acquire ſuch a ſplendor by recording your
exploits, whatever ſucceſs may attend you in future fail not to communicate to me by a letter.

EPISTLE XVI. *

I CAN ſcarce believe that, than which nothing
can be more certain. Departing from you,
in obedience to your order, and on an urgent
occaſion, I am both willingly and unwillingly
abſent from you. For I think I could be ſooner
negligent of my life than of your commands.
Any labours, however great, ſeem trifles ; however
ſmall, when deſired to undertake them for you, I
have been uſed to think them ſweeter than ambroſia.
To this it is owing, that, were you to command me,
I would depart not only from you, but from myſelf.
But as I conſider you as my deity, without you
nothing ſeems pleaſing. You conſtantly occur to
my mind : whatever I hear repeats the voice of

* This alſo is publiſhed only in Latin by Zambicari.
It is the XIVth of his IId book.

Julian ;

Julian; whatever I fee reflects the image of my
venerable deity. And when a fweet flumber re-
frefhes my languid limbs, you feem fo prefent to
me, that, by the kindnefs of the immortal Gods,
feparated and loofed from the body, my mind
feems to fly to you, to embrace, accoft, in fhort, to
worfhip you; fo that if I were to be deprived of
life, I would wifh that to be my laft day. Farther,
that I may no longer be thus tormented, I intreat
you to give me your permiffion to return to you,
and in your prefence to adore your deity, which
abfent I at once admire and venerate. If not,
as by your indulgence it may be effected, I could
eafily confent to be banifhed, not only from the
city I fo much love, but alfo from the world *.

* In the Latin, *non modo interdici mihi optatiffimâ urbe,
fed ipfâ etiam urbe facilè patiar*—which I do not underftand.
Perhaps *ipfâ urbe* fhould be *ipfo orbe*. I have ventured fo
to tranflate it.

*** Thefe are all the Epiftles of Libanius to the Emperor
that are extant. Of the others addreffed to Julian
(of which there are ten more), one is to his uncle the
Count of the Eaft, and the reft to fome other perfon,
or perfons, of the fame name.

I N D E X

T O

V O L U M E I.

VOL. I.   A a   *Antoninus,*

Dominus,

JULIAN,

Quintillus,

INDEX.

END OF THE FIRST VOLUME.